CELG

THE STANDARD GRAND

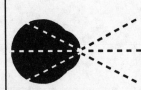

This Large Print Book carries the
Seal of Approval of N.A.V.H.

THE STANDARD GRAND

JAY BARON NICORVO

THORNDIKE PRESS
A part of Gale, a Cengage Company

Farmington Hills, Mich • San Francisco • New York • Waterville, Maine
Meriden, Conn • Mason, Ohio • Chicago

LIBRARY OF CONGRESS CATALOGING-IN-PUBLICATION DATA

Names: Nicorvo, Jay Baron, author.
Title: The Standard Grand / by Jay Baron Nicorvo.
Description: Waterville, Maine : Thorndike Press, a part of Gale, a Cengage Company, 2017. | Series: Thorndike Press large print Bill's bookshelf
Identifiers: LCCN 2017028682| ISBN 9781432843229 (hardcover) | ISBN 1432843222 (hardcover)
Subjects: LCSH: Large type books. | BISAC: FICTION / Literary. | FICTION / War & Military.
Classification: LCC PS3614.I3548 S73 2017b | DDC 813/.6—dc23
LC record available at https://lccn.loc.gov/2017028682

Published in 2017 by arrangement with Macmillan Publishing Group, LLC/St. Martin's Press

Printed in the United States of America
1 2 3 4 5 6 7 21 20 19 18 17

THE CONCERNS

THE SMITH FAMILY
Antebellum Smith (Bellum, Bang Bang, Ant), Specialist, US Army, AWOL
Travis Harmon Wallace, her husband
Increase Smith (Crease), her father

THE EMPLOYEES OF IRJ, INC.
Evangelína Ixchel Carrillo Canek (Evy), company landman
F. Bismarck Rolling (Bizzy), chief operations officer
Marisol Soto-Garza, executive assistant to Mr. Rolling
Ray Tyro (Reverend, Early Bird), private contractor
Ellis Baum, real-estate lawyer

THE VETERANS OF THE STANDARD GRANDE
Milton Xavier Wright, owner, Sergeant, US Army, Vietnam vet

5

Paul Vessey (Vess), Sergeant, US Army, Vietnam vet

Dereemus Stotts-Dupree (STD), Specialist, US Army National Guard

Samuel Stone, Private First Class, US Army National Guard

Jeffrey Luce (Screw), Specialist, US Army

Jairo Merced, Private First Class, US Marine Corps

Jacko Botes, Lance Corporal, US Marine Corps

Abdul Alhazred (Luckson Merisme), Private First Class, US Army

Ferdinand Wisenbeker (Wiz), Petty Officer, US Navy

THE DEAD

Ada Wright (née Teplitsky), Milton's wife

Nehemiah Teplitsky (Chema), Milton's father-in-law

Santiago Nabor Fuentes Carrillo (Papí), Evangelína's father

Maryam Tyro (née Jalal), Ray's wife

Sammy Davis, Jr., entertainer

THE BEASTS

Foxtrot (Foxy-T), chocolate Labrador

Egon, Belgian Malinois

Fulan and Fulana, raccoons

Wile E. Prince and Sue, alpaca
Son of Gizbar, cougar

THE VETERANS OF THE BAGDAD GRAND

Asa Goodman (Goody), Airman, US Air Force
Ruffin Steed (Steady), Private First Class, US Army
Ike Dopp, Lance Corporal, US Marine Corps

THE REST

Ramona Aahal Canek Gómez (Mamí), Evangelína's mother
Ira Lependorf, estate lawyer
Sharyn Tyro, Ray's mother
Dean Tyro, Ray's brother
Esperanza, Increase's sixth wife
Carlos (Charles, Charlie, Victor), Increase's step-son
Shoshanna Roshanda (Jinx), dancer
Caryn and Kip, residents, Rip Van Winkle Motor Inn
Joe Ginsu (TrapAvoid), hacker, former colleague of Ray's
Meena Mohammadzai (Zamda), role player, National Training Center
Al Franken (Chairman), US senator

for the weak or fainthearted,
all of us ultimately;
for the strong or fierce-hearted,
the one and only Thisbe

Here they come,
returning from the road,
Thirsty ghosts, skirts desert swept,
Their mirage breath smeared, burnt,
Bad-i-sad-o-bist-roz dry
and dust-blasted,
Here they come,
returning from the road
— NADIA ANJUMAN, "The Deserted Voice"
translated from Persian
by Meena Mohammadzai

Because the keys to the Kingdom
got locked inside the Kingdom
And the angels fly around in there
but we can't see them
I got a girl in the war, Paul,
I know that they can hear me yell
If they can't find a way to help her
they can go to Hell
— JOSH RITTER, "Girl in the War"

■ ■ ■ ■

SUMMER
2012

■ ■ ■ ■

Specialist Smith gunned the gas and popped the clutch in the early Ozark morning. Her Dodge pickup yelped, slid to one side in the blue dark, then shot fishtailing forward. The rear tires burned a loud ten meters of smoking, skunky rubber out front of the stucco ranch house on Tidal Road.

She felt thankful for her bad marriage. It allowed her the privilege of living off base; she could go AWOL without having to bust the gates of Fort Leonard Wood. Her four-barrel pocket pepperbox, a COP .357 — holstered, unloaded — rode on the passenger seat.

To be sure she was doing right, she drove by Big Papa's Cabaret, a soda-pop strip club that entertained lonely soldiers and unruly locals. Half a dozen men loitered outside, swigging from bottle-shaped brown bags.

Sure enough, Travis's rusted-out, rice-burner pickup still sat in the dirt lot, its

Browning Buckmark decal, in Stars and Stripes, peeling from the rear windshield. A display of American pride on his Japanese truck.

Unemployed, entrepreneurial Travis, inside somewhere, waited for the final lap dance to grind to a halt. Then his business got busy: pillhead happy hour.

Smith could practically hear the last-hurrah clapping and thigh-slapping, the hands of the soldiers not always paired. The dented steel door swung open and out staggered the pokes. There was Travis, a townie, bringing up the rear. Travis Harmon Wallace, her civilian husband. Overweight Travis. Travis under the influence of lord knew what Travis. Shiftless, automatic transmission Travis. He got blown back a step by the sunrise, shielding his eyes. He regained himself and made way to the milling men.

She gave a long thought to killing him, Travis.

The powerful derringer on the passenger seat was a gift from him — he tried so miserably hard to be hard — a gun he thought sexy in her grip and gangsta in his. What he'd bought them for their last anniversary. His-and-hers concealed carries. Had them engraved *I'm your huckle bearer.*

16

When she'd tried telling him it was huckle-*berry,* he got in her face. Near pistol-whipped her with the present.

The idea of loading the gun raised a clot of bile into her tight chest.

On her way out of town, she drove back by the house — its sham mortgage they'd started falling behind on the day after their incomprehensible closing. She slowed, tried to hear Foxtrot pawing at the doorframe. Nothing. Likely asleep under the butcher block.

She admired the twin tire marks she'd made earlier. They would be her lasting goodbye to Devils Elbow, where every street name started with T. Steering clear of 66, she took Tidal to Teardrop.

Smith, keeping to country roads, chan-neled her daddy's crass drawl. Antebellum, he said in her head, you ever find yourself on the lam, you shunpike it, hear me, grrl?

Shunpike, Daddy?

Shun the turnpike, dumbass. Bumpkin county sheriffs a hell of a lot easier to outrun than revved-up state troopers. I should know.

She sped east out of the hotdamn Ozarks through the Mark Twain National Forest. She threw her ringing phone — *Travy* — out the window and into the parched summer. It smithereened in the rearview. She used her teeth to pull off her wedding band and engagement ring. Spat them into her hand and shoved them into the trash-crammed ashtray, mall-bought diamond solitaire be damned.

The temperature was already near ninety and Evangelína Ixchel Carrillo Canek savored the sopping warmth of the morning air like a sauna. She strode through it looking for a syrupy café con leche. Far as she could tell, she'd been assigned to the Mantenimiento Marino de Mexico project initiative because she was Mesoamerican. Possibly as punishment for botching Fort Worth. She had no training for the Tampico job. Oversee the replacement of two winches, a slew bearing, and the tugger hydraulic pressure unit on the *LB Lacie Bourg,* routine maintenance on a maintenance vessel. A week ago, she couldn't've picked out a slew bearing in a pile of yoke hoists.

She found an open stall the size of a Texas outhouse, ordered in Spanish from an old Huastec woman missing a finger. Evangelína had little of her ancestors' language. That didn't stop her from offering a Maya greeting, "Bix a beel?"

The woman, shorter than even Evangelína, nodded but gave no indication of understanding. Ten minutes later, clutched in a scaly hand like the foot of a ten-year-old hen, she held out the steaming coffee. Perfectly sweet and scalding hot, the split stalks of sugarcane brought to boil with beans pulverized in a guayacán mortar and pestle.

The domestic retrofitting crew was still not at work aboard the liftboat moored in the diesel-slicked Puerto de Tampico. A teenage infante de marina with a wispy moustache stood guard, a submachine gun slung over the shoulder of his baggy fatigues. The negotiations with the local union, backed by the Cártel del Golfo, called for a ten-to-four workday. Labor agreement or no, she was on Tampico time.

Evangelína spent twelve days seeing the sights, fending off the advances of the locals, known as Jaibas, Crabs. In the evenings that lasted for ages, she shrugged on her jogging vest, loaded with twenty pounds of steel weights, and ran. Masochistic with her runs, she needed to make the most of her time.

Later, in four-inch heels, she wandered Calle Aduana, bemused by the aspirational Old World buildings, their balconies accented with English cast iron.

After her strolls, every night for an hour or more, she talked to her mamí back in Houston, who worried about Cártel del Golfo or Los Zetas beheading her only daughter.

Between girlfriends for too great a stretch, Evangelína considered going home with the butch owner of La Gula — a waterfront restaurant that served one of the slowest, best meals she'd ever eaten. The excessive after-flan course, served with a glass of sparkling rosé, was a plate of percebes flash boiled in squid ink for as long as it took the chef to say the Lord's Prayer. Evangelína chased the briny, elastic goose barnacles with puffs on a habano Bolívar Inmensas.

Drunk but not desperate, not yet, she entertained the older woman's advances but, confident Tampico was tranquillo, she walked alone through the dark back to her hotel, pulling heartily on the Cuban cigar to fend off the bugs, a pack of feral dogs in tow. The tremendous teats of the yipping bitches brought her to tears. Maybe she was desperate. For the last six months, despite costly assistance from a Houston fertility specialist, Evangelína had been failing to get pregnant.

With each mile it got harder to turn back.

20

Smith had done it, quick and simple. Absent without leave. She'd miss the dog most, was already wondering why she didn't drag him along. Foxy-T would make for good company and decent protection — not as good or as responsive as her M4 carbine but for damn sure warmer.

This was simpler — alone — this was necessary. She had no girlfriends to talk her out of taking off. A tomboy raised by a hooligan single father, a dog person drawn to the doggy company of men — this disposition lent her advantage over the catty Army women.

Done two tours driving mostly men. Two tours more than most Americans. On her first, reassigned to Charlie Company, 321st Engineer Battalion, she made fuel runs. Al Asad to Camp Ramadi right after Op Murfreesboro. Then, K-Crossing up to Mosul. More than once during that first tour, she'd been on MSR Tampa behind the wheel of a HET hauling sand imported to the desert. Local sand was too fine for concrete. Sand everywhere and not a single grain to mix. Had to transport sand from UAE to make a blast wall for fucksake. As if sand was a form of government, and what the Iraqis had at home just would not do.

In Afghanistan, tour number two, assigned

at the support battalion level moving cargo to P1 units, it was a lot of Ghazni to Bagram Airfield and back. Got so she sometimes forgot where in BFE she was, Iraq or Afghanistan, engaging urban ex-Ba'athists or rural Taliban with terrible teeth, hearing Arabic or Pashto. The Hindu Kush mountains in the distance helped get her bearings; most of Iraq was flat as Florida. On both tours she saw a good bit of checkpoint detail. As a woman she got to pat down women and kids.

She'd been reassigned and set to deploy once more; third time's a charm. Two turns playing grab-ass with circumcised women in burqas. Driving disposable half-million-dollar trucks on those clusterfuck roads. Getting two kilometers per gallon of diesel. Having had her unfair share of wrecks. She couldn't stomach risking her life yet again. She didn't want to drive, the one thing she was good at.

Didn't even realize it was the driving till she got back stateside over a year ago and a quick giddy-up to the grocery store sent her into a longwinded panic. Spent a panting lifetime picking out a pre-wrapped head of iceberg lettuce from the pyramid of identical heads only to leave it in a magazine rack before bolting the checkout line with what felt like a heart attack. Didn't even like iceberg lettuce.

Diagnosed her with PTSD — big surprise, who wasn't — prescribed her Ativan for her anxiety, Risperdal to calm her, plus an anti-depressant. Mix her a prescription cocktail and send her on her hazy, libidoless way. That was their idea of maintaining troop morale. US military become a pharmacological force. Soon soldiers would be wearing Pfizer patches on their uniforms. It made sense. It'd been grass and junk in the jungle, allowed if not approved, and a generation later designer pharmaceuticals had been sanctioned for the sandbox, where the recreational drugs of choice were domestic hash in cubes like beef bouillon easing you down off all the imported caffeine and methamphetamine, cans of Red Bull more important to the Surge than mortar rounds.

Once her scripts kicked in, she'd lost a year and a half, little idea where it went. Here she was readied to redeploy, just like that. Medicated, she felt as though her life had been pirated and broadcast over the internet, without her permission, at a crappy connection rate on an ancient computer, audio muffled, video pixilated and herky-jerky. Her old life — high-definition, painfully vivid, sexually driven — was available if she wanted to pay admission. The price was her posttraumatic stress.

As she sped along, doing 75 in a 55, half wanting to get busted and turned back, the degrading voice of her crackerass daddy was replaced by the calm monotone of her shrink, Major Olmstead: You internalized the war, Smith. Attuned yourself to the tensions and stresses of grave danger. Doesn't make you dysfunctional. Makes you a good soldier.

But Olmstead's aim had been to ready her for a return to a drawdown war forever flaring up. In addition to his scripts, he kept giving her reading assignments, self-help books with embarrassing titles. An advocate for the power of positive thinking, he said the simple act of reading was an exercise in creative visualization.

She instead engaged in destructive visualization. Daydreaming ways to kill Travis. Then there was a scene — one she thought unrelated to her husband — she evoked over and over. She's in the heart of the Islamic world, infidelling. When she confessed the fantasy to Major Olmstead, he suggested she imagine doing something constructive there, something helpful. She said it was helpful cussing Muḥammad in Mecca, helped put her to sleep. Her honesty earned her another ridiculous reading assignment.

That's when she started plopping her daily dose in the toilet, birth control and all. Sure enough, back came her bad case of the war jitters, where the sudden sound of Travis yelling her name about bounced her out of her boots. But her desire also came roaring round the bend, and she felt a bit like her daddy's reconditioned '70 American Motors Rebel Machine, the V8 engine with its four-barrel Motorcraft carburetor.

Smith gave a thought to visiting the old bastard of a biker — all his Warlock buddies called him Crease — wasting away with wife number five along a rural length of the I-4 corridor, bitching about spics this, wetbacks that. She hadn't seen him since she shipped out for boot camp — she'd rather hang herself with a rusty length of concertina wire.

Instead of turning south, she could head north, toward Canada. Seek asylum. She'd have to steal across the border. All she brought was her driver's license and military ID.

Ray Tyro opens his compact. His camouflage cream is spent. He tosses the tin into the dying fire. Barehanded, he picks out a couple of warm coals. Cups the embers and blows till they glow. They catch. For a moment, he holds a flame wavering in his palm.

The burn, its seared-skin smell, flashes him back — fighting toward the torched Opel SUV on the low-slung bridge. Green I-beams angled over the muddy Euphrates. He stuck his hand through the shattered driver-side window, like reaching into a preheated oven. Two colleagues. One on the board of the International Peace Operations Association, a trade union for private military contractors. The other a former SEAL and personal trainer to movie stars, had his own line of workout videos. Both men, dead. Strapped into the front seats, charred and smoldering, smelling like pigs forgotten on a spit. Their throats slit *after* they'd been burned to bubbling black. Ray forced to leave behind their bodies. An atrocity, a violation of the Ranger Creed. To be dragged through the streets. Strung up from the riveted spans. But before Ray abandoned the remains of his teammates, with AK rounds ripping all around him, he drew his curved trench knife and gouged open one of the smoldering cardboard crates. There, he found package after melting, shrink-wrapped package. Stamped-steel forks, spoons, knives. The mission: make a delivery for subcontracted food caterers from Baghdad to a recently established forward operating base west of Fallujah. They were ferrying flatware — Ray resists the memory, refusing his murderous fury. He strives to stay present. Pain helps.

He drizzles canteen water on the cinders in his burning hand. Fizzle and smoke. With his thumb, he crushes wet coals into a warm mash he smears over his face. He's vanishing. He must be careful — anonymity permits everything.

This ritual erasure once evoked pride. Bound by brotherhood, backed by the resolve of a nation under siege. These days, his thirtieth birthday lying in ambush, his long hair thinning, his beard ever thicker, he's a sad, aging white dude. More clown than commando. A bought-and-sold soldier. Gone from fighting a right war — ready to notch kills as payback for the obliterated 3,000 — to waging a wrong one. After which, Ray let himself be poached by one and another private security company, figuring if he was going to fight for wrong reasons, he should be sorely compensated. In terms of pay grade, entering the private sector was like getting promoted to one-star general. He put the money to good use. After his in-laws, the Jalals, were killed in the Al-Rashid district of Baghdad, he started sending 10k here, 5k there, to his mother in Jersey without so much as a note. He could tell how she was doing by how long it took her to cash his checks — the longer the better. When he was recommended for the Standard surveillance job, he'd been pulling down a thousand dollars a day for a three-months-on-one-month-off schedule. From that there to this here, earning half his rate but over a full 365, selling his skills in the States to who-knew-who, and toward what end he has no idea. But he would damn sure find out.

Smith woke with a neck crick as the sun rose. Little notion who she was. Tired with travel. The stinky, humid cab of her truck parked at a gas station. Hearing the *shoosh* of semis outside and the morning sounds of her empty stomach, a nearly audible ache to pee.

She slapped her face and hupped to, at attention behind the wheel, her sense of self partly restored by the sting. With it, a sense of purpose: she wanted to go for a swim in the ocean, get clean. She'd grown up splashing between the Gulf of Mexico and Florida's Space Coast, and she'd been landlocked or sandbound since she enlisted. She had a couple hundred bucks. Enough for four more tanks of gas at ten-miles-per.

She spent the last of her cash at a BP in Pennsylvania she thought to boycott because of the *Deepwater Horizon* mess but she had no choice. As she approached the East Coast, her jaw aching from all the gas-station jerky she'd been gnawing, she couldn't steer clear of interstates — all roads and signs leading the way to New York City. Might not be so bad to have some hustling bustle after the isolation and military monotony of Leonard Wood.

Her truck got her over the Tappan Zee before it sputtered, died, and coasted to a stop on the shoulder. Relieved, she ditched the three-year-old Dodge Ram for whoever found it first. Her 10k signing bonus for re-upping all went toward the down payment on that pickup instead of paying down some of her debt. From the ashtray she fished out her rings, planning to pawn them. She removed any trash that might identify her. Unscrewed both license plates. Popped the truck's VIN plate off the dash. This would only buy a little time. VINS were stamped on every major car part. Law enforcement would eventually process, trace the truck, and alert AWOL Apprehension.

She slipped out of her jeans, pulled on her last clean tank top, flashing traffic, and climbed into her dirty camos. She'd draw more attention in uniform, but she'd be safer. Earn a little sympathy, maybe a handout. She clipped the leather holster of the small, weighty pepperbox pistol at the small of her back, shouldered her field pack, and humped it through the outer boroughs. Took her a couple days to thumb and bum her way into Manhattan — she wasn't getting on no death trap of an underground train — and got dropped off in the West Village at nightfall during a July heat wave.

The Christopher Street celebrities deadbolted themselves into air-conditioned townhouses. Out came the trannies done up like vampires, reedy black boys in bras.

Heading farther downtown to get sight of the ocean, she found her way to the southwestern-most pier, between the New York Council of the Navy League and the terminal for the Staten Island Ferry. The water's edge lapped against the pylons. A dim Statue of Liberty in the distance. Hand up like she had a question.

The nighttime temp had risen from ninety-odd degrees at midday — humid, heavy — and Smith stank from high heaven to hell's cellar. Couldn't tell the smelly soup of her self from the odor wafting off the water.

She tucked her holstered pepperbox into a pocket of her field pack and draped her digicams overtop, a pixilated camouflage heap in a shadowy corner. If someone stole all her stuff, so be it. Hopping the banister, she dangled, then plunged into the black Atlantic.

Frigid, dreadful, and dark, the ocean was a withdrawal dream. She scrubbed and rinsed as best she could, gargled and spat while she treaded salty water. The current was strong and suggestive, coaxing her — away from the rearing, beaming center of Western civilization — into deep water. The draw of it more frightening than any sea creatures below the surface. She floated a moment, let the current carry her. If she did nothing, if she relaxed too long, she'd be shuttled out to sea past Lady Liberty, who, come to find, didn't have her hand up to ask a question — she was waving. Bye-bye, Bellum.

When the maintenance and retrofits of the liftboat were finished, twelve days late, Evangelína stayed a week in one of the *Lacie*'s two cramped VIP staterooms, like a stowaway in a teak closet, during the slow, sickening motor out to the *Veslefrikk Z* platform.

At platform, the *Lacie* had trouble with the preload. The ROV driver was a twitchy techie from British Columbia — pimply and pálida como el hueso. Entirely incompetent, he took a week to find firm seabed before they could jack up.

During the delay, she ran weighted laps around the heliport. Eight and a half circuits about equaled a mile. After each mile, she changed direction or she became queasy. As the delay reached its seventh day, the roughnecks turned overly deferential, which made her increasingly suspicious. She memorized each of the international crew's names, first and last, but she addressed them by their jobs: Driller, Derrickman, Shakerhand, Mudman. Helped keep them in line — in the face of her gender, despite her height — if not under control. A few she gave nicknames. They found them endearing even though insult was her intent. The slippery South African tool-pusher she called Atún, Tuna. The floorman and motor-man, rotund Algerian twins, hairy and happy-go-lucky, were Alegrías. When they asked what it meant, she told them joyous, and kept to herself that it was slang for testicles.

The American roustabouts were worse than the grabby Tampico locals, whistling and winking, behind her back whispering, Shorty this, Shorty that, but they dealt an entertaining poker game. The youngest and tallest among them claimed to be a bayou shark, and he did have a wide, white smile that seemed sharpened.

Evangelína refused to trust a word he said. Her dismissive disbelief made her mull — for a minute — taking the lanky boy to bed. She'd be done with the tens of thousands of dollars in bills for doctors and sperm donors. Her mestizo child would have a sound chance of growing taller than five feet. But she didn't. She wouldn't. "Bayou roustabout," she said, reconsidering her strong hole cards — pair of jacks — before the flop came down and checking her bet to give the false impression of weakness, "you think maybe just this once you could *not* deal me a hand like a chicken foot?"

He shuffled his chips like a professional, said, "I might could," and yet he had the tells of a mark — closing up his hand a minute before he mucked it, fingering his stack well before he raised — and she only lost money one night, the last.

On her way uptown in the Day-Glo night, Smith felt cold and ashamed. Her hair dripping the length of her spine. She'd lost control. Then it hit her. She wasn't under control; control was hers to lose.

She marched up Broadway through Times Square at midnight, every bit as gaudy and egregious as the Vegas Strip, only it sprawled up instead of along.

All in one place at one time, there were more people of every persuasion moving hurriedly about in the middle of the night than she'd ever seen in her life. She tired of juking the motley lot. Made herself a cardboard sign. Worked in a misspelling. The dumber they thought you were, the more they gave — *Lady war vet could use assistence, peace!*

Soon she had enough to buy herself a five-dollar hot dog tonged from gray water by a man who smelled stronger than she did and occupied a cart that, on its side, read, *If you love you're Freedom thank a veteran.* When she held out her fist filled with pocket change, he shook his head. "On house. Nice one with Bin Laden." He gave her a hamming thumbs-up. "Next, you get King Abdullah. Mindmaster nina leven. Send all drones. The better the more. Waterboard him one time for Ahmadis."

She said, "Well alright, Amadeus," and, "Hotdamn," returning his Lynndie England thumbs-up.

He smiled and said, "Hot dog."

She deposited the coins into her pack along with her sign. Bit the nasty-looking, delicious dog, ate it plain and fast and nearly choked it up when she saw the box of a building in front of her, neon Stars and Stripes on its side, was a recruitment office.

Fighting back a panic attack, she focused on her breathing exercises. Hastened east on Forty-Second, cut down around Bryant Park, then up Fifth. She strode north toward Central Park, and it took a couple of wandering, sleepless days before she got comfortable with her bivouac, or was too beat to care. Not hard for a soldier to camp out, she told herself, especially in summertime. More police than people in the park after dark. Its deepest uptown reaches seemed remote as Ocala Forest, except for the sirens wailing out of ambulances caught in 2 a.m. traffic and the admonishing burps belched from cop cars with wicked indigestion. Eventually, she found the perfect tree for her tree hammock, an out-of-the-way beech northwest of the North Woods, near the old stone fortress of the Blockhouse flying a threadbare flag.

To keep rats, raccoons, and possums from ransacking her roost, Smith peed duckwalking around the base of the tree. She climbed up and reclined beneath the canopy.

While she lay swaying, exhausted awake, she told herself she'd get her daddy to wire her some money his broke ass didn't have because he owed her bigtime. Roughing her up and chasing her off the way he did. She'd run from him and into the arms of the Army, and here she was running from the Army. Shit, she'd rent a little studio, or a loft, whatever that was, like they did on TV. Maybe she'd even *be* on TV. That didn't come to pass, she could hang herself from this here beech. Sure way to wind up on all the newsstands.

Trying to put herself to sleep, she came up with tabloid headlines that would run over the picture of her dangling body. One she liked best was *No Jessica Lynch.*

Staring through the dark spangled leaves of her tree, she returned to her recurring fantasy — she sneaks into Islam's holiest place, Mecca, wearing a black Gulf-style abaya, covered head to ankle, barefoot. Mixed in among the throng, she undresses. Removes first the niqab from her face. Then the hijab from her head. Lastly, she pulls the abaya off her body. She wears nothing underneath. The mob gasps, parts, goes silent. Naked before the bearded men and covered women, here she usually starts cursing them and their prophet. This time she sees herself raising her open hands to her ears, palms forward, fingers slightly splayed, as if signaling the crowd to stop, asking them to hold their stillness.

When they do, she lowers her hands and folds them across her bare chest, right atop left, overlapping to the wrists. She's doing what she's seen Muslims do a million times. She unfolds her hands, bows at the waist, hands on knees slightly bent, spine perfectly parallel with the ground. Poured water would not fall from her back. She rises. Then settles to her knees, bowing again, knocking her forehead painfully against the ground, feeling as much of the ground with her nose as her brow. She holds this pose and waits for the first stone.

A lusty Ada danced the jitterbug with little Sammy Davis, Jr., in the Stardust Room of the Berle. The scene she brought to life was silent, motion picture in a time before talkies, more memory than dream — getting difficult to distinguish the difference.

Milton Xavier Wright's next thought was the same as it'd been for thirty-five years: Ada was dead. Slung from the giant two-door coupe, Ada skipped across the tarmac. He could see himself there at the crash site, though he shouldn't've been, couldn't've been, she facedown in tall grass on the shoulder, burbling her last breaths into a blood puddle. He'd been afraid to move her, her neck kinked like a canvas fire hose; he'd been afraid not to move her, she drowning in her own fluids. But he hadn't been there. Had he?

Milton roused — hungry, coming to in the deprivation chamber of the oubliette, an egg-shaped hollow below the armory cellar, discovered as part of the caverns when the basement was blasted and pick-axed. Excavated bluestone became the armory walls.

Modeled on the one under the Bastille, the oubliette once stored dynamite, then ice. The room remained a constant 50 degrees, needed no heat in winter or cooling in summer. An efficient space. In it, Milton was nearer the inner elements. Closer to the core. Here, the cavernous air, the weather underground, felt therapeutic, even if he worried about the noxiousness and flammability of the earthly emissions.

Ada forced her way through his newly occurring migraines, his occasional blackouts, or she was their cause. His reflections were becoming painfully vivid, continuous. Hallucinogenic. More like flashbacks, they overtook him. The vapors. Then they vanished — he felt like himself. But they were becoming more frequent. The visions swelled like balloons in his brain, caused him considerable confusion.

He'd spent decades gaining a measure of control over his intrusive thoughts. Here he was, in his dotage, losing control. Especially when those thoughts concerned Ada, who was domineering in life. Willful as all get-out. Why should she be any different in death?

Every morning Milton made this same transition. Primordial lungfish emerging from muddy water: sluggish, hesitant, the pull of ages drawing him back into the primitive ooze. He spent time between two elements, amphibious — the past present, the dead alive.

This carried him to his next daily realization. He was dying.

The thought shook him stark awake. He held his breath, pounded his sternum with his fist. Far before dawn; he hadn't gotten more than four hours sleep in decades.

How strange. He must rediscover his looming mortality morning after morning.

Two years ago, he received a partial laryngectomy, endured the removal of twenty-six lymph nodes. Convalescing after the surgery, his neck stitched, glued haphazardly

39

back together, he got his stage-IV diagnosis. Dealt the death card, ace of spades.

To discuss treatment, the oncologist brought in reinforcements. Visited with the radiation and chemo staffs, outnumbering Milton five to one.

They took turns describing a harrowing narrative of trial and pain without promise of redemption. Seven weeks of intense radiation therapy, when a sore throat so severe would develop that swallowing, eating, and talking would be difficult, if not impossible, for upwards of a year. Another staffer added: And we'll mix in chemo once a week beginning with radiation therapy. Each treatment —

His voice, like a hacksaw, rose hurtfully out of him: Not interested.

Sergeant Wright, quality of life is an important factor in this decision, but we need to be perfectly clear you understand what it'll mean to refuse further treatment.

Surgery was one thing. You all are trying to drop the atom bomb on me now. Not putting any more toxins in this body. What got me here in the first place. Didn't have a say that go-round. This time, I got a say. I say zap some other poor sap.

Maybe you should take a little time.

Just tell me one thing. Without treatment,

how long I got?

The radiologist turned to the oncologist, a small, waistless woman who looked like a teenager. Milton didn't understand why most of the VA doctors were residents of SUNY Downstate, kids who wouldn't know Basic Training from potty training. She turned to Milton reclining in his hospital bed. Without treatment, Sergeant Wright? Her voice was loud, insistent. Six months to two years? We simply can't know. Could be longer, but it could also be shorter. Your cancer's metastasized. It's sure to continue spreading. To the lungs, maybe the brain. After that, it's pretty quick, and not painless.

Consider it my contribution to lowering the costs of healthcare.

In all seriousness, Sergeant Wright, the short end doesn't give you much time.

Most folks I grew up with are long damn gone. Life expectancy for black men aint what it is for the rest of you all. Survived me a war, a wife. Outlived my parents and hers. Got no living siblings, no kids. I've some loose ends, same as anyone, but I have zero desire to spend my last days too sick to talk. We got work to do, a shelter to run. Whose big idea's it anyway?

The five healthcare professionals shifted

41

and shrugged uncomfortably in their baggy scrubs. The fingers of a small hand doing delicate work in an extra-large glove. His oncologist, the thumb, offering her opposition, said, What big idea are you referring to?

He tried to clear his throat, couldn't. He sat up, unsure where he was. In a neglectful VA hospital or his tumbledown Catskills hotel. In the living past or the dying present. The thin line getting thinner all the time. Had he said all that, and right after surgery? If he hadn't, he should've. Should've said all that and then some.

Wind was hiring landmen away from petroleum. Evangelína had entertained two good offers for management positions from upstart outfits in an industry where her womanhood was at a premium. The wind rush in the windswept West Texas plains, especially the Llano Estacado, was allowing ranchers and farmers to lease their land to wind developers for a set rental per turbine, or a percentage of gross annual revenue. Wind offered a clean revenue stream to supplement farming income without disturbing planting, harvesting, and grazing. Cows chewed and cotton grew all the same beneath the great, gradual sweep of the tri-blades, even if they swatted migratory birds out of the air by the dozens.

Part of the wind recruitment pitch had been: Don't do harm. Do good. Wind was a greeny, crunchy culture less inclined toward discrimination. That was why she hadn't made the jump. She wanted the challenge of succeeding among the ts'ulo'ob, those-who-are-not-us, starched, determined white men with high hairlines, boxy shoulders, and shovel chins.

Since the start of the Arab Spring, IRJ had reconsidered every alternative. Shipping employees off, letting people go, despite record profits. There was the split with Halliburton. The $2 billion contract to rebuild Iraq's oil infrastructure neared completion. Everyone save the corporate officers feared for their jobs and felt the company's mission to be adrift.

We're a global engineering, construction, and services company supporting the energy, hydrocarbon, government agencies, minerals, civil-infrastructure, power, industrial, and commercial markets — we also do laundry! IRJ had become a business of barracks builders and trash burners, handling logistics and operations for the US military. As the larger wars in the Middle East petered out, the company offered services to newly militarizing nations looking to cut costs and outsource some of what IRJ called the logistical Ls: lunches, linens, and latrines. This straying afield led to a crackpot company initiative, Sunrise at Seventeen Seventy.

Earlier in the year, the pdf announcement went round. Her colleagues quoted it to one another in nasally voices: *The first truly sustainable land development program in Queensland, Australia, surrounded by a national park, marine park, a recreation reserve, and a conservation park, Sunrise embraces ecological sustainability throughout in the management of the carbon, water, energy, and waste cycles. With IRJ's own next-generation wind turbines, built to outcompete Siemens, the wind farm at Sunrise is only the beginning of the greening of the business we will grow.*

Evangelína was, admittedly, oversensitive to appropriation and cultural ventriloquism of any kind, but this was absurd. And who'd written the copy that made it sound like a petro-industry theme park? When, in passing, she'd asked Bizzy, IRJ's COO, about the project, he said, Call it an experiment in appearances. He sighed — something about him altered. He lowered his voice: Between you and me . . . He shrugged a shoulder, touched her forearm, said, Please, Evy, be patient. Someday soon you may understand.

At the Nourishing Soup Kitchen on 110th off Fifth, Smith sat alone. A ham sandwich sagged in her hand. A strange face — hers — scowled up from a room-temperature bowl of broth.

An old brother with swagger and a trim white goatee interrupted her lunch, introducing himself as Milton Wright. His voice was a harsh rasp that rattled in his neck: "Billet homeless vets in the Catskills. Help get them off these here streets." He thumbed the brim of his cap. On it, a sun and star, split by a lightning bolt — the 75th Ranger Regiment insignia.

"They say you got neck cancer."

He sucked on something that clicked against his teeth. "Sore throat."

These down-and-out vets, she'd learned, were worse than ugly cheerleaders when it came to their gossip. She swirled her broth with her cheap spoon. "Say you run some sort of camp in the mountains. Forced labor."

"Indentured servitude's more like it. We do some alpaca ranching, good bit of farming. Lot of work." He told her it was tough to get vets to shift their standard operating

45

procedures. "Get them fretting over the Fedco seed catalog instead of Brownells gun parts. How to keep the old chainsaws well oiled and firing cleanly instead of worrying over the actions of their weapons. Make them care about the health and hygiene of their alpaca. Lot of my soldiers end up going home afterwards," he added, "or making a home for themselves in the Catskills, where they come to feel secure."

Her hands — aged a year in the last few weeks. Her fingernails stank no matter how hard she scrubbed. The city was turning her dirty and mean and in a hurry. How many hundreds, thousands of bottles and cans had she sorted for their deposits?

He ahemmed, sounding a little like the territorial, caterwauling Asian women she'd been fending off from streetcorner garbage bins, women who smelled and looked clean and surely had a warm bed, a hot bath, tiny women who could cough up and spit lungers with the precision of varsity outfielders.

She asked, "This camp a yours got a name?"

"The Standard Grande. My not-for-profit's called Standard Company." A charity, he explained. Said she was talking to the owner, executive director, president of the board of trustees, and commander-in-chief.

"Inherited the place from my wife when she . . . well."

"I'm with the 58th Transportation Battalion," Smith said. "Was with. Our motto's *We Set the Standard.*"

"Take it as a sign."

There was a scuffling in one corner of the cafeteria, a nonsensical shouting, some man arguing aloud with himself.

"Got turned away from a shelter last week," she said, "after nearly getting mugged. Told me I had to be homeless for a year to qualify for a bed. Don't matter. I'm 88-motherfucking-mike. Motor transport operator. Always on the move."

"Means there's nowhere you're safe."

She lifted her stamped metal spoon, thin and bendable as foil, folded it in half, and splashed it into her plastic bowl. "Trying to scare me?"

"Not scare," he said, "warn. War comes home. Every soldier humps it in his ruck."

"Her ruck."

"Right. Usually I focus in on the handsome Johnnies." He looked around. "Seeing more of you homeless Jodies out and about. Been meaning to retire. Told myself no new recruits. Then I saw you. Thought, What's one more? Try to be a bit more . . . what do they call it? Gender neutral?"

47

Around them, men and women shoved bland, starchy food into their unshaven faces, most of them black or brown, the white faces tanned or sunburned.

"If I'm homeless," she said, "it's by choice."

"Easy to say here in summer. Take some advice. Go on down to the VA office. Get yourself a disability determination. Sit through the Comp and Pension, you walk out with a lifetime of income. Takes time to start collecting. Once you do it don't stop. You'll know you're homeless when you can't list an address. That's when they'll give your application the stamp of approval. Once you're squared away, I got a PO box upstate you can use."

"What's Comp and Pension?"

"Psych exam. You go in. You apply for a total. Total disability compensation for PTSD pays out about twenty-five hundred a month. You got your DD 214?"

She sniffed hard. Deserters didn't get a Certificate of Release or Discharge from Active Duty.

"You got someone —" He coughed, a cough that caused him some pain. "Scuse me. Someone who can maybe get you a notarized copy? Mail it to you. Or to you care of me?"

She'd had about enough of this know-it-all old brother. "Nobody. Nothing. No father, no husband. Don't got no dog nor a care in the hootenanny world."

"What, you get a dishonorable?"

She turned her look from mean to murder. All he did was nod. Didn't bother to give her the snappy salute he'd given a few of the men.

He made rounds, slapping backs and touching shoulders like a career military man — high-ranking but no general — a soldier who hadn't pawned his soul for a gold star.

Smith stopped paying attention.

"Got an idea, downhome girl." His low-throttle growl close to her ear made her gasp, his breath herbal, warm and bad. "Let me take you out, buy you a real lunch."

"You trying to date me?"

"Call it a date with an edible sandwich."

Willing to do just about anything for a decent meal, she slapped the bread back on top of the shimmering slice of meat and said, "Homeless lady vet eats lunch — take two!"

"We'll go to the Carnegie Deli. New York City institution and a rite of passage both. Do me a favor first. Slip that bent spoon in your pocket so management don't see it."

■ ■ ■ ■

Alone, applying his face covering — so black it's blue — Ray feels like his employer, Baum, the Kingston lawyer, is redacting his features.

As his face-black dries and cools, it contracts, drawing tight his skin. He's bound by his current contract. The work — a combination of field consulting and covert information gathering — mostly accomplished. The retainer he's on is set to expire with the arrival of his replacement. He's the boots, next come the suits. The only feeling more distressing than being confined by a contract is not knowing where or when the next contract will come.

He isn't cut out for undercover work. He's conditioned to go in silent and strong, with utmost tactical discretion, camouflaged but in uniform. Passing as homeless was easy at first. Had no problem with lying. But maintaining the lies ground him down. He kept notes, made outlines and charted chronologies, until it got to be too much. He'd gathered enough intel from inside, and he decided that as an outrider he could keep a better eye on Wright and his herd. Up here, Ray can watch silly Standard Company from high ground.

Wright and his Simon Says. His furry uniforms — that Wright didn't deign to wear — intended to demean and embarrass so he could maintain the upper hand. Squeezing headcase grunts, capitalizing on the weak-willed, every bit a war profiteer. Worse, because he's turning no profit. Wright's more mercenary than Ray. Deeper in the hole because he refuses to admit it. His cancer's surely a ploy, way to get more disability to pay down debt.

Here at camp, Ray has the books he kept in Baghdad: broken hardback of Lattimore's translation of Thucydides' *History of the Peloponnesian War;* soggy Signet paperback, *Henry V;* falling-apart copy, his fifth or sixth, of the *Ranger Handbook.* Page by page, he feeds them into the fire.

When done, tired and hungry, he lets down his guard, allows the past to con its way through the security checkpoint he's set up, where it's sure to detonate in his face —

Over a decade ago, in his last battalion OPORD briefing before redeployment, Ray's Ranger company was told by their top-heavy CO, a gone-to-pot veteran of the first Gulf War, My best piece of advice to you all is as follows . . .

A long pause as they waited, most of them, like Ray, antsy to exit the hangar, cross the tarmac, board the commercial 747 contracted out as part of Operation Iraqi Freedom.

Finally the CO said, You'll only hear me say this once, men. And after I've said it, I'll deny having done so. He took a breath that sucked the air from their lungs like a close-quarters explosion. While you're there, men, you make sure you have a plan to kill every-one you meet. I mean everyone.

Here Ray is, more than a decade later, sitting cross-legged on American soil in the blue mountain morning, hours before dawn, a civilian still living in accordance with those deadly wartime orders.

When he's starved and sleep-deprived, he puzzles out these terrible contingencies.

He asks the faint fire, "Where would you do the lawyer?"

Snatch him on one of his late Kingston nights leaving his Stockade District office, weight him down and drop him like an anchor into the Ashokan Reservoir. Let the entire City of New York get a taste of him. But first, drain him of information.

"What about Wright?"

Where he sleeps. Draw up his rope lad-der, pour in a gallon each of Hi-Yield lime

52

sulfur pesticide and Kaboom Shower, Tub & Tile Cleaner. Let the liquids mix in the pour. If he wakes, he'll think it's a prank, one of the vets pissing into his hole. There on the floor of his single-sleeper dungeon, the puddle will produce hydrogen sulfide, found in natural gas, known to percolate through fractured fissures in rock and leech into water wells. Wright'll be unconscious in seconds, dead within a minute. One of the kindest ways to go.

"And the other Standard vets?"

Too damn easy. Like a herd of mad cows sound asleep in a tinderbox barn. Slip a wick into the fuel tank of the generator kept in the Esther House lobby. Light it. Bar the exits with braces sure to burn. Bonfire of the PTSDs.

The veterans of the Standard Grande had been back from their wars for some time, trying to figure out how to live lives in the face of newfound civilian freedoms. No one barking orders but their girlfriends, wives, and mothers. Fuck them. The vets could do anything they wanted anytime — they were Americans in America — though what they wanted wasn't what they needed.

They had good cause to bolt home and wind up straggling in the streets of New

York City, where they couldn't qualify for HUD/VASH benefits, having exhausted the good graces of the DOM program, unable to uncover any information on Project Torch, given the runaround by the administrators of Operation Home. They had multiple DUIs, student loans for what the GI Bill 2.0 didn't cover to attend the University of Phoenix, credit cards with 20 percent interest rates. They were drug addicts, closeted queers, amputees, alcoholics. They were Born Again. They were Black Muslim. They were violent offenders and ethical vegetarians. They'd done short time in county lockups, charged with violating restraining orders, lewd and lascivious conduct, six counts of animal cruelty for selling a litter of kittens with pierced ears over the internet. To say they all expressed both the loss of physical integrity and a response to an event that involved terror and helplessness — the hurting-for-certain hallmarks of PTSD — would've been too easy. The harder truth was that they were men unmanned. More than the sum of the bullet points in the revised *DSM-5,* they were the very reasons for some of the revisions. They were outliers. They hadn't fallen through cracks. The ground opened up and they dove in face first — *hooah!* But they could only live like beasts for so long, so they'd gone with Milt, who gave order to their days, even if his orders were crazy.

The vets mustered at the center of the Alpine village. Over their secondhand camos bought in bulk from Liberty Military PX, they wore full alpaca pelts fastened with lengths of catgut. The pelts, worn casually, were their uniforms, part of Milt's PSYOP campaign to ward off trespassers while keeping alive the legend of the Catskills Sasquatch.

The packed Carnegie Deli thrummed like a hot hive. Smith sat in front of an unbelievable stack of deli meat. The piled-high gore flayed her, opened her wide before she knew what was what.

"You alright?"

She caught herself staring at her untouched heap of sandwich. Pushed away the plate. "Didn't get DDed," she said. "I'm AWOL."

"Alright then."

"Officially deserter," she confessed. "Couldn't do another tour. Done two." She knew things were winding down, getting safer all the time, that shit had hit the fan and this was the clean up afterwards. Her mind said that. But her body sat there fac-

55

ing down a sandwich, practically paralyzed. "Did mouth-to-mouth on a face like that. Could only tell it was a mouth for the few teeth that hadn't been blasted down Toose's throat."

Milt had a look like he'd seen it coming. Take a fresh vet out to lunch, get a shock-and-awe story or two. He pinched his lozenge from his mouth. "Toose?"

"Our interpreter. Haibitan. Just Haibitan." Afghanis were like Brazilian soccer players. No last name. So they'd whipped one up. "He thought all Americans danced the Watusi. Haibitan Watusi. Even had a nametape made. Toose for short."

"Wife used to dance a mean Watusi," Milt offered. "What happened? I can take it."

"How's it a pack of cigarettes costs twelve bucks here? There, you get a carton for pocket change, counterfeit Camels rolled by legless orphans. Watusi smoked Pines. Loved him his Pines. He'd been having a hard time finding pottable water."

"*Potable.*"

"Huh?"

"Don't mind me. Sometimes I just got to prove I put the GI Bill to fair use."

She had no idea how Toose afforded cigarettes. No running water but all the men smoked. "At checkpoint," she said, "filled my canteen cup, handed it to him. From about a klick away, out of some school we were supposed to have secured, a sniper shot my can —" She swung her open hand, smacked herself in the chin and rocked her head back with the mimed force. "— pow into his face." She stared at her sandwich. "What we looking at?"

He got that klicks-away gaze she knew meant more than shared tears. It amazed her how contagious anxiety was among the war-torn, like clap in wartime. She knew Milt'd been a serious soldier. Putting some of her emotional burden into his ruck settled her a little. He looked confused and upset, not at her but for her.

"Mine's the Woody Allen," he said eventually, "corned beef and pastrami both. I'm an honorary Jew, you know. You got —"

"Like what's-her-name on that show *The View*?"

"We rough it at the Standard. Primitive as can be. No electric, never mind TV."

Took Smith a moment. She found the face on the Wall of Fame: "Whoopi Goldberg."

"Whoopi's no Jew. She's got an opportunistic stage name. Smacks of Uncle Tomism. Now Sammy Davis is another story." His look was a plea. "Sammy Davis, Jr.?"

She shook her head and pulled her sandwich carefully toward her.

"Used to do one heck of a Sammy. Been known to finish it off with a few lines from 'Mr. Bojangles.' But I'll spare you." Milt pointed. "Yours is corned beef. But we can leave these plates sitting right here and get on outside if you'd feel better."

"You just bought me a twenty-five-dollar sandwich, on your charge card. Here's what. I'm'a take one bite of the corn beef. See what a twenty-five-dollar sandwich tastes like. Eat the thing that threatens to eat you, right? Then score a couple boxes and get em to go. You take mine on up to your Camp David, feed it to hongry-ass Bigfoot. Cause I gots to banana, man. But first —" Smith hefted the sandwich-half with both hands. Nearly a pound of flesh. She stretched her jaw and bit. Chewed. Choked down a mouthful. Meat, warmed blood, rusty, salty, she feeling a tongue lolling in her mouth, her tongue — giving mouth-to-mouth, she'd gotten burned on a hot shard of her canteen cup buried in the exposed bone of Watusi's chin. When she'd lifted her head for air, Watusi burbled, trying to tell her something, kept reaching upward, his mangled mouth saying what sounded like Many piss. Many piss. She told him not to talk. Found his topi, a square cap intricately embroidered with dots of mirror, deadly, that flashed in the sun. Surely what the sniper aimed for. Knowing she was doing wrong, but not knowing what was right, she placed the cap on his crotch, which wasn't wet. He pawed his chest, trying to reach into his vest. She was losing him. His eyes filled. He looked at her, into her, and, in English, said, My number three wife. She only understood because he'd said it to her a hundred times. She laughed, painfully, said, My number two husband, if you're proposing, you're gonna need a ring. American women don't settle for sheep. He nodded. From his eyes alone, warm and crimped, his mouth a wet red mess, she got the sense he was smiling. He tapped his chest. She said, Too tight? He shook his head, placed his open hand over his heart, and turned away from her. She unbuttoned his vest. Into the lining of the vest was sewn a plastic window, like in a wallet. Behind the window was a photo of her: standing in front of the Abu Hanifa mosque, scaffolding around its rebuilt clock tower, making a peace sign.

Later she asked around. Other terps told her he was probably saying, Maní piss, my father. Watusi was from Zaranj. Village one klick from the Iranian border, a place coalition forces didn't go, a place she couldn't get to, to say sorry to his father, so she let it rest.

Milton was watching her in a way that made her want to wipe her mouth, her face. She set down the sandwich. "I got a pattern. Going AWOL on you."

She left him sitting between the two towering sandwiches about to topple, and it was a few weeks before she mustered the courage to ask about him. The manager of the soup kitchen said she could send him word, that a week or so might go by before he got it, deep as he was in the Catskills and entirely off the grid.

Took him a few visits over a couple months to cajole her upstate, and she caved after he confessed to having cancer, albeit in remission. Just like she'd done with the Army, she committed herself before knowing what she was in for. Milt had a contract for her to sign, and she flipped through without reading. The fact of it was enough; it made him seem legitimate. So she signed on the solid line, but first, he said, he needed to lay the foundation for her arrival.

The Standard vets called their hides ghillie suits, except for Stotts-Dupree, who called his a yowie, which was how they referred to

60

them at Camp Robinson, Army National Guard Sniper School, where Stotts-Dupree flunked out after contracting a bad case of the yips.

Most of the vets were accustomed to the notion that in uniform they looked like Germanic shepherds being retributively raped from behind by a herd of lanky sheep. Come winter, they'd again be grateful for the warmth the pelts provided. But here it was, end of a scalding, droughty summer, and they were in furs. They were uncomfortable and irritable.

Their routine had been busted. They hadn't eaten lunch. Midday Simon Says — part military drill, part camaraderie builder — had been canceled, the daily briefing pushed back to evening. All so Milt could make one of his weekly milk runs.

Scratching their beards of varying lengths, the Standard vets stood at a remove from the old fountain pool they used to contain their cook fire. The two Marines of the company climbed in, kicked over the sewer grate that served as a grill, and stomped out the coals. Smoke tumbled up around them. They sought to settle a grudge and, despite the disruption, the entire company was glad for a diversion from their standing orders — split wood; set snares; see to the meat

61

rabbits, chickens, and alpaca; gather their droppings to age, mash up, and water down to fertilize the three-acre garden after they tilled; weed endlessly, harvest, seed the fall crops, on and on. Readying for winter was a nine-month means they got a break from only while trying to survive its end. This unrelenting work distracted them from their real-world guilt over the families they'd abandoned, and from the certain knowledge that these families were easier off for their absences.

In charge was Sergeant Paul Vessey, the highest-ranking officer of Standard Company and, as the only other Nam vet, the most senior man after Milt.

Vessey was a year north of sixty with nothing to his name — nothing except his dog, Egon. Right before Vessey's life had collapsed on him like a coalmine with no oversight, he'd managed one decent thing: he put his name on the waitlist to adopt a retired military working dog. Just before HUD foreclosed him, he got a call from Lackland Air Force Base. They had a Belgian Malinois, Egon, a sniffer who'd served six years, surviving four tours and two handlers, before hip dysplasia got him declared excess by the Department of Defense. The other vets understood that old-ass Vessey had been brevetted because of Egon. Everybody loved Egon, everyone save Private Stone, whom everyone hated.

The two Marines untied their pelts. One of them, Merced, lay down his walking stick, mumbling, "Improvise, adapt, overcome." The stick, carved with runes only Merced could read, was expertly topped with a five-point antler like a bony hand. MWD Egon barked at the stick, bit one end, and tried to drag it off.

Vessey got a handle on his dog's choker. He made rounds, using Egon's ailment as an excuse to go slow, his knees every bit as grating as the dog's hips. He tallied heads. One missing. Reverend. Absent yet again.

For months, Reverend had been slipping in and out. They all figured he'd split. No surprise, but Vessey wanted to have some intel to report back when Milt returned.

Specialist Dereemus Stotts-Dupree, the baby at age twenty-two, stood alone.

Vessey walked, Egon at his heel, over to him. Stotts-Dupree scuffed a sole of the hobnailed boots he swore by, back and forth — *scri, scri* — over an exposed slab of bluestone. With nearly every pass, the cleats shot sparks. His scruffy cheeks were sucked in under his high cheekbones — he wasn't wearing his top teeth.

"STD, you got any info on Reverend's whereabouts?"

Stotts-Dupree started straight in on the Second Coming, and Vessey turned away from the lisping prophecy, catching enough to feel crazed: how the four happy horsemen of the Apocalypse were bound to come riding down out of the Catskills and into the babbling City of New York on the backs of the Standard alpaca.

"Luce, howbout you," Vessey hollered. "You set eyes on Reverend?"

Specialist Jeffrey "Screw" Luce couldn't quit scratching the itch at the tumescent end of the stump rounded off just below his elbow. He wore army-green, button-down shirts he'd tailored himself; the shortened right sleeves boasted cuffs with cute corduroy buttons, which he claimed made them easier to manage one-handed.

Luce shot a brown rope of chaw spit into the grass, dabbing his mouth with his stump before going vigorously back at the itch.

Vessey gently pulled Luce's hand from the raw nub. "Go gentle."

Luce jerked his arm out of Vessey's grip. "Fucking touch me, Vess, you two-handed homo-ass motherfuck."

The dog flashed his yellow fangs but didn't snarl.

64

"Egon, gîter, boy."

"You and your French-speaking gimp of a German shepherd, you're a goddamn —"

"He's a Malinois, Specialist Screw Luce. You'll address me by my rank or I will sic Egon on you. Watch while he goes to town on your chew toy of a scrotum. Got me?"

"Yeah, shit, I got you. Hearts and minds." Luce leaned over, reached, and held himself with his stump. "Got you right here."

Vessey unclipped the leash from Egon's choker.

Luce stood at attention, clapping his heels together, and saluted with his stump.

Vessey reclipped Egon's leash, returned the salute and hailed the next man, "Stone, you seen Reverend?"

"No I have not seen no Reverend Ranger." Private First Class Samuel Stone was an Army National Guardsman who, in summer of '01, signed up for *One weekend a month, two weeks a year,* and wound up getting twenty-four months of mobilization for his six-year fine-print conscription. He kept his eyes trained on the Marines. "Mighty beautiful thing."

"What, two jarheads about to bust one another over nothing?"

"Nah, man. A meth rock. It's a rough opal."

"Tell it to your sponsor."

"Sponsor's been dead going on two years, which incidentally's how long I been sober." He squatted and held out his open hand to Egon. "Meth's got more names than a freelance pole dancer."

Egon hesitated, whined, and flattened his ears.

Stone said to the dog, "Egon, you know methamphetamine was *the* drug of choice for bombardiers in the Deuce? How's that for testament to its righteousness." He reached into his pocket, brought his empty hand out again, and rubbed a greasy finger on his palm.

Egon sniffed, then licked, and Stone grabbed the dog's tongue, held hard, and gave him a shove in the hindquarter.

Egon yelped, snarled, and leaned into his bite stance.

"Gîter, Egon." Vessey tugged the choker.

Stone said, "Damn mutt chewed a hole in my canteen."

"You got it coming to you, Stone." Vessey pulled Egon along.

On one thigh, another vet smacked out a fleshy drumroll with battered drumsticks.

"Luckson," Vessey said, "you got a bead on Reverend?"

"It's Abdul Alhazred, Vess. How many

times I got to tell you? It's official. Milt's lawyer made it legal."

"You becoming Muslim's like me turning communist."

"Didn't you do time on a commune?"

"Dandelion up in Ontario. Maybe the best year of my life."

"There you go." Alhazred played another run on his thigh, this one quicker, closed, the fast beat saying, *Move along.* "Now if you don't mind, I'm working."

"On?"

"My freestyling. Check it. *My rap occupies a gray area, verbal malaria —*"

"Anyone ever told you you're white?"

"I'm high yellow." *Ba-da-tshh* — Alhazred's joke-roll rim shot was two pats on his thigh followed by a mouthy cymbal crash. "Where Milt at?"

"The city."

"Must say, stupid as his Simon Says is, and much as I hate it before I'm doing it, it's a fine way to start the day. Hearts and minds. Way he leads it, it's like foot drill."

"Beats watching Marines grope each other in the cook fire."

"Hope the brother's seeing a good lady medic. One moment he his ol' sharp self, the next he's gone Airborne without packing a chute. Brother's fighting cancer with cough drops. Shit aint gonna win the war. Hearts and minds, damn."

"They're herbal."

"Vess, come off it. Least the brother could do is get a script for some medical marijuana. Then share, shit. Hearts and minds."

"Hearts and minds. You boys even got any idea where that comes from?"

"Comes from our war. Said it over there a little ironic like."

"Comes from *my* war, not yours. Lyndon B. Johnson. Know who he is?"

"Yes, sir." Alhazred grabbed himself in a lowball salute.

"You young guns all got the same cocky attitude." Vessey tugged Egon's leash and motioned over Petty Officer Ferdinand Wisenbeker, their only sailor and the only vet besides Merced who wore his fur to full effect. Wisenbeker tipped the alpaca face off his head like it was the bill of a ball cap.

Vessey said, "Let's get a fire lit, Wiz. Everybody'll settle down once we eat. You're on KP. Afternoon eggs."

"Don't eat eggs, Vessey, my man. Even if I did, what'd you want? Me to cremate Merced and Botes?"

Private First Class Jairo Merced and Lance Corporal Jacko Botes stood naked from the waist up. Merced had an epic Día de los Muertos mural, tattooed in Technicolor, up his back and across his shoulders. Botes's torso, covered in coarse black hair, looked like the lean body of a wild boar. They bounced on the balls of their boots at opposite ends of the short fountain pool. Merced smacked himself, raising red handprints on his face, his chest; Botes flexed, stretched, and popped his neck.

"Didn't know Filipinos could grow body hair," Luce yelled. "Botes, in a fag bar you'd be a bear!"

When Stone shouted, "Let's roll!" Merced and Botes thwacked together at the center of the ring like two colliding sides of beef.

Wisenbeker leaned in and lowered his voice. "Been made to understand Reverend's being paid by George Soros, who's funding a Standard splinter group. Set up an outpost a couple klicks from here. Amassing forces. Gonna lay siege to the Standard. Shit you not. Know what else he told me?"

Alhazred, Wisenbeker's straight man, offered, "Wait till you hear this, Vess."

Egon lay down and rested his chin on his paws, and Vessey readied himself for another veteran tirade. Grunt talk was a feedback loop. Gossip, prophesy, conspiracy theory, pipe dream. In the information age, most soldiers operated with limited information. So they told stories. Like most Americans. Just trying to make sense. Of a US secretary of state displaying a fake vial of anthrax at the UN General Assembly. Of WMD spirited, eleventh-hour, over the border to Syria, a convoy of presents to President Assad. Or Uday Hussein's snuff videos, showing him feeding the bodies of his victims, sodomized brides kidnapped from their weddings, to his pride of pet lions. Or the neatly severed heads of suicide bombers, some of them women wearing hijab, that were booted around while survivors and soldiers like Merced took photos with their phones.

"What you want me to say?" Wisenbeker said. "Reverend's a stuck-up special ass. Thinks he's better — fucking wannabe West Pointer — cause he read *Art of War*. Whoop-de-do. Dude can do eighty push-ups in two minutes. Aint no operator. *Rangers, lead the way,* my cockeyed dick. Dude's Mossad."

"All this time we been calling him Reverend" — Alhazred clicked his drum sticks — "when we should've been calling him Rabbi."

Wisenbeker said, "Guy sold his gun for corporate sponsorship. And that tomahawk? Come on. Shit's a prop. No one trusts him. Tell him, Abdul."

"I don't know. Seen him lodge that toma-hawk in a tree from far-ass away."

Wisenbeker told Vessey, "Merced says he's got a one-man FOB up a nearby peak. On some high-alt psychotropic psychedelic psilocybin trip. Balancing rocks for enlight-enment. Thinks he's Bruce Lee in *Game of Death*. He knows the dim mak, my foot."

Alhazred said, "I know dim sum."

"Not talking," Wisenbeker said, "bout no cross between oriental buffet and bingo. Talking the dim fucking mak, man." Wisen-beker shoved two fingers into Alhazred's neck.

"Ow."

"The death touch. Said it literally means *press artery* in Chinese."

Alhazred rubbed his neck. "So what's dim sum mean?"

"Fuck if I know," Wisenbeker said. *"Press dumpling?"*

They watched the Marines tangle a min-ute, deadlocked. For most of them, the Standard was their last potshot at a decent life. Once they left, they'd be on their own, and most of them wouldn't make it alone.

Like Luce, who will leave in the middle of a biblical plague of bats to bum his way out to Greenport toward the end of the North Fork of Long Island. There, he begs his ex-

wife, on a Tuesday, on his knees, on her
sunken front stoop, to let him in, and when
she does, as soon as the door closes behind
them, he's back to begging her, back on his
knees. He wants to get her off with his
stump. She can't believe it, and against her
bad judgment, she undresses and lets him.
Despite her reservations and the ugly,
unsanitary look of the thing, she appreciates
it, enjoys it even, the bizarre behavioral
therapy. Trying to turn loss into love. This
alone gets them through the first month,
but it doesn't erase her suspicions. In month
two, she catches him picking up Asian men
on Craigslist, using her computer, and she
throws him out. He rents a room in River-
head at the Peconic Inn, next door to a pizza
parlor, a long commute to Greenport for a
job crewing aboard the Shelter Island ferry.
Before work, he buys a fifth of the cheapest
vodka at the closest package store. Nipping
from the plastic bottle, he walks to the Riv-
erhead train station. Moments after a train
passes, he can be seen, on his knees, as if in
prayer, resting one cheekbone, then the
other, against the tracks. The vibrations
jostle, warm, and loosen the mucus in his
sinuses, the tracks heated on the iciest days
by steel wheels worn to a mirror shine. For
a few seconds, his head clears. He can go

about his day crossing and re-crossing Peconic Bay.

One blustery winter morning, he rises off the track lightheaded and chases after an unloaded freight train picking up speed. He heaves himself aboard with his good hand, his only hand, and settles into an empty unlocked stock-car, its floor covered in frozen manure. There, he eases into the long, windy ride, sub-zero, kept company by a fifth of Kasser's Kavkaski, and twenty-four hours later he's found dead, no ID, his one hand rigor stiff and curled through an opening in the steel slats. The responding firemen and medical workers are confronted with the choice of cutting through the steel wall of the cattle car or breaking the poor hobo's wrist to free his body. An EMT tries a forearm massage to loosen up the hand. Nothing. Guy's hard as rebar. After a call to Anacostia Rail Holdings Company, they decide against cutting the cattle car. With a hair dryer, they take turns thawing the wrist and fingers, the freight train outrageously late by the time John Doe lets go.

■ ■ ■ ■

FALL
2012

■ ■ ■ ■

Evangelína woke hungover — a mescal-induced migraine. In the watery dark outside the porthole, a helicopter jounced onto the platform's heliport. Next came an unexpected knock and an Aussie holler from the other side of the reinforced door: "Whirlybird's all set, Miss Canek!"

Cursing in Spanish, she hurriedly dressed in a business suit that was asinine aboard an oilrig. She packed her suitcase, jettisoned what was left of the pound of dried apricots she'd brought with her. Her mamí, a curandera, claimed they were a fertility food. Evangelína had yet to tell Mamí she was trying to get pregnant.

As the helicopter approached the coast, the dawning Texas haze thickened. They whirred over the countless platforms and tankers offshore. Beyond the beaches, refinery row: retention pools, storage tanks, the eternal flames of the flare stacks burning waste gas.

They flew above the suburbs. Finally, Houston. While the sun blistered over the Gulf of Mexico, the helicopter touched down atop IRJ Tower. Evangelína — sick to her stomach, off balance — disembarked refusing the hand offered her by the copilot.

No one was at the helipad to greet her. She spent a moment gathering effects, checking her phone. A weather alert. Harris County was on the western end of an unseasonal *continental haze episode.* Sounded like a PR concoction designed to put a measure of abstraction between a catastrophe and how to address it. She gazed over the yellowed city parched and dusted by an unbreakable drought.

Wanting to work out some of the mescal, she bounced her suitcase down three flights of stairs. She waited in the understated lobby on the thirty-seventh floor for her shotgun meeting, called by her boss's boss, F. Bismarck "Bizzy" Rolling, with whom she was close.

Unsteady on her sea legs, head splitting, unshowered, she sniffed her hair. Whiff of the platform, oily and oceanic, but it had a nice shine, a springy bounce. She wore her jacquard cap-sleeved skirt suit, something her mamí would call el vestido de una piruja, because it shamefully cut across the back of her knees and offered up a small wedge of cleavage — Ay, Dios mío, ayúdame, Evangelína.

She tugged down her skirt hem. Bizzy liked and lobbied for her. Papí had worked under Bizzy most of his adult life. Papí'd been among the first Mesoamerican landmen in the States. Evangelína, the lone female graduate in her class at Texas Tech's Petroleum Land Management program, was one of a few dozen women in the American Association of Professional Landmen, and the sole constituent of the AAPL lesbian caucus.

Evangelína didn't know why she'd been summoned. Neither did she understand why she'd been sent offshore. Her specialty was not managing the reconditioning of offshore rigs, out at sea; her expertise was securing leases for drilling and mineral rights. She preferred the water from a sandy beach, daiquiri in hand, or paddling a kayak downriver, in view of both banks. A phenom in the field, she was a failure as a manager. Landowners were more trusting of a woman, which made fellow landmen more distrustful.

With peeptoe pumps nudging the floor-to-ceiling window, toenails unpainted, she looked dizzily out, her breath condensing on the glass in the overly air-conditioned lobby.

Bizzy's executive assistant, Marisol, approached. Evangelína, about to ask for an aspirin, was cut off: "Señor Rolling está listo para tu, Señorita Canek."

Evangelína felt a dull confusion. The feeling sharpened into fear. This wasn't how personal assistants addressed prospective management. It wasn't the informal tu that worried her; it was the señorita, as if Evangelína were a wayward schoolgirl.

Bizzy stood backlit by the Houston morning. He didn't believe in sitting at work, kept to his feet all day at that high desk, practically a podium. Bic ballpoint in hand, he looked more like a philharmonic conductor than chief operations officer of IRJ, Inc., formerly Irvine Raus & Jost. Promoted from a decade-long tenure as Group President, Government & Defense, Infrastructure & Minerals, & Hydrocarbons, Bizzy would likely spend the next five years as COO and retire at seventy-five.

He didn't even glance at Evangelína as she stood beside her luggage. She'd known him all her life, and he'd gained appeal with age. He was a charmer but not smarmy, a caballero. Of an older order: no computer, dictated all correspondence to Marisol, conducted business face-to-face, by phone, at lunch, or on the front nine. There was little documentation of what F. Bismarck Rolling said or did.

His attention was fixed on his small desktop, where rested an imposing corporate document, the bound pages stacked high as a little legislative bill.

The cold reception, absent eye contact, not a nod of acknowledgement, after being yanked off the *Lacie,* made her fear for her job. Why was this just occurring to her? In these tight times, the larger the salary, the less the security. Her salary was significant.

He was stalling, allowing her time to figure this out on her own, so when he spoke the words — Evy, sorry to say we're going to have to let you go — they wouldn't come as a shock, and she wouldn't make a scene. She wondered how long her savings would last. She owned the Montrose two-bedroom townhouse she shared with her mamí, who had no income, and she'd intended to put her savings toward the start of in vitro treatments. If in vitro didn't take, she'd adopt. That had been her plan, but maybe she needed a new one.

"Mr. Rolling," she said, "you asked to see me."

Bizzy looked up from behind his standing desk. "I'm sorry, Evy. Troubling morning." He told her to have a seat, as though she were going to need it.

"I'll stand, Mr. Rolling. Thank you." She felt a burning burp rising inside her like a bad decision she was bound to make. "Like you like to say, sitting's for Sundays."

"And kneeling, Evy."

She nodded. A Presbyterian, he'd attended her Baptism and First Communion; she never made it to Confirmation. Papí's melanoma had taken him by then. Mamí was Maya Catholic, more a devotee of Ixchel and the Virgin of Guadalupe than Christ and his pope.

"In Tampico," she said, "I visited the Temple of the Immaculate Conception. I lit a candle for my father." She was grasping for purchase. It embarrassed her, but broaching the subject of Papí with Bizzy occasionally brought out anecdotes she'd never heard.

He asked if she wanted something. Coffee? "Know you take it light and sweet, just like your old man."

When she didn't answer, he said, "You sure?"

She wasn't sure — she wasn't even sure what she was unsure of, but she nodded.

She learned this from her immigrant parents: when lost in conversation, nod. If you've committed to something you shouldn't have, you can always get out of it later.

His old hiking boots were ridiculous, tan leather and canvas paired with his tailored suit, boots he'd supposedly tied on for his first assessment trip to the Middle East in '03, boots he'd worn to work every day since. They said he kept them on because at a moment's notice he could be called away to the Emirates to negotiate a billion-dollar project.

She studied the haze out the window. The haze wasn't Houston's; the haze was hers. She needed water. "I'm sorry, sir. It's just, the helicopter ride . . . I'm feeling a little nauseous, so if you're going to fire me, please get it over with and let me go home — where I haven't been in a month — so I can make sure my mother's still alive."

He leaned back, hands on either side of the desktop, and a spark of something — empathy? epiphany? — warmed his eyes. A grin turned up the corners of his mouth. "You want Marisol to get you a ginger ale?"

She shook her head.

"How is your mother?"

She nodded.

"What makes you think I've called you all this way to fire you?"

She thought of Marisol addressing her as señorita. "The helicopter before dawn," she said. "The delayed preload. The Fort Worth lawsuits."

"The drinking and gambling aboard a company vessel?"

She felt dulled. After a moment, she reached an understanding: word of her carousing traveled faster than helicopter. She suspected the *Belle of Baton Rouge* dealer was a company plant. On each platform, there was usually one, reporting directly to the snitchy strivers of middle management. "I really fucked up Fort Worth, didn't I?"

"Easy, Evy."

"Any word on the lawsuits?"

"All settled. Out of court. Not small sums. Price of doing business."

"So, wait, just so we're clear here — I'm not being fired?"

"Not today," he said.

She shook her head, woozy.

"We've invested in you, Evy, and I have a vested interest in you."

She thanked him.

"This industry's come some way. This company's about much more than petroleum now. Paradigms shift. Whale oil gets scarce, gets costly, and, voila, save the whales. But think how our predecessors, a short century ago, used a eucalyptus trunk to drill a well in what's now downtown LA. That well produced forty BPD. We went from forty barrels a day in Los Angeles to 260,000 a day in Veracruz, all in the space of twenty years."

To hasten the conversation, she said, "Yes, please, I understand."

"Evy, your father was a good Catholic. Your mother, on the other hand, who was an extraordinarily beautiful woman, tends toward idolatry."

She felt her legs wobble on her heels. Any accuracy in Bizzy's statement — putting Mamí's beauty behind her and her idolatry out front — didn't lessen the insult. Yet it turned her momentarily against her mamí growing ever older and more irrational. "Idolatry, sir?"

"Never met an educated woman with so many superstitions. I hope she's not ready-ing for the upcoming apocalypse."

"In December," she said, "one cycle of the b'ak'tun will end, sir, not the world. It's like flipping the calendar from 1999. Time to party. Ancient Maya knew how to have fun. The doomsday scenario's gringo gossip."

"Sorry if I touched a nerve, Evy." He winked, and she reminded herself that when Bizzy liked you, he needled you.

She told him that her mother, who was still beautiful, would be getting ready for the End by making her mole sauce and enough tamales to feed an army. "There will be leftovers."

"Tremendous admirer of your mother," he said. "Love to hear her tell those stories about shape-shifters. She has a word for them, the changelings."

When Evangelína wanted a bedtime story, Mamí recited passages from the *Chilam Balam,* one book of which she'd translated as a student at Universidad Anáhuac. Evangelína couldn't do justice to "The Interrogation of the Lady Xoc," and so she stood silent.

"She was a sight, your mother."

"Still is."

"It's different when you get old, Evy. You'll see. Your father was a much better prospector than I ever was. But times change. Technology upends everything. Nothing more so than a codger like me. We're so far removed from the land these days we can't even get the lay of it anymore without the aid of instruments and experts — that's why this company's run by engineers — and then we need advice from a gaggle of lawyers and approval from a slew of politicians. Used to be, you could grease a couple palms and start drilling. Bankroll a cathedral if you absolutely had to. Not any more. God has given way to golf. It's still horse-trading and back-scratching. The Suite 8F attitude is old hat. The Lamar Hotel's a parking lot. Now it's goods and services. It's all about government contracts. We employ more American private contractors, and hold a larger contract with the US government, than any other firm in Iraq. We built the US embassy in Kabul. We're responsible for the renovations at Gitmo. Our work in Cuba's nothing to brag about, but we made that facility safer for the troops and detainees both. Not something to brag about, but something to be proud of. So don't let your lack of an engineering degree slow you. There's a place for you here, but it's up to you to determine where you fit in. I'm speaking to you not as one of your bosses but as a family friend." Bizzy stared into her eyes for a long moment, then turned and faced the window. "Been in and out of Texas off and on for all my years now — this drought — never heard of anything like it."

He turned around. "Let me get to the point. The *Lacie* and Forth Worth didn't play to your strong suits, Evy." He looked at her over his bifocals. "We've got you in mind for something else."

"Should I be concerned?"

"Always, Evy." Bizzy eyed the TV screens. Here was the reason she was having trouble reading him. She mistook distraction for dismissal. He slapped the open portfolio on his chest-high desk. "We want you in New York. Make a play on a plat in the Catskills."

"I didn't do so hot with the Barnett Shale," she reminded him.

"We're giving you a second shot. You got Fort Worth riled up and raring for a fight. But this isn't shale gas. This is . . . something other than."

"I don't like the sound of that."

"Sending you north's a gambit." He winked. "New York's no Texas. Lived in Manhattan when I was at Irvine. City was a meaner beast then. But you'll be upstate. You've served us well for nearly a decade, Evy. We owe it to your father. I owe him."

She waited.

"We want to purchase a private property. Under one of the subsidiaries, SW&B Construction. That's who you'll broker for. It'll all be in the portfolio. Marisol has a copy for you. We want to build a luxury golf resort in the Catskills. We've an agreement with the PGA, corporate sponsor for what will be a Tour stop, the whole shebang."

"But SW&B specializes in paper mills. First Sunrise at Seventeen Seventy and now golf?"

"Our critics said the same thing about our part in the Great Man-Made River Project. Oil exploration led to the discovery of that aquifer under the Sahara. Oil technology makes the retrieval possible. You've been with us long enough to know it's crucial to keep an open mind. Intents rarely align with appearances. What this country's all about. Put another way, Evy, you must try to trust me."

"Why not use a subcontractor?" She hesitated, then added, "Someone who plays golf, and knows the Marcellus. One of the outfits working Pennsylvania, say."

"We want a company person on this one."

"And not a company *man.*"

He looked at the screens, then back to her. "We'd like a woman's touch."

"Something about the landowner I should know?"

Bizzy folded back the cardstock cover of the portfolio and showed her a color photo, obviously taken on the sly with a high-power

zoom: the landowner looked like a malnour-
ished Kofi Annan. "African-American wid-
ower," Bizzy said, "inherited the property
from his wife. Old Borscht Belt resort,
defunct for decades. He lives there, has
converted some of the buildings into a
halfway house for troubled war vets. On the
surface, it looks legit." Bizzy flipped pages.
"Swamped with back taxes and late fees as
early as '84. Multiple liens. Six, seven, eight
maxed-out credit cards. Some time after the
wife died, he brought in an auctioneering
outfit to sell off the holdings of the resort's
game farm. According to this — I'm quot-
ing now: *The Game Farm was the first pri-*
vately owned venture to achieve official status
as a zoo from the Department of Agriculture.
Huh. Two rhinos sold for six thousand and
nine thousand dollars to the International
Rhino Foundation. Three wisent went for
sixty-six hundred — what on earth is a
wisent? On and on. The auction brought in
1.7 million, after taxes." Bizzy read silently
until Evangelína grew uncomfortable and
began shifting on her heels.

"I'm sorry, Evy, this is all very interesting
to me. I remember the Standard — I'm
almost certain it's G-R-A-N-D-E." He
flipped to the cover, then back. "Brother.
What does that tell you? We can't even spell

the name right. Marisol! Hell. Edith tried to get me to go. Not the place for a goy, not unless you were Rocky Marciano training for a fight. We'd drive by on the way to the ski slopes. The TV commercial was in heavy rotation — this was back in the days of three channels — I could probably sing you the jingle, but I won't subject you to that indignity." He flipped pages, forward then back. "Zoo spanned more than 900 acres, about half the Standard parcel. Proceeds from the auction got him mostly through the nineties. Granted 501(c)(19) tax status for a nonprofit at the end of '01. Maybe some fraudulent doings. Maybe embezzling the veterans he's supposed to be helping. Finding that out will be part of your responsibility. Could provide leverage. He's claiming annual income in the 200k range, but property taxes take the lion's share. He owes on equity loans. He's all upside-down. A lease won't make a bit of difference to this gent. We'll shoot for a sale. That doesn't work, we'll get more imaginitive. The numbers are showing a couple million in the red, and we understand the county's about to start foreclosure proceedings. Where is Marisol?" Bizzy took off his glasses and glared at the closed office doors. "There's also some indication he's unwell."

"Physically?"

"Could be an insurance scam. Claims Agent Orange exposure."

"And we know all this how?"

"How do we ever come to know anything, Evy? We suss it out."

"And I can't go in straight why?"

"You are going in straight."

"And if he doesn't accept golf money, am I going to offer gas money?"

"If you can't seal a sale for a golf resort, we'll consider a plan B. But we're ready to exhaust all possibilities for a sale. Understand? The risk's worth the reward on this one."

"Even though Cuomo's balked?"

He smiled.

"The governor isn't by chance a golfer?"

Bizzy's smile faded; when he lost patience, he got quiet.

"There's something you're not telling me."

"You don't get to be in my position by being a tell-all, Evy. But I will say, given your vested interests, that it's a safe bet — and I know you're a betting woman — you've been following things pretty closely up there. Let me clue you in, because, like I said, politics is now most of what we do. Cuomo signed same-sex marriage legislation back in June of last year. Week later his administration announces they're seeking to lift the ban on horizontal hydrofracking. You can raise your bet that some of our execs — mind you, not all are as socially accepting as I — never thought they'd live to see the day they'd be supporting gay marriage. That's a connection the *New York Times* didn't report. You with me?"

"I'm playing catch-up."

"Cuomo traded drilling for gay marriage. A win-win. Democrats downstate get concessions on a civil-rights issue. Upstate Republicans, mostly live-and-let-live Libertarians, get jobs in an area hard hit by recession. But Cuomo will backpedal be—"

A knock rattled the door, and Marisol entered without waiting for permission.

"Almost done here, Marisol. Evy, you'll find the information you need in the file. And, Marisol, it's *Grande* with an E for goodness sake. Who's Ellis have working on this?"

Marisol shrugged.

Evangelína said, "Is that all, sir?"

"Let me stress one more thing. Any purchase agreement's for todo el tamal." Bizzy's Spanish was beautiful, too beautiful — he had the condescending pronunciation of a criollo.

"It's not a worthy golf resort if it doesn't

include mineral rights."

"At's my girl."

"The schedule?"

"Posthaste. We want you started yesterday. That's why we yanked you off the *Lacie*. You've got little more than two months. End of the calendar year. Afraid you'll be gone for Armageddon." He winked. "If you need to get back here to Houston, to check in with your mother for any reason, you have the use of a company jet, so long as it's not excessive."

"One more question?"

He waited.

"Am I still being encouraged to apply to the executive program at Darden?"

He didn't answer right away, and the hesitation told her more than what he eventually said: "IRJ always encourages employees to further their educations."

As she turned to go, she let slip her phone. It clattered to the floor. She kicked it. Bending, she stole a look at the TV console. All the screens, some ten or so, displayed a series of dust-blown video streams. Desert vistas. Drone's-eye view. A couple crumbling urban settings. Pockmarked sandstone. A few displays showed pipelines stretching through sand to hazy horizons. Others focused on road crews. Then there was one frantic live-action shot televising what she guessed were IRJ contractors outfitted like Zapatistas: flak-jackets, black balaclavas, assault-rifles. A muzzle flashed and she looked away.

She grabbed her phone and stood, tugging down the hem of her skirt, shrugging her jacket up her shoulders, sickened. She wondered if IRJ chief operations officer was a job she'd ever be able to manage.

Bizzy was regarding her. "Evy," he said, "how are you feeling?"

"Sir?"

"I mean your stomach. You've gone a little . . . blanca."

She tried to swallow the acidic burp caught in her chest. "It's passed."

"Any luck yet?"

Another jab at her card playing. "Luck with?"

"Dr. Heller."

Her fertility specialist. She hadn't told anyone. "Not yet, far as I know, but I'm putting all my poker winnings toward treatments."

"Must play for big stakes. Cost a pretty penny. Worth it if it takes. It's not easy, juggling something like that with a full workload, especially alone. You let us know if there's anything we can do to make things easier. I'll check in on your mother."

She thanked him in Spanish.

"And, Evy. Don't go up there worrying about lawsuits. You give it the hard sell. No pulled punches for fear of reprisal. This landowner's hard to get hold of. You're going to have to be creative. You know the drill. Pun unintended. Our out-of-house legal council on this is a local boutique firm. The thinking was — keep a low profile till we saw how Cuomo was leaning. He's someone we've worked with in the past."

"Cuomo."

"Ellis Baum. He, Baum, practices —"

"Land-lease?"

"Real-estate. With a land-lease background — that doesn't concern you. He's your supervisor. He operates out of an office in Kingston, knows the area, over and under. We've got you on a company jet. A driver will meet you at the airport and take you to Ellis. If you have to use the loo, you hold it till you've seen Ellis, understand? He's more than your boss on this, he's your eyes and ears. He speaks for me. He'll make approval of any offer before you present. He's already got a small team up there information-gathering in anticipation of your arrival so you're not wasting time in the courthouse digging up county records.

They put together what's in the file, misspellings and all. But it should be trustworthy, mostly. Chain of title's all right here."

She turned to go.

"And one more thing, Evy. There's also a chance Wright murdered his wife back in the mid-seventies, so take precaution." He cocked his head, fixed eyes on the TVs. "One last thing." He didn't look at her. "You fuck this up the way you did Fort Worth, I will fire you."

Marisol walked Evangelína wordlessly, solemnly, to the elevator, cradling an inch-thick corporate report.

Before the elevator doors dinged open, Evangelína asked for an aspirin. Marisol simply shook her head. She waited till Evangelína pushed the L button before handing over the heavy portfolio. Bizzy hadn't given up the one on his desk. His contained information she wasn't privy to, but that was nothing new.

Trying to ride out the weather, Smith huddled in her tree hammock. Cold. She burrowed beneath her plastic poncho. Icy rain yanked yellow leaves from their branches and slapped them down on her. When she felt a seepage, warm, between her thighs, she knew: of fucking course. Made her miss being at war, where you skipped your sugar pills, jumping straight to the next cycle. Last thing soldiers needed, they'd joked, was more bleeding.

Shivering and swaying, she dug a Ziploc freezer bag from her field pack. Her toilet paper, her pepperbox pistol, and the bandolier that held her tampons and a dozen .38 Special rounds. All still dry. She pulled herself up, untied the hammock, climbed down from her tree, and packed her effects. She had an afternoon date to meet Milt on the southwest corner of Central Park North and Fifth. With nearly a full day to kill, she started walking to warm herself, looking for a place to change.

On the corner of 100th, distracted by a black Lincoln crashed into and wedged under a parked FreshDirect truck, no drivers in sight, she almost broke her nose running smack into the clouded window of a phone booth, surprised to find they still existed. Last time she was in a phone booth was on FOB Ghazni, where soldiers lined up backwards and facing away from the phones to give callers the privacy to cry.

She closed herself inside the booth. The pissy stench, ammoniac and potent as smelling salts, snapped her awake. Undressing, she danced on top of her boots, trying not to touch the floor with her socked feet, climbing into her damp, hand-washed fatigues, wanting to be in uniform to meet Milt. *If* she decided not to stand him up.

Changed, she was exhausted. At her thighs, the yellow receiver of the telephone swung from its cord. She picked it up and dialed her husband's number. A recorded voice instructed her to please deposit four dollars and sixty-five cents. She hung up, opened the door on the slowing rain, lifting her face to the cold spittle and drawing a few clear breaths. A cop cruiser was double-parked at the corner. She closed herself back in the booth and raked through a pocket of her field pack: about seven heavy dollars.

She let go of the last nickel, knowing that at this hour Trav would be as good as dead after mashing and snorting his bedtime Oxy. She didn't want to talk, all she wanted was to hear his recorded voice. To do so, she was willing to pay a begged-for four-sixty-five.

When Travis answered on the third ring — "Who's it?" — the words, slurred together, were a comfort. For a second she was happy, nearly hyperventilating with homesickness, her heart full and fast as the house music *whumping* in the background. He could say something to keep her from going into the wilds with a black Airborne Ranger three times her age. She said, "It's me. I —"

Another voice, female, on his end. Over it he said, "That you, Bellum, you cunt?"

Her breath caught; his cussing her was nearly a reassurance.

Sprawling silence passed between them. Then: "Don't just call me after all this time and breathe, bitch. Or quit breathing why don't you. Slit your own shit throat. Fucking cowardly cooze." He sighed or blew smoke. "You know I'm only kidding, baby. I'm just upset's all. You know I love you more than me. You know —"

A man's voice, booming over a PA, drowned out Travis: "Let's have us a round of applesauce for Ms. Golden Delicious and her pet iguana, Sir Licks a Lot."

"That's right," Travis said. "Out having me a hoot here at Big Papa's. Got a stack of dollar bills. What? Hold up a sec." The music faded a moment, came back full blast. "Shoshanna says hi." Shoshanna Roshanda, a sweet-tempered dancer — her stage name was Jinx — had a daughter, LaLa, who Bellum and Travis had sat for some nights. "Oh yeah, we've got real friendly. Hope you're happy cause I am." In his loose jabber-jaw, he sounded jacked-up and brought down both — coke, meth maybe — probably a half-empty fifth of Goldschläger in his Carhartt pocket. "MPs're hunting your ass down, if you're you." He hawked out a wet smoker's cough and spat. "Couple of mooks come by the house twice saying they was with AWOL Apprehension. Said a notice went out to law enforcement the world over. You there? You hearing this? Don't matter. They even sent a letter to your old man. Been visiting him. I read it. Hysterical. Bunch a fried baloney about duty, honor, yada yada la-de-da-de-fucking-da. The joes said they dropped you from the rolls. Gave you a separation something-or-other. Told me you can't apply for any college. Had me a chuckle at that one, dumb as you is. Hey, you still there? I love you, baby. Let me step outside for a sec so you can talk to someone."

The music stopped and she wanted to hang up but she held fast to the receiver pressed painfully to her ear.

"Here, say hi to Mama. Say hi." Snuffling, followed by a sliding sound. "That's gross. Goddamnit!" A yelp. "Said say hi not slobber all over my fucking smartphone. You hear that? Foxtrot says hi. Hey, you crying?

You sound asleep? You ODing? You want to quit, gohead. Wither up and die, you witch." He coughed. "You got nothing? Four years married and four months gone and you got zip to say? Know what? Matters not one squatting iota. We had shit to say to each other since you got back. Fucking everybody in the Stan but the bearded Taliban. Them too, for all I know. Foxy-T, quit your fucking whining. She don't give two shits bout neither of us."

The more she listened, the less she held her edges — Travis saying he had a side business going. Worked it out with your pops. Come to like ol' Increase. He could give a hoot though. Been two suicide-by-cop in Devils Elbow since you left. Sometimes I even catch myself thinking you did right to bolt stead of going back for the triple dip. But don't worry about old Travis, who — hey, man, sup. Yeah, hold up. I'll catch you inside soon as I'm done talking to my bitch wife who done split on me.

A voice, inaudible, was followed by Travis's girly laugh. Then, an explosion of bass-heavy music before all got quiet save the whines of sweet Foxtrot. Foxtrot helped her regain some of herself. Helped get her perimeter secured, Travis on the outside.

"Hear that?" he said. "Dude said least you

didn't do like his wife and take the dog. That joe won't pay but thirty for these jelly-nose pills I got. Say, if you —"

A recorded voice cut Travis off: "Please deposit another —"

Smith depressed the chrome tongue.

The cop car was still at the corner, rain turned snow. Had to be getting close to dawn. If she got herself arrested, or shot, she wouldn't have to decide what to do next.

She crossed the street and stood at the driver-side door of the police Impala. On the other side of the glass sat a white woman in blues puffed up by a ballistic vest, staring into her lap. Texting.

Smith rapped her knuckle on the window.

The cop looked irritably up from under finely plucked eyebrows penciled back in, her only makeup. Through the closed window, she said, "I help you?"

Smith tapped her own wrist. "Got the time of day?"

The cop took a long look at Smith, then shook her head.

"Obliged." As Smith turned to go, she heard the window power down.

"How long you been in that phone booth?"

Smith's heart got jump-started. She didn't turn, kept crossing the street, about got

103

bowled over by a cyclist who shouted as he whizzed past.

"Hey," the cop said. A metallic *clatch* as the car door opened, then the *chic-clunk* of it slamming shut. "You answer me when I ask you something."

Stepping up the curb, Smith shrugged her field pack off one shoulder. When she turned to face the cop, the bag wheeled around and came to rest hanging at the front of her hip — the pocket, holding her pepperbox pistol, unzipped.

The lady cop was young, younger than Smith, and alone. There had to be a partner nearby, probably fetching coffee. The cop stood at arm's length, hands ready by her hips. A name bar engraved *Cole.* "How long you been in that booth?"

"Was I breaking any laws?"

Cole reached and depressed the button on her radio clipped to her shoulder but didn't speak into it. "You in there when the accident occurred?"

"When I went in, that's how they were."

Cole's hand rested on the butt of her holstered sidearm, a Glock made of mostly plastic. "What happened there?" Cole touched her own eye.

"Some schoolgirls hit me upside the head with a rock." Smith nodded toward the cop car. "Here comes your partner. They always put females together?"

"Move along, soldier. That's an order." Cole crossed the street to the cruiser and her breakfast delivered in a bag by her partner. The officers exchanged words. They looked at Smith and gave her sloppy salutes, cop salutes but salutes all the same.

As a return gesture, Smith reached in her field pack and gripped her gun, staring through the pair of lady cops to Travis at her funeral, blubbering like a chubby girl, her daddy consoling him, father and son-in-law all buddy-buddy as "Taps" was blown from a bugle. A snappy three-volley salute. Then they'd receive her folded flag from an honor guard on bended knee after a tear-jerker thank you. But burial honors were reserved for veterans discharged under circumstances other than dishonorable. Dead, she'd be interred unceremoniously, same as any civilian.

She pulled her hand, empty, from her field pack and waved. The cops waved back. Smith didn't care to continue on. Nor did she want Travis or her daddy to have any sort of satisfaction. She would abide to spite them, because they'd both tried to kill her, Travis by increments and Increase all at once. Her death would somehow prove them right about her.

If she couldn't kill herself, she wondered if she could go home. Back in Devils Elbow, there'd be one outcome. She wasn't worried about the court-martial. It was Travis. Not what he'd do to her but what she'd do to him. She'd rather face the possibility of being raped and dismembered by a Catskill serial killer than confront the certainty of committing a domestic homicide and spending the rest of her life in jail.

She double-timed it toward her rendezvous point. As she jogged, a cadence, the original jody call, came to her. She sang loud as she could:

Aint no use in lookin' back,
Jody's got your Cadillac.
Aint no use in lookin' blue,
Jody's got your husband, too.
Aint no use in feeling sad,
Jody's got the job you had.
Sound off: one, two.
Sound off: three, four.
Sound off: one, two . . . three, four!

Smith stopped at the public restroom overlooking the Harlem Meer. Sitting on the toilet, she broke the breech of her pistol and dropped in four rounds. Some six hours

106

early, she felt ready to meet Milt.

Astounding. A short episode in a life could become a life's obsession. Milton's memory of the jungle heat, heavy, burdensome as a sodden quilt, was like fighting against a greater gravity. Then the chill during a snap monsoon that lasted a month. Entire team with trench foot. Nothing as exhausting as a twelve-hour shiver on soaked ambush. When he got C-rats, a reprieve from freeze-dried LRP rations, he dug a hole and buried the four cigarettes that came with the accessory pack. An offering to the land that was not theirs. Spur-of-the-moment superstition become a pre-mission ceremony for whatever six-man team he was part of. All of them gathering to jokingly bow heads, someone saying: Who do you voodoo, Doctor Cockadau?

Someone scatting back: And the doowop girls go, *Doo do doo do doo do do doo.*

Someone else chiming: Howdy Doody, hocus-pocus.

And, finally: Izzy-wizzy, Milton, baby, let's get busy.

Then they all fell silent and lay to rest four fresh smokes in a mini mass grave.

Next, he might summon a few of his countless close calls. The cauterized hole punched through his rain poncho by a friendly tracer. Friendly hands patting his back to put out the friendly fire he wore. Funny as hell at the time, calling him HIR — the human illumination round — for the rest of the mission, code-named Greensleeves. How, on a later recon, he set the four-position selector switch on his CAR-15 to burst. Hopped, firing, from the hovering skid of a Huey into a hot LZ. Waves of elephant grass like a churned-up lake. Only to have his first-aid kit shot clean off his belt. The force of the enemy round at his hip making him do the twist. Spinning him 180 degrees as he squeezed the trigger. Three measly bullets striking the fuselage, rendering the chopper inoperable. Having to establish and secure a perimeter so the Huey could be airlifted by a lumbering Chinook. The sight awesome and absurd. A helicopter giving birth to a helicopter. Then to have the Chinook shot down with the Huey in tow — two birds, one RPG — killing both crews. Getting redesignated a Ranger partway through his second tour. Becoming a Ranger meaning zilch at the time — he was a recon man first — being a Ranger meaning everything now. All the intimacies with the NVA, a fighting force that made the Vietcong seem like a ragtag company of farmers, orphans, and widows, which they mostly were. And then the scene in his mind where he expended the most attention: his untimely attachment to the Screaming Eagles of the 101st and his small part in the futile defense of Firebase Ripcord.

On an on, near miss after hair's breadth, and, in the end, the irony wasn't lost on him: he was bound to be a casualty — decades late, a couple million dollars short — and his downfall wouldn't be a sexy, leaden-eyed sapper of a suicide mamasan with a toe-popper in her cooch, nor getting snakebit by a pair of communist pit vipers mating in his foxhole. Instead, he was bound to be a belated fatality in the War on Weeds, nixed by military-grade Roundup, zapped by friendly spray thanks to all his wartime exposure to the rainbow defoliants — the Orange, but also the Blue and White — while he was on recon through Thùa Thiên — his mind straying to Monsanto at four-odd-o'clock in the morning. Monsanto, along with Dow Chemical, was a main producer of Agent Orange.

Sterilized, Milton couldn't have children. Surely that was one reason he ran a halfway house for vets acting like buckquick, cutup kids in the Catskills. After years of deliberation, over the ramifications of bringing a half-black half-Jew into the tumult of a world unable at the time to fathom a future that promised a mulatto president, he and Ada tried to make a baby. After two miscarriages and a stillbirth — third time done harm — they gave up, he relieved, she heartbroken. They blamed her age — thirty-three with the last loss — but then, gradually, reports trickled in, after her death, about dioxin and the fifty-five gallon drums of defoliant with the orange stripe painted on the sides, and just what, exactly, this chemical agent was doing to the post-war generation of Vietnamese. Modern warfare needed another statistical designator: WAA, wounded after action. Last count — 500,000 Vietnamese children born with birth defects. In his mind, the five followed by five zeros was a long white digit chalked on a blackboard. Soon, Milton Xavier Wright would be tallied among the KAA.

Milton massaged his throat, searching for the lump that'd been concerning him for months. Size of a golf ball, it had a bad lie, buried behind the strings and cords of his neck. The lymph nodes he had left felt swollen, but not painful.

There were people who knew, or estimated, how much defoliated jungle, how much manmade wasteland, he'd stepped stealthily through. When on base, he killed plenty of time around the buffalo turbines, trailer-mounted systems used for roadside spraying and camp applications that shot herbicide from a fire hose. Even did some spraying himself. On his first tour, he scored an occasional rearguard assignment — no easy task for a black grunt — and one such privilege was spraying perimeters with a backpack dispenser.

Lying on his underground cot forty years later, he could hear the *slosh, slosh* rushing after him over the ages.

Milton's mouth was nasty, his lips ashy and chapped. On the nightstand stump, he felt for his water flask, a gift from Ada. He drank deeply, threw off the heavy, unshorn alpaca hide that was his covers, and got up fully dressed in yesterday's clothes. He kicked back the fur rug, doused with tea tree oil to temper the stench, and urinated painfully into the grated drain in the floor, passed gas, and replaced the rug.

The only access to the oubliette came from the trap door at the dome of the ceiling. From it hung a rope ladder that served as a trust test. Anytime, one of Milton's vets could stand over him and cut his tie to the surface. A fact he pointed out to new arrivals on their introductory tour. Wanting them to trust him, he needed first to show them trust. He hadn't yet been proved a rube and left for dead, though he had one resident, Reverend, who'd become a concern before he checked out. Milton didn't bother to tell his vets there was a drain in the floor big enough for a man to crawl through that he used as a latrine. He was proud he'd never been forced to shimmy through his own piss to find where it led.

Milton climbed the rope ladder like a healthy man half his age, pain spurring him to climb harder. That afternoon, at 1600, he needed to pick up the girl. She showed promise. He held out the desperate hope that maybe she'd take up the torch when it fell from his hand — he'd hoped the same thing of Reverend — but Smith would need first to clear her record, get her deserter status resolved, which would take time, time he didn't have.

Standing in the basement, he switched on the red-filtered, right-angle flashlight. Brown bats flitted about, their squeaks like the gritting of teeth. This year, the bats seemed to be later to hibernate, insomniac.

A primitive carpenter's chest held his clothes, his sidearm, and sundries, many of them contraband. He didn't exactly practice what he preached: total self-sufficiency. He gave himself some slack — he was the only Standard lifer.

In the dim disk of red light, he changed his camos slowly in the chill, rubbed unrefined shea butter on his elbows, the fatty balm smelling like nuts about to burn. He brushed his teeth with dry baking soda, swigged the last of the water from his flask, gargled, and swallowed. He popped a lozenge into his rotten mouth. Before he laced up his jungle boots, he gave the thin leather of the toes and heels a quick shea-butter polish. He picked out his natty hair and covered it in a wool stocking cap. He checked his calendar — hard to keep track of the days living like he did — today was in fact his day to pick up Smith.

He sat on the lid of the carpenter's chest, turned off his flashlight and, by feel, he field-stripped the M1911A1. Placed the parts in sequence beside him on the chest. One by one, he went at them with an old toothbrush. Took more care with them than he did his teeth. He oiled and pieced the sidearm back together. The whole, its weight and potential, terribly greater than the sum of its parts.

He holstered the gun at his hip and felt his way through the black basement, skirting the maze of halls he knew by heart in the dark, passed custodial rooms and the vast laundry center long defunct, where came to rest the glorious passing bell bought by Nehemiah, Milton's father-in-law. The thirty-eight-ton cast-brass behemoth had busted its coupling and crashed through every landing of the tower and every floor of the armory's four stories.

The bell had been legendary in the Catskills. Guests said it had the power to disperse storms and sickness, drive away golems, and extinguish fire. It'd been tolled to ward off evil. The bell was a reincarnated Maccabee king. The bell was the voice of God. At the start of the War to End All Wars, the bell had been ordered melted down and cast as a cannon. Beaten for days, it would not bust. When the tollers finally gave up, it buzzed for a week and then cracked but refused to break.

Milton reached the stairs ascending to the first floor, a single open area that originally provided main storage for military surplus and munitions bought at military auction. When Nehemiah acquired all the property surrounding the upstate warehouse site of his father's Manhattan-based Army-Navy reseller, turning the location into a world-class resort-cum-game-farm, the great room of the armory castle, Masada, was reconditioned and designated Zero Mostel Hall. Reserved for special banquets and decorated with an Elizabethan theme, the Zero was the venue for summerstock presentations of Shakespeare plays, and every year without fail there was a production of *The Merchant of Venice,* Nehemiah's favorite, what he referred to as Shylock after the Shoah.

Milton stepped over the defunct tracks of the private freight line that deadended just inside the portcullis. He shouldered open the warped wicket in the great door and, like a man coming up from the fathoms, drew a full breath of brisk fall air.

Aboard a company jet for the first time, Evangelína studied the grain of the wood tabletop. Rolling and opalescent, more like polished semiprecious stone than a length of lumber. On the tabletop rested the closed Standard Grande portfolio, its title misspelled. Meticulously bound but sloppily compiled. Filled with too much information gathered over years, some surely scandalous, some wildly inaccurate, some plainly plagiarized, overwritten in places, sketched in others. These documents frustrated her, something decidedly gringo about them: sprawling, arrogant, excessive. The time and money expended to gather and distribute the information in the document — it was morally degenerate. Though without it, she'd have a harder time doing her job, never mind living her life. She felt the same way about el gran Estados Unidos.

She was the only passenger on the Bombardier Global Express, which probably cost IRJ $45 million. Ferrying her to Stewart Airport in Newburgh, New York, was a three-person flight crew — captain, copilot, flight attendant. Back at the office, a popular conversation topic, while awaiting the beep of a microwave, was the price of these executive runs. If her colleagues were right — some had seen the numbers — the 1,500-mile one-way trip cost in the neighborhood of 15k.

The jet could've accommodated twenty coach seats comfortably, but the cabin was laid out with leather-appointed berthing for six, a forward club arrangement with foldout tables, a divan, a café table and a credenza adjacent to a galley with two coffee makers and a convection warming oven. The lighting was romantic.

Evangelína sipped her strong Bloody Mary, thinking of her mamí. The hola-adios the poor woman had gotten from her here-and-gone only daughter. Evangelína was aboard a jet more luxuriously appointed than Air Force One; her mamí had never flown. She couldn't help but feel a pang of pride. In the space of one generation, her family had gone from a border crossing, albeit legal, to jet-setting.

She opened the portfolio, flipping pages like she would a mail-order catalog. Turned to the chapter "Medical Health." A hundred-plus pages of forms — claims, request-for-payment, dozens of grievances, appeals, forms for approving a representative for appeal — Evangelína wasn't ready to wade into the sickening bureaucratic morass.

Included was a copy of the police report from an accident in 1977, where Mrs. Wright was killed. There was some discrepancy over who'd been driving, Mr. or Mrs. Wright. Mr. Wright had a BAC level of 0.19%. There was an investigation. Not murder. Charges of manslaughter were brought, but Wright got off with a plea bargain, admitting guilt to DWI and reckless endangerment. He paid a $500 fine. A footnote: *In 1977, a person convicted of a drunk driving offense in New York paid an average fine of $11.*

She didn't read with purpose till she reached the last fifty pages of the nearly

400-page document. Invariably, that was where the crucial information lay buried, in an appendix. There, you found the facts that didn't fit into the story IRJ was trying to tell. If you were the so-called independent lab commissioned by the J.R. Simplot Company, whose phosphate mining operations polluted Idaho creeks with selenium, the appendix was where you hid pictures of the two-headed brown trout.

She stopped at Appendix VI: "Grassroots Opposition of Alarm for Catskills Region Development." What caught her eye were the redactions. Bizzy's version surely didn't have text blacked out. A note read: *Any future investment should take into account the strong regional resistance to development of any kind, no matter how environmentally sound.*

The appendix included an email from James Sherry, New York's Acting Commissioner & Director, Office of Counter Terrorism, Division of Homeland Security and Emergency Services: *We want to continue providing this support to the* ███████████ ███████████ *stakeholders, while not feeding those groups fomenting dissent.*

The Sherry email cited an FBI bulletin: *Environmental extremists continue to target the* ██████ *industry. Although the incidents have mostly involved vandalism, trespassing and threats by environmental activists . . . this pattern is morphing — to more criminal, extremist measures.*

The redactions weren't subtle. But they weren't what she expected either. The IRJ redactors hadn't blacked-out all overt mentions of Marcellus shale gas, just those that were a part of other commercial groupings. The withheld information had to involve some other part of the energy industry. Filling in the blanks was like doing a contextual crossword. *Nuclear* might fit the redaction — *target the* ███████ *industry* — the word had to be five, six, seven characters at most. *Gaming,* maybe. Could simply be *energy,* or *golfing.*

Her cover was shoddy — she didn't know a putter from a pitching wedge, but this was business: know just enough to get by, and then move on to the next concern. Maybe she'd play a few swings, take a crash golf course. Bad as the cover was, she thought that by it Bizzy was trying to keep her safe. The Earth Liberation Front didn't torch golf carts. They saved their Molotov cocktails for heavy industrial machinery.

Included in the Sherry email — under a subheading called "The Concerns" — was a list of names, their affiliations, meetings they'd attended, websites visited, contact information, and driver's license photos like mug shots. Some of the activists were familiar.

Another appendix stated that the opposition monitoring, commissioned by New York State, had been contracted out to the Terrorism Research and Response Institute, operated by Total Intelligence Solutions.

A regional, privately run center subsidized by the Department of Homeland Security, Total Intel's office was a suite on the ninth floor of IRJ Tower. It was a known secret that they engaged in domestic surveillance. Ten or so analysts, half-reformed Anonymous hackers in their twenties and thirties, hunched in cubicles beneath the panoramic blue glows of desktop monitors big as picture windows. They were looking in not out. Trolling for personal information on message boards and in chat rooms, using aliases familiar to the targets to befriend them on social networking sites. Then feeding gathered information into databases that spat out spreadsheets sold to corporations and municipalities.

Working for IRJ worried Evangelína — about her privacy, her perceived freedoms — but working the Barnett Shale in Fort Worth had made her paranoid. The citizens organized in a way that was scary, and a group of domestic ELF eco-terrorists took charge of the resistance and shook her crew. The ELFS practiced a brand of radical environmentalism. They were like treehugging, club-wielding Teamsters, willing to shatter glass and crack skulls.

Deeper in the "Grassroots Opposition of Alarm" appendix, Evangelína read that a splinter group of the Sierra Club's Atlantic chapter had merged with New York Residents Against Drilling (NYRAD) to form Occupy Marcellus — this made Evangelína snort into her Bloody Mary. She could see grimy gringo teenagers, matted blond dreadlocks dangling over the fronts of their Che T-shirts, packing the bowls of their water pipes in underground caverns. Strike a match and blow themselves to kingdom come. Suicide bongs.

She knew it wasn't funny. For every pot-smoking teenager looking for a cause there was a desperate landowner looking to get even for a perceived wrong. Someone aggrieved, who knew where to look, could find that a plane owned and operated by IRJ was flying from Houston to the airport nearest the NY Marcellus. The thought was panicked but it made Evangelína wish she'd flown commercial.

She closed the portfolio, finished her drink, and tried to nap.

The jet touched down with a bump and a squeal. Evangelína thanked the flight crew and stood in the open doorway, freezing. The air was bracingly cold. The flight attendant said the temperature was 52. She hadn't packed for this weather.

At baggage claim stood a young gringo, tall, holding a sign, *Canek,* and he bore a resemblance to the former riverboat casino dealer aboard the oil platform. The sight of him stopped her, but it wasn't him; it couldn't be. She felt the presence of her papí, who used to joke that all gringos look alike. Papí was warning her with this case of mistaken identity, but the voice resonating in her head wasn't her papí's. It was Marisol's. At the last moment, Bizzy's assistant had thrust the portfolio into the elevator at Evangelína, tripping the safety sensor — the doors jerked back open.

They stood staring at each other. As the doors reclosed, Marisol had said, Evangelína, cuidado.

Recalled, those last words weren't a warning — be careful — they were a threat.

Evangelína slipped into the airport restroom and used her phone to arrange a car rental. Half an hour later, when she came out, her driver gone, she wondered if she'd just fucked-up and got her ass fired.

Masada hulked behind Milton, a gothic citadel sprung from a mead hall. Four-story bluestone walls. Empty bell tower. Pair of ramparts overrun by reddening leaves of poison ivy and Virginia creeper. He spent a moment listening and breathing, synching his senses with the out-of-doors. The sky in the southeast glowed vaguely orange, an illuminated immensity that might be mistaken for the sunrise. It was New York City, reaping benefits of midnight oil burned along its outskirts, down in Jersey and up the Hudson.

At the old Alpine village, he took Standard Hill. The bunny run made history in the fifties: first ski slope in the world covered in manmade snow. Six still-standing buildings — clapboard and half-timber sided with hipped roofs and shake shingles — were set to collapse, a smorgasbord for carpenter ants. The lodge, more grand Adirondack cabin than Austrian chalet, leaned precariously downhill. Over the years, with help from his company, Milton removed and stored every fixture and piece of furniture from the doomed buildings of the Standard, which once boasted its own post office and airstrip, a power plant and synagogue, its own press and social daily, the *Standard Tattler.*

The Standard Grande had been a testament to assimilation, a Diaspora collage of designs and themes borrowed from homelands left behind. The Alpine village always seemed to Milton the most out-of-place. Like a recreation Biloxi plantation in Liberia. Here in the Catskills would gather a thousand Jews escaping, for a few days a year, the cramped trappings of the Lower East Side, Brighton Beach, Flushing, and Yonkers, most of them Ashkenazi, but also Mizrahi, Sephardi, Bukhari, and Italkim, having survived pogroms and purges, having lived through the Holocaust, vacationing at a resort where they could enter into a large-scale Aryan architectural diorama and be served huge portions of wurst and sip schnapps after zipping down the slope on Alpine skis or bent into toboggans. To Nehemiah, that had been the point. Jews couldn't go to the Austrian Alps and feel welcome, and so he determined to bring Hallstatt, Salzkammergut, not far from Lake Toplitz in the Totes Gebirge, to the Jews.

What remained of the Alpine village was horseshoe-shaped. As long as the structures stood, they sheltered wind even in winter.

Here, Standard Company cooked.

Milton built and lit a fire in the small former fountain at the village center. He strained to replace the sewer-grate grill. Over coals he set the big coffee boiler, rusting beneath its chipped enamel, filled with stale grounds and clear, clean water from Trout Creek fed by the Neversink Reservoir of the New York City watershed. While the coffee heated, he checked the animals.

He picked through lessening darkness. His old eyes, in the weak light, scanned the ground for wild mushrooms, difficult to distinguish in full sun never mind near night. After decades of training his eye, he couldn't shut off the foraging reflex even when fruitless. There still could be found hearty bracket mushrooms, young Chicken of the Woods growing in the cold like stacked Styrofoam plates from the trunks of oaks.

In Vietnam, this scanning reflex had been a few feet higher, his eyes darting along the treeline, the search pattern of a soldier seeking out the enemy, or hints of him, before being seen — an instant the difference between shooting and being shot.

The chickens kept the squad in eggs three out of four seasons. Thirty hens, give or take, stocky, plucky Rhode Island Reds —

the Commies, they called them — with blistery combs. Their coop was the listing pro shop of the overgrown golf course. Their roosts were wood-handled wedges and irons.

Milton clucked through a window screened off with chicken wire. The hens clucked a response and followed with their pleased trills like the slipping of thirty loose fan belts.

The alpaca paddock and pasture was the fenced-in former fairway of the tenth hole, a dogleg par-3 once renowned for its sucking water hazard and a bottomless sand trap, Hell Bunker. Milton had never played a single stroke. The closest he ever got was carrying clubs for Sammy Davis, the only caddying he ever deigned to do. It still surprised him, the way old age worked. He woke with a person from his past in mind, and that person kept him company for days, a not unhappy haunting. Sammy made sense — Milton had been thinking more about him — Sammy died of the same thing that was killing Milton.

As he stood before the unidentifiable tenth hole, a conspiratorial thought occurred to him. He and Sammy contracting the same cancer two decades apart wasn't simple co-incidence. Larger forces were at work. Such forces weren't God, they were government. You didn't get syphilis because the Good Lord was punishing you for frequenting the brothels of Tuskegee; you got syphilis because the Man subjected you to the disease to better understand long-term effects on white folk. Maybe dioxin exposure, and the increase in incidents of sterility and throat cancer, was part of a larger plot against black Amerika. Take away our ability to reproduce and, at the same time, deprive us of a voice.

Milton shook his head hard and got his legs going, kicking through the browning grasses and fallen leaves. The minute he stopped moving, ceased working, his mind receded into dismal places. He dismissed his cancer conspiracy as paranoid, though justifiably so, something his crackpot vets would cook up round the campfire. There were so many cover-ups, so many vagaries and opacities — MKULTRA, the fifties CIA program that targeted subversive Americans, Paul Robeson the most notable among them — that it was hard to maintain trust in human goodness, never mind the decency of the US government.

Milton focused on his surrounds. No birds flitted. All quiet save for a hushed rustling. Falling leaves settled on the fallen. When the Standard was in operation, under the tutelage of impatient Ada, he'd learned to ski and play tennis. Golf was a bourgeois line he refused to cross. He'd ribbed Sammy, told him his saving soul-brotherly grace was that he was no good at the game. In response Milton didn't get a cutting comeback — hard to imagine that was forty-plus years ago — instead, he got Sammy's disarming sincerity, which always carried a whiff of the stage. When he took you into his confidence, he did so with flare and a tad too much minstrel poetry, yet he rambled in a way you knew wasn't scripted. Like the time Milton lugged Sammy's clubs for eighteen holes while Sammy and Nehemiah went at it over their huge handicaps. A wager made between them for a whopping dollar, Sammy calling it a big bet between Jews. He told Milton and Nehemiah how he and Altovise had, earlier in the year, gone to DC. There, they'd been the first free black guests in history invited to sleep in the White House. That didn't happen under Kennedy's watch, short as it was. No, man. John, God rest him, snubbed little ol' me, and after I helped him secure the Negro vote in '60. Cold-shouldered, all cause I was married to May at the time. This when unions between whites and blacks was still illegal in thirty states. Sanctity of marriage my skinny ass. Sight of a one-eyed Negro Jew hand-in-hand with a blonde-haired, blue-eyed Swedish model a foot taller than me? That was too much for John, man. Those Kennedy cats were always caught up in appearances. That's Catholics for you. Frank's the same damn way. Shiny surface hides a shit substance. Too much pomp. Their pope's basically a pimp in a pointy hat, man. He aint far from furs. Don't never trust no white motherfucker in a pointy hat.

Anyway, point is, it took Nixon to get a Negro an invite. After Nixon put me and Altovise up, his boy Don "Rummy" Rumsfeld, who's running Nixon's War on Poverty, where I'm on the advisory board — this Rummy was in Vegas giving a speech while I was doing my hundredth gig at the Sands. Hundred's a big deal, now. And I took him and his wife to see a show. Didn't tell them who I was taking them to see, just said I was taking them to see the greatest entertainer in Vegas, and they were game, man. So we go see Elvis at the International, right, and he's the King of Kings. He's got a collar like a count. Scarlet scarf and a belt buckle big as a license plate. And poor square Rummy's looking a little hound-dogged. After the show, I take them back-stage, and it was a party, man, gorgeous girls everywhere, and I look up, expecting to see Elvis mobbed by honeys hanging all over him. But no. Elvis's towering over Rummy alone in a corner, and he's grilling him about the Army and the draft, and it's not like you think, Milt, militant as your Black Power ass can get despite living up here with the Lost Tribes. Cause Elvis is a big sup-porter of the draft. And he loved him his time in the Army, man. I served in the Big Deuce. Drafted in '43.

This is all going somewhere, and coming back around. This all ties in, don't you sweat. Then I'm a make a run on that dollar over these here back nine, Chema. You wait. When I arrived for Basic, I was strapping on a watch my father gave me, and it slipped to the floor. And this white motherfucker, Jennings — I'll never forget his name or his face — he crushed my father's watch with the heel of his boot. Looked down at me and said, Don't worry, boy, you can always steal another. This Jennings was the ring-leader of a group of racist motherfuckers who made my life living hell. After a show I did at the Officer's Club, Jennings motioned me to join his table, said he wanted to say sorry and slid a pitcher of beer my way.

Apologized for it being warm but he wanted to make peace. When I poured a glass and started drinking, his cronies fell out laughing. I was drinking a pitcher of their piss. Well, when Altovise and I arrive in our limo at the White House, guess who's guarding the White House gate? That's right. Jennings. Can't make this stuff up, man. This is God at His mysterious Motherfucking work. So I says to him, Don't I know you? Know what he says? He says, No sir, Mr. Davis. What I'm sure to hear at the entrance to the Pearly Goddamn Gates. *No sir, Mr. Davis.* Out front of the Nixon White House. Not the Kennedy White House, mind you. Nixon. Took crooked-ass Dick to get a nigger a bed in the nigger-built White House. Say what you want, Nixon's got no care for appearances. What you see is what you get, like it or not. And when we got inside, Dick offered me and Altovise the option of sleeping in the Lincoln bedroom. I said, Mr. President, I appreciate it, but I don't want ol' honest Abe visiting me in the night talking bout, I freed them, but I sure didn't want them sleeping in my bed, and Dick let out that laugh like a horse shot in the hindquarter. So we opted for the Queen's room, where you best believe Altovise and me made love in that big bed like it was nobody's business. But we both had a good cry first, cause I remember back when I was a hoofer having to soft-shoe around, *Yes sirring,* and *No sirring* my way on and off every stage I graced, and that Klansman Jennings out front guarding us while we made love in a —

A dismaying bleat snapped Milton out of his Sammy Davis invocation. The calls of the alpaca, high-pitched and whiny, were sweet complaints even when aggrieved. He slipped achingly between the timber fence rails as the sun nudged up over the Gunks forty miles east, igniting the turning leaves of the trees from here to there like Milton had called in a napalm strike on the Mohonk Mountain House perched atop the Shawangunk Ridge.

The vista looking out and down was spectacularly spangled. The piney greenness. Maples reddening. The yellowed ash, bur oak, and elms. Colors of fall put him in mind of his Pan-African days, made him think of his flirtation with, his near immigration to, Liberia shortly after he got back from Vietnam. That was before he met Ada, who made America feel like home for the first time in his life.

In the paddock, two male alpaca neck-wrestled, an exertion that usually waited till after their morning feeding, such that it was. A three-sided loafing shed offered shelter but, like some of his vets, they preferred the out-of-doors. He'd seen them sleeping in the open during the hardest rain and on the coldest night, sub-zero, a layer of frost on their fleece. Evolved in the Andes, they found the Catskill climate mild during the worst winters.

Milton was in command of two squads. Each consisted of a dozen-odd members: his veterans and the alpacas they were assigned. There was a chain of command. A vet and his alpaca constituted a team, the vet the team leader. Milton kept thirteen animals, one for each resident plus two extras, which he cared for himself. Their number was down from nineteen at the start of the summer. Two crias birthed in June didn't make it to August, one dead of what was probably a phosphorous deficiency and one eviscerated by a mangy runt of a coyote not much bigger than a cat. The squad had eaten one adult in the last two months, and three others had been carried off by someone or something. A tragedy, but Milton couldn't help feeling relieved, because the animals were slowly starving. He couldn't afford enough feed, and the cool spring preceding a dry, over-hot summer cut short by a wave of cold fronts made for poor grass growth and depleted minerals in their pasture. What was left of the herd was hurting.

He didn't take on a new vet unless there was an alpaca for him — or her. And he'd been weighing whether to wind it all down, stop taking new vets at all, let the whole enterprise peter out. Ten years was a respectable run. Smith might be his last guest. As a charity case, she wouldn't help his financial situation. At this point, he'd need to double the size of his company to start making a dent in his debt. He could no longer cover the costs of the interest, never mind reduce the principle, on all he'd borrowed. The esquires could sort it out when he was dead. With the help of his lawyer's estate planning and finesse as executor, the Standard might even live on as a shelter. He reminded himself he had some life in him and that he wasn't going to waste it on financial worry. Toward Nehemiah's end, the old man had often said, Make sure to send a lazy man for the Angel of Death.

Milton approached, clicked his tongue and whistled. The two males disengaged, unwinding their necks and standing at attention, ears perked. The rest of the herd gathered in a tight pack at the center of the paddock, whimpering and warking. Sue, the youngest male, sixteen months old, tiptoed over and nipped Milton's forearm.

Milton jerked away, and Sue jumped back bleating and rejoined the herd, burying his head between two fleecy haunches. Something was wrong, and the absence of jays, finches, and woodpeckers at their noisy morning tasks told him a predator of size was in the area. Milton counted heads of his herd: four, six, seven, ten, twelve. Someone was missing. He went through again by name. Zsa Zsa van Winkle, Four-Legger, Bandera, Al-Pac-Man, Diddy Yah Diddy, on down the line. Reverend's animal, Wile E. Prince, was gone.

Milton scanned the dark treeline, scouting along the perimeter of the paddock. The sun was low, and the horizontal, high-contrast light accented every nuance of the ground. Tracks of a scuffle showed in the soft soil near the loafing shed. Alpaca had no hooves; they had two nails and pads like two heels of a hand pressed together. Scratch marks in the groundcover looked to come from the wrestling males.

A few feet away ran drag lines, four become three. Might've been feet while E. Prince was mostly upright. Lines ended at a broad swath — the body — as E. Prince was overturned. Wide track went under the fence. On the other side, the body swath vanished.

No blood trail. No tufts of fleece.

Black bear didn't enter hibernation dens till November in an autumn like this. Known to eat adult deer but not regularly. A penned alpaca was easier prey. Couldn't be coyote. Take a pack of three or more to kill an adult alpaca. Lone gray wolf could manage it, but they hadn't been verified in the Catskills for nearly a century. He'd seen lynx and bobcats. Both would have a hard time taking down an alpaca, couldn't've hoisted an adult off the ground. Would've eaten it while the other alpaca watched whining. Mess would be evident. The western cougar of the Rockies was steadily moving east, following the explosion of whitetail deer. Milton was certain they'd already arrived in the Catskills. In June a cougar was killed on the Wilbur Cross Parkway in Connecticut seventy miles north of New York City. A necropsy proved it to be wild and to have walked over from the Black Hills of South Dakota. Eastern cougar had just been designated extinct by the US Fish and Wildlife Service, which held the official position that any confirmed cougar sightings in the Catskills were released cats raised in captivity, most likely western cougars. Milton knew such cougars existed. Before he auctioned off the holdings of the game farm, he released a cougar, Gizbar, at a loss of some $10,000. The plaque still hung over her cage.

Milton approached Zum and Chewy, talking in his huffed rasp. Maybe his pretenses about Bigfoot and Sasquatch were becoming realized, because he couldn't explain this. No blood, nothing. Four adults vanished, poof, in two months. He would be forced to herd them into the big hay barn each night, yet one more chore to manage. Reverend came to mind, a conversation he and Milt had about —

A snap sounded, a scrape. The ears of Zum and Chewy pointed the same direction.

Footfalls, something being dragged. The thing being dragged sounded hollow.

Milton unsnapped the thumb brake, drew his sidearm, fingered the safety. He didn't disengage it, didn't raise the weapon. He took a knee, his popping joints nearly as loud as the noisy intruder.

A silhouette. A figure low to the ground dragged something beside it. Milton disengaged the safety. Applied a hair of pressure to the heavy, combat-weight trigger. Performing a snap assessment of distance, the background, his periphery, he prepared for the full-bore rush of a massive 200-pound cat. Sprinting at forty-five miles-an-hour. Capable of a forty-foot horizontal leap. Coming head on at high speed, the cougar would make a tight target almost impossible to hit. Milton might have time to squeeze off one potshot.

The hunched figure — on the far side of Milton's gun sight — reared up and emerged from the trees. "Aquí, vicuña, vicuña" — a woman's voice — "here, pretty vicuña" — an accent, Spanish but not Nuyorican, sounded like Southern Spanglish.

Here was Ada, his wife, speaking a foreign language, come home calling to his alpaca, which had once been hers. A wash of dread — he wasn't *thinking* he saw Ada. He was observing it. Here she was. Young, displaced. Then, as soon as she was, she wasn't.

The voice belonged not to Ada but to Smith. Smith had hitched her way up here to save him a trip. He lowered his sidearm — he re-raised it. The trespasser, the woman, was young but not white, wasn't rangy and athletic like Smith. Stepping into the sunlight, she was short but not squat, a Latina, busty and hippy, early thirties, her hair in a dark ponytail coming undone. Her new blue jeans were muddy and wet to the knees and she held out a phone like a wafer of black glass, pointing it at the herd on the far side of the paddock.

His instinct was to run her off without her getting sight of him. Normally, he'd fire a round, a sounding of the alarm sending his squad on high alert. They'd resort to their assigned scare tactics in his ongoing PSYOP campaign against scrappers and vandals, but his squad were all asleep.

He could shoot over this short woman's shoulder. The more fear that surrounded the Standard, the more people would stay away — that'd been his intent, implemented since the shuttering of the resort. He wanted to leave trespassers with the impression that the Standard was haunted, that Bigfoot, Sasquatch, and Yeti dined on over-curious hikers drawn to ruin, that crazy Catskill mountain men had the run of the place and were willing to hunt down hunters trying to take deer from private property, or murder meth-heads seeking to yank every last inch of copper wiring from the walls to sell for next to nothing.

His voice wasn't strong enough to command this lady's attention from where he kneeled. He holstered his sidearm — this was what disease, more than age, did to a

man, made him timid and soft, too compro-
mising. He stood, bit down on the cuticles
of his pinkies and let out a catcall.

She jumped — "¡Ay, Dios mío, ayúdame!"
— and dropped her phone. It landed on the
ground beside her kayak — that's what
she'd been hauling. She looked around to
locate the whistler. She hollered, "You
scared me," bending over at the waist in
what seemed to him a cleft offering, suggestive, found her phone in the fallen leaves,
waved and said hello.

He stood ground and glared.

She leaned against the fence and perched
her new hiking boot on the lower rail, at
home on the range. She was too comfortable; she'd mistaken his whistle for a flirtation.

"This is private property."

She cupped a hand to an ear. "Beg your
pardon?"

He strode to the fence and swiftly kicked
her foot off the rail.

"¿Estás loco?"

"You're on private property." His breath
was bad and he employed it like an uncon-
ventional weapon.

She took a step back. "I'm sorry. But that
doesn't warrant assault." Barely over five
feet, she gestured to her plastic boat that

had a store sticker still on it. "I'm portaging."

He set his hand on the butt of his holstered sidearm, still warm from his grip, his heart yet to settle after the misplaced fear, the painful confusion, she'd stirred in him.

Her eyes went to his hip. She took another step back.

He said, "Portage elsewhere."

She shot a look at her boat. Protruding past the seat was a black shotgun barrel and in one motion he opened the thumb brake and drew his sidearm with a zipping sound as the sight scraped the nylon weave. He held the .45 down at an angle. She was saying, "Tranquillo, easy, please," before he realized the gun barrel in her boat was a paddle.

He was making mistakes he wouldn't have made ten years ago, but he kept the gun drawn and lowered. "Dangerous for a woman to be trespassing up here alone. Could get you shot. Or worse." He wanted to fix some healthy concern in her, make her muddle-minded, the way she'd done him, but didn't want her running to cops with a wild story about an armed and dangerous quick-draw old Negro at the Standard.

"Take it easy, would you please? I'm passing through is all."

"You're trespassing and I'm tempted to have you arrested."

She raised her chin and squinted at him, defiant. She was more Indian than Latin, with a sharp-featured face, beautiful in its severity yet warm, like the head of a hatchet still red on the anvil. She tucked her phone under her chin, pulled her hair out of its ponytail, shaking free leaves and twigs, and retied it. Her tightened scalp drew back the corners of her dark eyes. Meaner. She pulled her phone from under her chin and said, "You can't."

Despite her certain appeal — tight jeans, buttery smell — he was losing patience. "Get on out of here before I have the police come escort you out."

"Down home in Texas, people show a little more restraint with their firearms."

"You're a long cow ride from Texas."

"You the landowner or just some squatter hermit?"

He sniffed and didn't holster his gun.

"If you're the landowner," she said, "you should know the laws. This isn't trespassing. You couldn't have me arrested if you wanted to. You've got a river right there that's navigable-in-fact. Anyone has right-of-way on that river even though it cuts through the middle of your property — assuming the property's yours."

"You a lawyer?"

"I'm no lawyer."

"Then which gas company you work for?"

"Seeing as how I'm not breaking any laws, would you mind being a bit hospitable and give me a hand? Where I'm from, we take more kindly to strangers."

"How's that, by hanging em high?"

"The only thing we hang high is our piñatas, now if you please."

She was a strange mix that caused him confusion. She wouldn't've been possible a generation ago — one part Southern belle, one part Menchú Tum — and he pointed to her flimsy boat that had been recently poured and pressed into its present shape. "If your canoe's too heavy for you, you shouldn't be out alone."

"Kayak. And I'm not. Got my phone to keep me company." She slipped the slick device into her tight back pocket, and he felt himself relax.

Her futuristic phone was a dark window into everything he'd missed over the years. With it he could access his every ignorance, if he only knew how, and he knew, with dread, he would never know how.

Her eyes fixed behind him. "One of your

143

friends approaches."

Milton awaited reinforcements he was in bad need of, Reverend coming on strong and overblown, taking too much pleasure in running folks off. Then he remembered: no one had confessed to seeing Reverend in nearly a month.

Milton ignored the alpaca, keeping his back turned, and the animal, Sue, butted his head into Milton's hip, knocking him off balance.

"This one's lively, and cute. They're scraggly. Like they're starving. They supposed to look so wasted-away?"

Sue wasn't fat, but neither was he wasting away, not with his coat coming in. Milton wondered what was telling her they were underfed. "Someone's just carried off one of my herd. Thinking maybe it was you."

"Me?"

"If I can't have you arrested for trespassing, maybe I'll try a lawsuit for poaching."

Sue nudged Milton, wanting a pull from his flask.

"I don't want trouble," she said, "legal or otherwise."

"What, they don't cultivate a sense of humor south of the Mason-Dixon? Let's get your canoe in the water so I can see about solving the mystery of my vanishing camelid." He ducked between fence rails. A complaint escaped him. He sounded like whiny Sue.

"You okay?" She offered her hand, saying, "Evangelína," and he didn't take it.

He gave her his back and grimaced, the twinge more along his ribcage than his spine. He needed to stretch, needed a minute before lifting a boat. Crouching, he untied the lace of his boot, concerned he'd need help to stand. "That true, that spiel about portaging and . . . What'd you call it? Navigable-in-truth?"

"Learn something new, don't you." She had an authority he found reassuring in a woman so short.

"Been here since the seventies." He stood, slowly but without help or support from the fence. "Been running off trespassers of one kind or another. You're not the first person to portage on my property, but none've ever made your argument." He lifted the bow of her boat. A pain stitched between his ribs, like he'd popped a suture. He dragged the stern as he went. There was the hollow scraping sound he'd heard earlier. Another rustle, this one receding, came from the far treeline. Not trusting it, he was losing faith in his senses, and the world.

The woman chased after Milton, raising

the bow, unable to let their silence last more than a moment. "Most people aren't informed. Me, I'm paid to be informed."

He dropped her kayak and faced her. "By who?"

"I'm a right-of-way agent."

"Not just out for a joyride in your canoe, huh? Right-of-way agent. Sounds like a lawyer by another name."

"Kayak. I'm on company business."

"Gas company business."

"I'm under contract with SW&B Construction."

"Looking to build a casino?"

"My employer's interested in this property. We're considering a few holdings in the Catskills. Not a casino. Too much risk before next November. We want to build a high-end golf resort that's no more than a long drive from New York City."

"That part of your marketing campaign?"

"We're trying to decide if we should recondition an old property, like this one, or if it would be more cost-effective to buy an undeveloped parcel and start from scratch."

"You give me a few minutes?"

Her eyes widened, as if she thought he might sell her the whole lot right there on the spot for some duffel cloth, ax heads, wampum, a few Jew's harps, and a fistful of Dutch guilders. "Take your time." She pulled out her phone. "No reception up here."

Maybe she was alluding to his lack of hospitality. He leaned against fence rails he'd raised from trees he felled, looked beyond the spooked alpaca that would soon be starving.

He'd entertained offers over the years. One in '87 he would've taken from the Koch administration, in a failed bid to turn the Standard into a city-owned-and-operated 600-bed homeless shelter. Local officials beat back that proposal, and it eventually led Milton to enact the idea on his own, on a smaller scale. Then there was the offer that sounded a lot like this offer; he'd already heard the one about the high-end golf resort, in the mid-eighties, from a boomtime Japanese investment firm. In bad financial and emotional shape, he'd been physically fit, even drunk, which helped him endure the boozy dinners, where three Sumitomo salarymen in Italian suits talked to him about nemawashi, digging around the roots, a process of discreetly laying the foundation for some proposed change or new project. Milton bonded with one of the men, Kensaku, who, weeks earlier, lost his wife and two teenage daughters in the Otaki earthquake when the south face of Mount Ontakesan by the Magio Dam crashed through the pines and carried his home and his family into the reservoir. Yet here he was, Kensaku, talking tee shots and bad lies, proclaiming a love of lox, sipping sake, saying Kiso-Ontakesan resembled these a Cat-a-skills. He bowed his head sharply, raised his masu, a wood box of a cup. He told Milton he would begin to mourn when he returned home, once the sale of the Standard was finalized, but Milton, after deliberation, declined, bowing his head, saying he wasn't ready. His wife was here, dead eight years then, but still here. The other two salarymen, furious, stormed out. Kensaku stayed to pay the bill, and the two widowers finished their cold sake in shared silence.

Milton thought to offer this Evangelína a cup of coffee, get a sense of her seriousness, but the squad would be gathering round the cook fire for morning briefing. He was to let them know that a woman, Specialist Antebellum Smith, would be joining their ranks that evening. One woman was plenty. He didn't want a short sexpot to get his vets riled with her talk of a purchase. Make them think they'd again be homeless — he wouldn't let that happen. Offers like this came to nothing more times than not.

Staring at the leaves falling around his dwindling herd, he determined to turn her down, run her off, but he'd do so with some measure of reluctance. He understood his role. A business deal was a courtship, she was the suitor, and if she was serious, she'd be back. He said, "I would kindly like you off my property."

"But, wait, what just happened?"

"Nothing happened. I'm not ready to sell yet."

"How could we help you get ready? We're prepared to make a sizable offer."

He wanted to say: Go on over to the Mohonk Mountain House and offer size to the Smileys. See if they bite. You also got the Concord and the Nevele nearby. I'll give you directions. Now scat. What he said was: "If I wanted to sell, I wouldn't sell to some construction company with plans for a golf course. I'd sell to some hydrofracker for a whole heck of a lot more than you're willing to offer."

"We're offering a purchase, clean and simple."

"This what they call the hard buy? You have a tough time hearing no, don't you?"

"Here's my business card. I'd like to be in touch."

He took the card. "Let's get over to the Mongaup and launch you in your tippy canoe, Menchú Tum."

"Menchú who?"

"Kids these days. If you're not reading it off your phone, it's dead to you."

They portaged together without talking, finding a walking rhythm, she synching her choppy steps to his rangy strides. The sunlight rang his ears, making him want to beat a retreat back to the dark and curl in the void of the oubliette. Bright light had gotten brighter, was audible, like the tolling of a bell. Into the treeline he followed a well-trod deer trail heading to where the Mongaup gossiped in the woods. Deer trails wending through underbrush from water source to water source. Deer trails become hunting paths, first for indigenous Americans, followed by Europeans and their slaves. Paths for hunting become wagon roads become Main Streets and Broadways. The story of America was a story of roads, and all the roads said the same simple thing: we want and will go to get.

At the bank of bluestone slabs, she climbed in her kayak. He shoved her off, nearly dumping her into the water. He stood watching, refusing to wave, as she drifted downriver, waving. He caught a chill, pain behind his eyes like a cold icepick slipped into his temple — a wave of déjà vu that was more clairvoyance than remembrance. Milton felt watched. Tracked not by a person but a presence, stalked by the lost past. On this very spot there surely stood a former Dutch slave — father of Isabella Baumfree — sending off the daughter of a Lenape chieftain making an offer of too little, too late.

Ray takes the quick route from the Standard grounds, a five-mile sprint downhill beneath the zipping sizzle of the high-tension cables, where he feels secure. Under the thrumming electromagnetic field, invisible yet tactile, like ionized air before a lightning strike, there's no need to wear a tinfoil beanie to keep his employers from reading his brainwaves.

The scraps of metal, killer confetti scattered under the skin of his hip and thigh, burn as if still hot from the VBIED blast that projected car parts into his person. Earned him his last Purple Heart and the lifelong pledge of partial disability pay — a check that, for the past year, went straight to Wright.

His throbbing pain lessens the farther he runs. There's a stat he can't get out of his head: IEDs caused over 60 percent of coalition casualties in Iraq and Afghanistan. Ray pulls up. Takes a knee and gives his thigh a hard rub. Sometimes he can't believe he made it out alive. Sometimes, he's certain he didn't. He died. This here, his American afterlife, is but a bad dream, a living hell, the everlasting sentence he's serving for his war crimes.

Consolidated Edison maintains the broad service road, keeps it well cleared. In the sunken valley below him, the Neversink Reservoir stretches its dark avenue. The spangled trees, splashes of yellow, orange, and red broken up by the spires of evergreens, spread to the tinselly Hudson River and beyond, reaching the hazy foothills of the Berkshires.

He resumes his run. At the third mile, he reaches the bank of the reservoir. He takes a few minutes to skip stones on the surface, beneath which lie whole drowned towns. Big freshwater fish, walleye and trout, trolling for little fish in churches. Soft-shelled turtles the size of tires cruising over Division Street and Old Post Road. Lives and livelihoods deluged, all so residents of the five boroughs can drink clean water.

He walks the bank till he finds the narrow point over the Neversink River. Sweaty and ready to place his call, he enters the hamlet of Neversink, relocated after the original town was sunk. The antediluvian naming of the village, circa 1800, surely sealed its fate.

Ray makes treks into the neighboring small towns every week, to place a call, to loiter in the public library, where he uses a computer to conduct research, or visit yurt-forum.com, sometimes simply to catch sight of another face, sometimes to nurse a can of Coke at the Citgo in Neversink, where there are no bars. After the end of Prohibition, the civic Neversink elders passed a quaint dry law still in effect.

The payphone stands outside the fire department, where two firefighters use a pressure washer to scrub and spray the big Volvo diesel pumper.

Watching them watch him, Ray dials the real-estate lawyer who for nearly a year has issued Ray's orders, received his briefs, and paid him in tight bricks of cash.

The male receptionist answers, "Baum Law Office."

"It's Early Bird."

Silence, followed by throat clearing. "One moment. Can you hold?"

"Got all the time in the world, sweet-heart."

The fireman holding the pressure washer

regards Ray from across the twenty meters separating them. He's Ray's age, pushing up on thirty, Ray's height, a couple inches short of six feet, but he's over-inflated, his bulk built by heavy weight at low reps, his strength slow. Ray's strength is his speed and stamina, increased by calisthenics, distance runs, and survival work. His body provides all the resistance — he's proud of his bushman's physique.

He must be giving the fireman the shit-eye, because the guy aims at Ray down the barrel of the pressure washer. He winks and shoots. The jet of water arcs up and over but falls short. The implication doesn't: Ray's a dirtbag in need of a wash.

Ray sniffs his underarm. He does stink, his hair long and greasy, his beard thick and filthy. He hasn't been clean-shaven in a decade, facial hair grown out to blend in first with the Taliban and then Iraqi insurgents.

The other fireman, tall, all sinew, is leaning on the pole of his scrub brush. He smacks a hand on his partner's slab of a chest.

Ray raises his arm and waves, flashing them, if they care to see, the tomahawk sheathed snug in his sopping armpit, concealed when his arm is at his side.

They don't wave back. They're on guard. Ray can't blame them. The population of the village is a couple hundred souls. These two see an unwashed mountain man — soul long sold — come down off his precipice as a threat to the soulful.

Over the receiver, the receptionist says, "Mr. Baum on the line."

"Yes, hello, this is Ellis."

A click as the receptionist hangs up.

"We need to meet."

"The usual place?"

"No."

"Can you come to the office after hours?"

"I name where."

A clatter of keyboard keys in the background. "Okay."

"I want to go fishing."

"Is that code?"

"It is not."

"You have a New York State fishing license?"

"Howbout you score me one, as a perk."

"Where you want to fish?"

"On a boat, on the Ashokan."

"It's far for you."

"Don't assume you know where I am."

The *clack, clack* of fingers over keys. Then silence, and Ray imagines Baum getting up from the mod desk positioned against the wall of the pre-Revolutionary stone-house-cum-commercial-space in the former capital of New York State, going to the window and looking out at the payphone cattycorner to his office, a phone Ray has used.

"Since September 11th," Baum informs him, "you need a Public Access Permit to use DEP land in the watershed. The PAPS aren't easy to get, and you have to have one before you can apply for a Boat Tag. Once you get your Boat Tag, then you're free to fish on the Ashokan."

"You have a Public Access Permit."

In the pause that follows, Ray nearly hears Baum's synapses recoiling into the curlicues of question marks: What else does he know about me? That I'm married? That I have two kids, one adopted? That before I opened my Kingston real-estate office, I worked as a land-lease attorney in a Pennsylvania mining town?

Baum says, "I do."

"You also have a Boat Tag. And a boat. On the north bank off Onteora Trail."

"You've been checking up on me."

"You wouldn't be paying me so handsomely if I wasn't capable of due diligence."

"We'll have to get you a guest pass. The DEP's everywhere out there. I've never been on the reservoir and not gotten carded."

"Then get me a guest pass."

"Can take up to two weeks. I'll need a valid driver's license number."

Ray pulls out his Jersey license. He reads the letters and numbers, transposing two.

"I'll arrange it."

"Do better than that. Expedite it. I want to meet, at twenty-four hundred hours, three days from now."

"We're supposed to be getting more weather. Early November nor'easter."

"We'll go blizzard fishing."

"Twenty-four hundred hours is midnight?"

"That's right."

"Midnight blizzard fishing on the Ashokan. Can I know what this is about?"

"My replacement made contact with the target."

Another pause filled by keyboard clacking. Probably dashing off an email to some hydrofracking higher-up. "You're sure."

"She's a sexy Mexican midget in a kayak."

"Is this some kind of joke?"

"If it is," Ray says, "it's on you. This is where I get off. Tour's up. Be sure to come with my final installment. You're supplying the gear and the bait. Twenty-four hundred hours, at your boat, three days from now,

Thursday, guest pass or no."

Ray hangs up. He watches the firehouse, not yet ready to make the hike uphill. Uphill is harder on his leg.

When the burly fireman stomps from the firehouse holding a yellow hatchet and a whetstone, Ray, wanting to work out some frustration, decides to let himself go berserk.

He walks to the Neversink Citgo and buys two cans of Coke. Then strolls over to the firemen, approaching slowly, casually, a Coke in each hand. He grins and nods.

Their fists whiten, on the scrub brush, on the hand ax.

Ray offers a slight shake of his head, to set them mistakenly at ease, and says, "Make you boys a wager."

Near dark, Smith shivered at the assigned rendezvous point. A frigid wind blew through the chasm of East 110th at the northeast corner of Central Park.

A kidnapper van pulled up, exhaust huffing from the tailpipe. From out of the van's driver-side window blared a whistle like an incoming tow missile. The van drove around the traffic circle and slowed to a stop in front of her. The passenger door opened. Behind the wheel, Milt hissed in his scratchy rasp, "Come on in out of the cold. Supposed to start snowing again any second." He looked alone.

She listened to the van's engine: a steady, uncongested *gurr-urr-urr* as it idled. It sounded a lot like the voice of its owner. The body of the Econoline looked bad — polka-dotted with splotches of sanded, unpainted Bondo — but there wasn't a spot of rust and the old die-cast heart that made it run was rumble fit.

On the side of the van, she could make out the words *The Standard Grande* in faded rainbow pastels and a groovy font with fancy caps overtop an airbrushed scene. A gray castle perched on a washed-out green mountain. Under it, a slogan: *Where rest sets you free.*

She regarded gaunt Milt in his trim white goatee. He looked good, considering, like a senior marathoner. She climbed in. She made a show of faith — in his decency, in her decision-making — by dropping her field pack between them where he could reach it.

He pressed his thumb against his temple. "Want to drive?"

"I'm done driving."

"My wife never learned. Spent her whole life being driven. Died driving." He seemed to wither as he said this.

"Hope for my sake you weren't the one behind the wheel."

Again, thumb to temple. "Her lawyer —" He winced.

"Her lawyer? That sucks." She reached to touch him but didn't. "You okay?"

The pained silence caused her to call everything into question. Then he asked if she was hungry.

She was starved. "I could use to eat."

He shifted the van into drive but kept his foot on the brake. Her door was open.

She stared into the back of the van — windowless, tidy, and empty. "Half expected to see me a bed back there outfitted with leather restraints."

"Been on my fair share of prisoner snatches. Couple of them successful. But here in my civvy dotage, I'm no longer the abducting type. Don't worry."

A gray old-timer's hat rested on the center console. "Makes you think I'm worried?"

"Old Negro picking up a white gal? Take into the woods? Call it nigger's intuition."

More out of spite than desire, she pulled shut the passenger door. Her closed window had a crank and she gave it a turn to let in some air.

He cut the ignition; the engine coughed and went quiet. He swiveled to face her.

His gaze felt like a hard frisking. "You know something, Specialist Smith, since our first encounter, I've been waffling. Because bringing a woman up to the Standard might be a horrible idea. My vets can be a volatile bunch. But they're mostly harmless to others. It's themselves I worry about. But I figure they came up in a co-ed military. If I can keep the company of a lady vet, so can they."

"You tell them I'm coming?"

"They know someone's coming."

"They know this someone's a female?"

"Not all of them, no. Was set to tell them, at morning brief. Something came up."

She reached and grabbed her field pack. She didn't bolt, not yet, in part because Milt was taking his time, allowing her to weigh options.

He must've sensed her softening, opening, because he reached and, tenderly, pressed her hand gripping her field pack.

She fought not to flinch. Almost lost it — here was the first sympathetic touch she'd received in months, the first touch not a grope or an assault since she fled Leonard Wood, longer even, cause Travis'd been rough with her ever since she got back from Afghanistan and confessed her infidelities.

Her eyes got swimmy and hot under Milt's

attention. She wanted him to hold her. This made her furious. "You make any advances, Pops, I'll take it as an act of aggression. I'll introduce you to my sidekick. You got me?"

"Not sure if I should be offended or flattered you think I want to bed you."

"Be whatever," she said. "Flattered or fended don't make no never mind. Just wanted to get that — and this — out in the open." She let go of her field pack and reached in the small of her back with her off hand. The pepperbox was in his face, at the end of her cocked arm. She was steady. For the first time in the van, she felt at ease and in control.

Milt stared up the quad barrels. "Might have to start calling you Bang Bang, liable as you are to go off over next to nothing. You did see that clause in the contract you signed that specified no firearms, right?"

"Didn't read the fine print." She lowered the gun.

"Litigious as everybody is these days," he told her, "clause's there mostly so I don't go getting sued. Far be it from me to want to limit your Second Amendment rights, but I've found that guns don't mix well with my crowd. Seeing as how you'll be the only female, I'm gonna make an exception. Do keep in mind" — he reached and opened the glove box — "you won't be the only one packing." The door dropped down, and inside was tucked an old-school M1911, a holstered .45 caliber automatic. He slapped the door shut, picked up her field pack and held it out to her. "You don't have to do this."

"Beg pardon?"

"Could leave you here. You could go back to that tree of yours. Must say, something awful comely about a wild white girl living in a tree in Central Park."

"My tree's got all of two leaves left. I'm an easy target for every schoolgirl in Manhattan." She fingered the scab in her eyebrow, glanced in the sideview, bag under her eye a fading yellow — she looked terrible. Haggard at twenty-five. She holstered her pistol.

He produced and unwrapped a Ricola. "Could take you to Port Authority. Buy you bus ticket back to Ar-Kansas."

"Missoura. And what, face a firing squad?"

"They don't shoot deserters."

"Court-martial then. Spend the rest of my service in the brig. Yeah, no."

"It aint like that."

"How do you know how it aint?"

"I've made some calls on your behalf."

"My behalf?"

163

"They hardly prosecute deserters anymore," he told her. "Couple years back, there was a crackdown. Prosecution rate tripled, to something like six percent. Most deserters — if not on deployment orders — get dishonorably discharged without being prosecuted. Different if you high-tailed it in a combat zone."

She plucked his fedora off the center console and donned it at a rakish angle. "Probably part of their ploy. Turn myself in expecting a slap on wrist and wind up getting a bullet in the back of the head."

"Yeah, you're gonna fit right in."

"What's that supposed to mean?"

He pulled the hat off her head and dropped it back on the console. "Bus ticket would set me back, but not really, cause I'd just charge it."

She buckled her seatbelt. "Come on, Gramps. Show me your Rust Belt resort."

"Alright then." He cranked the ignition. "Not rust. Borscht, something you're gonna develop a taste for might quick. Got a recipe passed down through the generations, on my wife's side. Winter sets in, we eat a lot of rodents, rabbit, and root vegetables."

She rested her head and tried to doze, and then they were stopping at one of the members-only, big-box wholesale retail warehouse clubs for obese Americans on supersize condiment diets. Milt, putting on the gray fedora and cocking it, said he needed some things they couldn't produce themselves.

She caught some shallow sleep, and when she felt a lurch, she woke gasping.

"You're safe." Milt's grumble, coming from the driver seat.

Cardboard boxes brimming with sacks — of rice and ground coffee, pasta, something called quinoa — were bungee-corded to one wall of the van. She'd gotten the most restful, secure sleep she'd had in months, despite the bad dream, the particulars of which were already vanishing. Snow coming down hard.

Dropping her guard, she stared at the fine profile of this old man she was coming to trust. Handsome, he was weathered in a way that expressed a wildness settled by wisdom. Something becoming about Milton Wright, his trim goatee, small silver hoop in his ear.

He shot her an unamused, uncomfortable look. To break the spell he plucked something off the center console and held it out to her — a sardine tin. "Will be your survival kit. Every vet gets issued one, just in case. Might get you through a long lost weekend on your own. You pack it yourself, seal it with duct tape. That'll be the first duty you pull. Keep it on you at all times." He sniffed in various directions like a dog with cataracts in a changing wind. "Smell that? Burning rubber?" Then he strained his face and winced hard. "Got to pull over." He made his way to the shoulder, where they rumbled to a stop. "Been having dizzy spells." He threw the gearshift into park but didn't cut the engine. He reclined his chair and closed his eyes.

"Ah, excuse me?"

"Give me a minute." The color spilled from his face, from rich brown to deep yellow, his lips fading till they blended with his gray goatee.

"We need to get you to a hospital?"

Without opening his eyes, he said, "Trade seats. I'll point the way."

"To the hospital?"

"To the Standard. It'll pass. Trade seats."

"I don't think so." Her breath shortened and her gut soured, burbling acid up into her chest. "I told you." She shook her head and hard. "Done driving. Specially not in snow."

Eyes closed, he pushed himself standing, hunched over in the cab, unsteady. "I'm not taking no." He fumbled for and grabbed a fistful of her sleeve and yanked her up.

They did a slumped waltz, stepping on each other's Army-issue boots and, then, there she sat, behind the wheel for the first time since she'd abandoned her Dodge Hemi along the highway all those months ago.

"What you waiting for?" His eyes were still closed.

She cranked the ignition — *grrrt* — and jumped at the grinding of the already started engine. "Shit. Out of practice."

"Don't go breaking the gear teeth now. Your daddy just bought this vehicle."

"My daddy would vote before he bought an automatic."

He pressed his thumb into his temple, not massaging it, more like testing a soft spot on a melon. He tapped his forehead and said, "Tokhes."

"Huh?"

"Your daddy, when he said something clever, touched his head and said, Tokhes."

"You don't know my daddy," she said, "and my daddy don't know no tokhes." She adjusted the seat. "Thought I was gonna be on the receiving end of some hospitality. Here I am, hospice." The highway was wet, snow not sticking. Her breathing was short but she wasn't hyperventilating, not yet.

She loved being on the road, when that

road wasn't going to explode beneath her. She gave it more gas. Milt leaned back as the van accelerated — slowly, surely — and reached the speed limit, 55. There she coasted. She was driving like an old lady. What state's motto was *Live free or die?* Freedom was like war that way: if it didn't make you nervous, you weren't truly engaged in it. Driving, she felt anxious, she felt alive.

Evangelína sat parked in her roving office of a rental car, engine idling, heat blasting, deliberating a run. If nothing else, it would warm and calm her.

The B&B, Bed by the Creek, was cosmic punishment for traveling by private jet. The online reviews warned it was filthy, smoky, and cold — *Don't stay here, stay away!!! You'll leave feeling like one of local Lenny Bee's smoked trout packed in dirty dry ice!!!!!!!* — but the bad reviews made no mention of the biohazard.

Evangelína had been seduced by the sunny images on the website and, once in the driveway, despite the shady look of the place, got sucked inside by fatigue, the pride of a proprietor willing to fly the rainbow flag out front, and her limited cash. She didn't want her billing on the company card

— they'd know right where she was — didn't even want it on her debit card. It'd be cake for an IRJ techie to hack into her bank account. Changing lodgings at this point was one too many tasks to manage.

She diddled with her phone — five voice-mails; seventeen emails; the photo she'd taken of the alpaca was bug-eyed and blurred; the extended forecast showed highs in the low 30s and 20s lows with snow for five straight days; in Houston, the temperature was an enviable 77 degrees. Her laptop charged in the passenger seat. A tablet computer and a portable laser printer lay on the backseat next to a box of SW&B stationery and literature.

She listened to her voicemails. A fertility appointment she would need to reschedule. Messages from Marisol, each more urgent than the last, imploring her to call, to meet with Ellis Baum, to contact Bizzy. And one concerned message from Mamí. Bizzy had telephoned to invite her, Mamí, to lunch and asked if she'd heard from Evy.

Her mamí's worry was warranted — Evangelína hadn't gone twenty-four hours without talking to her since Papí died — but the company concern wasn't.

She'd done what made her different from other landmen: she went straight to her boss. The way she saw it, out in the field, the landowner was boss. She thought if she closed a quick deal, her stock would rise with Bizzy. She'd be back home and warm with her mamí in Houston before the Catskill snow set in.

But here she'd been in New York for not yet one full day, made contact and got nowhere. She'd already played her navigable-in-fact card. Now she would introduce herself to this Ellis Baum late and without a handshake agreement. Maybe she was trying to get herself fired. And on top of it all, she was sure she was being followed.

She had one consolation: Mr. Wright showed a tell. His rough rasp was on repeat in her head — I'm just not ready to sell *yet*. She needed room to do her job. She needed some distance, some perspective, to figure out how to help Mr. Wright get ready.

The company reaction to her being incommunicado heightened her paranoia, made her think she was in danger, which compelled her to hole up, not reach out. And Bizzy calling Mamí to invite her to lunch? As far as Evangelína knew, they hadn't talked in years.

Sitting in the car lit by the glacial glow of her phone, she felt drained. Couldn't shake the dread that weakened her at the airport. Felt unhealthy engaging in corporate espionage. Golf? A racket worthy of the Golfos was more like it, and she was neck deep. Expendable, she'd been dispatched on the chance that Mr. Wright was desperate enough to sell for golf money, saving the company tens of millions of dollars at least.

IRJ sought to capitalize on the infirmities of an arthritic war vet who so happened to be a person of color. And Bizzy, with his excruciating pep talk while distracted by that bank of TV screens showing what must've been IRJ security contractors — her boss was in command of a private army, in control of privatized natural resources. IRJ, with its right to free speech, its federally mandated license to influence elections, stood firm on the platform of corporate personhood. The more involved Evangelína got with the IRJ executives, the more it seemed like playing God.

She told herself she was being melodramatic. It was the cold. She needed to acclimate. Hadn't gotten in a run since she arrived. But it was more than that. This assignment felt like a long, hard slog while lugging a great burden. She could hear her colleagues gossiping around the microwaves: Remember when she won Landman of the

Year? Seems like ages ago. I never liked her anyway. And those four-inch heels? Who's she trying to kid? What'd you expect? Send in the midget when you want to fall short.

She stared out the windshield into the dark woods, so alien to her. The trees looked dead. That was all she could think at the Standard, while portaging. Everything's dying. It wasn't the first time a landowner had waved a gun at her — regular physical threats were part of the job description, especially in Texas, which was why most of her peers carried concealed weapons — but afterward, she'd been traumatized, couldn't stop shaking.

She needed to make a choice. The thought felt like asphyxiation. Fatigue, lightheadedness — was exhaust seeping into the cab? She turned off the heat and cracked her window. It'd been a long time since she'd known these sensations — endless wavering, paranoia, the tight chest, tense internalized talks, constipation and sleeplessness, the magical thinking. Right after Papí died, when she came out to her mamí, who'd tsked and said, Oh, Evangelína, we've known since you were four years old, and Papí didn't care, hija. He said you were hok'ol beh, on another road, just like my sister, Tia Crescencia, whom he loved.

172

A visitation by Papí, at a rinkydink airport, it was absurd. She was becoming her mamí. She breathed deeply, her mouth at the cracked window, drawing cold, clean mountain air far into her. She needed to run, needed reminding that each new assignment felt this way at the start — the same fears. She'd overcome them in Mexico. But those fears arose in a place she felt at home, felt warm. Here in the icy, unknown Northeast, she needed to hear a familiar voice. She called her mamí.

By the time Smith pulled up to the Liberty post office, Milt seemed — mostly, strangely — recovered, the color returned to his face.

"Need to run in, get my mail," he told her, "back in a quick," and he was, standing at the driver-side door, telling her to slide over.

He climbed in behind the wheel with a thick stack of envelopes dusted with snowflakes, sat with a *hrumpf* and walked his knobby fingers through the stack — bill, bill, junk, bill, bill. As he sorted, every piece seemed to go into the same pile, until he stopped at one with a slickly styled return address: *SW&B.*

He set the oversized envelope in his lap and hefted the other mail, some falling to the floor. She picked them up: *Wickes Arborists. Bank of America. Chase. Wells Fargo. The State Assembly of New York. Lependorf & Associates.* As she handed them over, he shoved them into a grocery bag dangling from the center console. He held the SW&B envelope to the snowy daylight.

He dug into the pocket on the door, stuck his hand in the cup holder. He opened the glove box. "Here, hold this." He handed her his holstered .45, heavy as hell.

She drew it out, and he paused, studied her, saying, "Aiming your gun at me's one thing, go aiming my gun at me, you're in for it," before he resumed tossing the van. The semi-automatic pistol was older than she was but beautifully maintained. The technology was far more advanced than her throwback pepperbox. She asked, "What you looking for?"

"Reading glasses."

"What you need read?"

He looked at her and squinted his muddy eyes. "Don't know if I can trust you with what I have here." He fanned himself with the big envelope. "But if I'm going to expect you to trust me, it's incumbent on me to first show you trust, so I'm gonna take a chance. You've taken a chance on me."

She nodded.

"What I'm gonna tell you goes in the vault, understand? You make no mention to the others. Don't want them riled. At this point, I'm reasonably certain nothing'll come of it." He held out the envelope.

When she reached for it, he pulled it away saying, "Not one word."

She leaned over and snatched the envelope. Tore into it. Inside was a page-long cover letter. The paper felt as thick and durable as cotton-bond cash. Paper-clipped to a hokey brochure, pictures of women in hardhats, smiling men with tool belts who hadn't broken a sweat. She read, "*Dear Mr. Wright:*

"*With a focus on small to medium-sized projects between $5 million and $25 million* — lot of money — *we are capable of delivering developments in all phases of construction, including new installations, retrofits and maintenance.*

"*We began expanding our presence in the late 1990s, experiencing success in the areas of customer products and building services. Now as a wholly owned subsidy —*"

"Subsidiary?"

"Yeah, *subsidiary,* sorry — *SW&B continues to support our clients while also building our resume* — I mean *résumé* — *in other industries.*

"SW&B has developed a diverse list of clients since the company first started in 1987. Year I was born. *Today, many of its clients are Fortune 500 companies that cover hospitality and heavy industry. We have done business in 33 states and have completed more than 280 heavy industrial projects* — can I stop now? Goes on for another paragraph. What's all this about?"

"What's the name at the bottom?"

"Evangelína Canek."

"Let me see that." She handed it to him and he studied the postage through narrowed eyes. "Stamps," he said, "not metered mail. Not postmarked. Probably bribed the postman to put it straight in my box."

"What's this about? They use all those words but never say nothing."

"Tell me something, Specialist Smith. Why'd you enlist?"

"Serve my country."

"That's what you tell yourself once you're in. I'm asking why'd you enlist."

"Get away from my daddy."

"Get away from Daddy. That's something gets you in the door. Once you're there, they don't take no. Once there's no escape, and they're screaming in your ear, serve my country starts making sense. Start wanting to give your all for the good ol' US of A. Maybe that gets you through the first year or two. After year three, four, six? By the time you've done your service, you come out feeling owed. Owed a job. Owed insurance. Owed disability. Want to be compensated for your time served. You've risked your life, on multiple tours. Now it's time to collect. I should know," Milt said. "Felt me the same damn way. Felt it even stronger, cause I was drafted. But then you get out. Looky here, no jobs. VA's giving you a hard time about benefits. You're owed, but they don't make it easy to collect. Lot of hoops, some on fire. Makes you mad. That attitude — I'm owed — is ruinous. At the Standard, we try to be at least self-sufficient."

"I can do that."

"See," he said — leading her one way only to yank her the other — "thing is, self-sufficiency aint enough. You know, you're an 88-mike, motor transport operator. Remaining neutral gets you nowhere, doesn't get this country anywhere, doesn't get humanity anywhere. You got to keep it in drive. Get a move on. Status quo don't cut it. Got to be better than that. Must be more than self-sufficient, have a little left over, to give to your brother, your child, your neighbor, and not just because you're gonna be old and infirm someday and are gonna need an assist, but because the world as we know it will unwind if you don't. The Standard's a company. We pull together but not because we have to. You got a choice. You pull cause you want or you scat. That's it. The spiel."

"Sounds scripted."

"Scripture's more like it."

"Gospel of Wright?"

"Been honing it ten years. Most vets climb in this here van for the trip upstate with me're lucky not to be headed to Sing Sing or Wallkill, but you are a captive audience."

"Why'd you start it?"

"Long story."

"Come on," she said. "I told you why I enlisted, now your turn."

"Should rest my voice."

"Scratchy as it is, you don't seem to mind the sound of it."

"I can take a hint."

The phone rang four, five times, and just before the machine was set to pick up, Mamí answered, "Ba'ax ka wa'alik?"

The familiar sound of her Maya, the wet clicks and soft pops like water boiling in terra-cotta over an open fire, nearly brought

Evangelína to tears, and yet, in Spanish, Evangelína responded, "Mamí, answer the phone in English."

"Bix a beel?"

Evangelína loved this greeting, despite her mamí's obstinacy, which was Evangelína's obstinacy. *How's your road?* If Evangelína ever married, she'd be ts'okan u beel, which meant *finish her (wife's) road.* She answered, "Ma'alob, Na'." *Fine, Mother* — that about exhausted her command of her mamí's mother tongue.

"Dios bo'otik." *God pays.*

Evangelína replied in English, "The devil pays better." She added, "It's freezing up here, Mamí. Hace frío." The older Mamí got, the more time she spent in Maya, which had no word for yes. If you asked a Maya, Is it cold? the reply will come as a rephrasing of the question, It's cold. Maya assumed you had all the time in the world. "Were you awake?"

In Spanish, Mamí said, "I was outside. Feeding the aluxo'ob."

This word, aluxo'ob, had no Spanish equivalent. The nearest Evangelína could get was duende, supernatural forces in the form of goblins, or bush spirits, but it was more than that. In English, she said, "Mamí, must you always act like a superstitious old

Indian?"

In Spanish, Mamí said, "Your ancestors were ajaw. Your relatives fought alongside Zapata. Don't forget your revolutionary blood."

"You've been watching reruns of *Aló Presidente* again."

"Don't get smart."

"If Bizzy knew Chávez was on the TV in my house even for a minute, never mind eight uninterrupted hours, I'd be talking to you from the unemployment line."

"I know that not to be true."

"Mamí, when Chávez nationalized the oil projects in the Orinoco belt, he put us out of business in Venezuela."

"Chávez is us."

"Chávez is loco, and dying."

"He thinks Estados Unidos is the cause."

"His Cuban cigars are the cause. Aluxo'ob. What on earth are you feeding them?"

"We have ants. I'm enticing them out of the house."

Evangelína couldn't help but laugh, which was progress. There was a time when her mamí's superstitions made her cry, or scream. Mamí's spirituality, like her politics, was a crazy-quilt. Ancestors weren't more important than ants; ancestors were ants.

Never mind how they'd managed to march up to Texas from the Yucatán. The guayacán bowls — holding the jellied papaya seeds that drew the ants to the maize — told the weather of the ancestors. The wood grain delineated not just their years but, if you looked closely, her mamí would admonish, you'd see the seasons they lived through and how long a drought lasted, yada yada, nada y nada, exhausting Evangelína with her infinity in everything.

A howl came through the phone. The sound of Mamí's copper kettle — dented, a dull green patina over it. Mamí had brought the kettle with her from Quintana Roo; it, too, was aluxo'ob, the ghostly voice of Chichí, Mamí's mamí.

"Ants," Evangelína said after listening to Mamí fix her saffron tea, the tinkle of the spoon as she stirred in honey. "Call the exterminator."

"Your boss — ch'akat beh — invited me to lunch." *He's a forked road.* "This errand he has you on, it means you won't be home for Día de los Difuntos?"

"It's important work, work that'll keep me here awhile, unless I close a deal in record time, which isn't seeming likely."

There was another silence, and in it Evangelína heard a strange clicking. She thought it was the engine cut off and cooling, but there was more to it. The sound was glorious, the shattering of a million minuscule bells blown from glass. She strained to hear it. And then she saw it — snow! On the windshield. The crystalline flakes bursting as they landed. Amplified by the kayak strapped to the roof. Her eyes welled up. "It's snowing, Mamí."

"I've never seen snow."

"It's beautiful. It has a sound."

Mamí sipped.

"Did you tell Bizzy you'd have lunch with him?"

"I told him I was an old widow who can date anyone she wants."

"You did not."

"I did. I tell him that every time he calls."

"How many times did he call?"

Mamí sipped.

"Mamí?"

"You work very hard, Evangelína."

"What does that mean?"

"You're gone a lot."

"Mamí."

"We go to dinner occasionally."

"Mamí! He's my boss! He was Papí's boss!"

"He speaks beautiful Spanish. We go to his country club. He has Edith's blessing."

"Here I thought the last time you saw him was ages ago, at Papí's funeral. Don't you blame him for Papí's melanoma?"

"I blame the sun."

"I don't know what to say. I'm . . . shocked, Mamí. Not appalled, that'll come later."

"Don't be."

"How long has this been going on?"

"Stop talking about it like it's an affair, hija. It's a friendship, an old one. Older than you. I'm his charity case. We talk a great deal about your father. He likes to hear stories about the Yucatán. He can be a tremendous bore, but if you tell him to quiet, he quiets. He's well-trained by his wife." They fell silent, and Mamí said she should go, she had the bougainvillea to contend with.

"Be careful."

"They're just thorns."

"I'm talking about Bizzy."

"I don't have to worry about his feelings. He's not my boss or my husband."

"Mamí, when you see him, do me a favor?"

Mamí sipped.

"If he asks about me, tell him you haven't heard from me."

"Is everything okay, Evangelína?"

"I should go too. Tak saamal, Na'." *Until tomorrow, Mother.*

"Ya," Mamí said and hung up. Ya was Maya for love, a root word that could also mean pain, sickness, or a wound.

"After Ada died," Milt said, "her father followed close on her heels. I was in a bad way for a long while. Lost two decades to drink, depression. All but checked out. My father-in-law left me the family business. Was no business, and no family, left. Felt responsible for Ada's death. Was living like a hermit. Nothing to keep me company but my animals. News of 9/11 reached me a week late. After, I went to my wife's lawyer —"

"One who killed her?"

"Killed her?"

"In the car accident. I was paying attention."

He went quiet again. This time didn't seem by choice. He stared at the snowy highway rounding the bend of a foothill. When he didn't come to, she prodded: "You went to her lawyer . . ."

His look — pleading, confused — opened her up like a boiled peanut.

She welled with affection. She also felt shamed; his deep love for his dead wife made her feelings for Travis seem shallow.

184

She reached and gave Milt's forearm a pat. Awkward, clumsy. When that didn't do it, she pinched him, and hard.

He swerved the van in the snow. "Damn, girl." He sniffed, hacked into his fist, and rubbed his forearm. "You nip like my alpaca." Then he told her: "After 9/11, some folks went looking for revenge. They'd call it justice. Me, I pulled the other direction. Wanted forgiveness, make peace, more with myself than anyone else. Owed something to my wife, her memory. Thought to turn the Standard into a shelter for vets the way my father-in-law made it a haven for Jews. Knew me a couple guys, Nam vets, not guys I served with just hardluck guys I met on trips to the VA in the city. The Standard was collapsing all around me. I needed help and these guys wanted to get far away from Ground Zero. We worked out a deal. They sign over a portion of their disability to go to overhead, room and board, I give them a place to stay, work to do. Thought, if I can keep at it, maybe it'll be around long enough for vets of newer foreign wars. Had no idea we'd be getting into a situation that was two Vietnams at once. If I had the manpower, and the money, maybe a grant writer or two, I could put up a couple hundred hurting vets. Cause when these boys're done —"

"And girls."

"Took me two decades after discharge to get right. Not all right, mind you, but right enough to make a second go at making some contribution." He looked away from the road, nodded at her. "This time's different, different from my time, hell, maybe different from any time." He turned back to the road. "Cause now it aint only the men coming home from war needing help. It's the women. There's progress for you."

After a silence, he told her they were almost home. He wasn't bunking her with the other vets. She'd get a room of her own. "You begin feeling comfortable enough that you want to make the jump to the library — in fall and winter, everyone sleeps together —"

"Excepting you."

"Except me. That's right."

They were on a back road that was a series of steep switchbacks. She asked, "What're those tipped over drums?"

"Barrels of sandy salt. Once the snow starts to stick, switchbacks're damn near impossible to get up. This here snowfall's supposed to last for days, so get ready to be snowbound. Crazy what's become of the weather. Okay," he said, "we're here."

There was no sign at the front entrance. They turned past a leaning guard house, empty and covered in *No Trespassing* postings. Milt drove up the crumbling drive. On either side stood two stone-and-mortar columns. Spanning them was rusty iron, simply wrought, spelling out: *FREIZEIT MACHT FREI.*

"German," Milt said. "Means *leisure frees.*"

They drove toward a tower rising to the tops of the towering white pines. She counted floors, nine. The rundown cylinder was Cape Canaveral meets Hotel California. It was funny, a vision of the future left behind.

"Standard Tower," he told her. "It's starting to Pisa."

Next came a castle that looked covered in camo netting. She asked, "FOB Camelot?"

"Masada," he said, "the old armory."

She craned her neck to see it from the far side as they drove by and came into an architectural hodgepodge stretching on for a few village blocks. It was like the main street of a tiny town that never figured out where it was, in time or space.

"Underground passages link most of these buildings," Milt said. "Used to connect all the kitchens, laundry facilities, and storage areas so the staff could move about and wouldn't be in the elements. More importantly, so they wouldn't be seen. Those passages are mostly off limits. They were reinforced ages ago, and we don't trust them."

"And that's where you sleep."

"Right."

"And all this is yours."

"What's left of it."

"Why'd it go under?"

"Haven't you seen *Dirty Dancing*?" He pointed. "Buildings were built in each decade, as the resort expanded. Development came to a halt right around 1970. Beginning of the end," he said. "I arrived shortly thereafter. That block of a building like a Soviet dormitory there, erected in the fifties, that's Esther House. Now the cold-weather barracks. Library's in there, where everyone beds down. You're free to borrow any books, just make sure to note it in the log. Over that hill, which was once a ski run, that's where you'll find the Alpine village. That's where we muster and take meals. The company should be gathering ranks. That's where we're headed."

A ringing reached her, the tolling of a church bell.

"That's assembly call. We've been spotted."

Most of the windows of the barracks were boarded up and, at ground level, she saw a figure, lumbering and furry, what looked like livestock that was upright, strange, a little scary. When she asked Milt what was that, he answered, "That'll soon be you."

With the voice of Mamí still in her mind, Evangelína pulled up Ellis Baum in her phone's address book. She didn't touch his work number. The time was just after 6 p.m.; she doubted he'd be in his office. She climbed from the car, stood in the strengthening snowfall. She turned up her face, let the flakes land, frigid, on her cheeks. She trembled.

She would go for a run over the Standard campus, sticking as best she could to the old logging roads mapped out in the Standard portfolio. They, like the rivers and streams, were passable without trespassing, public access as long as she didn't wander off them. She'd be as conspicuous as possible, and if she were lucky enough to meet Mr. Wright again, she'd make an offer worthy of gas not golf. Then, she'd give Ellis Baum a call. He and Bizzy could sort out the details with the lawyers.

Smith couldn't make sense of two outright oddities, so she did her damnedest to ignore them. She stood shivering around the cook fire, snow swirling, staring hard into the black hole of her cowboy coffee — burnt and hot as old engine oil at the end of a long desert haul. She wore her field pack pulled tight over her shoulders. Her pepper-box clipped at her hip.

Nine men including Milt, a squad-sized group of former soldiers uneasy at ease, and a dog. Nearly in tears with the want to let that shepherd slobber her face, she waited for Milt to make introductions.

The scruffy men shifted weight from boot to boot, warming their hands on their enameled tin cups showing the faded Standard logo and motto — *Rest Makes Free* — all of them shooting looks at her, the FNG.

One vet stood with his back to her. The hide he wore was all one piece. The front legs of the skinned animal reached down the man's arms and were tied at the elbow with what looked like translucent cord. The hindquarters draped down the backs of his legs and were likewise tied at the thigh. The two belly flaps of the animal were drawn around either side of his torso and tied. But the most extraordinary, and downright terrifying, part of the getup was that the former face of the creature, eyeholes and all, rested atop the man's head and was tied under his chin. He looked half man, half eaten. The others wore theirs more casually, like shawls shrugged over their shoulders.

If not for the caveman capes, the scene could've been on a firebase in the Hindu Kush. But then there was the other oddity: the backdrop of the Alpine village.

Milt quieted his troops with that piercing whistle. "Listen up," he rasped. "I want to introduce Specialist Antebellum Smith, who I've taken to calling Bang Bang."

She shook her head and waved a hand.

"A motor transport operator. Fifty-Eighth Transportation Battalion out of Leonard Wood."

"I prefer Bellum."

"We'll take it into consideration," Milt said. "Most of you boys know better than me, transportation's one of the deadliest jobs in these here wars. Show Bang Bang due respect." He went around the tittering group, naming them. "Bang Bang's our newest guest," Milt said. "Make her feel at home. Vessey, you're dismissed as Brevet General. You'll give Specialist Smith the lowdown when we're done here. Anything to report?"

"Nada," said the old vet, Vessey, with his dog, Egon. "No sign of Reverend."

Milt nodded. "We've been lax of late. We want to get back on full alert. We need to be more vigilant about trespassers. One in particular. Want you to keep an eye out for a woman, about yea tall, a Latina."

The vet wearing the full hide, Merced, said, "Better call la Migra."

"She's not an illegal," Milt said. "She's on a business trip. She expressed some investment interest in the Standard. Caught her kayaking on the Mongaup. Got a hunch she'll be back. If you spot her —"

The vet with the Muslim name said, "Scuse me, Captain."

"What is it, Brother Alhazred?"

Alhazred. Alhazred. "Anyone seen my drum sticks?" When all he got was shaken heads and shrugged shoulders, he said, "Thanks, fucks. What about Simon Says?"

"Not today," Milt said. "We got a late start and a lot to do. Now, this woman returns, give her the full Standard. Someone spots her, sound the big bell for emergency muster. Gather up for a quick brief, then go all out. Scare bejesus out of her. Run her off."

Merced said, "Affirmative."

"Don't make sense." The other Marine. Botes.

Milt said, "Now anybody see signs of E. Prince?"

"Found what looks like a crop circle in our cornfield," Alhazred said. "All indications point to alien abduction. But, Comandante?"

"What, Alhazred."

"Don't we have time for just a short Simon?"

"Luckson," said Vessey, "howbout we play Red Rover instead."

Smith asked, "Who's Luckson?"

Stone said, "Red rover, red rover, send Bang Bang on over."

Smith rested her hand on the butt of her sidearm.

"Chief," said Botes, "I don't get why the little Latina's got to get a trespasser's treatment. Sounds to me like she's a purchasing agent maybe looking to make an offer. Why don't we invite her over for coffee?"

Milt let Botes's gripe settle over the group. When the silence started making them uncomfortable, he said it was no secret he wasn't well. He was gonna keep at it as long as he could, but he needed them to start thinking ahead. He said he was putting things in place to make sure the Standard didn't fall into wrong hands. It was also no secret he was way in the red. "If you haven't noticed," he said, "I'm not getting rich off your disability. This woman who crashed our party says she's representing concerns that are interested in buying the Standard. But she did not make an offer."

Stone said, "You're sitting on a goldmine, General. Why don't you just lease some of this place to frackers and take us on a vacation to the Bahamas?"

"Cause I'm unwilling to poison people's water's why. This woman's company," Milt added, "wants to turn the Standard into a golf resort."

"Let me get this straight," Vessey said. "If this woman comes poking around, you want us to scare shit out of her so she takes her big check and never comes back?"

Milt said a business deal was a seduction. "We don't play a little hard-to-get, she'll lose interest. If we run her off, she wasn't interested in the first place. If after trying to run her off, she comes back with an offer, we know she's dead serious. We get a sense of how hard we can haggle. Maybe we can work in a provision that preserves Standard Company. Establishes it as an official half-way house for New York vets, maybe something that offers some sort of work release. Big projects are always looking for built-in tax breaks and community enrichment to get the local votes they need to proceed."

The youngest vet, Stotts-Dupree, failing to grow a beard — maybe all of twenty — said, "You trying to turn uth into caddi-eth?"

"You know without your teeth," Stone said, "you sound like a sexy Mike Tyson."

Merced said, "Milt, don't know about these putas, but I'm going nowheres."

"You won't have to, Merced."

Alhazred said, "How about just a quick Simon, Captain? Get the blood flowing."

"They thart fanthifying thith plathe," Stotts-Dupree said, "we'll get evicted."

"Not going back to Hoboken," Merced said. "My wife and kids don't want me, don't want them. I'll hold up in these here woods."

Vessey said, "Don't start, Merced, and we got to find STD's denture cause I can't understand a fucking word he says."

Smith felt her hand gripping her sidearm — she wanted to shoot herself in the face to put a stop to these proceedings.

Milt said, "We're gonna get you fitted for a new one, STD. Few of you are due for visits to the VA Center in Castle Point anyway."

Alhazred said, "You sell this place, maybe you gift STD some permanent teeth."

"Didn't want to mention it," Milt said. "But we try not to keep things classified. You boys — and girls — know, despite certain strictures, we run this outfit more as a cooperative than a military unit." Milt's look turned drill-sergeant stern. "Because I'm not going to be around forever, I need you guys to start considering contingencies. Understood?"

Merced said, "I'll take Tamal to the mountains. Waters rise, we'll be dry and high."

"I can see you now," Vessey said. "Riding your alpaca like in *Last of the Mohicans.*"

Botes said, "Last of the Mexicans."

Smith raised her hand.

Milt said, "What is it Specialist Smith?"

"I'm freezing."

"Almost done," Milt said. "Now, weather forecast says this snow's just the start. We're getting dumped on in the next few days, so we got cords of wood to split and stacking to do. You know the drill —"

"Really quick, Sarge, Simon Says."

"Quit it, Alhazred. Now Bang Bang here's gonna be on the big bell from here on out. Bang Bang, big bell gets sounded for musters. Vessey'll give you details."

Merced said, "That thing's haunted."

Alhazred said, "I thought I was on the big bell."

"Luckson, you're relieved of big-bell duty. Alright, boys and girls, fall out."

Inside the B&B, the proprietor, Bruce, sat at the breakfast nook. He didn't look up as Evangelína came through the front door. He was morbidly obese, a varicose diabetic who wore compression sleeves on his legs and, cold as it was, nothing but shorts and tremendous white T-shirts.

Here he was, shooting up, his insulin works on the table. "Excuse me," he said. "Let me wash up and I'll make dinner." He stood, with a lightness that was alarming in a man so fat, and went to the kitchen island, over which hung, suspended from the pot rack, a leather cord with a small noose for bleeding guinea hens.

"I'm going to skip dinner."

"You're paying for it."

"I can't eat right before I run."

He told her there were some wonderful trails. "Be great for cross-country skiing if this snow keeps up. We're supposed to get over a foot in the next two days."

Maybe she'd go for a ski over the Standard

campus instead of a run. She'd need to revisit Morgan Outdoors. Return the kayak and exchange it for cross-country gear.

"Be careful of the black bear. Whole family traipsed through here last month. Ate every last one of my guineas. Know what to do if you encounter one?"

"I do not."

"Bear sees you, start speaking in a low, calm voice — doesn't matter what you say — and retreat slowly. Stand tall, even if he charges. Do not play dead. Show no fear or weakness. If he charges, stay where you are. First charge is usually a bluff. If you stand ground, he may turn away. If he makes contact, you have to fight. Only chance. Other type of bears, it's best to play dead. But a black bear will just eat you. Odds are against you, but a bear that attacks is often young, or starving, maybe wounded. He might be scared away if you pop him in the nose. Aim high."

Feeling nullified by the briefing, Smith watched Milt walk over the hill and disappear in falling snow.

Merced circled toward her carrying a small enamel pitcher. The hollow alpaca face hovering over his face bore a resemblance. "Cream?"

She held out her cup.

"Say when."

The milk was off-white and thick as snot. She nodded, and he stopped pouring. She swirled her cup, looked in, sipped, and grimaced. The other vets laughed.

"Alpaca milk's sweeter than cow milk." Merced gestured the pitcher toward her chest. "Like breast milk. When my wife gave birth to our first, got me a little fixated."

Smith sipped; it wasn't bad once you expected the sweetness.

"Don't you want to know why I'm not with them?"

Smith shrugged.

"Cause they're dead, or good as dead. We all are."

Smith nodded.

"You know," he continued, "we're practically standing on a crater. Just like the Yucatán. Catskills was struck too. Shooting star half-a-klick wide. Came crashing down not far from here. Impact was like a hundred thousand A-bombs. Look on a map. Circle of Panther Mountain just north, Esopus and Woodland creeks, they're the edge of the crater. And we're due for another one." He nodded. "Cause me," he said, "I'm like a meteor magnet. We're next, mira."

A couple of the other vets laughed, and

Vessey said, "Merced, we haven't saddled you with a nickname yet. Howbout Nostradamus?"

Botes said, "Howbout Nostravamanos."

"He's never been married neither," Vessey said to Smith. "Never had kids."

"Yeah," Merced said, "it'd be nice though, having em. Petting em. Feeding em. Tying their tails in knots."

"FNG," Botes said, "if you haven't noticed, Merced's shooting with a bent barrel."

"I've tinnitus is all, puta. And Lyme."

"Got headbutted by the head of a suicide bomber," Vessey said. "Hasn't recovered."

"Wasn't headbutted. But I did boot that puta's burqa'd cabeza like Cuauhtémoc Blanco in the World Cup against Belgium. *¡Gol de Blanco!*"

The mean-looking vet, Stone, said to her, "FNG, we need a tool before we get started on this evening's operations."

She didn't respond.

"Could've stopped that girl," Merced said. "Chest all wrapped in duck tape. Didn't cause she was a kid. Zits and everything."

Vessey said, "Hearts and minds, Merced. Don't mean nothing."

"Reverse-angle bluestone planer," Stone said. "Find it in the Quartermaster's Store under R. Can't miss it."

"Milt tells me," she said, "I'll go. Don't know yall, so yall can go blow."

"Yall," Botes said. "I love it."

They watched Milt march up the hill carrying what looked like a bear cub. As he drew near, the bear became a hide, beautifully colored, creamy with honeyed highlights. When he reached Smith, he told her turn round.

"Hope it aint hunting season," she said. "Don't want to wind up shot and strapped to the hood of someone's pickup."

Stone said, "Makes me wish I was a pickup."

Milt said, "We're the ones do the hunting round here."

"Why you don't wear one?"

Stone said, "All part of his PSYOP campaign to win our hearts and minds."

"It aint so bad," Vessey said. "Sure given me more sympathy for poor Egon here in summertime." The dog opened his eyes at the mention of his name. "Once you try it on, you won't want to take it off. Specially not in this weather."

Milt draped the hide over her shoulders.

"Heavy," she said.

He tied the hide high on her sternum, then around her waist.

The feeling that settled over her when he finished came as a surprise. Short of superhuman but not by much, it seemed elfin. The hide warmed her, lent the hint of invincibility without the terrifying immobility of the Army's Improved Outer Tactical Vest.

"Feels good," Vessey said, "don't it?"

Botes said, "Welcome to the wilds."

Stone said, "That's a nice color for her. She looks good enough to eat. Now, oh Captain, my Captain, tell the FNG we need a reverse-angle bluestone planer from the Quartermaster's Store before we get started on tonight's operations."

Milt said, "You tell her."

"I did. She won't listen."

"There's a chain-of-command here, Specialist Smith, and you abide by it."

"Quartermaster's is up over the hill," Stone said. "Here, you'll need this."

She caught the flashlight, clicked it on and headed in the indicated direction, relieved. She was more exhausted, and more demoralized, by the company of these crazy men than by her months of solitary homelessness. She worried she'd made a mistake.

When she found the building, she wended down moldering halls, using the tags of bad graffiti as points of reference. Lots of swastikas. Wondering how the vandals had gotten past Standard Company, or if the vandalism was an inside job. The verbal hate crimes of shocking succinctness: *Hang Obama. Smoke the 6,000,000. Gays rape gays.*

Through doorways were masses of insanely organized clutter. A room of wall-to-wall bathroom vanities, the basins resting on the floor, their porcelain pedestals standing like severed legs. A room stacked floor to ceiling with bathtubs, one on top of the other, staggered and interlocking, as if arranged by a giant toddler with OCD. Room of mirrors leaning against every wall, reflecting reflections bright and broken in the flashlit dark. Walking through the Quartermaster's Store was like entering into the failing memory of the resort, and she could not remember what she'd been sent for.

She came back to the Alpine village an hour later empty-handed, half-blind, blown away and hoard-headed. There were six vets around the cook fire. Stone saw her, started singing, and then they all broke into a raucous chorus:

There are beavers, beavers, beavers
Wielding rusty cleavers
In the store, in the store

There are quar-ter-masters
Hanging from the rafters
In the Quartermaster's Store

Ray kneels before the fire hissing in the snowfall. For his trek down to the Standard in the dark, he readies his kit, three blades, simple and severe. He hacks up phlegm, spits on the whetstone, and sharpens each edge. Using his leather belt as a strop, one end looped around the toe of his boot, he hones the edges until they can shave long whiskers off his neck. With his curved trench knife, a corvo, he whittles the tip of his walking stick to a point. For every hike, he finds and shapes a new stick, and discards it once his leg is loose.

In the small of his back, he conceals the three-and-a-quarter-inch fixedblade Bloodshark, hand-forged by Tracker Dan, a Navy SEAL and sometime knife maker.

To one thigh, he ties the corvo given him by a Zeitgeist colleague, a Chilean commando turned private security contractor after the ouster of General Pinochet. Every time he ties it on, he hears Diego's voice: For you, compadre, a corvo for Tyro. Muchas gracias for what you done con mi escoba at the Baiji refinery.

Over his tank top, Ray shrugs on a camo

204

buttondown. Lastly, he straps to his chest a Kydex holster and slips in the tactical tomahawk, a Sayoc-Winkler RnD Hawk. The carbon steel head is snug against his sternum and the butt of the curly maple handle reaches his bellybutton. He tries and retries the quick-release bungee retainer — each time, the tomahawk slides out smooth. The weight of it in his fist is primeval.

A snowy wind, unseasonal, moves over the dark features of the mountain. Once he confirms the arrival of his replacement, his job for the lawyer is finished. He'll collect his last payment, but he won't leave straight-away. He's determined to hang around, see to what end his work will be put.

He could use some R&R, has given thought to a catty-corner road trip across the continent come spring, but, first, a rough winter alone in the Catskills will help settle and center him, get him back to es-sentials. Strange to think that his family's a hundred and fifty miles south, in Jersey. A rundown mother and two busted-up broth-ers who've got no idea he's been stateside going on a year.

Trees scrape and rasp. The doors of Baby-lon open into dark dimensions — a place he spent time on recon, Hillah, Babil Gov-ernorate, Iraq, eighty-five klicks south of

Baghdad, patrolling the rebuilt ruins shortly before the Iron Tigers of 2nd Battalion, 70th Armor Regiment, took Hillah. While there, Ray experienced recurring waves of déjà vu. They were the most intense when he passed a mound of raised red earth on the western edge of the ruins. Felt like part of him died defending that dirt. It hurt to watch the jarheads of Camp Alpha use their KA-BARs to pry bricks from the new buildings on the site, bricks stamped: *This was built by Saddam Hussein, son of Nebuchadnezzar, to glorify Iraq.* When those souvenirs were gone, they went to work on what was left of the Ishtar Gate, weathered figures of dragons, having lasted two-and-a-half millennia, vanishing after a single season of the US Marines.

Early snow bends and breaks branches of trees, unfallen leaves catching the weight. The wind dies, the fire goes out, the only sound the trickle of the rivulet that passes along the outskirts of his camp and collects to become Conklin Brook, one of the many sources here at 2,500 feet atop Slawson Mountain before spilling into the Neversink Reservoir.

At 0300 hours, Ray smacks on his assault helmet. Affixed to it are his CANVS retrofitted AN/PVS-15s, color night-vision goggles.

He tips them down in front of his eyes. A civilian caught in possession of the covert eye-gear would bring a great deal of heat and the heat would be federal. Likely in the form of a DHS bureaucrat in an ill-fitting suit, instigated rather than impressed by Ray's service to his country.

Ray assumes the NSA are tracing his movements. Whoever's assigned to Ray is surely being shadowed and documented. Dossiers on top of dossiers into infinite oblivion.

He tips up his goggles and begins the hike downmountain toward the Standard grounds, the second time in four hours he's made the trip. The odd pieces of old horse tack slap and clack, giving away his position. He makes adjustments, tests his sound signature. His next steps are stealthy. He first fashioned the tack into a harness-and-sling that could carry a slack-bodied adult alpaca, which weighs about as much as a woman.

Smith's second serenade came later. Milt toured her around, introduced her to her alpaca, Sue. She'd be entirely responsible for him, in addition to her other duties. She'd feed and brush him twice daily, trim his horny nails, file his fighting teeth, shear him next spring, and butcher him come fall. She'd wear the hide of her alpaca to humble herself. No part of an animal — alpaca, chicken, rabbit — went unused. They rendered the fat, offal, and bones to make lard, soap, and schmaltz.

She excused herself, found a spot shielded from Milt and the snow. You'd of thought she committed a capital offence when he intruded on her burying a tampon. "What you think this is," he barked. "So in love with your own womanhood that you go conducting funerals every time you bleed? Off your knees. Give me that. That's got uses."

"You've got to be kidding."

"Hand it over." He received the bloody tampon in his bare palm.

She wasn't squeamish — prissiness was for civilians, a privilege soldiers couldn't afford — but she avoided Milt the rest of the day, disgusted. The morning after, she kept her distance when he took her on frozen dawn patrol in two feet of snow, until he called her over. A fresh possum, still warm and soft, killed in one of the company's countless snares, snares illegal in the state of NY — ITDs Milt called them, improvised trapping devices — and from the corner of the possum's bloodied mouth dangled the white string of her tampon.

At the cook fire, snow still falling, Smith wonderfully warm under her hide, she and Milt shared a look and a wink over their possum stew, a look that none of the other vets caught, save Merced, who got irate. He funneled his anger at Botes.

Minutes before lights out, Stone broke out an old-school cadence call none of them had heard but Vessey and Milt, cause it'd been banned before they'd all enlisted:

Rich girl uses Vaseline,
poor girl uses lard
But Bellum uses axle grease
and bangs them twice as hard.
Bang Bang Bellum. Bang away all day.
Bang Bang Bellum. Who ya gonna bang
   today?
Rich girl uses tampons,
poor girl uses rags
But Bellum's cunt's so goddamn big
she uses burlap bags.
Bang Bang Bellum. Bang away all day.
Bang Bang Bellum. Who ya gonna bang
   today?

She'd heard worse, and to shut them up, she drew her pepperbox, aimed it at Stone's gaping face. One by one, they went silent, smirking, their smirks saying her pistol was too cute to kill a man.

After a ten-mile, off-trail hustle in the snowy dark, Ray approaches the outskirts of what was the thousand-acre Standard Game Farm, its fall-down separation barrier a twenty-foot-high fence erected to prevent animal immigration. The corrugated sheet-metal panels, corroded, have parted like curtains. He slips through an opening used by a division of deer. He hears movement to the east, some hundred meters off.

Adrenalin fizzes through him. He regulates his breathing — in through nose, out through mouth — allowing himself the benefits of the endorphins without succumbing to a debilitating amygdala hijack. Time slows. His periphery contracts and his focus tightens. He draws his tomahawk, crouches and scans the perimeter.

He catches a shadow low to the ground, a nocturnal carnivore. He tips down his night-vision goggles — a raccoon at the base of a tree pulls on its paw with its front teeth.

Ray's in a hurry. His objective: snag a woodstove from the Standard Quartermaster's Store, hump it up to his camp. It'll be the hot heart of the nearly finished yurt that will get him through winter.

He needs to get the stove before insomniac Wright starts busying about, but Ray hasn't eaten protein in weeks. In this, he's a fundamentalist. He strives for autarky — a closed system — like Afghanistan under the Taliban. He would starve to death before he bought provisions at the Price Chopper, and E. Prince, in the cold weather, must hang for another week before Ray can slow smoke him the way he'd been taught to prepare cabrito.

Here at the promise of a more immediate meal, his weakness takes shape as need. Better to be rushed and nourished, or faint but with the luxury of time?

He lets fly the tomahawk — strikes the raccoon squarely in the hindquarter. The blade lodges in the tree trunk with a wet *tock,* pinning the raccoon. It yelps and gnaws the handle, pulling and pushing with paws that are practically hands, hands that horrify Ray for an instant — small, black, and spindly, the hands of a baby scorched by the blast of a 500-pound smart bomb, a bomb guided by Ray, he the one laser painting the target with the SOFLAM — he wills the image away and draws his fixedblade.

He pins the coon's head with his boot. A fingertip locates the tiny atlas bone. Top of the spine. Occipital bone, base of the skull.

There, he slips in the blade.

Ray tells himself that the lump in his throat is hunger, not anguish. Then he's willing to acknowledge it: he's sad for the kill, clean as it is, in a way he refuses to be with armed men done in by his hand.

From the canopy overhead comes a warbling bark, like a lapdog being drowned. A run of trills follows a whine. The raccoon kit, hiding in plain sight, sways like a drunk. It's weeks old, weighing two pounds at most.

The little critter fixes him with bandit eyes and pleads like a pup. Ray mimics the sound. The kit sniffs in his direction. It complains again and its whines are answered by a second kit that waddles around the tree and noses at the mother's belly, trying to nurse.

Scavengers. Like him, trying to survive any way they can. The other kit climbs clumsily down and snuggles into its sibling, who barks. They already seem to him like brother and sister, the latter runty and aggressive, the boss.

They watch as he dresses their mother, riled by the terrible conflict of odors — mother meat. Ray removes the kernel-like scent glands from under her arms and legs. If left in too long, the glands give the meat the flavor of hot asphalt. Hungry as he is, he chokes down the nutrient-rich organs, swallowing hard and fast in between gags.

He uses the intestinal casing to bind the dressed carcass, dangling it from the branch of a tree, too high for coyotes, too long for the kits to negotiate. On his return, he'll claim his kill. If the kits are still around when he gets back, he'll worry about them then.

Making up lost time, Ray dashes toward the center of the Standard campus. Winded, his leg loose, he approaches the ivy-covered castle from the front. Its façade — two flanking turrets and its empty bell tower — looks like a steam paddleboat bearing down on him. He sprints toward a half-collapsed utility shed, pop-vaults onto a wall, and dynos onto the slate roof that crackles beneath his boots. He crouches and breathes.

From a hundred meters in nothing but scattered starlight, through the night-vision goggles, he studies the wicket cut in the great door of the castle armory. The rotted branch he leaned against it hours earlier remains in place — Wright hasn't surfaced.

Ray tips up his goggles, jumps off the shed, and double-times it.

At a window, in the drafts that whistle through the gaps, Ray smells the Standard vets. He flips down his goggles and peers inside. Fine woodwork and floor-to-ceiling shelves on every wall. The spines of tens of thousands of old volumes. He can make out their striped pastels in the light source at the center of the library. Looking into the hearth nearly blinds him even though it's burned down to a few dim coals. Around the hearth lies a circle of heavy furs pulled over sleeping bodies.

He counts seven, eight. Counts again. Someone missing. He moves to another window. Still eight. There're ten vets, including Wright and the new woman he's heard talk of, and Wright is underground, unless he surfaced by some secret exit.

Ray turns tracker, checks exterior doors. Finds the west-facing exit propped open with an atlas. The first place he looks is the latrine. What Wright calls a composting toilet is nothing more than a scrap-lumber shithouse emptying down an old water well.

From the outhouse comes the sound of someone passing troubled gas, no privacy nor decency at the Standard.

Ray finds cover and waits.

"Oh, for christsake!" A woman's voice. "What do yall wipe with up here, Milt, your dang left hands? You're every bit as bad as the Taliban. Shit." The outhouse door kicks open. Out she comes walking like a detainee. Pants and panties shackling her ankles. The triangle of her dark pubic hair. She's hardly more than a teenager, her legs long, toned and shapely, her face fatigued. She squats and rakes through snow to reach the layer of dead leaves.

She looks up, her eyes gray through his goggles, staring right at him but seeing nothing. She winces, wiping.

He pulls off his headgear and hangs it on the branch of a box elder. The woodstove he wants hasn't gone anywhere in years — it can wait a little longer — because here's the perfect chance to introduce himself.

Ray crouches into a three-point stance, leans, and scrapes his boot to get her attention. When she looks his direction, he charges her across the ten meters separating them, howling like a rabid dog who's slipped his choker.

Toppling over backward, her ankled pants tripping her up, she crab-crawls in reverse through snow.

He rears over her, huffs his chest and snarls. He can smell her, her every intimate odor, heady. Her eyes are wide and worried, and he lets himself smile.

Her eyes narrow. Gone from pleading to pissed off, and all because he showed mercy, a sense of humor. She says, "Scared the piss out of me." She hikes up her panties, her camo trousers, nonchalant as can be, like a girl who grew up with seven or eight bullying older brothers. "Now if you'll excuse me."

He's smacked by her openness, her accent. He offers her a hand up. "Your gut'll get used to the primitive Standard fare. Hit up Wisenbeker for some of his homemade alpaca-milk yogurt. Don't know how he keeps vegetarian without wasting away."

Glaring at him, she takes his hand.

He helps her to her feet and then he squeezes, hard. She's got a good grasp and she gives back some of what she's getting. He tightens, sees the slightest bend of her knees, and she squeezes in return, what he guesses is the last reserve of her grip strength. She's hurting him. He grins, and she says, "Look at you. Look like the dang dominatrix of SEAL Team 6. Look ready to tie me up, murder and rape me." She yanks back her hand.

"In that order?"

She shrugs, even though he was trying to be personable, likable, and then there's the voice: How would you do her?

To suppress an answer, he asks, "I look like a killer to you?"

"Face painted black, hatchet strapped to

your chest? Yeah, you look like a killer."

"Sadly, nothing confirms you're alive and well in the world like killing a person."

"You're the one's gone AWOL."

"That what Wright says?"

"All he said was no one's seen you in almost a month, not that they'll admit to."

"You keep a secret?"

She shakes her head.

"Don't tell Wright you saw me."

"Why'd you leave?"

"Cause I can't trust Wright."

She says, "What's not to trust?"

"The list is long."

"Yeah, well, he's been good to me, and for me." She blows a couple breaths in her hands, warming them, then cups them over her ears, saying, "First thing I'm gonna do is tell him I saw you, so just beware."

"That case, tell him I borrowed one of his woodstoves to get me through winter. Figure he owes me." Ray nods and backs away. He raises a hand, and blacked-out the way it is, it seems to him more like a threat than a farewell.

On Smith's third whiteout day in residence at the Standard, Milt pulled her aside. "How'd you feel about chauffeuring me around in the snow?"

She told him Vessey had her and Stotts-Dupree shoveling off the roof of Esther. "Vess's worried about it caving in on our sleeping heads."

"Vessey can find someone to shovel who's not a motor transport operator."

In the van, behind the wheel, when she asked where they were going, Milt said he'd tell her when they got there.

"Last night," she said, "I met Reverend."

"You met him? For what, dinner and a movie?"

"You sound jealous."

"Just surprised. Haven't seen him for a while. You've been here a couple of nights, and we have a Reverend sighting?"

"He asked me not to tell you."

"Everything's a secret with Reverend."

"Why's he called Reverend?"

"That too's classified apparently. So what was the occasion for your meeting?"

"Caught me coming out of the latrine," she said, "in the middle of the night. Face and hands all blacked out. Looked like he was on night raid. Said to tell you he took a woodstove. What's his story?"

Milt told her how Reverend sought him out. Milt reluctant at first, but then it started to make sense. Reverend was eager. Milt started to groom him. Never told *him* that. "Maybe if I had, things would've worked out differently and he would've stuck around. I don't know. Was almost like, after a time, a switch flipped and he needed to mistrust me. Like you, he doesn't fit with the rest of my vets. You're all outriders, but Reverend rides outside the outriders. High-functioning but could not get along. Thought that might work to his advantage, and mine. Leader can't be too close to those he leads. But it didn't work. Being a Ranger counted a strike against him. Being a merc was strike two. The guy's self-sufficient, and scary smart, but he's got hangups. Got a good heart, it's just atrophied. The brother's suffered some loss, loss he has a hard time acknowledging. Reminds me of me," Milt said, "after I got back from my war, after Ada. Plenty of differences, but it's the similarities that matter. He could use some looking after."

"You asking me to —"

"I don't care *what* he's doing," Milt said. "Just want to know *how* he's doing."

They drove for a while, Milt pointing the way with hand gestures like they were out on patrol. Then she asked, "Any news on the missing alpaca?"

"I'm thinking it was Gizbar."

"Another vet I haven't met?"

"Gizbar's a mountain lion I released. Before the game-farm auction. Was actually the second Gizbar. Morning I opened her cage, she refused to go. Couldn't chase or entice her out. She'd been born at the Standard. I finally gave up. On the third day I went back, she was gone. Haven't seen her since."

He told her the first Gizbar had been bred from the daughter of the last known Eastern cougar, the Ghost Cat, trapped in Maine in the thirties. "There's a chance it's some other cougar. But if I'm feeding Gizbar with my herd, that's alright by me. Someone should get fed." He pointed to a commercial building and had her park the van outside the law office of Ira Lependorf, Esq., & Associates, Estate Planning and Elder Law.

"I'm gonna ask you to come in."

"No."

"Sy specializes in estate planning," Milt said. "He won't turn you in. He handled the reading of Ada's will. Then we did it again for her father's will. When I die," Milt said, "I want you to be the one called before Sy. To inherit the Standard."

She reconsidered the sign. "Is Sy one of the associates?"

"This is Sy's law office," Milt said. "Sy Blackstone. Used to book talent at the

Standard. He was Ada's agent for acting gigs."

She pointed to the sign. "Then who's Ira Lependorf?"

"Have I been saying Sy?"

"You have."

"I mean Ira."

"You alright?"

After a long moment, he said, "No, Specialist Smith, I am not."

She opened the door. "Alright."

"Just give me a minute." He closed his eyes.

After a minute, she said, "You've got to be cocked if you think I could do what you do. Those vets wouldn't follow one order I gave."

"Those who don't like the succession plan," he said, "would be dismissed. You find new recruits who know you as commander-in-chief. That don't work out, you move on." He rubbed his temple. "You're good at that." He opened his door. "Hup to."

The country club at Cripple Creek was ramshackle in a way that never failed to surprise Ramona Aahal Canek Gómez. Drug-addict gringas and exhausted Mexicans waited the tables. The sunburnt golf course was private but the membership dues were paltry, a formality, and the rabble that played rambunctiously through, bringing their own booze in plastic bottles, was Bizzy's connection to his dirt-floor past. Edith Rolling, a wonderful golfer, was not a member. She'd come once, decades ago, and refused to return. This, Ramona knew, was the reason Bizzy brought her here.

They spent an hour drinking the cheap bottle of chardonnay he'd ordered, digesting their light lunches, and catching up in Spanish. Everyone they knew was dying or dead. They discussed their own aches and pains, ailments that brought them to the topic of what to do after lunch. "When I drive you home," Bizzy asked, "will you invite me in?"

"I will invite you in."

He reached in his blazer pocket, produced a pill bottle and, with some trouble, trouble they both found amusing, he opened it, popped a pill into his mouth, and downed it with the last swallow of chardonnay. He paid the bill.

Inside the law office, no receptionist sat at the reception desk. Stacks and towers of file folders teetered, a few on the floor.

A middle-aged man, in a loosened tie,

entered the room. He seemed harassed and, also, amused by his harassment. "Please excuse the mess," he was saying. "Fired two temps in three days. I'm winging it here. How you doing, Milton?"

"I'm dying."

"When was the last time you saw your oncologist?"

"Been awhile."

"Who's this?"

"Want her to have power of attorney."

Before Smith could protest, Ira was saying, "Excuse me but who're you?"

"She's with me."

"Can she speak?"

"I can speak fine."

"How long have you known Milton?"

She looked at Milt.

"Don't look at him. I'm asking the questions."

"About three months."

"Ira, please," Milt said, "no need to cross-examine."

"Milt, if you'll excuse me, let me do the job you don't pay me to do, because —"

"You'll get paid when I'm dead."

"If I'm lucky, if I'm quick, I might get a fraction of what's owed me." Ira sniffed and suggested they stick with the will the way it was. "When time comes, we'll hold an estate auction. Raise some capital. The bankruptcy proceedings are slow-going. County's so far behind that a delay may work, unless you live another five years. There're liens on the property. I'm talking with a couple land trusts. They're concerned about the debt. I'm talking with a forester. Have the plat logged before a sale. If the auction and the logging get you close to black, Mountain-keeper might move in and make up the difference. Because if they don't, and the plat passes into foreclosure, at the bank auction, a gas company will snap it up. If the Marcellus ever opens, they'll develop it for drilling the following day. That or a gaming company. So we're copacetic? We're not changing the executor?"

Milt shook his head.

"Power of attorney? Not sure you're capable of making that decision at this point, Milton. What I'm seeing here is evidence to the contrary. Doesn't look good." He shrugged at Smith, who was desperate for a chair she knew wasn't going to be offered — they were all occupied by stacks of files. "Sorry, sweetheart. Nothing personal. But I don't know you. I've been working with Milton and his family for half my life. I owe it to them to be a bulldog."

Smith said, "Might it be alright if I ask a

few questions now?" When Ira shrugged again, she asked, "You used to be Ada's agent?"

"Me? No." He looked at Milt. "That was Sy Blackstone. Sy's been dead for years."

"Milt told me his wife died in a car accident. But he's hazy on the specifics."

"With Milton's permission."

Milt nodded.

"This was before I went into estate planning. They'd gone for a drive one summer night. Milton'd been drinking. That right, Milty? This was in the bad, old days. Ada wanted to try driving at night. One of a —"

"She'd get behind the wheel," Milt said, rallying some, it seemed, now that they were talking about the past, "and you'd tell her do this, do that. She'd do it, but she'd do it while driving five miles an hour."

"Well, Milty let her drive, and they hit a deer."

"A deer, right. Forgot about the deer."

"How could you forget the deer? The deer got him off. That deer saved your life."

"Deer ruined my life."

"Not for that deer, you'd still be in prison."

"I was aiming for the deer."

"You were not *aiming* for the deer."

"Think I might've been."

"You couldn't've been. Ada was driving, Milt. A fact he failed to mention during questioning. They were both thrown from the car. Officer on the scene assumed Milt was driving. Bit sexist of him. Milt here didn't bother to correct him for the record."

"Worst night of my life, and I've had some bad ones."

"Ancient history. Case closed."

"Tell that to my conscience."

Ira told Smith that the 1970s were a different age, up here on this side of the Hudson especially. Milt was under suspicion just for being black and alive standing over a dead white woman, even if she was a Jew. Cops spent a week investigating, and they turned over what looked to them like a motive. "You alright for me to continue, Milton?" Without waiting for an answer, Ira said there was a nice insurance policy. "That upped the ante of suspicion. Then they conducted interviews. She'd been having, shall we say, a dalliance."

Milt closed his eyes and pushed his temple.

"It was the end of the seventies, Milt. Everyone was wife swapping."

"Not you."

"Yeah well, I don't go in for all that woman nonsense, no offence. Anyway, long story interminable, cops interview Milt here, and they don't buy the deer story — this was before deer were everywhere — and they didn't buy that he didn't know about the . . . well."

"Dalliance?"

"And, Milt, you stubborn ass, you didn't do much to help convince them. He was hurting. His young wife — sorry I'm talking about you as though you're not here — is killed. Week later, investigating officers tell him he's a suspect in her death? This they do by cluing him in that she was fucking around? The dirt they dug up was, it was smutty but in a very seventies way. I won't go into gory details. I'll just say, Ada was a free bird on the edge of extinction. No one else like her."

"All these years later," Milt said, eyes closed, "I'm still trying to get a clear picture."

"Well," Ira continued, "I called in a favor. Had someone go over the car with microscopes. They turned up the tiniest tuft of fur. Found in the undented fender of that indestructible Toronado. Don't make em like they used to. Carcass of the deer was a few hundred feet from the crash site. Cops relaxed after that. We settled for reckless endangerment. What year was that?"

"Seventy-seven." Milt shook his head.

"She was how old?"

"Thirty-three."

"Terrible tragedy. But Milt cleaned up his act, eventually. You were a mess for — I'd go up and check on him a few times a year — you got it together in the end, and you've had a good run doing good work."

"Already using the past tense on me."

"Well, good thing you came by. I need to update you. There are interested parties, Milt, parties with vast legal resources, which means vast financial resources."

"Young woman? Canek?"

"No. Local lawyer, says he's working for a development firm. Been making inquiries for a year now, and we're not counting them as a legitimate part of your estate plan, but it's ramped up over the last month or so. In your best interests, I've been forthcoming, providing them information, none of it confidential."

"Is this interested party SW&B Construction?"

"Don't know who's behind the Kingston lawyer. He hasn't been transparent. Gives the sense it's big. Could be gas. Could be a Native American tribe backed by one of the international gaming cartels. But that casino vote this time next year's a big gamble." He looked at his watch. "I've got another client coming by in five. If either of you have any more questions, you know where to find me." He sighed. "Power of attorney."

Bizzy, aided by his Viagra, and Ramona, helped by her plug-in consolador, made old love, love-making that was flatulent and fearsome — threat of heart attack or stroke a presence in the room, like the third party in a ménage à trois who, at the last moment, decides he just wants to watch — and their achy, inflexible sex was all the more pleasurable for the fear.

In the passenger seat, Milt shook out five, six pills from a bottle of aspirin, popped them into his mouth. With eyes closed, leaning back in his seat, he chewed. "Don't want you to tell any of the others what just happened in there."

"Howbout you tell me what just happened in there."

"Not entirely sure." He looked at her with sad, sick eyes.

"You think you have the start of Alzheimer's?"

"Got a feeling what I'm feeling between my ears won't be slow-going."

She wasn't sure what her duty was. Confronting Milt with the facts wouldn't fix anything. She'd seen enough death, as it was happening, to know that facts had no place at the end. At the end, the truth was whatever you needed to help you over to the other side — the Saydabad boy, his torso crushed by the tremendous HET tires. She kneels over him. He's saying, Z'ma mor. Z'ma mor. The boy's not asking for his mother; he's calling Smith his mother, and she plays the role. Tells him it's alright, repeating again and again, Allahu Akbar, Allahu Akbar, until he's dead.

She didn't want to play any more roles. "Milt, look at me."

He did.

"Are you the one who killed Ada?"

His response started as a nod. The nod grew vigorous. He winced, a spasm twitching one closed eye, as if a current surged through him.

"It was an accident, Milt. Even if you were the one driving. An accident."

He shook his head, and then his whole body began to shake, convulsing, his arms paddling, his mouth contorted. A sound came out of him, and that, more than his thrashing, scared her, made her realize he was having a fullblown seizure. He was passing gas, drooling, and wailing all at once.

She looked for something to force into his mouth. By the time she had his hat brim at the ready, he was easing up. Relaxing. Then she smelled him, knew she'd need to get him cleaned up.

She held his hand, petting him. The seizure subsided. After ten or so minutes, he said, "Sammy I'm fine with, but Sy's another story."

She didn't engage him. She waited for it to pass like a storm, the heat lightning in his head. Tiny tumors like raindrops taking shape in his cloudy brain.

He opened his eyes and found hers, was able to focus. The look there was horrible — terror and anguish — the dread of a child, the confusion absolute — and he squeezed shut his eyes. Two tears dropped, missing his sunken cheeks, catching in his white goatee. "I killed Ada?"

The question in his voice split Smith. "No, Milt, you didn't."

"Who then?"

"He did."

"Who?"

"Her lawyer, Sy."

"Suspected they were having an affair. But it was far worse."

Ellis Baum woke whimpering, sounding to

himself like an old, overweight Weimaraner. When he raised his head, a drooled-on brief stuck to his cheek, and he peeled the sodden page off his face. He needed to leave for his midnight meeting on the Ashokan.

First, he checked email: two from the IRJ executive assistant he'd done most of his dealing with, Marisol Soto-Garza. He skimmed them. Still no word from Canek. Maybe that's why Tyro'd called this meeting. Maybe he had information on, or had, the landman.

He sent himself an email: *Going to meet Ray Tyro for a midnight rowboat ride on the Ashokan — Ellis Baum, 10:55 PM, 2 Nov. 2012.*

He loaded the car with gear, allowing a half-hour at his office to count out and ready for transport the cash that would be Tyro's final installment.

As he swerved around the reservoir in a dark, steady snow collecting on the white roads, Ellis tried to spot police cruisers and DEP SUVs. There were none. Only a snowplow, its amber lights flashing, its plow raised, scattering salt. He'd exaggerated the official presence to deter Tyro, but the authorities were here and in force, just never when you needed them. They jumped out the moment you unzipped your fly to relieve yourself against a tree you had no idea was on the endangered timber list.

He turned onto Onteora Trail and parked, worried that if the steady snowfall kept up, he wouldn't be able to pull out of the spot. Here it was weeks before Thanksgiving, after one of the driest summers in recent history followed by the annual superstorm of the century, and he already needed snow tires. He left on his brights, kept the car running. He didn't want to give the impression he was staying.

A man emerged from the trees holding a head-high walking stick. Whitened vapor rose off Tyro in thick wisps as snow whirled down around him. Ellis was afraid of the kid and in awe of him. At that age, Ellis had been studying sixteen hours a day for the bar.

In camo cargo pants and a khaki button-down shirt with the sleeves perfectly rolled, his jacket under his arm, his head uncovered, he wore a small pack slung over his shoulders and clipped high on his narrow waist. He flashed his hand, more halt than wave.

Ellis powered down his window.

"Cut the lights," Tyro said. "Let's not attract attention."

Ellis turned off the headlights.

"Parking lights, too. Come on, Baum, this isn't amateur hour."

"Volvo doesn't see fit to let me turn off the parking lights without cutting the engine."

"So turn the damn car off."

"No."

"No?"

"I've got your payment in the trunk, but I'm not getting in a boat with you."

"Mr. Baum, I'm offended. I've never even considered hurting you."

"Why are we meeting out here like this — and don't tell me it's about your replacement. I know she's arrived."

"Want to run something by you," Tyro said. "It's sensitive. Need to be sure there aren't prying eyes and ears. Sides, I like to scare you. It's easy but it's fun."

"So run it by me."

"Let's fish. I could use a little R&R. I've earned it. We're here and I'm hungry."

"We could've met for sushi."

"It's a glorious night and it's — shit."

"It is shit."

"Hope you wore your tango shoes." A wash of yellowed light swept through the car and over Tyro, who squinted against the glare. "Just DEP. Not real cops."

"DEP's more real than real cops. He goes

through the trunk, we're done."

"Relax, we're fine. This'll be a blast."

The white SUV parked behind Ellis, blocking escape, flooding them with its high beams.

"Prick." After a minute, Tyro, standing at Ellis's window, said, "What's taking him? You got any outstanding warrants?"

"Do me a favor, just don't say anything."

"My record's immaculate, man. Makes Mother Theresa look felonious."

A clean-shaven cop, jowly and ruddy, a face like a just-smacked ass, climbed out and left his vehicle running. Ellis felt relieved, calmed by an interaction with someone heavier and more out of shape than he was. Over a white shirt and a loosed black tie, the DEP official pulled on a green parka but didn't zip it. Training a flashlight on Tyro, he approached, leaned down and shone the beam of his Maglite into Ellis's face. "Gentleman. Inclement weather for night fishing on the Ashokan."

Tyro said, "We're diehard."

"Two must be. Got permits?"

Tyro pointed at Ellis, who extended them out of the window. Tyro, quicker than the cop couched in goose down and fat, snatched them, flipped through the documents, said, "All's in order," and passed them to the officer, who shot Tyro a who's-this-guy look as he tucked the flashlight in his armpit and studied the paperwork. "Ellis Baum?"

"That's me."

"And Ray Tyra."

"Tyro. Sounds like Chino. Or Keno."

The cop narrowed eyes at Tyro and addressed Ellis: "Line of work."

"I'm a lawyer."

The cop looked hard at Tyro. "And you?"

"Unemployed."

"He works for me," Ellis said.

The cop said, "Can't be both."

"He works part time. Does consulting."

The cop asked, "Kind of consulting?"

"Private investigation," Ellis said.

"Let him answer."

Tyro said, "Like the man said."

"We're between contracts," Ellis said. "He's never been fishing on the reservoir, wanted to get out before it froze — I fish but refuse to drill holes in ice — so here we are."

"Alright," the cop said, "so let's see your gear, make sure you've not already got your limit or're over, that you're not transporting dope, firewood, gypsy moths, emerald ash borers, or snakeheads. Then you can be on your snowy way."

"Snakeheads?"

The cop told Tyro that it was a kind of fish. "Crazy thing, in middle age, develops what they call a labyrinth organ lets it breathe air. See them flopping their way over land. Can survive a four-day crossing so long as they stay moist. Been known to migrate a quarter mile. We call them Fishzilla."

"I promise you," Ellis said, "we have no snakeheads. We haven't even gone out yet."

Tyro said, "Just refuse, Mr. Baum, you're a lawyer."

"You're a lawyer," the cop said to Ellis, "so enlighten your partner here. Right now, I'm looking at a Terry exception."

To Tyro, Ellis said, "Game wardens have more leeway than regular cops to conduct warrantless searches." Ellis said, "The ax?"

"His ax gives me cause to search the car and any containers. Not that I need the ax. You're on the reservoir in the fucking snow. That's probable cause enough." The cop shivered. "Alright, enough of the runaround. Let's pop the trunk. We're done dallying."

Ellis cut off the engine. He climbed out of the car and shambled to the trunk. Opening it, he watched Tyro, gave his head a slight shake. If things started to go bad, the ex–

Army Ranger in his employ would go rogue. Ellis would be facing an accessory to aggravated assault charge — the least worst outcome. He opened the trunk, slowly, his heart about to blow. "Here we have poles, broken down and dry. Brand new lantern."

"What's in the cooler?"

"Not snakeheads." Ellis flipped the lid with a shaky hand. "Nothing, not even ice, which I apparently forgot."

"It's snowing out," Tyro said.

"No bait? Only thing hitting in this cold's the walleyes. For them you need shiners."

"We don't believe in bait," Tyro said.

"Or you aren't here to fish."

"I've got a couple jars of egg sacks," Ellis said, "a tackle box of lures."

Tyro said, "Who needs bait when you have diaper wipes."

The cop said, "Diaper wipes?" He leaned into the trunk. "Little old to have an infant."

Tyro's hand reached behind the small of his back.

Again Ellis shook his head. When Tyro didn't stand down, Ellis said, "My two kids are grown. My age, you don't have wipes for an infant. You have them for accidents."

The cop said, "Accidents?"

"You need me to say incontinence?"

"Yeah?" The cop's grin dimpled his big

cheeks. "Didn't take note of a birthdate. You don't look a day over fifty."

"Very kind. But, you wait, you get to be my age — I'm fifty-eight — you too will start driving around with a tub or two of wipes in your trunk. And a change of underwear."

"Alright," the cop said. "Seen, and heard, about enough. Just don't go tossing your crappy wipes in my reservoir." He closed the trunk, told them to stay safe, and warm. "Remember, three trout. Season ends on the thirtieth. Three walleye. That's your limit. Land a snakehead, come find me." He left them and climbed in his vehicle but didn't drive off.

"Guess you got no choice but to get in the boat with me now, Mr. Baum. Don't want to ruin our cover."

"How are you gonna go calling attention to the Wet Ones?"

"Worked, didn't it. And you were quick on your feet, self-effacing under the gun. Be careful, I might get to like you."

"He's not gone yet. You could still get us arrested."

"This guy? Nah. Now let's catch a late dinner. Spend a little quality man time. Do us both good. Could use some seafood in my diet."

■ ■ ■ ■

The cougar stops on the deer trail. Opens his mouth. Tastes snowy night air. He huffs, licks whiskers. Late-born fawn. Many nights ago. A tang wets his mouth, twists his empty gut. Then, there's what he's after. The odor dizzies him. Fallen apples when soft. He pads along the path through snow. Whiffs of creatures. Oily scent of stags, high sweetness of does. Hollow of a downed tree, he rears away. Blinding smoke-musk of sleeping skunk. Nose to the path. Bumps it against snowy ground. Sight fails when closest. Wet soil under snow. Rotting leaves. Sulfur of bird droppings. Rodents mostly, foul. Squirrel, mouse, vole. A scavenger, he ate them before he mastered the hunt. Farther downtrail, rubbings of a male mink. Other hints. His hackles twitch. Dogs. Fainter, days old. Catching wind of a lone vixen. Smelling sinewy. Trunk of a great tree. Here he spent entire days. Edge of a meadow. Overlooks a deer scratch. Home of his greatest catch. Two deer at once. Killed at dusk. The male pounced on from above. Bite to the back. Doe trapped beneath the stag. He ate the doe's innards. Dragged the warm carcass, open, to his mother's den, cold. No scent of her. He called. Her scream a confusion. He calling into her den, she calling back. Weak, sounding like him. He fled trembling. He returned to his stag. Spent days eating. Gamely chasing off the yipping dogs. Dogs he usually flees from.

The vast reservoir. Dark like sleep, like death, thought Ellis. His sleep, his death, and Tyro the boatman. They floated through snowfall. Shadowy mountains reared around them, more a force, gravitational, than a sight. Barehanded Tyro rowed. The surface of the water lay placid, the wind barely there, snow falling to become the reservoir. The fathomless abyss — overhead, underneath. Ellis felt pressed between two slabs.

The oars splished, oarlocks grinded. "Wasn't being totally honest, Mr. Baum."

"Why doesn't that surprise me." Ellis had trouble striking a match. "What are we talking about?"

"When I said I never considered hurting you. Has occurred to me. Occurred to me that I could kill you and sink your body out here."

"You do anything to me," Ellis told him, "it'll take the authorities an hour to pin you down as a suspect." There were five, six dud matchsticks in the puddle under his boots.

"That how you think I operate?"

"Just know I've taken precautions. I turn up missing, someone will go through my recent filings, see I applied for a guest pass. Your name and driver's license will be there."

"You think that information will lead them to me?"

"The DEP aren't just on the roads," Ellis told him. "They're up in helicopters. They use satellites. They patrol the reservoir with drones. They're always watching. Besides, I know from your file you've worked interrogations. Cross-examinations use the same tactics. You're not going to hurt me. This is the intimidation before the ask."

"I don't need details at the outset, Mr. Baum. Just give me a target and —"

"Some cash."

"Makes the world go round. Thanks to you, I can relax for the next few years."

"So, what," Ellis said, "you want to know who's paid you a hundred and eighty-two thousand dollars?"

"For starters."

Ellis shook his head. "Can't. I'm bound by certain principles."

"Don't give me that attorney-client privilege crap."

Ellis holds his hands to the lit lantern

throwing heat, vaporizing snowflakes that land on its hood. "Let me ask you something."

"Shoot."

"Where's my landman?"

"Thought you arranged for her to be here."

"I did."

"Well?"

Ellis said, "Haven't seen or heard from her."

"Funny you should bring her up."

"What'd you do?"

"Let me make my pitch. If, after, you tell me I'm being irrational, that I've gone overboard —" Tyro reached his hand over the gunwale, cupped water and rubbed his beard. "— I won't be offended."

"Where is she?"

"Where's your phone?"

"You won't get reception out here."

"Just give it to me, Ellis."

He produced a phone as thick as a puck. He handed it to Tyro.

"A BlackBerry? Tell you what, I'm gonna help you out."

Ellis waited.

Tyro flung his arm out over the reservoir, his hand empty when he set it in his lap. A moment later — *splash.*

"You did not."

"Did."

"That's my whole entire absolutely everything."

"Need to make sure you're not recording this conversation."

"How would I be recording this conversation with my Stone Age phone? You could've just shut if off."

"Don't you have everything synched with your computer?"

"I don't know. My daughter does that stuff for me." Ellis started casting his pole in the direction of the splash.

"What will you pay me?"

"Haven't I paid you enough?"

"For a rendition. Say I did kidnap this lady landman of yours."

"Kidnap my — no, no, no. You were hired to watch, to listen and gather information. There is nothing illegal about what you've been contracted to do. Unethical, maybe, but criminal? No. We're not careering into first-degree felonies here."

"Just wanted to hear it from the horse. Thought maybe if your bosses really wanted Wright out of the way, it wouldn't be hard to pin a kidnapping charge on him. Probably wouldn't stick, but an investigation could add enough pressure that he'd cave."

"You mean set up the landowner?" Ellis stopped casting. "Make it look like he took my landman?"

"Now wait just a second, Baum, what you're suggesting is decidedly criminal and I don't want any part of it. I, too, live by a creed, and part of that creed says that *under no circumstances will I ever embarrass my country.* You asking me to embarrass my country?"

"Cute."

"What if the girl got kidnapped wasn't your girl? What about the new lady vet that Wright's now billeting. What if it was her went missing?"

"No women will go missing, understand?"

"Easy, Baum, you're gonna tip us. We are not close to shore, it's cold and I'm in much better shape."

"I'm fatter. More buoyant, better insulated."

Tyro's fishing reel whined, something pulling out line, and he jerked it. "Might have something." He reeled.

"Look," Ellis said, "under no circumstances are you to kidnap anyone, understand? These people are backed by a great deal of capital, both financial and political, but they do not engage in illegalities here at home. Outside the homeland, rules are different. Here at home, they're willing to pay people, to lobby like crazy, give millions to Super PACS, to change laws if need be, but they don't break laws. Bend them, sure, but only in a white-collar way. Times've changed. I don't need to run rendition by them. Jesus. They don't kidnap Americans, not even if they're Mexican Americans. So if you've got this woman, I'm advising you, release her. Understand?"

"I haven't kidnapped anyone."

"Then where's my landman?"

Tyro said she talked with Wright for a time, about what Tyro wasn't close enough to hear. "Didn't have my Detect Ear on me. They talked, then Wright helped her carry her kayak and shoved her downriver. That was the last I saw of her."

"You swear to that?"

"On the bodies of all of the fallen Rangers I've dragged to safety under fire."

"Tell you what, I'll extend your contract, same rate but under —"

"You think just because I've hired out to you I'm always for rent?"

"Double, thousand dollars a day."

"Deal. What am I doing?"

"You find me my landman."

"You got a file on her?"

"I've got a file on everyone. Can we be

done here? I'm freezing."

"Not till I land this thing."

"Cut the line."

"Absolutely not," he said. "Paddle us that way. I'll reel, you row."

They were quiet, the only sound the uneven slap of the oars.

Tyro's line grew perpendicular to the water. He reeled and his pole curled. "Think I might have something, Ellis." He reeled quicker, then stopped. "Think it's your phone?" He reeled in the last of the line. On the far side of the red-and-white bobber, at the end of the leader, was a small walleye.

"Not a keeper," Ellis said. "Not even close."

"But I'm starving. How big does it have to be?"

"In the State of New York, fish has to be bigger than your penis, otherwise you have to throw it back. Can we go now?"

"I'm keeping this fish."

"Come on, last thing we need is to get busted for having an undersized walleye."

As Ellis rowed toward shore shaking his head, Tyro gutted the gasping fish with a black-blade knife that zipped through scales, through bone. He tossed the head overboard but not before plucking and eating the eyes.

With his teeth, he pulled off a hunk of belly meat. Chewing, he offered the cleaned fish to Ellis, who shook his head, trying not to gag.

The bottom of the boat scraped the bank of the reservoir. "How're you getting back to your camp?"

"Was planning on killing you and stealing your car. But now I've come to like you. Didn't have a contingency. Didn't have a father growing up, either."

"Where'd that come from?"

"Just opening up a little, Ellis."

"How about I give you a lift."

"Was hoping you'd say that."

"We'll stop by my office for the Canek file. But first, wash those hands."

The autumn snowstorm, officially a nor'easter, dumped historic amounts of snow on the upper Catskills. Hunter and Tannersville reported receiving over four feet in forty-eight hours. Evangelína couldn't get out of the B&B driveway. She had no phone reception. The internet was down. When the snow eventually slowed, Bruce offered her the use of his snow blower; he failed to offer her help. She felt more like an employee than a guest, but after two cooped days with nothing to do but pore over the Standard portfolio, she was grateful for the hours it took her to excavate her rental car. Then came the long drive to the sporting-goods store twenty miles away. She got fitted for winter cross-trainers that the salesman billed as the shoe for people who run even when the postman stays in, socks that boasted graduate degrees, futuristic snowshoes, trekking poles, a pulk, an LED headlamp, a watch, a lime parka, and a pair of pink-and-black bib snowpants, the brighter the better. She demanded that her snow attire be able to comfortably accommodate her weight vest, which she brought with her to the store. The salesman, a scruffy Catskill treehugger no older than twenty, told her, "You're hardcore." The manager wouldn't let her return the kayak, which she'd paid for in cash. She charged the bill on her debit card. Now that she had a plan, she was less concerned about being traced, and she saved the receipt to be reimbursed.

The cougar pads into fresh snow. Birds complain, flit overhead. His hunger a bird. At a rock outcropping, he lingers. Traces of a coyote pack. Rank bitches. Reeking of scat and the dead. Darkness after deer. Smelling prey in snow, not seeing, not hearing. Under the deer odors, the thickest, headiest of all. Human. Powerfully spicy and sour. Men make a rank wind. Not terrible, not as repulsive as dogs. The smell of the men is his fear. His muscles tense. Then, another scent he's on. Newer, stronger, a surprise. It doesn't push away. It pulls along. A human bitch.

In the early morning dark, the blue hull still strapped to the hood of her rental, Evangelína parked as close as she could to the Standard, three miles from the north gate. All but the major roads were still impassable. She geared up and headed out before the sun rose, a light snow falling, thrilled and already exhausted.

Her headlamp bored a tunnel through the icy dark, dark that opened a few feet before her and collapsed claustrophobically behind. The silence, insulated by a calm ocean of snow, was shocking. The first mile seemed to go endlessly on. Her snowshoes — part trampoline, part frypan — were clumsy and heavy. She'd chosen snowshoes to be louder, slower, her tracks bigger and more noticeable, but it was a hell of a workout, increased by the pulk pulled behind her and the added twenty-pound load of her weight vest, which was feeling excessive.

In her new gear over strange terrain, her pace was wacky, her arms flailing, her feet overburdened, one calf sore. The trekking poles burned her bi- and triceps. Normally, she ran like a chicken, arms tucked against her ribcage. With no sense of minutes passing, little notion of her route, she headed east, toward the Standard, in the middle of a white road not plowed nor disturbed by other tracks — during her runs, when she's most in the moment, she abides by a mantra: ts'oksah beh — *finish a road.* Now nothing counts, nothing save hitting her stride and sustaining it. She's found a rhythm in the shuffle-crunch of her snowshoes on the crusty snow — as though she's slogging across crème brûlée — starry impressions made by the plastic baskets of her trekking poles. She's absolutely present as she rounds a bend, stares up an ascent that's ultraviolet in the blue glow cast by the LED lamp elastically affixed to her forehead, projecting a long cone of light that becomes her vision. Her pace slows as she climbs against the grade, half-speed, demanding twice the effort, her torso, canted forward, nearly perpendicular to the incline. Summiting the hill, there's no wind. The breeze she feels on her cheeks is of her own making. She trudges past scat of some kind, like a huge hamburger in an icy divot along the road-side, tremendous tracks running toward and away from it — bear?

At the risk of being found out, Ray turns on Baum's phone. The BlackBerry rings more than sixty times in twenty-four hours, the Tri-State area codes uncompelling compared to the unlisted callers coming from 713, Houston.

He goes through the email inbox. Most messages real-estate related. Then there are four from an IRJ executive assistant, Marisol Soto-Garza, each more frantic than the last, all of them mentioning Ms. Canek.

He finds a chatty message from the person Ray takes to be Soto-Garza's boss, F. Bismarck Rolling, Chief Operations Officer, IRJ, Inc. The email, transcribed by Soto-Garza, includes contact information, and Ray jots it down.

The battery's about to die. Before it does, in response to the last email in Baum's inbox, from the address marisol.soto-garza@irj.com, Ray sends a message, impersonating Baum, knowing there's a good chance Baum'll discover it and realize Ray palmed his phone: *Our contractor has offered a safe rendition of Canek that can incriminate Wright. We interested?*

He wants to take a sounding of the bottom. Baum's response on the reservoir not only reassured Ray, it made Ray admire him. Now, he wants to see if the weight behind Baum is as upstanding as its legal council.

At a clearing in his camp, he finds a pocket of reception. The email sends with the sound of a little jet taking off.

The phone dies before a reply comes. Turning it back on would require a trip to buy a charger, and then a couple hours at the Liberty library. Or, for five K, he could overnight the phone to Fort Huachuca, Arizona, where a knob-turner former colleague and onetime Zeitgeist operator — a techie who spent a few years in direct action with the Activity before retiring, in his late twenties, to military training — does a little freelancing. The guy's a one-man army. Everyone calls him Joe Ginsu, though his hacker handle is TrapAvoid. He could infiltrate the infrastructure systems of all but the most technologically secure nation-states. In his spare time, he steals intellectual property from companies outside the US, and he sometimes plants incriminating information — false flags — for the fun fuck of it.

Baum's phone would come back in one

piece, accompanied by a zipped file on a thumb drive or, for an added $2,000, a bound, hardcopy ream of data: GPS positioning maps; spreadsheets of contacts, calls, and locations; a list of passwords; printouts of archived text messages and emails stored on web servers; transcripts of voicemails; tax information, answers to security questions, driver's license and Social Security numbers. But why bother.

The snow's here. He busies himself with the sundry tasks in the transition from bivouac to outpost. Working on the final phase of his yurt now that he's heaved the woodstove upmountain and into place, he bumbles and trips over the two coon kits barking at his ankles, scaling his pant leg if he stands still too long. His mind returns to a scene, an exchange of dialogue, that asks for more attention than it merits. He forces it away with little acknowledgement.

Back it comes. Here he is, days later, and Wright's lady vet — high-volt, low-current — is still whirring through his synapses.

The kits bop over in the falling snow, clawing and climbing atop each other, yapping. He moves his work, skinning a squirrel, readying it for a slow roast.

To the kits, he tosses the tail. They play with and fight over it before devouring it.

Then curl up together and laze near him, their eyes drifting open every time he moves or makes a sound.

He fits together the last length of chimney, supported by an exterior stanchion and piped out the bowed wall of the yurt. The box stove is an ancient three-legged Ransome Rathbone that's rusty outside but sound in. Where the pipe meets the wall of the yurt, he wrapped it in a cuff of asbestos insulation pulled from the basement of Esther House. With the shelter complete, he lights a low fire to break in the stove and to see if the whole thing will blow. Once it's burning, and the yurt warms without drawing smoke, he wants to share what he's made.

Evangelína's downright hot. Amazed by the vaguely miraculous heat her body radiates in the cold. She unzips her parka. Soon she'll take it off in the Catskill chill before sunrise. If she didn't know better, she'd think it was after sunset — no real difference between before the beginning and after the end. Then there's the pulk, which she forgets for stretches now that she's loose. Harnessed to her waist, she pulls the sled beast-of-burden behind her over the flats, poling up the steeps, down the broad snowy swath of blanketed road. The sled holds a slushy half-gallon of water, a few energy bars, her phone that gets spotty reception in the whole region, and the Standard Grande portfolio, with all its privileged information, in a gallon Ziploc freezer bag. She considers shucking her weight vest, but she'd still have to lug it in the pulk, unless she left it trailside. She continues on as she is.

The overcast sky is silvering. Her downhill pace is steady. She has little idea where she's going as she tries to remain on the narrowing road, switchback after switchback obscured by snow. When she tires, if the landowner doesn't accost her, all she'll need do is turn round and retrace the swath cut by the pulk through the snow. Her return will be mostly downhill. She looks at her watch. She's tromped for nearly an hour and hasn't reached the Standard. Worried she's lost, she stops, rests, takes out the Standard file and checks the topographical map, finds Wittenberg, Slide, and Peekamoose mountains, Reconnoiter Rock. She should be coming into the Sundown Wild Forest. The white road will pass the Neversink Reservoir, depositing her at the property line of the Standard.

For Mamí, for Maya, the road is all-important. Maya cities were networks of sacbeob, white ways, raised boulevards paved with limestone stucco over rock and rubble fill, some of which stretched for hundreds of miles connecting city to coast, temple to cenote. Maya roads were hallowed white paths through shadow country. To Maya, the Milky Way was White Road, route into and out of the underworld, and the night sky was the reflective surface of the water in a sacred cenote, the pool below mirrored overhead. Cenote Sagrado was upside-down entry into the heavens, and the road was the way. Not only the beginning of life, its end and what came after, the road was life.

Slow, noisy. Men are cows. Throats exposed. Ever on hind legs. Offer their organs and entrails to him. More than deer, men are made to be fed upon. Fat as pigs. Men should starve. More plentiful than deer. The cougar fights his urge. Easy prey. For dogs and men. He's hungry. The bird in him. Snow deep, early. The odor he's after. Stronger on the trail, closer. Mixed with opened wood. The human bitch makes him hungry, a new way. He flattens his ears, puffs his tail. Crouching, he approaches. She holds a small tree. Makes human sounds. The creek where it's shallow. Closer, he knows her smell. In heat. He shows himself. Telling her he could take her. One way or the other.

As Smith worked in the snowfall, her mind stirred everywhichway, a dissociative mess, her ADD overactive, her thoughts like snowflakes in the storm.

She was used to being the only woman outnumbered by a wild bunch of hooligan Boy Scouts. Getting the crap jobs. But this, this was worse than a hazing. Could be an honest-to-god curse. "Split sycamore." So impossible was it. Yet she was doing her damnedest to appreciate the task as part of her education.

The temp was well below freezing yet she'd worked up an honest lather. Sweaty, she shrugged off her full fur and searched for the wedge in burying snow.

She stopped to consider an idea that seemed not hers. More like it emerged from the Catskills. She was reasonably certain her brain would be contained in her skull till her dying day. She'd always assumed her mind would be too, but she was learning otherwise. Her mind ventured outward, went on scouting missions, its limits defined not by her body but by her interactions with her environment. The birch, the white oak, the elm, they were extensions of her while she considered them — one of the trees moved in a way that should've been impossible. Made her feel hallucinatory.

Milt still hadn't surfaced, not since they'd gotten back from visiting the lawyer. The company was worried, some of the vets scary in the severity of their instability. Even Vessey, the most together of the scattered bunch, seemed unbalanced.

She raised the maul and swung it down and it lodged there till she yanked it forcibly out — splitting sycamore was like counter-insurgency. You couldn't just drive a wedge into a wheel of sycamore and watch the whole thing come apart. "Need patience and finesse," she told the wheel. Get to know it intimately — not only how cells of resistance grew but why — and this was best done by women. The feminine side of war.

Sycamore was a tree like one gnarly knot. With Vessey's help, she was becoming a forestry buff, understanding how trees lived, thrived, what slowed their growth and killed them off. Past couple of nights, soon as the sun went down, the vets huddled around the library fireplace. She buried her face in a woodsy book so she didn't have to interact. She was trying to know one tree from the next. Not just type from type, but developing relationships with individual trees, which had personalities and attitudes all their own. Like this here sycamore, hollow at its core, gutted by generations of carpenter ants till the tree crashed down under the weight of an earlier storm. From the outside, the sycamore looked healthy, sturdy as could be, but inside was another story. So it was with Milt.

Vessey had handed her a coverless copy of *Know Your Woods.* In it she kept returning to the entry for American sycamore. Read how wood grain was determined by the arrangement of cells. In easy-to-split woods, cells gathered on a straight plane. American sycamore not only twisted as it grew, it changed direction year to year, the cells interlocking as they spiraled clockwise and counterclockwise in successive years — resistance ingrained in it. Made her think American sycamore was America. Turn right for a time only to torque left. Back and forth, year after year, a split America grown ever more resistant to splitting. Only to be brought down by ants.

Beyond the short stack of sycamore, the forest was beautifully black, gray, and white in the snow. Scene from an old movie. She never had a favorite kind of tree, never knew enough to care. The American sycamore, the ghost tree. Could be the totem of Standard Company. Ghost platoon stationed at a ghost resort. Lost firebase in the falling snow. Spooks trying to scare off trespassers in a region of the country left for dead. Untouched bowls of ghost borscht in ghost hotels at the edge of ghost town after ghost village. Ghost mills and quarries. Ghost tanneries. Ghost industry in a Ghost Belt all but forgotten by a nation gone to hell under a ghost God.

A noise in the hushed treeline. The snow muffling everything.

The more aware she became of a living, breathing natural world absent of people, the more people made sense. She was getting the hang of divining their motivations and inclinations even if she couldn't tolerate them. Maybe that was what it meant to grow up, earn some seniority and a bit of perspective. She felt ancient. War did that to you. Each day — even the down days when nothing much happened — was a lifetime anxiously lived.

She assessed the work she'd done. All the woods, each when freshly split, had distinct smells: the ash, green olives; the oak, mustard; the maple, vanilla. The top inch of her chopping block, a wheel of hickory, had gone matted from countless cuts.

She didn't love it up here but she appreciated it, where you could be hot in the cold, a beautiful feeling, much better than the redundancy you got in the desert: hot in the heat.

One of her wrecks, on MSR Tampa. Nearly killed a mother and a couple of boys — she's tipped the HET into a culvert. Can't get her M4 out of the rack. When she climbs from the overturned truck, one boot sloshes strangely, a boy in her face, teary and screaming. She's sure the preteen runt is going to shoot her square in the teeth with what looks like an old shoe. A Marine shouts and has a mean bead on the boy. Turns out to be a flattened soccer ball — probably cost his family a month's wages, that or it was given him as part of a coalition win-their-hearts-and-minds campaign — goddamn soccer ball nearly gets him shot in the chest.

The boy gawks and points, goes silent. She'd been swinging her arm out the open door as she drove, pounding the side of the truck to scare off the bleating goats — so damn skinny their ribcages like canvas over radiators. The goats got immobilized by the sound of the air horn, stood there in the road till someone carried them off or plowed through them. Smith glances where the boy points: her upper arm has acquired an additional, odd-angled joint. The bone, white as a new tooth, busted out of her skin, tore through her sleeve. Blood seeps down the length of her and pools in her desert boot, sloshing with each step. The boy whispers a word in Pashto and runs away — she woke nights hearing his voice. Or the voice of the other boy, one she did kill in Saydabad. Woke to the voices of all the boys and girls of the wars — Afghan, Iraqi, American — like a choir lost in a dust storm.

She listened to the trees around her. Her attention got stuck on a large snag centered on a trunk. The snag, an old amputation that bark had grown over, became a face. Two deep-set eye sockets, one dark, one gold verging into green, both eyes beautifully lined, high tawny cheekbones over an orange anvil of a nose, a full lipless mouth, grinning. Inhuman. When she made out ears, triangular, her skin whizzed. She froze. A big cat. Identification animated it. The beast looked to be missing an eye. It turned and offered her its profile, as if deciding she was no threat, and then prowled ahead, its body looking like the felled trunk of a tree moving between trees. She said, "Florida fucking panther in the Catskill Mountains?" and felt her hip for her sidearm, which wasn't there. It was meters away on top of a stump, gathering snow.

Evangelína's burning calf feels better when she's moving. She sprints up the next incline. Charges downhill. Here's the runner's high, a wellness she only comes upon occasionally, on long distances, but she's never worked this hard before, and soon she starts to struggle, to tire, weaken. She considers giving up. Go out again tomorrow, wait till the plows have done more work. She's making deals with herself. Reach that tree, turn back. She reaches the tree and keeps running forward.

She cuts off Neversink Road onto Burnt Ridge Road. Finds a trailhead that leads to a high corrugated fence, wide gaps between the metal sheets — she's found it. Beyond, she can pick up one of the many old logging roads crisscrossing the nearly 2,000-acre Standard plat. She has a moment of fright, like at the airport. Someone's watching.

The panther licks its whiskers, shuts its open eye for a slow second.

Without looking away, Smith takes slow steps to the stump. Pulls her pepperbox. Slides the latch that pops the breech of the quad barrel. She checks the four cartridges and snaps it closed. When she looks up, taking aim, there's no target.

She needs to run the image from her mind. Something out there — the cat maybe — gives her the feeling of the calm before the bomb. She'll check on Milt.

As she gathers the wedges — cold and rusty chunks of steel, carrying the maul at Right Shoulder, Arms — she hears something. She stops, listens. She squeezes the ax handle, then drops it to redraw her sidearm.

After an hour of tracking, taking risks being spotted — Vessey and Egon keeping a distant watch — Ray catches Wright's lady vet alone splitting wood.

Her alpaca hide hangs from a tree branch, and she's steaming in the snow.

He takes his sweet time creeping to her. Inside three meters, he decides to redo their last encounter, their first encounter, to see if it plays out differently. He scuffs his boot. She drops her maul and wheels around.

There's a metallic glint at her waist that trips in him an autonomic response — he lunges and chops his ulna on her radius, torqueing up her wrist, then wraps her arm in the bend of his, his hand slipping behind his back and gripping his belt to keep tension on her trapped arm. With his free hand, he pries the small, weighty pistol from her grip, lets go her arm, elbowing her in the solar plexus to force her backward, make space, a delivered blow that drives him into a quick half-spin. He faces her. She stands doubled over. He aims her sidearm at the crown of her head, his finger searching for and finding no safety catch.

He waits without hurry for her to regain her breath. This encounter is a force escalation of their first; that time, he hadn't touched her except to offer a hand.

When she stands upright, short of breath, facing her own firearm, she doesn't register recognition, only fear, and he remembers they met while he was coal black.

He assesses her weapon: .357 pocket pepperbox. Looks like a cop dropgun. He breaks the breech. Loaded with .38 Special rounds. Mean little gun poorly cared for, showing some spots of rust. An engraving on its barrel.

"I'm your huckle bearer?" he asks. "Hell's a huckle bearer?" He flips the gun around and offers it to her butt-first, saying, "Want to show you something."

"Who the fuck . . ." She raises her arms over her head, stretching her diaphragm.

"Thought you were a big cat come to eat me." She lowers her arms, holds her ribs.

He wants to apologize, wants to tell her his name, but he withholds. "We met," he says. "While you were . . . indisposed."

"You're the asshole."

"Get the Standard grand tour yet?"

She says she's still going through the hazing phase. "Been poking around some. Snow's slowed things. Everyone preoccupied with winterizing."

"How long you been at this?"

"This here's day two."

"Who gave orders?"

"Stone."

"Wright assigned me the detail my first day," he says. "Had blisters on top of blisters. After a week, I marched over and told him to fuck himself. He could split his own damn sycamore. Know what he said? Said, What took you so long?" He wags her gun at her. "Name's Ray."

She takes and holsters it at the small of her back. "Why they all call you Reverend?"

"You been by the indoor pool?" he asks. "Pool house is something to see in the snow. Like a Siberian terrarium."

"Can't."

He tells her it'll take five minutes. "Then you can get back to your splitting sycamore, a job you'll never finish. No one does. This tree finishes you. One of Milt's psychological snares. This one a game of Uncle. Point's to make you give up. Gauge is how long it takes."

"Could use a break," she says, and he leads her on a short, silent walk through snow. At a dark stairway underground, he tells her it's the basement door to the pump room.

When Smith hesitates, Ray says, "Sorry. Don't mean to scare you. No reason you should trust me. We'll go in the front door."

"You don't scare me." She draws her pistol. "It's okay, Ranger. Lead the way."

Evangelína's rapid heart accelerates. It must be close to 200 BPMs. She's giddy again, has gotten a fourth or fifth wind. Races ahead, noisy as possible, to draw attention.

She finds a trail that forks down a bank to a dry creek-bed. She charges the bank and slips. Skis a moment on her snowshoes. The toe of one catches a crag. She goes heels over head. As she falls, the sled of the pulk clips her calf — wedges into the back of her lower leg. A wet *pop*. Snapped against the heel and the calf with a broken bungee cord. Her hip and elbow slam against snowy ground.

■ ■ ■ ■

Ray's on point through the dank network of pipes and pumps that once heated and filtered the Olympic-sized pool. They take the stairs and ascend through a door in the floor. Noticeably warmer. The walls are windows four stories high, a glass gymnasium. Or a greenhouse gone wild. On the apron surrounding the pool, mature ferns grow over sprawling beds of plush moss. The green glow, iridescent against the snowy backdrop on the other side of glass, is otherworldly, a public pool in the abandoned Emerald City.

"My god," Smith says. "Gives me the feeling of being in a snow globe. Except the snow's on the outside."

Ray says, "Can't get over those chandeliers."

She looks up and gawks. "Chandeliers in a pool house. Wow."

Lichen-covered deck chairs circle the pool. There's a diving board, a bar. Sounds of water rushing inside — snow melting and leaking though the roof. She steps to the lip of the pool. A foot of swampy water at its twelve-foot deep end, a couple of deck chairs, trash.

"I should go," she says into the pool.

"I do something?"

She turns to Ray, her face twisted. "Milt's not gonna make it."

"Why so sure?"

"Saw him have a seizure."

"So what are you gonna do?"

"Me? Fuck you, I just got here. What are you gonna do?"

"VA hospital's probably the best place for him."

"That aint what he wants."

"And what's he want?"

"Curl up in the dark and die, I think."

Ray asks, "What's Vessey say?"

"Milt told me not to tell anyone. Also asked me to keep an eye on you."

He laughs.

"You're just like him, you know."

"What." He spits on moss. "Washed up wannabe operator? One-time black national-ist and LRRP with a Jew fetish? I don't think so."

"Well I'll be," she says. "Looks like I just found me the sore spot."

"Sweetheart, I've got more sore spots than a leper colony."

"You got the same tendency as him," she says. "Only difference is he goes under-ground. You retreat to higher ground."

"You sound like a shrink."

"What happens when you been well shrunk."

"Come with me."

"Where?"

"Higher ground."

"I'm married."

"How's that going for you?"

"Ever see my husband again, might have to murder him."

"Honeymoon's over?"

"Honeymoon was my first deployment."

"Spent mine in Amman."

"Your first deployment?"

"My honeymoon."

"You're a liar." She leans over, hands on knees, starts breathing heavily. She yells, "Oh why's the bottom always got to fall the fuck out of everything!" She grips her chest. "Feeling anxious."

"Let's walk it off."

"Real easy to take advantage of me when I'm like this. Get real passive. When my husband would take it upon himself to mistreat me."

"Sounds like he deserves a talking to. Maybe we pay him a visit. Subject him to an enhanced interrogation."

Again that stricken look, more deaddog and hangdog.

"I'm sorry," he says. "No more jokes."

When she starts shivering, he says, "I made you something."

"What?"

"I'll show you."

She lets herself be guided outside, but not before one final look over her shoulder at the pool house like a deserted island in a glass bottle.

Evangelína pulls off a mitten. She finds a knot at the base of her calf. Another knot, smaller, at the top of her heel. No entry wound, no blood. No bone stabbed bluntly through the skin. Her hand has gone immediately numb in the cold. She can't be sure of what she's touching. Can't flex her foot forward or back.

Using her poles, she stands. Upright, she's afraid her calf might burst. She hobbles over the creek-bed to her tossed snowshoe and, sitting, tries for a few minutes to pull it on. She spits. She gives up. It won't matter; she can't put any weight on the foot.

Mitten off, her middle finger is the first to pass from numb to burn, as if she'd run it under scalding water. Stupid, the way the body senses a freeze and a fire in the same way. Further evidence it can't be trusted, especially not with pain. This attitude, her mistrust of the body's overprotective alarm system, allows her to be extreme in her exercise. She's tempted to force weight onto the foot. First she settles her calf on a mound of snow to ice it while she unfastens the bungee cord from the tarp. She checks her phone — no service.

She drinks from the CamelBak of slushy water, chews and swallows an energy bar like a nutty length of rubber, considers jettisoning the dead weight of the Standard portfolio. The temperature must be below zero. She takes it on faith that the sun has come invisibly up behind the cloudcover. Switching off her headlamp, she stashes it along with the thrown snowshoe under the tarp that she bungee cords back over the sled. She considers removing her weight vest, but its bulk will help keep her warm. She pulls out a few weights the size of candy bars before it becomes too much trouble.

She can't tell how long it takes her to scrabble over the low bank, but when she finally does, she's exhausted in a way she's never been. The trail from here is mostly downhill to Route 55. She descends it gradually, clumsily, falling often. Every time the toe of her hurt foot touches the ground, the anguish is so absolute she nearly blacks out.

■ ■ ■ ■

Their hike felt more like an advance than a retreat, and the man on point, this Reverend Ray, was a compelling contradiction. Made Smith think of Basic Training: in his company, she felt safe and frightened both, challenged in a way that was intimidating and intense, life-changing even, but not deadly. Travis was more like war. The threat was real.

On the trail, they passed a set of tracks in snow. She read them as a person pulling a sled, but her mind jumped to the panther. To test Ray, she told him something was taking the alpaca, adding, "Milt said it was some cougar he released."

"He is losing it."

"That's what I thought. But then, right before you ambushed me, I saw it."

"Probably a bobcat."

"This thing was female-lion big. Florida panther big. The tail was two feet long easy. We're talking 200 pounds."

"Could've been a cougar I guess."

"Cougars and panthers the same thing?"

"Have to ask Wright," he said. "Some serious tracks up here that aren't bear. Paw prints big as a wok. Mud and snow amplify tracks. Cougar track is supposed to be twice as big as a bobcat. Cat tracks show no claws. Bear and dog — coyote, Egon — show claws."

After a time on the trail, mostly uphill, her legs burned, her toes numb, but her body was aglow with its self-made warmth. Then, Ray left the trail.

She stopped, looking for some sort of marker. "Where you taking me?"

His answer came as a quickening of his pace. She felt a pang of terror: she'd soon be cooked and cannibalized according to some classified appendix of the *Ranger Handbook.*

"Home," he told her, and the simple sound of his voice calling back to her — earnest and scratchy — put her at ease.

They came up a ridge onto a reach of level ground. A dense stand of old-growth white pines, a barrens, dark, the trees over a hundred feet tall, two hundred years old. The treetops wove together and only a hint of light, a dusting of snow, reached the ground, where the carpet of needles was so deep it had bounce. Every tree looked the same as far as she could see. A piney maze. The air smelled like Christmas, felt thicker, wetter, a frost pocket, the humidity high. A creek must run nearby. Many of the treetops were reddish, their topmost branches like rusty flags. When she looked closer, a number of the trees, maybe half, seemed to be dying or dead. "What's killing these pines? Been reading about blister rust."

"Some weevil."

Soon the stand thinned. Stack of stones, what looked like blocks of slate, stood next to the trunk of one pine. A precarious balancing act. Another stack, more precarious than the last, and then another. Countless of these stone towers, most only three or four stones, but a number stood chest high and must've been affixed with adhesive. Then there were two or three that defied not only gravity but believability. An oblong boulder balanced on a pebble tipped on a shard. Two massive triangular slabs perched point-to-point.

"My cairns. How I relax."

They summited at a tremendous wet shelf of bluestone shielded from the snowfall or cleared of it. At the far end of the plateau, no trees grew, indication of an overlook. Near it stood a small circular structure, some kind of domed tent, stovepipe sticking blackly out one side. Lattice exterior and, inside the latticework, the walls looked suede. Like the Bedouin goat-hide tents she'd sat in sipping tea. She touched it —

taut enough to bounce a rock off of. She rounded the leather tent. It came within inches of a sheer drop-off and — she gasped — a mountain view like a gut punch.

Falling snow filled all the volume of the valley, and she intuitively knew how many snowflakes occupied the air, like white beans in a glass bowl. The number, finite, filled the limitless space of her imagination. When she tried to name it, the number, she lost it.

In the stirring valley currents, drifting snow coursed like white-water. The most substantial and lasting things in this world were not. This mountain holding her up was little more than the crest of a wave. Bound to break and crumble, washed away by weather.

The mountain made her wonder if anything she'd done would survive her. She had made nothing lasting. Offered little. What if, in her small part, she'd done more harm than good? Hadn't sacrificed, for the war efforts, the way she'd been told. Hadn't given something of value but had taken, and by force. A burden on this wild blue ball and the people busying about it. Here she stood at an edge, gaping at a brimful valley, space and time nearly comprehensible, and she had nothing to give.

Maybe in the end, all that mattered was not how much you did but that you simply did. You were. There would be no grand tallying. There would only be a slow, imperceptible subtraction. Like this mountain, this moment, eroding under her feet.

She hoped there was more. She didn't want her life to be a draw, a depression, a pull toward the downward spiral of chaos and disorder. She wanted to add order. To uplift. But she needed to start small, and maybe the place to begin was to make one supportive relationship and go gradually upward and outward from there.

She faced Ray, long beard and wild hair. "You built this, made this, by yourself?"

He nodded.

"The wind won't blow it over?"

He told her the white pines were a natural windbreak, and the beauty of a dome was its low drag coefficient. "Wind makes downward pressure that keeps the structure in place."

"Who are you?"

He took her by the sleeve and brought her to the far side of the shelter, where was stacked a face cord of split ash collecting snow. He pulled back the shearling flap.

The yurt was entirely fur-lined save for one section of floor against a wall, where, on a foot-high slab of bluestone, crouched a cast-iron box stove silhouetted by a window and the snowy valley beyond. It was easily, undoubtedly, the coziest space she'd ever seen. She wanted to curl up inside and hibernate.

Here was the absolute opposite of Milt's sleeping quarters. The difference between the billet of a man at the end of his life and that of a man in his prime.

When she moved to enter, he grabbed the waist of her pants and yanked, stopping her cold. "What," she said, "no women allowed?"

"Boots off."

His touch — firm — got her roiling.

He said, "Any dirt gets in there stays. Can't exactly plug in a vacuum."

She unlaced her boots in the falling snow, taking off the heavy alpaca hide and draping it over a clothesline that ran to a tree.

He began unhitching his kit. Off came his tomahawk. Followed by a crazy-curved sacrificial knife. Last was a short fixedblade, iridescent black with a knotted-cord grip.

"Why not just carry a gun?"

"Gun wants —"

"Tell me inside. I'm fucking freezing."

He held open the flap for her, and when she ducked in, he followed carrying an armload of firewood. Without a match, he got the fire going in a quick, magical minute.

"Growing up," she said, "I had this picture book, *Little Fur Family*. Had a fake fur cover. This is like being inside that book."

In his hand he held what looked like a pair of rats connected by a length of curved, whittled wood. He held the rodents out to her, and she reared back. He pulled them apart and placed them on her head — earmuffs. They were snug and warm and smelly, and she said, "Stink like road kill."

He reached and jerked them off her head, yanking her hair.

"Ow, hey, no. Just because they're smelly doesn't mean I don't want them. Christ almighty. This what you made for me?"

"Forget it."

"Give them back. Thank you, that's . . . What kind of fur is it?"

He whistled. A moment later, from outside came a whine and growly barks.

"What the hell was that?"

"Florida panther."

"Fuck you."

He opened the flap and made a whining noise, and in filed two small raccoons, side-by-side and leaning against each other while they lumbered like little bandit hunchbacks.

"Fulan and Fulana."

They looked inseparable. Then, they separated. One of them came up and gave the earmuffs a sniff and whined.

"These two gonna become a fur bra?"

"Your earmuffs are their mother."

"Oh that's awful."

"Had I known she had two pups, I wouldn't've killed her. After, I thought I'd bring these two back to camp. Fatten them up first before eating them. That upset you?"

"Please," she answered. "You're talking to a Florida Cracker. Eaten me plenty of coon stew." She told him how, when stationed at Leonard Wood, she was always trying to get Travis to go to the Gillett Coon Supper held in Arkansas ever year.

When he got quiet, she said, "Tell me bout your wife."

"What are you, all of twenty-four?"

"Twenty-five going on fifty."

"In the eyes, you do look middle-aged. But that's war. You got the stony stare of a combat vet. But you've got the long, lovely body of a standout on the swim team."

"Played soccer in high school, center forward. Wanted to be Mia Hamm."

"I took judo and jiu-jitsu. Wanted to be Royce Gracie."

"That why no firearm? You all hand-to-hand?"

He said a loaded gun wants to go off. "In a warzone, same as in the movies, always does. Coming back to the States, knew I was gonna have a tough time with that." He mimed pulling a trigger. "Finger gets itchy," he said. "Specially after ten years as a shooter. Coming home, every soldier's confronted with the dilemma that a loaded gun shouldn't go off." He closed the damper on the woodstove. "You have to fire your weapon?"

"More times than I can count, and all I was doing was driving truck."

"One of the most dangerous jobs in the service."

"Wish someone at the recruitment office woulda made mention."

"How's it feel to get behind a wheel?"

"Milt's been helping me, but I'm skittish, to say the least."

"Ever ride a motorcycle?"

"Practically conceived on a Shovelhead."

"Wait, I'm trying to see it. Okay, got it. You have some kinky folks."

"My mother's dead."

"Motorcycle accident?"

"Found burnt to a crisp," she told him. "Mattress on the floor of a Parramore crack house. Say she probably passed out with a lit cigarette. Instead of putting her out, the other crackheads simply split. Sometimes I wonder if she wasn't murdered."

He apologized.

"Nothing to be sorry about. Never really knew her. Hooked when she had me. Couldn't even bother carrying me to term. I was a crack baby. Born at thirty-two weeks. Weighed all of four pounds eight ounces. Tiny. My daddy's got a Polaroid he took of me sleeping in a cast-iron skillet, room in it for an omelet. Spent a month on the NICU. Daddy was there every day. My moms didn't visit once."

When he apologized again, she said, "Quit your apologizing. Lot of people got it a whole lot worse. Least I had me a daddy to watch over me. Granted, he fucked me up in other ways. But not many Warlocks willing to change a diaper and raise a baby girl on his own. Did the best he could. Which, mind you, wasn't good, but he kept me alive."

They were quiet for a time, watching the raccoons paw each other.

"I should probably go check on Milt."

A pup stood and shambled behind Ray's back. Ray winced. The pup appeared on his shoulder, whining sweetly and sniffing his ear. "Don't think I'm gonna be able to eat them."

"Oh, come on. Don't tell me you're gonna let a little affection get in the way of a coon stew. Other vets at the Standard talk about you like you're a stone-cold killer."

"Like a professional athlete, career of a stone-cold killer's a short one."

They were quiet again — she basked in it like the first sunny day of spring after a winter the likes of which she'd never known. The only tension came from her resisting her want to touch him, be touched by him.

There was a single decorative note, an artful line drawing. "Why the pair of starry eyes up there?"

"That's the Third Star."

"There's only two."

"You make the third one with your mind."

She untied her hair and shook her head. "Show me."

"An eye exercise," he told her. "Two Rub el Hizb symbols. You refocus your vision on a point between them and kind of push them together. When you get it, the third star looks like it's floating in space. Takes practice. Helps keep my vision sharp. My acuity's deteriorating. When I took my MEPS physical, scored 20/9 vision."

"Bullshit."

"Back in my youth," he told her, "assuming you're 20/20, I could see you at 600 meters and you'd have to close in to 300 to see me. My recruiter, after seeing my score, tried to push me toward flight training, but all I wanted was to be a pair of boots on the ground."

"You cold?" she asked.

He shook his head.

"You're shaking."

"Nervous."

She smiled. "I do bite."

"The doc," he said, "after he praised me for my vision, made fun of my ears."

She turned and regarded him, ear to ear.

He put on the coon earmuffs, and the coon kits perked up and whined.

"Now I see why. They're furry, and smelly."

"Ears don't line up," he told her. "Never noticed before. One's a quarter inch lower. Got all self-conscious. Few months back," he said, "found this book in the Esther Library, doing some reading up on birds of prey — we'd lost six chickens in two evenings. Barn owls," he said, "have asymmetrical ears. When they hear a noise, they can pinpoint the location because of the slight time difference it takes to reach each ear."

She felt herself loosen, a localized warmth and relaxation in what she imagined was her uterus. Opposite of a cramp. She'd felt the feeling in the early going of her courtship with Travis. Forgot all about it, how it came this close to queasiness but stopped just shy, like the ratchet up right before a rollercoaster drop. But here with Ray, there was more to it. Maybe it was just the yurt, the cozy fur, his owl anecdote, a warm stove, the glorious view. She said, "I should go."

He nodded.

"Before I do, tell me bout your wife. Bet it's a sob story. But I think I can take it, in here, with you. This about the most at ease I've felt in years."

"Some other time."

"Reverend — you can tell me that at least."

"After I lost my wife, I was done. I was . . ." They both can nearly see his thoughts arc up and out of the yurt, over the Eastern Seaboard, across the Atlantic, the European continent, like an intercontinental ballistic missile, to land in the Middle East.

She prodded, "Go on."

"Right. Well. Seriously considered becoming Log Cabin. Get discharged under Don't Ask, Don't Tell. Want to know how out of my mind I was?"

She wanted to believe him. "Yes."

"Became a minister."

"Get out."

"Man of the cloth. Talking to an ordained member of the Spiritual Humanist clergy."

"Reverend."

"Made the mistake of telling Wisenbeker. Sometimes I was the Reverend Right Honorable Ranger. Sometimes R&R. They love their nicknames. Certificate of ordination's in storage in Liberty. But that alone wasn't gonna get me out of an active duty enlistment contract, even if it was almost up. But it strengthened my claim. Gave grounds to request conscientious objector status. My CO was unimpressed, but he took pity on me after I confessed to marrying a local national. Figured he wouldn't care now she was dead. I was right. I'd already carried my load and then some. Took a couple months to process, but it got me my honorable with a little bit of disability and a life insurance policy."

"I'll be."

"Left Baghdad," he told her, "went straight back to Amman. Spent all of two weeks not participating in warfare or assisting the military. Met a guy at a strip club and got a job as a shooter for a security start-up. Hopped companies three times in as many months. By March of '04 was getting ambushed in the private sector, with the best outfit operating. Stayed in Iraq another seven years. Was an EC, expat contractor. Didn't even come home on leave. Took all my off time in Amman."

"Reliving your honeymoon?"

"Sullying it's more like it. Stayed in Sweifieh at the Turino Hotel. Spent my days, and a lot of money, across the street, at Valentine. Topless bar. Ogle the Syrian and Lebanese girls. Never find a Jordanian working there. Lot of Russians. Chinese. Trying to recast my experience, or outnumber it. Only made things worse."

"What brought you back to the States?"

"A job."

"How'd you lose it?"

"Didn't," he said, "still doing it."

"What, they let you work from yurt?"

He opened the woodstove but didn't put another log on. A wave of dry heat flooded the air. "Being paid to find the woman who's here to buy Wright out."

"Paid? By who?"

He shrugged.

She reached for her alpaca pelt on the floor — it was a part of the floor. Hers, she recalled, hung outside on the line.

He grabbed her wrist.

"I'm listening," she said, "if you got something else to say."

"Spent the last year spying on Wright."

"What do you mean?"

"Mean I've been paid to be here."

"By who?"

"Does it matter?"

"If you're gonna come clean, come."

"Some Kingston lawyer working as middleman."

"How'd you get this job?"

"One of my bosses said the parent company was looking for a vet collecting disability to do a little stateside work. Good pay, low risk. Was already far past toast, so I said sign me up."

"What was the name of the company?"

"Zeitgeist."

"That was the parent company?"

"No, parent company was . . . I don't remember. They're all shells and subsidiaries over there. We were doing a lot of securing pipelines and refineries. But the company who swooped in and made the two SEALS who started it millionaires a hundred times over specialized in infrastructure."

"Construction company."

"Maybe."

"SW&B."

"Don't think so."

"You sure?"

He told her that the company was some sort of service provider, one of those names intended to be forgettable, more generic the better. "When the company bought Zeitgeist, they changed its name to Secure Solutions — they seemed oblivious to the fact that we then became the SS — but we still went by Zeitgeist."

"So you've been here nearly a year doing what exactly?"

"Observing. Gathering information. Building chain of title. Vetting Wright."

"And you pass along this information for pay. Okay. And what am I, part of your cover? You playing me to help you weasel more information from a dying man?"

"My work on Wright's done. They got all they needed. Moving to the next phase."

"Which is?"

"Purchase I would guess. They've sent in a right-of-way agent to make an offer. But they lost her."

"What's that mean?"

"Means they can't find her."

"You have anything to do with that?"

"Come on, what do you take me for?"

"I don't know. I thought I was getting an idea, but you've just . . ." She started forced exhalations, beating back her panic with her breath.

"Think they're trying to leverage Wright out of the Standard if he refuses their low-ball offer" — she was having a hard time hearing what he was saying — "lot of money behind it."

"If you're done digging up dirt on Milt, why they still paying you?"

"Lawyer wants me to track down this missing woman."

"So you stood to gain by her disappearance."

"Hadn't thought of that. Had thought her disappearance, the possibility of it, could be useful. Even floated it by the lawyer. Told him I could subject her to a domestic rendition program. Kidnap her and pin it on Wright. Easy now. I see that look. No need to worry. I would never. I offered it as a way to see where the bottom is on this whole thing, take a sounding. Even offered you up when he shot down option one. See if the ethics got murkier with less loyalty. Not that I would. I was fishing. Trying to see if they'd bite."

"I'm feeling sick."

"I would never hurt you, or any other woman."

"You only kill men."

"Armed men that have it coming to them, that's right."

"What if the lawyer'd said yes?"

"I might've killed him."

"You're not joking."

"If he'd said yes, at the very least, I was planning on working my way up the chain of command, find who's giving the orders. Maybe kill that guy."

"How do you know a woman's not giving the orders?"

"These days, it's possible."

"It ever occur to you that *I'm* working undercover, sent in by the same company who's been paying you?"

His look darted toward the door. Then he leaned back and squinted. "I'm trying to be honest and open with you, like you asked, and now you're fucking with me."

"You're a whore. You're not to be trusted. Look me in my fucking face. You have any idea where this woman is?"

"None whatsoever."

She kept quiet. It was all sinking queasily in. "Where'd all these pelts come from?"

"Milt's herd. Alpaca fleece is warmer than wool, hypoallergenic. Even flame-resistant."

She counted the hides that made up the floor and walls, at least ten — there was the zipping feeling, hairs on end. "Where's

E. Prince?"

He pointed to the door flap. "You walked through him."

She stood. "Milt's convinced his cougar took him."

"He gave me the go-ahead to take E. Prince."

She reached for the door flap and flinched from it.

"Where you going?"

"See Milt. Tell him he's got a traitor. Before I do" — she pointed a finger an inch from his face — "I need to tell you, Go the fuck to hell."

His dark laugh troubled her more than what he shouted after her as she tore out of the yurt: "Hell's not somewhere you go, sweetheart, hell's someone you become."

Evangelína comes to. Freezing, sodden. Blackness gives way to gray, watery. Bracken sways lazily overhead. The ellipse of un pez, a fish, swims near her face. She's shivering. The dead are cold — she is dead. Staring up at the icy underside that is the frozen surface of the reservoir. Or not. Cloudcover. Too early for the reservoir to ice over. Not sediment falling on her — snow. Not bracken — trees, leafless. And not a fish but a face — familiar, or not familiar, but friendly. Dark-skinned. Dark-eyed. But bizarre. A face topped by a face, one human, one not — a wayob, shape-shifter.

"Mamí," she says.

The lower face, the human face, speaks. Something kindly, something reassuring.

A human hand — rough, dirty — reaches and touches her neon parka. The hand recoils, the lower face, human, twists, like an old vine. Another hand, holding something, a young tree, a sapling topped by a skeletal hand, rears up. Quick strike that snakes down and into the pit of her pelvis.

The wayob struck her with its sapling — it all makes terrible sense — the sapling became a snake. The snake is a nauyaca, Mexican viper. A hot, venomous agony blooms below her bellybutton. When the wayob yanks back the snake, she hears a wet rip, fatty. The wayob has torn her bib ski pants, or the nauyaca has been pulled in two. Pain in, and over, her pelvis sparks a blinding brightness behind her eyes.

The face under the face wavers. The face of her papí, younger, leaner, worn, a thin beard. The face — concerned, confused — grows. Closer. Her jacket flings open. She's being undressed, readied for bed. She tries to say something, reach out and touch this man she's missed so desperately, so dearly.

He rears back, terror on his face, dropping the sapling-become-snake in the snow. In his hand, he holds a weight pulled from her jogging vest.

In the swirling flurries, Smith passes cairns topped with snow like stocking caps. A few tower overhead. Stony sentries sure to collapse. The cairns, their precariousness, make her anxious and, when at her back, they leave her with the sense she's being watched. At the cusp of a panic attack, she enters the pines.

After untold minutes, she's staring over the edge of her composure, looking dizzily down into the coiled void of her anxiety. She's comatose somewhere, catatonic, airlifted to a CSH cut into a stand of Afghan pines in Ghazni Province, awaiting transport to a fixed-facility hospital, having suffered a catastrophic head injury after one of her wrecks. She didn't kill the Saydabad boy. She died to avoid him. This, all that's come after, is make-believe, a drawn-out dream — her conscious mind coping with extended unconsciousness.

She fights this rabbit-hole notion with her breath, as if her breath were the ultimate weapon. Draws big, vast pulls of sappy air to combat the condemned thinking, the claustrophobic falling. She's freezing. Losing herself. She left behind the earmuffs. Refused to touch her alpaca hide. Inside it hid her sardine-tin survival kit sewn into its own little pocket. The only thing she brought in her flight from conniving Ray and his hurt-locker yurt was her sidearm and bandolier. She increases her pace to warm herself.

Again, she comes to the cairns like a sprawling small-scale Stonehenge. She can't believe they're the same ones, can't believe Ray hasn't used some trick to keep them upright. Can't believe he's been royally bullshitting Milt for the last year. A plume of blue smoke rises from the flue of the yurt. Fuck. She turns a 180. The cairns mock her and seem to wobble. She side-kicks one — her anxiety abates. She front-kicks another. Feeling relief, she boots over cairn after cairn. They come clopping and thudding down, sliding and cracking. After she's toppled every last tower, she feels wretched, stupid.

More lost minutes. Ten, maybe twenty. Then, the trees thin. She arrives at her juvenile aftermath: bluestone kicked haphazardly about. For the third time, she's found the fucking yurt. She's feeling crazy, hopeless enough to slink back into camp and beg directions. Her alpaca pelt no longer hangs on the clothesline. Sickened, she stands before the door flap that is the hide of poor poached and skinned E. Prince. She throws it open.

Inside, the two coon kits wake and whine. They lie curled near the stove. She doesn't see the earmuffs, and Ray's gone.

Her shivers grown to shaking, she pulls and tears the hide of E. Prince off the yurt and drapes it over her shoulders. She tromps past the once-were cairns and reenters the pines dragging a dead branch that cuts a swath behind her. After another fifteen or so minutes and a few more missteps, she finds the trail down toward the Standard.

Evangelína puts her hand to her stomach, below her navel. Her fingers touch something slick — her papí made an offering. Left a gift of food, his favorite. He set on her a coiled chorizo fresco — on their annual family road trips into Mexico when she was a girl — she is a girl, Papí insisting they make the dry, dusty drive to Toluca to gorge on, and then stockpile, chorizo verde, locally made pork sausages stuffed with tomatillo, cilantro, chili peppers, and garlic. She's never seen her papí eat so much and so pleasurably. When sated to burping, he buys ten kilos he smuggles across the border in an ice chest shut into a battered valise. Evangelína and Mamí are nervous as mojadas, wet ones, crossing the Rio Grande on a moonless midnight, Papí saying in Spanish, Easy, girls, it's only food. If they find it, they'll confiscate the chorizo, not me.

Papí's offering, warm, raw, slips from her grip. Her fingers come away wonderfully red — Mamí's poppies in a subtropical downpour. Maybe the drought has broken, maybe she can go home, to Papí, to Chichí, to a place in a cenote where all the wants and wishes of her life are met like basic needs.

She hears Papí tromping away through snow. She must face the end alone. But his face, fatherly, under a face, feral, still hovers before her. She's staring through the memory of it, the past painfully becoming her present.

Seasons ago, his mother killed the other cubs. Cubs the cougar calls for some nights. Together, they ate them. After, she clawed his eye. Screamed and hissed him off to hunt on his own. The eye dried. Fell from his head. A bad berry. His mother, old, weak. Seasons since he last caught her trail. He pads through deep overturned snow.

Hears an answer to his emptiness. Kill the bird. Big, clumsy tracks. Injured bear. Huffing and grunting its hurt. Closer, not bear. Human. Warm, already open.

Vessey shuttles split wood into the lobby of Esther, grunting and aching, cursing his bones that grate and whine like chalk on rock.

Egon stands, barks.

"What is it, old boy? Lunchtime already?"

The lobby door flies open and Merced, heaving, leans against the doorway. He bends over, hands on knees, the door smacking him in the rear. His alpaca face hoods his long black hair. To the leafy floor, he says, "Vess. Vess."

"Merced." Vessey sits on the old, leaky generator and waits for the spew of nonsense. If only Merced had a pull-cord and a choke to close.

"Un autogol, Vess, un autogol. ¡Ay, Dios mío! Un autogol."

Egon barks.

"Con permiso, Egon, usted perro digno."

"Asseyez, Egon." When Egon sits, Vessey says, "What the hell's an autogol?"

"Un autogol. ¿Cómo se dice? Autogol. Auto. Own! Own goal!"

"You were playing soccer?"

"It's football, Vess, and, no, I hurt la bonita."

"Bonita. That's *little bone* right? You hurt your pecker?"

"¡Ay, carajo! Not my pecker, Vess, the pretty Latina."

"She's here?"

"Aquí, yes, damn."

"Start from the start. In English. You speak perfect English. Hurt how?"

"My short-timer's stick. Pulled her right open. Guts come pouring out. Pensé que iba a explotar." He made a pouf sound, his hands expanding outward. "Thought she . . . shit. Don't know what I thought, Vess. Her jogging vest, one of the weighted ones? This cabeza." He fired a thumb-and-finger pistol at his temple.

"Okay, okay. Where?"

"The high trail."

"Take me."

He shook his head. "No way, Vess. I got to run. Voy, adios."

"Merced, you take me this fucking instant. That's an order. Understand?"

Merced looked through the cloudy glass of the Esther lobby for a long moment. He butted his head hard against it.

"Merced."

Egon went to Merced, sniffed his red

fingers, then licked them.

Merced looked at his hand. He nodded to the out-of-doors. "Vamanos."

Evangelína knows a new pain, this one blue, a quickening pain, a pain that snaps her awake, yanks her from delusions of apocalyptic grandeur to deposit her in the snowy mountain woods, a pain that makes her think it's not the world that's ending — the end is hers alone.

Sounds made at her throat, but not by her throat, confuse her. A low rumble. She needs to get free. She flails, strikes a body. Recalls, vaguely, some instruction about fighting for her life, that playing dead was a sure way to die.

She strikes. Finds fur, fur too short to grab a fistful of. She hears screams, feels screams, and, just before she blues-out, she's not sure if the screams she hears are hers.

An instant later, she's back, the blue burned red. She opens her tearful eyes.

A broad brown wedge of a face, inches away. The two faces of the wayob have merged. Her papí winks at her, a jaguar fully transformed. Papí sniffs her neck. His whiskers tickle beneath her chin, just like when she was a girl. His unwinking eye, the gold of a Libertad coin.

She reaches up.

He swats away her hand with an open paw big as a sombrero. His claw snags on her coat sleeve, hung up on the band of her watch. Papí jerks away his paw and growls. He sniffs her mouth, inhaling her breath, his mouth parted. His breath rank and metallic. He licks her neck with a tongue like a sea urchin. Her neck feels nettle-stung, tingly and burning. He clamps his mouth over her throat — she can't breathe, again goes blueblind.

She fights. Thrashes with more than she has. Draws resistance from the sacred cenote of her self.

Papí doesn't let go. His growl vibrates her vocal cords. He growls through her.

She shoves hands into pockets. Something to fend off Papí, gentle Papí, doting Papí, Papí to be feared only when angry Papí, anything Papí, finds nothing, Papí, nothing but price tags pulled off and tucked away. She yanks at the pouches of her weight vest, fumbles, finds purchase on a weight, drops it in snow. She's using both numb hands, searching and grasping. Each hand opens a flap and removes a weight. She's aware of her awareness, but only because she's losing it, her presence of mind slipping out from under her, her grip loosening on the gripped weights, one in each hand, she gazing up at the overcast, a snowflake landing and melting in a spangled blur on her open eye.

Smith arrives at the tracks she and Ray encountered going up-trail. They're snowing over. Fresh tracks, boot tracks, come and go. She's eager to check on Milt, both excited and saddened to convey news of E. Prince, to relay the info that Ray's been spying for corporate interests. She's also afraid, afraid of what she might find down in Milt's tunnel-rat hole. She sees him stiff with rigor, stinking of the —

A dulled scream, muffled by snow, reaches her numbed ears. Could be wind. Could be the sound of frostbite setting in, her blood freezing. Unsettling, how in the silences and the noises up here, she hears all sorts of ghostly voices.

She heads away from the tracks, away from the scream, toward Masada, the snow underfoot screeching and singing like the sugar sand on Siesta Key in Sarasota.

The second scream stops her, turns her, a jolt. Her vestigial hackles rise icy under the warm hide of E. Prince. The scream is so terrifying, so dreadful, that it spurs her to sprint through snow in its direction. She's barreling ahead before she knows what she's doing. At a dead run, she reaches her hand to steady the holstered pistol banging her hip.

She follows the tracks. Muddle of boots, one or two pairs, snowshoes, a sled. Then out of the woods, joining the other tracks on the trail, are prints of a creature of such size that they stop Smith skidding cold, not out of fear but disbelief, she slipping and falling in snow. On her knees, she inspects the paw prints from inches away. Polar bear. Before she has time to correct this thought, another mad cry, clearer, washes over her.

She's back on her boots and running. As the trees thin, the cries hit her as more than simple sound; the cries become as solid as the strike of a hand. The cries shove her away, try to turn her the other direction, the fear in her a physical assault.

The Florida panther stands across an opening. Fifty meters away. The great cat bends over its find, biting and pawing. A loud neon fabric, puffed green and pink. A sleeping bag. Some hiker's camp in a clearing.

Hearing Smith, the panther turns its head. Its face, the wedge of it, is a fierce yield sign. But friendly somehow, confiding. Winking. Its open eye, across this distance, is a dot of vivid green-gold, a drop of antifreeze. The panther hisses, flashes four pink fangs. It belts out a roar like a redlined engine.

The cat's one-eyed, same panther she saw while splitting wood. When he turns back to his camp rations, Smith retreats, places painstakingly slow steps away, careful not to show her back. Let him have his pilfered goodies. Whatever trespasser left them deserves to come back to his camp hungry and foodless. One more thing to report to Milt.

As she backs away, the panther bites and pulls, lifting the two-tone neon off the ground. Tan face buried in the neon green, sweep of black hair. Person. Smith's vision keys in, tightens on the cat trying to drag the body into the treeline. There's no fight, no resistance whatever, in the hiker.

Smith draws her pistol. She aims, braces, elbows bent, fires once. The recoil jumps the gun over her head. She recovers, aims at the unfazed panther, fires again.

The panther releases its bite and nearly speaks a roar, a roar more like a plaintive sentence than word of warning. A beard of venous blood, deep red, covers his chin.

Smith advances. Ground underfoot broken and rocky, made slick by melting snow.

When the panther crouches to spring at her, she fires a third round.

The panther flinches, ears flattened, but doesn't turn, doesn't run.

Unsure which barrel to aim over for her last shot, she tries to recall the firing sequence. She has reloads but no time. Still too far for much accuracy. She continues advancing, sighting between the top two barrels at the panther's chest tipped low, its body recoiled, readying to rush her and making a tighter target. Just outside range, four body-lengths maybe, she fires her final round.

The cat roars. Doesn't withdraw. He rises and charges, kicking up a spray of snow.

When Vessey and Merced hear the first faint shot, they stop. Hearing the second shot — muffled by snowcover — they both sprint in the direction of the reports, Egon leashed and whining at Vessey's side. The snow slows them, Vessey's worn-away joints slowing him further. By the time the third shot's fired, they see the gunman — gunwoman — Bellum absorbing the recoil of her pepperbox with bent arms, then moving in.

They enter the clearing, the snowcover thin. A cougar crouches over a small hiker bright as candy. Vessey can't tell the screams of the hiker from the cougar.

Egon yanks hard at his choker, fighting in

the direction of the cat that's three, four times his size, the cougar unbelievably big, its tail as long as Egon.

When Bellum fires a forth shot, and either misses or does no damage, Vessey unleashes Egon, commanding, "Sortez-le!"

The cougar charges Bellum, its speed at that size astounding.

Egon sprints, not toward the sprinting mountain lion but toward Bellum, Egon trained to attack gunmen.

Vessey, about to yell Gîter, heel, hesitates. Egon isn't heading for Bellum — he's on an interceptor line, not charging after the cougar, but where the cougar will be.

Egon barks and barks again.

With a plant of massive paws, the cougar tries to change course at a full run with a side jump. Its feet kick out from under it, skittering rocks, and it slides on its side like a derailed locomotive. The cougar is up on its broad paws in an instant. It leaps, stretching its long, limber body at Egon.

The cougar and the dog collide, Egon looking like a toy terrier. Their growls and barks are distorted and bent by the twisting. Then a roar, a howl, are each muffled by mouthfuls of fur. They both release their loose, initial bites. They circle around one another, close range. The cougar claws at

Egon. Egon pulls back then lunges, is swatted toward the cougar's flank but manages to clamp his bite on the muscled hindquarter. The cougar pulls away, dragging Egon. Again it pulls, drawing Egon on his paws over snowy bluestone. When Egon doesn't let go, the cougar torques its body, reaching its huge head around, and clamps its mouth on top of Egon's narrow head.

Vessey and Merced, stunned, watch the cat and dog fight. Vessey's snapped to by Bellum's sudden proximity to the fray.

Bellum continues her advance, hissing, waving arms at cougar and dog. She stumbles over the uneven ground, a loose slab of bluestone. She lifts the sharp slab overhead and hurls it. She grabs another slab like a long shard, closing on the cougar.

Merced finds a chunk of bluestone, throws it, hitting the cat, and Vessey rains down cold rock after rock.

Only after Egon slumps with a yelp, limp, does the cougar release the dog's skull. The cat backs away from the collapsed dog, feints toward Bellum, who lifts her arms, splays the fingers of her empty hand, rises on tiptoes, and screams.

The cougar backs away, takes a step toward the hiker who hasn't moved. The cougar gives its own berserker scream, and

Bellum responds, even louder, lower and higher both, from the floor of her pelvis up through the bony bridge of her face, a war cry so visceral that Vessey shrinks from the sound.

The cougar pulls in its tail, raises its ears, turns its back, and bounds into the trees.

As Merced looks on, Vessey uses both hands to scoop and shove the indígena's intestines back into her. Vessey says, "Help, Merced."

"Como?"

"Zip her vest, while I'm here holding everything in, then her jacket."

Merced doesn't move.

Bang Bang strips to her tank top, starts biting at the shoulder of her jacket.

Merced says to Vessey, "Bang Bang's eating her shirt."

She tears off one sleeve, then begins biting the other.

Merced says, "Egon."

"Triage," Vessey says. "Now help. I got my hands full. Zip her the fuck up."

Merced takes hold of both open ends of the jogging vest. Just a jogging vest. Dios mío. He fits the zipper parts together, and zips.

Bang Bang pulls plastic wrap off a couple of white plugs. They look like cotton dummy rounds. She pushes the plugs into the largest puncture wounds, then wraps one camo sleeve snuggly around the indígena's neck. Without instruction, Vessey holds it in place while Bang Bang folds, wraps, twists the ends, and ties tight the other sleeve overtop.

Bang Bang grabs the indígena's wrist. The beds of the indígena's nails are blue. Bang Bang puts her ear to the indígena's mouth. "Faint pulse, steady breathing. We've got to move. She's in shock."

Vessey picks up Merced's carved stick, rubs the end of the antler with snow. To Bang Bang, he says that the gut wound looks godawful, but it's not losing a ton of blood. "That's not what's gonna do her in, not now anyway. Infection later might finish off what that cat started."

"Neck's a mess," Bang Bang says, "but the blood looks too dark to be arterial. Punctures in one or both jugulars, not the carotids. If it were carotids, she'd be already dead. We hurry, she might have a chance."

While Vessey and Bang Bang move the indígena onto her sled, Merced goes to Egon. The dog looks asleep in snow. Merced sees a steely glint, picks up Bang Bang's handgun, and slips it into his waist. He heaves the dog over his shoulders. When he says, "Bang Bang," she pulls her pistol from his waistband, touches Merced's scruffy face with her cold hand. She leans in and butts her head against Egon's brow, pressing her head to his for a moment, then she kisses his black nose.

She and Vessey drag the indígena feetfirst, limp on her gear in the plastic sled. Bang Bang's alpaca hide thrown over and tucked under. A sleeping Inuit, but for the blood.

Merced plods behind them with dead Egon passing gas on his shoulders. He can't take his eyes off the indígena's upside-down face that has lost its copper shine, gone gringa. Her long black hair sweeps the snow behind her like the dark train of a mourner's dress on Día de los Muertos.

Vessey uses Merced's short-timer's stick to help him make way with his small portion of the burden. Bang Bang, her leanly muscled arms exposed to the shoulder, wears the indígena's waist harness to pull more than her share of the weight.

Merced grips Egon's legs, wet from snow. The black pads of the dog's paws are soft yet rough as sandpaper. Merced presses one against his cheek. The dog's head lolls against Merced's shoulder, dripping blood off the point of an ear, leaving a dotted red line in the snow behind their procession. They're a sad parade, Merced thinks, and he can't shake the sense that this is how the end of the world begins — they're bearing the first bad news of it.

In front of Standard Tower, Vessey takes quick charge. "We got to get her to a hospital," he says. "Closest one's Catskill Regional in Harris. We've got no way to call 911."

Bellum says, "She might have a phone on her. Anyone go through her stuff?"

"Even if she does," Vessey says, "you're gonna have a hard time getting service. We make our calls at a payphone in Liberty. To drive there to stop and place a call's stupid."

"How far's the hospital?"

"Ten, twelve minutes, going the speed limit."

"I could drive her," Bellum says, "but whoever drops her off is gonna have to talk to cops. I can't. I'm a deserter, Vess. They'll haul me in."

"Okay, good to know. I'll drive. You find Milt. Think he's still down in the hole."

She steps to Vessey and hugs him hard enough to squeeze a *hunh* out of him. "Thank you," she says, still holding him.

He returns her hug. "You did good out there under duress. More than good."

"I'm sorry, Vess."

"Nothing to be sorry for."

"I mean about Egon."

"Go," he says, and she does.

Vessey checks the woman's pulse, weak. He gives orders the whole time he and Merced work to situate her in the back of the van: "Merced, when we're done, I need you to ring the big bell for an emergency muster. Bellum and Milt'll be along shortly."

"This is it, isn't it?"

"Roger that."

"They'll come for me. I'm just gonna split, Vess. I gutted that poor bonita."

"You didn't hurt that woman, you hear me?"

"I did, Vess. Opened her up with my stick like a wet enchilada."

"No you didn't, Merced. That cougar did."

"You mean jaguar. Jaguar came after, hombre."

"No one's gonna know a damn bit of difference." Vessey makes sure the woman's head tips to the side. "And I won't say a fucking word to anybody. Cause it's just like us whiteys. Come in here and stir the pot. Get things all roiled. Then the brown folks wind up trying to kill each other. Same here as anywhere. And this woman, if she survives, won't be able to make sense of what just happened. Now, dismissed."

After Vessey drives off, Merced heads away from Masada and the big bell, toward the former golf course and the chicken coop, where Alhazred, oblivious to the apocalypse underway, mucks out shitty straw, cursing and mumbling to his pitchfork.

"Alhazred! Vess wants you to go bang the big bell. Emergency muster. Bang like there's not tomorrow. Bang like it's the end of el mundo."

Ray's taking the suicide route off Slawson Mountain. He intends to place Bellum's alpaca hide and her earmuffs near the cook fountain in the Alpine village, but after spotting Stone, he decides to kill two birds. He hands off her things and passes on a little disinformation. Engages in a little PSYOP at Stone's well-deserved expense.

The way Bellum left, Ray's sure she won't be back. He's got their last conversation on a loop, trying to figure out where he fucked it all up. One thing she said — asking the name of the company that bought Zeitgeist — set him in action.

He hikes from the Standard to his storage unit in Liberty to get some cash and to roll out his motorbike. Then he rides to the Monticello Walmart, where he buys a charger for Baum's phone. He plants himself at a computer in the tiny Liberty public library. While the phone charges, he visits the credit-union website where he last maintained a checking account, thinking the company name might be there for each of his direct deposits.

He can't access the records. He closed the account when he got back to the States, liquidating his savings. He visits another site, Secure Aspects Group Inc., an industry resource for private-defense contracting. There, in their members' forum, he runs a search for Zeitgeist, the company name before they became Secure Solutions. In a few threads he finds the name of the company that purchased Zeitgeist: Allstates Technical Services.

The title of the first hit in a Google search is *Allstates Technical Services, an IRJ Company — full-service provider of professional staffing solutions including contract recruiting and staffing . . .* Fourth in the results is a page on the IRJ website, Subsidiary Operations, that lists Allstates alongside seven other companies. At the bottom is SW&B Construction.

The company paying Ray to gather information on Wright is the same one offering to buy Wright out. Whatever it might mean,

Ray has a location. If he feels the need, he can go to Houston and start shaking people down.

He picks up Baum's phone, partially charged. It's still switched off. If he turns on the phone, he might have a few quick leads, but he'll be compromised in four dimensions: longitude, latitude, elevation, and time. He decides he's in no hurry. It's in his best interests not to find Canek too quickly.

The underground air blew Alhazred back a step with its smell, funky and faintly sweet. In the cavernous darkness, he felt for the flashlight stashed in a nook of the passageway wall.

Knowing the sound of his own voice helped beat back the dread, he started free-flowing: "Burrowing after you, old Saddam, who's fully armed, you and your blinging gold-plated AK, but there's no where, no way, no how to hide from our side. We're on the dole, and we're gonna smoke yo scaredy-ass out your challah-hole. Check it, don't disrespect it, don't undermine the will of Allah . . . of Allah . . . Allahu Akbar, Allahu Akbar . . ."

Alhazred reached the old laundry room and was assaulted by the stench of rot.

From underfoot came a crackle. He shone his light at the floor. Wall-to-wall corpses, small, shriveled, a rodent killing field. He hopped involuntarily — the ceiling rippled like the surface of a dark lake. Bats. As many dead underfoot as sleeping facedown overhead.

He focused on his task. The great brass bell, upended. It seemed to swallow light, was covered in a green fuzzy patina of verdigris. Propped by debris from the four floors it fell through, the bell was big as an overturned Volkswagen Bug. Its inscriptions were in a language Alhazred couldn't begin to parse or place. In relief on the bell were warring figures, a crowned king of some sort and a great tree towering over a battle scene — all upside-down.

Milt said the bell was sacred, said his father-in-law bought it for the price of its scrap metal — $15,000 during the Depression — and there were archaeologists hunting for it and folklorists who'd written dissertations on its disappearance from the rubble of a Balkan cathedral bombed in the First World War.

Alhazred wielded the sledgehammer wrapped in burlap. "Allahu Akbar," he said, striking the upturned bell — a loud, broken knell made him ache for earplugs.

The veterans of the Standard Grande wanted to know what in hell they were doing making way toward the Alpine village for an emergency muster. With Milton not around to remind them, they were forgetting tasks, could not for the life of them keep track of the days. They'd started to suspect that the party was puttering to an end, but none of them knew that the assembly taking shape would be their last.

Stotts-Dupree and Luce arrived first, Stotts-Dupree's face filled out — he'd found his denture in a dirty coffee cup, suspected Stone hid it there to fuck with him.

Luce huffed a warm breath in his hand and cupped his stump. "Any idea what we're waiting for?"

"Waiting for word."

They stood aimlessly around the ash-filled fountain, listening to the erratic clangs resonating under the armory, cringing each time.

Luce said, "Hey, let's light this bitch. My stump's feeling the freeze."

Stotts-Dupree nodded and together they gathered kindling and seasoned splits from the nearby stack. When Luce started arranging kindling in a tipi, Stotts-Dupree shoved it over, saying, "Nah, log-cabin style. Way you build a fire makes a political statement."

"This aint a fucking filibuster, STD, it's a fire." Luce pulled out a brass Zippo and snapped it open with one hand. "I'm just trying to warm up my stump here." He held the flame to the end of his amputated arm.

Stotts-Dupree rearranged the kindling, stacked some timber; while he did, a bird landed in a drift of ash and snow inside the fountain. Stotts-Dupree lifted the creature by its wingtip. "Bat."

"Leave it be. Could have rabies. Especially if it's flying in the middle of the day."

"Dead. Just dropped out the sky into the cook fire, dead."

Luce clapped shut his lighter and inspected the bat pinched in Stotts-Dupree's ashy fingers. "Looks like it has rabies. White dust all round its nose and mouth. That or it's a bat with a bad coke habit."

Stone and Wisenbeker entered from the narrow passageway between two failing half-timbered structures, the Kosher Konditorei and Alf's Sportladen.

Luce said, "Either of you clowns know what's what?"

"Stone ran into Reverend," Wisenbeker

said, "who apparently has a crush on the lady cherry. Made her a pair of earmuffs."

Stone, wearing the earmuffs, held an alpaca fur in addition to the one draped over his shoulders. "If it looks like possum, smells like possum, must be possum." He repositioned the earmuffs between his legs, one muff over his crotch, the other like a cottontail. He dropped Bellum's alpaca hide in trampled, slushy snow. "Who's building a log-cabin fire? Log cabin's for gay Cub Scouts with Down syndrome." He kicked over the unlit stack of wood and began re-arranging it in a tipi.

A bat flew overhead. They all watched it skitter through the sky and disappear beyond the shake-shingled roof of the Schokoladenladen.

Botes came into camp holding a muddy hoe. "Anyone know what this muster's about? This aint SOP."

No one responded.

A bat flew cartwheeling over their shaking heads.

They all looked up at the same section of sky, their attention yanked as if by reins. A sound like the distant clapping of a mob of children, faint and wafting. The contorted applause grew louder. The quizzical look on the face of Wisenbeker turned from amused wonder to terror, and as he yelled — "Incoming!" — there comes a shift. The sight, once each of the vets gets a visual, offers relief: a fleet of bats flies a few feet overhead. As the colony passes, bats flop to the ground by the dozens.

Wisenbeker smacks Botes's arm. "Acrobats."

When Botes says, "Hardy har har," Wisenbeker starts humming what Botes recognizes as "Kill the Wabbitt."

The vets are laughing and yelping. Luce, too, until he catches a one-two combination, whacked in the ear and then walloped full-on in the face, the second bat's needle teeth piercing his lip. The sharp pain, the sight of his own blood, snuffs out his sense of humor, and, waving his stump overhead, he yells, "Medic! I need a medic!"

Stotts-Dupree hollers back, "Take cover, Luce! Reinforcements're coming!"

Merced runs into camp raking his short-timer's stick through the flying thicket. He shouts at the sky dark with bats, "You find yourselves among the pueblos indígenas of the world! El mundo is indígena! The árabe! The indígenas! The mestizos! The negros! The hajji! They know the apocalypse returns again! From the cenotes of Mexico! The caves of Tora Bora! The banks of the Tigris!

Where it all began, where —"

The cracked bell rang tragically. Hitting it felt like striking a living, breathing thing.

Alhazred banged and banged again, and between bangs, in the reverberation, he heard that other noise, miraculous. The flutter of a million little wings. As he banged, the burlap wrap came undone from the head of the sledgehammer. He tore it off.

Without the padding, he gave the bell a test whack. It clanged in a new way, a worse way, piercing, its gong become intelligible: *Gone.* Instead of stopping, he hit it harder, and harder still — *gone, gone* — his hands numbing. He slowed, tiring, and then he hit the bell a glancing blow at a bad angle, and the crack opened. The bell — in a shocking slowness of motion — began to fall into two unequal pieces.

When the ringing stopped in the air, he still heard the faint flutter of wings and a few squeaks so high-pitched they sounded like the splintering of his teeth.

"Loco-ass *Apocalypto* Chicano caveman," Botes says. "Surprised the bats aint flying *out* Merced's damn mouth."

Over the flapping mass die-off, there comes an ungodly clang, a ringing thunderclap like the big bell's been lightning-struck. The ground shakes.

Feeling the tremor vibrate up through him, Luce uncurls from the fetal position, checks his bloodied lip and shoves Merced off the short wall into the tipi wood stack. Standing over Merced splayed in the fountain, Luce yells, "That's it! I can't take any more! I'm the fuck out of here!"

Wisenbeker yells, "Where you think you're gonna go?"

"To get a drink! Then back to my fucking ex! Maybe she'll house me till it stops raining bats!"

As Luce exits the Alpine village, the bats begin to thin, and then the last few stragglers bumble overhead.

Stotts-Dupree asks no one, "This the end of the end of the world?"

Stone pokes out from under his alpaca hide. "The fuck's Luce going?"

Wisenbeker says, "Share a drink with his ex-wife."

"Now that Milt's dead," Botes says, "what you gonna do, Stone?"

Stotts-Dupree says, "How you know the good brother's dead?"

"Come on, STD, it just rained bats."

"That case," Stone says, "and if Luce is back on the bottle, I'm gonna go score."

"Strip club in Liberty?" Botes says. "Nice. What's it called?"

"You got a meth-head confused with a ladies' man. I'm heading straight to Neversink. I'll see you boys on the backslide." He unties his alpaca hide, steps out from under it, and files in after Luce.

The bright blather that filled the Stardust Room made Milt squint. Sputnik chandeliers — spindly, gleaming, sharp — pulsed over the crowd.

Backed by the big band, Sammy crooned "Polka Dots and Moonbeams." When the applause faded, he announced in his nasally voice, I'm taking five, fine people. Thank you very kindly. During the break, we've got a little something special planned, something far out — I mean that literally now — and we think you'll dig it. Shirt unbuttoned halfway down his birdy chest, collar spread-eagled, he folded himself over in a limber bow. Hopping off the circular stage, he strode in that short gait of his — part showtime hustler, part pulled muscle — to the Teplitsky table.

The band started a jazz standard Milt didn't recognize. In most every joint down in the city on this Saturday night, people his age — black and tan, brown and yellow, red, white and blue — were disco dancing. A year after Travolta took his turn as Tony Manero, king of the dance floor at 2001 Odyssey in Brooklyn, and America still had the fever. It should've been the summer of Summer — Donna had charted one hit after another — but there'd been a serial killer on the loose, and so the summer belonged to Sam.

But not at the Standard, where time slow danced.

Sammy tipped an imaginary hat brim to Nehemiah, winked at Milt, and, over his blue tinted glasses, he looked at Ada sitting between them. Care to dance, doll?

She said, Excuse me, Tateleh, touching her father's hand, and stood without a glance Milt's way.

They'd been arguing for weeks. Over his drinking, over her last miscarriage, over Nehemiah's reluctance to face the inevitable. Resorts were closing all around them — Youngs Gap, the Ambassador, the Flagler, the Laurels. Ada was also disappointed about her run in summer stock that just wound to an end, a run that didn't include one leading role. In a stage whisper to Sammy, she said, Married the one soul brother in America who can't get down.

Sammy flashed his perfect dentures —

Hahaa! — and shrugged a shoulder at Milt.

Milt knocked back his bourbon and watched the fuzzed scene like a soft-focus shot in the movies. He and Ada had met in a black cinema class that screened *Sweet Sweetback's Baadasssss Song.* Seven years later, the steady flow of Blaxploitation flicks had slowed to a trickle, and he and Ada had seen every one that opened in the city. *Mandingo,* her favorite, *The Spook Who Sat by the Door,* his. These days it was all *Star Wars* and intergalactic spin-offs, and it seemed to Milt that the only space-faring black man was a masked fascist with the ventilator voice of James Earl Jones.

His wife shimmied with Sammy. It was hard to feel bad about it. Not many places in this country where a black man, even a famous older brother like Sammy, could waltz around a white woman.

A busboy, last name Fishman, nice college kid from Brownsville, removed Milt's empty tumbler. He offered a generous hello to Nehemiah, bowing as he did. He turned to Milt. Hope it's okay what I told you earlier. It's just a story I heard, and my cousin's a storyteller.

You did right.

Mind if I try a little something out on you?

Fetch a cat a bourbon neat, I'm all ears.

The kid was back before "Lullaby of Bird-land" was through, and Milt half listened to a yarn about a senior gentleman the kid knew who'd started a business making mule-hair toupees. Milt caught the cue the routine was through when the kid was saying, Get it?

Done got.

Fishman shuffled away.

Overhead, the spacey chandeliers shifted, adjusting their orbits, and Milt gave his head a shake, rubbed his dry eyes. At the Standard, most everyone wanted into show business and bad — from the laundry ladies to the waiters on up to Ada — everyone, it seemed, but Milt and Nehemiah. There had been countless discoveries in the Catskills. You got your start on the service side and you were plucked out of obscurity and pushed into the limelight by the fishy hand of Sy Blackstone — house talent scout and booking agent responsible for the Standard airfield, built to fly in senators and starlets — and it took the anointed some time to realize they were still in the service industry, a high-class form of indentured servitude. But the reality didn't matter. They were all — everyone working this room — after the flashbulb fantasy.

Milt could foresee the stunted future

spread before him. Next, the bartender would be telling Sy a version of the mule-hair toupee bit, only a bit better, not so rambling and nervous. Soon Sammy would make it forever his own, confiding the very, very personal anecdote to Johnny Carson on national television, and tens of millions would feel compelled to accompany the late-night laugh track.

Ada's dress — sleeveless, snug, long and black with black sequins — made Milt take a conscious breath, turned him momentarily jealous. What right did he have? He didn't own her. Ada might be dancing with Sammy, might be fucking other men one after the other, or in unison, but she was married to him.

Sammy and Ada shuffle-stepped over the parquet dance floor under the beeping chandeliers reconfiguring themselves into crazy constellations — a whirling Chinook; then Ho Chi Minh himself, complete with grown-out goatee — Ada in the shimmering sheath of a backless dress cut low on her sweet sweetback.

The whole scene about bowled Milt out of his chair. Though it could've been the bourbon gone from his glass again. He signaled to no one, and in a moment his empty tumbler was three-fingers full.

She's the basmalke of the ball, Nehemiah was saying. He sipped his seltzer.

Milt considered his bourbon — he refused to drink white spirits — and shot it burning down the back of his throat. What's that make me, Chema?

You, my son, are a shvartzer schver arbiter. A hard-working Negro. Just like that one over there. But remember. Don't work too hard. Your people worked too hard too long. *Our* work didn't make *us* free. Made us docile. Kept us captive. What makes us free's our leisure. Our rest. Our contemplation, what most in this crowd would call prayer — that's why we observe Shabbos. That's why this place, all this, exists. You come here, you're freed from the expectations. He waved his spotted hand at the throng kept warm by the campy tummler. Look around, Nehemiah said. I've made a safe place for Jews. He brought his hand down on Milt's hand. And friends to the Jews. And anyway, a person's not a Jew because he has faith, but because he asks questions. He gave a squeeze. This is where the inquisitive come to rest. He patted Milt's hand. Even if we can't relax, eh? Practice for the end. That, he said with a raised finger knobby and bent, is the Shabbos. And that is the Standard. He motioned to a cocktail waitress, who discreetly removed Milt's tumbler without asking if he wanted another. But let's not overdo it, eh?

Milt flushed, his cheeks hot. No one could see him blushing, but that didn't lessen his shame. He stood to prove he could, wobbled, steadied himself on the chair back. He tugged down his blazer, buttoned the top of its three buttons.

On Milt's first visit to the Standard, Nehemiah found him a sport coat, helping him into it while telling him those three buttons were to be buttoned, top to bottom, always, sometimes, never. Remember, he said, always, sometimes, never. He brushed Milt's shoulders, patted his cheek and said, Now you can blend in with the Gentiles — they had a good laugh at that, the ice between them more melted than broken. A soldier in dress buttoned every last button.

In ways civil if not martial, Milt had been such a rube when Ada began bringing him up into these Jewish Alps, and here he was, part of the family. Felt more at home at the Standard than in smoldering Bedford-Stuyvesant.

Scuse me, Nehemiah, he said. I'm going to dance your daughter a turn.

You watch that first step. Nehemiah raised his seltzer glass. Hear it's the hardest.

Milt fumbled his way to the dance floor. Took him a long damn time. He parted Sammy and Ada with two hands and said, Husband has his privileges.

Thanks, doll. Looking at Ada with his good eye, he said, Milton, baby, she's all yours. I've got to get back to work anyhow. He caught Milt's glassy eyes with his glass eye. You know as well as me, young blood, Negro's got to earn his keep.

When Sammy was gone, Milt said, I don't trust that Blackstone. When Ada stiffened but didn't respond, Milt tried to instigate her. How'd your meeting go?

Fine.

He gonna get you any auditions?

He already has two lined up.

Lined up.

Both in LA. One sounds like a waste, but one could be good. A Buck Henry show.

You gonna be gone long again?

Couple weeks at most. But it's Buck Henry.

Who is who?

I have one word for you.

Okay.

Plastics.

Plastics?

The Graduate, Milty, Buck Henry wrote *The Graduate.* Maybe we should see a movie without Jim Brown in it every once in a while.

I've got one word for *you*.

Don't ruin this for me. You know my stance on this.

Remind me.

If we can't have a baby, I'm going to have a career.

With their resentments leading, they danced to a song Milt knew from Louis Armstrong and his Hot Seven. When it ended and Sammy strode onstage, the dancers took their seats, all except Milt and Ada, who stood holding each other, she more than him.

Let me tell you a little story, Sammy said, about my Uncle Morey's mule named Vanya. Sammy looked over his shoulder at the band. What? This is true now, so try to stay with me. Each time the beast passed gas, he'd flip back his tail. The tail, man, which was long and full for an old gassy mule, would come to rest atop Morey's bald head. He'd clop down First Avenue with the mule tail obstructing his vision. Sammy splayed his fingers and mimed bangs falling over his forehead. This was some time ago now. The tail, brushing his head like so, made him feel younger, more virile, man. So he shot the mule — pow! Some women

in the audience gasped. What? A mercy killing. Vanya was dying. He had terrible gas.
Put the poor beast out of everyone's misery.
Shoots Vanya and cuts off the dead beast's
tail. From it, man, he fashioned —

Milt said into Ada's ear, Let's go for a
drive.

You can hardly stand.

I'm not driving, you are. Get your purse
and kiss Chema. Meet you at the car. You're
not there in five minutes, I'm going on
without you. He left her standing in the
middle of the dance floor. Shoved out the
side door, hurting with the question he
needed to ask her. By the time he reached
the car, a brand new Oldsmobile Toronado
with power everything, he felt mostly sober
and like he could kill her.

Smith holds the flashlight with one hand
and pulls open the door in the passageway
floor. She shines the flashlight into Milt's
hole. The underground room, higher than it
is wide, with rounded walls, smells like cat
piss and pine tar. Then a thicker smell hits
her. "Jesus." It's like sticking her head into
a sewage tunnel under New York City. She
holds her breath. There's a tree stump
beside a cot. Milt lies curled up, uncovered.

"Milt, can you hear me? Milt. Milt, if you

can hear me, raise a hand." She waits. Nothing. She puts her face farther into the hole. "I'm climbing down to you."

She descends the rungs, jumps to the floor, landing on an alpaca hide that springs a bit beneath her feet. With two fingers, she touches Milt's scruffy neck. Pressing lightly, she feels no pulse. Pressing harder, it registers, but barely, and his skin is damp and freezing.

Milt lay on his back on the king-sized hood and watched summer stars over Vietnam until he heard Ada's heels tocking against asphalt. She was a beautiful, svelte woman who'd taken years of ballet, but she clomped around like a Clydesdale with a clubfoot on cobblestones. It drove him crazy. In the jungle, on patrol, she'd get everyone killed.

Let's not drive, Ada said, let's go to bed.

Have we ever made it in the Toronado?

You can hardly stand and you're talking about screwing in the backseat?

I need to lay down.

You are lying down, Milty. Let's go home and lie down in bed. No driving tonight.

I'm fine, sobered straight up. Nothing like a little rejection to kill a good buzz. He sat upright, stars swirling overhead. He found his feet and made way uneasily to the driver-side door, where he fumbled with the keys to the unlocked car. When he dropped them in the grass, Ada said, Where you planning on driving?

Around. Maybe swing on by the reservoir. Nice night, and we're not gonna have many more like this before the cold's on the ground.

A short drive, then bed.

I'll be back before you know it. He retrieved the keys, got the door open and plunked himself into the seat.

She waited to see if he might pass out as soon as he settled into a comfy chair. When he got the keys in the ignition and turned the car over, she went around to the open driver-side door and said, Slide your drunk stubborn ass over.

"How in hell are we gonna get you out of here?" Smith could recruit a couple more hands and fashion an A-frame, find an old pulley. With the Standard vets, a shared task like that might take a week. She sees the electric lantern and turns it on. "That's better."

She regards the mess that is Milt. Couple days worth of fouling himself. Wan and ashy, cheeks sunken. Flakes in his shaggy goatee with no clean lines. Hair all natty and matted. "You're not gonna be much help are you?" She stands, moves to pull the alpaca hide out from under him but sees how soiled it is. To cover him, she pulls the other alpaca hide off the floor. Beneath it, a cast-iron grate. She lays the hide over him, stands over the grate. Air draws down it. She steps off the grate, squats, grabs hold, and lifts using the strength of her legs. The grate comes up and she slides it aside.

She shines the flashlight down the hole in Milt's hole. A drop of about four feet to a slab floor that gleams with wetness. She pokes down her head. The ammonia of aged urine stings her eyes. She aims the light along a passage that's maybe three feet by three feet.

She goes back to Milt's bedside and tells him she'll be right back. She drops into the tunnel to see where it leads.

Ada's doing 25 in a 45 mph zone. Milt tells her to turn his way — she can't tell left from right. Tonight, this charming quirk of hers is ridiculous. His fury has him blurt the lead-up to the question he can't bring himself to form in his mind, never mind in his mouth: I'm hearing talk about Blackstone.

Talk's what people do best up here.

Milt reaches over, grabs the wheel, and tugs. The tires squeal.

Milton! What are you doing! Ada guides the car back into the lane.

Just a little simulated live-action. Now don't jerk me around, Ada. I'm not as drunk as I seem. I want to know what's going on.

Why don't *you* tell *me.* Tell me why it is you've lured me out here.

Because you're my wife and I don't like what I'm hearing about you and Sy.

Milton, Sy's my agent and a family friend. We go way back. Told you a thousand times, he was my first boyfriend. You know how it is up here with impressionable girls. That was me, fifteen years ago. Sy and I have a history. You're my present and my future.

Don't play me, Ada. I'm not one of your auditions.

She narrows her lined eyes and drives.

One of the busboys has a cousin trying to make it as scriptwriter in LA.

And?

This cousin got invited to a party.

People go to parties in LA, a lot of them, all the time.

At this party, they didn't have a coat check. They had a clothes check. Milt knows he's got her attention because she glances away from the road at him. Do I need to continue or can I leave it to you to pick up where I just left off?

She grits her teeth but doesn't answer.

Milt reaches out and takes hold of the wheel. If you think I won't yank us off this road and straight to our deaths, Ada, then you better buckle your fucking safety belt.

Milton.

You have regrets about marrying you a nigger?

Oh, Milty baby, no, God no. Don't ever say that.

What then? He slides over on the plush seat, part bucket, part bench, and kicks her foot off the accelerator. The car slows for a moment and then he steps on it. The big car pulls forward on the straightaway.

It's too terrible.

He pushes the wheel and veers into the empty oncoming lane. He takes his hand off the steering wheel and steps on the accelerator. You press the brake, I'll gun the gas. We'll wind up upside-down in a ditch.

They tandem drive in silence for a mile, the darkness around them dense as water.

We all do terrible things, Ada. I know that a hell of a lot better than most. Only thing makes it less terrible is if we can tell it. You taught me that.

It was just one thing led to another. A collapse of inhibition. With a little help. Something Sy said was safe. I, he —

Goddamn it, Ada. I knew it. Did Blackstone drug you?

I knew what I was getting into, Milty, more or less. They were handing them out at the door. It wasn't Sy's fault.

Whose then?

Milty, don't make me say it. Just know that I did it and that I promise, on all that is good and just in this world, I'll never do it again. Ever. It was a one-time thing.

This about that movie you made me watch on TV?

What movie?

One where Quincy Jones did the score. *Bob & Bill & Alice & Somebody?*

I forgot about that. Oh, Milton, who am I kidding? I'm never gonna catch a break. Sy's just humoring me for the Standard contract, but booking the hotel isn't what it used to be. Once the money dries up he's not gonna bother trying to find me silly sci-fi roles passed up by the likes of Ms. Van Dyke.

What are we talking about now?

We're talking about how we, you and I, slept, together, through the sexual revolution.

You want to swing, that it?

No I do not want to swing.

Cause if you want to swing, I can swing, baby. You know how many JAPS come practically begging for me to drip some honey in they honeycombs?

Milton, you'll never forgive me so just try to forget it.

He stomped the accelerator and they leaned back in their seats. No such thing as forgetting.

Milton!

He yanked the steering wheel and the two passenger-side tires skipped onto the grassy shoulder. Start talking, Ada. How many men?

At some point, I lost count.

I'm gonna be sick.

There were people making love everywhere.

That's what you were doing, making love?

It was a sex party. An orgy. Sex not love. Anonymous. Everyone wore sheer hoods. It was creepy. You could see out but not in. We all looked like naked executioners. That was the point. Part of the theme. The invitation welcomed guests to *Execute Inhibition.*

Sounds like my draft card.

Everything doesn't have to come back to Vietnam, Milton.

Hooded hooker at the receiving end of a gang bang? Sounds like My Lai fucking foreplay to me. He rolled down the window. Now I'm picturing the mess they must've made of you.

Don't, Milton.

Cunt overflowing with come. Were you getting two pricks at once? We know you take it up the ass like a pro.

If you really want all the gruesome details, I'll fucking oblige you.

Just tell me one thing. Did Sy get in line?

Sy was Sy.

What's that mean?

Means he watched and, afterward, lectured.

On what?

Some pet theory of his.

And how can you be sure Sy wasn't in line if everyone was in hoods?

When she didn't respond, he stepped on the gas.

Cause he and I used to be lovers, Milton. You know that. Besides, he's got the body of a parsnip. I'd have known if Sy Blackstone was fucking me up the ass.

You know, you're typecast for a reason. And you get no leads because you're shallow. Deepest thing about you's your twat. Which you'll sell on the cheap for some shitty bit-part in some sci-fi sitcom. But don't worry, Ada, cause if you don't get that one, I'm sure Sy's got some smut lined up for you behind the green door opposite Johnnie Keyes.

Johnnie who?

When Milt didn't answer, she said, He the black fellow giving it to Marilyn Chambers in that porno? He still didn't respond, and when she said, Careful of that deer, he pressed the accelerator to the floor.

Smith climbs back out of the tunnel and pulls Milt sitting upright. "Can you stand for me?"

He leans on an elbow. His eyes meet hers but he's not seeing her.

"I'm gonna have to get you out of here through your latrine."

He mumbles something, and she tells him to speak up.

"Careful of that deer."

"Careful of what, darling, your latrine?"

His look focuses on her for the first time. "Don't let me go back there. To Ada. I'm ready to be done." He nods. With tears in his eyes, he reaches and cups her breast.

"Come now, Milt, now's not the time to get frisky on me."

"Please."

"Stop, Milt."

"I promise, I'll never touch another

drink." He fumbles with the button on her pants.

"Milt, don't."

"Please, Ada. It's been so long, and I'm so sorry."

She leans in, not shutting her eyes, and, this close, Milt's eyes merge, forming a third. His goatee tickles her lips, his breath so bad his head seems yellow. He needs her help, she needs his. She kisses him, then comes up for a breath of air. "Come on, you old dog." She heaves him to his boots.

After a moment, he regains some of himself. He helps her help him into the drain tunnel. They make awkward way with the electric lantern. To distract him, and herself, she tells him she's solved the mystery of the missing alpaca. When he responds by saying what mystery? She says: "I found out who took E. Prince."

"Ray."

"That's right, Ray. How'd you —"

"While back," he says, "told him he could take some extra hides for a shelter he wanted to make. Told him he could have E. Prince to keep him company. Said he'd take him to keep from starving. Said if someone was going to kill E. Prince, he wanted to be the one."

They come into the old coal powerhouse.

Outside, the snow has stopped.

When Vessey returned from the hospital with the van, he was forced to climb out and salt the first two switchbacks. He couldn't get up the third. He waded through snow the rest of the way, found Smith waiting for him with Milt in front of Standard Tower, which seemed to be leaning a few degrees farther.

They were both filthy and stinking. "You two look —"

Smith shook her head. "That woman die?"

"Not yet." Vessey touched Milt's cheek, Milt's white whiskers rasping under Vessey's rough thumb. "Oh, Milt, my brother from another mother." Vessey looked at Smith through full eyes. "To the ER again? This another emergency?"

"He's sort of in and out. Responsive one minute, delirious the next. Confused. Keeps saying, No sir, Mr. Davis."

Milt mumbled, nodded.

"Hate to go right back. Feel like I barely got out of there. Closest VA Medical Center's in Castle Point. Another one down in Montrose." He checked Milt over, pushing on a few internal organs. "We should get him cleaned up. Change of clothes. Both of

you. Man, you stink. What've you been doing?"

"Don't ask."

"Both VAs are a little over an hour drive,"
Vessey told her.

"The van?"

"On one of the switchbacks. Not stuck
just won't climb. We'll sled her down. It'll
be fun. Come on. I'm thinking Castle Point.
They do a good job treating our Lyme
disease. Defoliate us with antibiotics. Milt's
oncologist's there."

"To a VA? Vess, they'll arrest me."

"I'm beat, Smith."

She closed her eyes.

"They're very discreet there with our
guys," he told her.

She, too, touched Milt's scruffy cheek,
and when he didn't respond to the touch,
she said, "Okay."

"That'a girl. How've things been here otherwise?"

"Stone and Luce bolted. Said it'd rained
bats in the Alpine village. Don't think they'll
be back. Both said their goodbyes to Milt.
He didn't even blink."

"Everyone else?"

"The four fucking corners."

Once they were on the interstate, Vessey

said, "Had a hard time explaining to the cops how it was I had tampons on me to stanch the blood."

"What'd you say?"

"First cop I talked to wasn't interested. Little later, a lady detective showed up and lit into me. Told her they're wonderful fire-starters. Showed her the place in my sardine tin where I kept them. She bought it, even though she was suspicious about the mountain lion."

"Wasn't a Florida panther?"

"Detective made a call to someone at the DEP. When she got off the phone, she wasn't gonna let me go. Think I was a suspect for about an hour there. Nurse came out after the first surgery, before they airlifted her to Vassar Brothers. Detective giving me heat backed off, a bit. Said they found a broken piece of tooth near her collarbone, piece of claw caught in her watchband, what looked like antler lodged in her pelvis. They were gonna run tests to make sure. Asked me if she might've been gored first by a buck. Told her hell if I know, and they let me go. Lady detective even called me a hero. Said it looked like she was gonna live if she survived all the surgeries. I said, You got the wrong guy. All I did was some field nursing. She said they'd be coming by

346

some time in the next few days to question everybody. Love to make you anxious with anticipation. Now this?" He unclipped his seatbelt, climbed into the back.

In the rearview, Smith watched Vessey take Milt's pulse.

At Castle Point, Vessey and Smith signed in Milt. They waited with him in Triage, Vessey answering the questions he could, and then more waiting in Admittance, until Milton Wright was called and the nurse saw he couldn't make it under his own power.

Smith wheeled Milt in and Vessey followed. They were ushered into an overflow care center, a gurney surrounded by curtains, where they waited. Three different nurses — all with the same puffy face floating above the V-neck of their scrubs — came and went.

An hour passed before they saw an internist who seemed to know Milt and have familiarity with his medical history. He introduced himself as Sudeep Mehta, MD, Oncology, Hospice and Palliative Specialist, asked about Milt's recent behavior, and Smith did the answering this time. Dr. Mehta nodded, took notes, and then said he was going to run tests, MRI, CAT scan, that there was an outside chance he was just critically dehydrated, but so far — he opened Milt's eyelids, studied one, than the other — so far he hasn't responded to the fluids at all. His best guess was that Milt's cancer had metastasized to his brain. "If that's the case, at most, at best, we're talking a matter of weeks."

"At worst?"

Dr. Mehta shook his head. "We'll take him for tests now. We should know more in a couple hours. You're free to stay."

Vessey said, "You bet your ass we'll stay."

Minutes later, Milt was wheeled away, and Smith and Vessey dozed in their chairs. Some time after that, Milt was wheeled back in, sedated. He'd been thoroughly washed and was wearing a gown. When Smith asked for an update, the orderly told them that Dr. Mehta would be back shortly. In the meantime, the cafeteria was in the basement.

An hour after they ate, they were given Milt's prognosis. His cancer had indeed metastasized to his brain. The MRI revealed a constellation of tumors, acorn size and smaller. The CAT scan showed a larger tumor on the brain stem, size of a golf ball, with a smaller piggyback tumor grown on it. "Tumors on top of tumors," the doctor said. "Not good. We've induced a medical coma, and his advance directives strictly forbid life support of any kind. We've contacted his health proxy. Now all we can do is wait."

"Wait for what?"

"The end I'm afraid."

Two days later, Vessey and Bellum sat at Milt's bedside, each holding a hand, trying to help him over, though they were the ones needing help. The painstaking, interminable conclusion to Milt's breathing was like labor in reverse. The contractions of his respiration grew gradually, terribly farther apart. When Milt took a breath, Vessey and Smith held theirs. Hours of anticipation, exacerbated by the beep of the EKG. A nurse came in and muted the machine. Milt's breath came and went, once every ten minutes or more. Half an hour passed. No breath followed. The line on the heart monitor was a horizon Milt had gone beyond. What marked his end was a stillness that ached and drummed in the two living bodies sitting vigil, a pair of lives left in the tumultuous wake of the passing of a life called Milton Xavier Wright.

Vessey and Smith visited Ira Lependorf, Esq., and when Ira greeted them from behind the reception desk, Smith said, "What, still no secretary?"

"These days," he snapped, "they're called legal aids. Apparently they don't make them like they used to. You don't happen to be looking for a job? Could use the order and organization of someone with a military background." He offered them a seat and told them Milton expressly stated he wanted no service, no military burial, not even so much as a toast to him. He's to be cremated, and he left no instructions for his ashes. He asked if they might want the cremains, and Vessey said fuck yes.

Ira said that every vet who'd ever been in residence at the Standard was mentioned in the will, including you two, but that sorting through what's ultimately left will take time. He also said that an offer had been made on the Standard, by a lawyer out of Kingston brokering for SW&B Construction, but it's low. Standing timber alone is worth more. Looks like SW&B are fishing, see if we bite to avoid the bureaucratic slog. If they can't get it for dirt cheap, they'll take their chances at the foreclosure auction. So we'll see what happens, and it's bound to take awhile. Questions so far?

She asked, "Was Milt stealing from his vets?"

"How do you mean?"

"I mean all the disability. Was he secreting it away into some offshore account?"

Ira shot Vessey a who's-this-crazy-bitch look; Vessey shrugged and leaned away from Smith.

"Let me give you some idea," Ira told Smith, "of what it's been to be the executor of Milt's estate, and things are only getting started. In his will, Milt stipulated that, after liquidation, which may take for fucking ever, I will get paid for a decade's worth of back-fees. That's first. After that, with what's left over, he wants to reimburse his vets for all the disability they paid in. I've done some prelim figuring, plugging in estimates, and I've found that if I write my fees off as pro bono — which is not simply out of the kindness of my heart, because I get a nice tax break — then after every last one of Milt's vets gets back every last dime they paid him for their billet, there might be a few thousand dollars left over. Could be significantly more, could be a lot less. Depending on the foreclosure. On the logging. On and on. I won't bore you. But you, Ms. Antebellum Smith — if that is indeed your name — should know that in his order of payments, after all the veterans' disability reimbursements, you're next. Now I've given myself a year to locate the hundred-plus beneficiaries. Which'll be like finding a queef in a typhoon. You know what a queef is? And where the fuck do I send checks to homeless men? I'm sure I'll go mostly to their next-of-kin. Whatever's left after a year, assuming that everything's been liquidated by then, will go to you. So to answer your question, no, he wasn't stealing from his fucking vets."

"And what about his wife?"

"Was he stealing from Ada?"

"Was he responsible for her death?"

"You're asking me if Milton was a murderer?"

"I guess I am."

"That I can't tell you, doll. That he took to his maker."

Smith drives the van to visit Evangelína at Vassar Brothers in Poughkeepsie, where she's kindly turned away after dropping off the woman's belongings, including a corporate document, thick as a phone book, in a gallon freezer bag. A nurse who helped with the surgeries — three of the four — informs her that Ms. Canek's in critical condition, and the nurse isn't allowed to say more. She then confides that when Ms. Canek was mauled, there was a perforation of her appendix. Appendix leaked bacteria into the abdominal cavity. Caused peritonitis, a serious infection. Performed a subtotal. Left in the cervix. Able to save the ovaries and fallopian tubes. The neck wounds were easy by comparison. And somehow she managed to rupture her Achilles. She's gonna have trouble talking and eating for a few months, and the scarring can be lessened with plastic surgery if she wants. "But the hardest thing," the nurse said, glancing over her shoulder, "hardest thing to recover from's the . . . well, I've already said more than I should."

"What are you gonna do now, Vess?"

"Squat here with Merced, Wiz, and whoever else till they toss us. You?"

"Thinking about going up to Reverend's camp. Maybe stay the winter with him, if he'll have me."

"He got on all right with STD," Vessey told her. "Merced was weird about him. All the other guys never liked him. Can't say I really did either. Something just plain off about him. But you know what? He'd get down on all fours and spend half an hour rolling around in the dirt with Egon, playing, wrestling, but gentle, careful of Egon's hips. By the end of it, that dog would be on his back, exhausted and ecstatic. Egon listened to me, because I fed him, but that dog loved him some Reverend."

Smith finds Ray's camp empty. After the monster nor'easter, there was a couple weeks of Indian summer, but the air's cold again, the last two nights getting hard frost.

Searching out the sound of running water she heard on her way up, she finds a rivulet drizzling between two rounded rocks. The moss growing on them is iced over, the rocks like a pair of small biospheres. A shin-high waterfall splashes into a mosaic blue-stone washbasin, its little dam built to hold a couple gallons of water before it continues on its way downmountain. She dips in her fingertip and it aches with the cold.

The yurt is warm. No fire burns in the woodstove but it's still throwing heat. She sets her sidearm by the door flap, a new hide, and relights the fire using a couple of smoldering coals. Once it's blazing, she strips off her clothes, soiled stiff, sour and gamey. She washes them at the brookhead basin and, naked, her teeth chattering, she rinses herself. Dashing back to the yurt, she hangs her clothes on the line. She hopes Ray will understand them as a white flag. She sits at the fireside and dons the earmuffs she brought with her. They smell like her half-rotting clothes. She feels ridiculous, desperate — what a shitty little planet — but the fur atmosphere enveloping her is a creature comfort like none she's ever known. She's sheltered in the hides of animals Milt cared for. Standard Company has disbanded, yet this yurt stands as a monument. She doesn't care if Ray poached every last alpaca to make it so. Doesn't care if he's a merc, a spy, a killer. She's made it this long, mostly on her own, and she needs some warm companionship.

Woken by a scratching sound, Smith thinks the cougar's come for her. She scrambles for her sidearm, unholsters it and waits. The sounds move around the camp, then fade.

She dresses, not bothering to tie her boots, finds the two coon kits, bigger, roughhousing at the foot of a white pine. They see her and scramble trilling into the woods. She follows them to Ray's field of toppled cairns. He hasn't restacked a stone. On a slab, she sets down her sidearm, starts righting the rocks. Hours pass before a dog bark makes her jump, and the cairn between her knees crashes down, a rock smashing the toe of her boot. She curses, hops, and there's Ray. He barks again, then whines, and the first thing that comes out of her is an aching apology.

He says what she hears as, "Hocus fogey."

Thinking of Milt — magical, old; disappeared, dead — and knowing she's misheard, she replays the sounds in her head until they become *Hope is phony.* She nods, near tears.

"My favorite place in all the world."

"What is," she says, "hope is phony?"

He laughs, and she laughs. He says, "Opus 40."

"Oh."

He nods and smiles, his eyes and shoulders rising at their edges along with the corners of his mouth. He's smiling with his entire body, at her, and she knows in her full chest she's forgiven, knows in her tired feet she's welcome, knows in her butterflied pelvis she could come to love this man. She steps toward him and her toe throbs.

"Opus 40's not far," he says, and there's her invitation, implicit but unmistakable.

She sees them wintering here, stacking stones and making daytrips, and it's not as if she never stormed off — never called him a whore and told him to go to hell — and yet it's okay anyway. She gets the sense that as soon as she said sorry — saying so while trying to right one of her wrongs — everything between them was settled, and not just for the moment. "I want to see it," she says. "Opus 40, whatever it is."

"Now?"

"Or not now. Later. We have time."

"We do?"

She shrugs and smiles, a warm flush filling her chest.

He says, "I'm no longer under contract."

She nods, then shakes her head. She feels happy, lucky; she feels like dying.

"Hope isn't phony," he says.

She nods.

"Heard about the landman."

She gives another nod.

"My lawyer told me."

She wants to say something, but if she opens her mouth she's afraid she'll scream.

"And Merced came up here and told me about you and the cougar. Guess you were right about what you saw."

She shrugs.

"What?"

She shakes her head.

"Wright?"

The tears come like an unyielding wall of water displaced deep in her, pushed out.

He picks up a stone roughly the size of a brick, and she waits, hands on knees, for him to bash her brains. The thought is crazy, and she can't help it.

He takes her hand, isolates a finger, places it on the rough gray rock. "Feel that?"

She wipes her eyes.

"You're running your finger over the head of a newborn. It's pediatric phrenology."

"Who the fuck are you?"

"Feel. Like reading Braille. A ridge that has three rises. A crevice, a nook. Anything that takes a triangular shape. You want a triangle for the same reason you want a three-legged stool. Three legs are more stable."

The more he talks, the better she feels. "You always talk like this?"

"Never talk like this. Don't have no one to talk to."

She laughs through her mucus.

"Want me to shut up now?"

"Please no."

"At Opus 40 — old bluestone quarry in Saugerties turned six-acre sculpture. It's drystone. No mortar. All made by one guy, Harvey Fite, over almost forty years. Somewhere into year twenty, he erected a nine-ton, fifteen-foot pillar at the center. Monster of a bluestone monolith. Rock like an exclamation point. Been standing for over half-a-century. He died at the site, fell off a ledge he —"

She kisses him. His beard is full and scratchy and she loves the coarseness of it, how it scours her skin, the smoke-oil odor in it. She takes his hand and pulls him to his camp, into his yurt, where they spend the night, the rest of the fall, and most of the winter.

■ ■ ■ ■

WINTER
2012

■ ■ ■ ■

They sleep spooned near the woodstove, Ray waking to feed the fire, she waking to watch.

Tell me about your tattoos.

Little intense pain in the moment. Makes you forget a whole load of past hurt. Problem is, don't last so you got to get another.

I see your meat tag. She touches his ribcage just below his left armpit, nine numbers overtop the letters *A NEG.*

We didn't wear dog tags. Too noisy.

Now I can steal your identity.

You can have it.

Our blood's compatible. I'm A-pos. What about this one? *We are shadows of . . . tendon fury?*

Tender. Gave myself that one. And this one over here.

You draw?

A little. Or used to. Painted a few T-walls in my time. Painted our unit's rock at

Painted Rocks when we trained at Fort Irwin.

Liked my time there. Almost got a tattoo off-base in — what's the town's name?

Feel like you're testing me.

Well.

Barstow.

Test passed. You give me a tattoo?

Maybe.

How you feel about dogs?

This is getting serious.

Well.

Think I've reached the stage where I'm more fond of animals than people. Part of the reason I'm up here. Rather have the company of a couple of rambunctious raccoons.

Naked in the warm yurt, they regard each other. For an instant, he seems virginal, tearful.

To be able to look on you like this? See you all so beautifully . . . together?

I'm smelly and hairy and, top it all off, on my period.

You're talking to a fellow soldier.

What's that supposed to mean?

I don't feel at ease unless someone's spilled a little blood.

Well I might mess your yurt.

We're pissing, crapping, bleeding beasts. Squeamishness over menstrual blood? That's crazy. Specially coming from a woman. It's the same sexist insanity of Sharia. To make menstruation an embarrassment? That's terrible. Sight of blood's a reminder of what we're made, how fragile we are. Nice to see some on occasion that's a sign of the potential for life. Instead of its end.

Okay.

Okay what?

You can fuck me now.

You got family?

Mother finishing out a life sentence behind the counter of a 7-Eleven. Two younger brothers. One's in East Jersey State, other at Monmouth University.

Good they're both getting education.

East Jersey State's a max security penitentiary. Once known as Rahway. Monmouth's more like a debtors' prison than a college. When I left for my first tour, my brothers spiraled straight down. Think I might've done to them just like our father did to us.

The first orgasm she has with Ray feels like one of those psychic surgeries performed in the Philippines: it's as if he goes in with bare hands and removes a mass from her. After that, they come easier, better, and their lovemaking — some hours long, some an intense minute, some all the increments in between — is the most satisfying of her promiscuous life.

In Iraq, when I was working for Zeitgeist, I bought a Russian Ural 650. Cost me 5 million dinars. The Fedayeen Saddam ordered a couple thousand of the bikes just before the invasion. Time the shipment arrived, Saddam was down in his hideyhole. Bikes were sold off one by one. Mine had a sidecar. Couldn't pay people to ride in it. Ural's a rugged, reliable little bike. Comes with two felt-lined clips in the sidecar to hold your AK. Used to ride it around the streets of Sadr City. Shiite slum that takes up most of eastern Baghdad. You put on a helmet, full face-guard, tinted, full beard growing out the bottom, and they don't know you're not Iraqi. You're nimble. Traffic in Baghdad got to be terrible. On a little bike, midsize engine, you come to feel safer even though you're exposed. Skirting lines of cars, threading through the lanes. Sitting still's the killer. Been in a fully armored personnel carrier, the Grizzly 6×6, V-hull chassis, 12.7 millimeter machine gun mounted on top operated from a remote weapon station. Felt less safe cause we were stuck in traffic. My days off, I'd ride over to the Mohsin Mosque, cut the engine. Wait for the adhan. Then he'd call the iqama, the summons, and 10,000-plus men came in carrying prayer mats for the outdoor sermon. The imam would start the prayer, and one little voice would call back, and then another, and then 10,000 voices were chanting in unison. Never failed to raise the hair. Was thrilling, and not a little frightening. Once I started empathizing with the men who were trying to kill me, knew I'd lost my edge.

With my daddy and my husband, my feelings didn't matter much. What mattered was making them feel good. But Milt? Milt made me feel good about myself —
You fuck him?
Don't. You didn't let me finish. And don't be like that. I've had enough of that kind of disrespect from the men in my life. Milt made me feel good about myself, but I don't want to just feel good. Makes the world a damn lonely place. You, you make me feel good about the place. Feel like things might just be okay for once.

He allows himself to imagine a future for them. This allowance feels dangerous, deadly even, something he spent years daring never do, look ahead. In this future, he and Bellum tour the Blue Ridge Mountains in a spring season breaking like a warm, rideable wave.

With all the fucking we're doing, we've got to talk about birth control.

Why?

And I thought you operators made plans to make plans. My periods haven't been regular, but pulling out's gonna get me an abortion. Don't want to go through that again.

In high school?

Right before my first tour. Military facilities only do abortions to save the mother's life. It was either Planned Parenthood, seek a pregnancy discharge — which isn't automatic anymore — or stay home with Travis and have his baby while the 321st went to war without me. I chose Iraq. Pro-life I guess I aint.

Here's the difference between us and them,

and I'm not talking about all of them, just talking about the men. Our men kill women and kids, same as they do, but women and kids are not primary targets. With their suicide bombs and passenger-jet missiles, they set out to kill women and kids. To them, there are no innocents. Infants are infidels first. Cut off their little heads with kitchen knives and be sure to videotape it with your phone and beam it to Al Jazeera. That's what we're fighting. That's the mission of the jihadi. And it's that prehistory attitude, after a decade of war against it, that some of the weaker elements of the US military succumb to. I'm talking about the Staff Sergeant Gibbs and the other pawns from the Stryker brigade stationed at fob Ramrod, murdering Afghan civilians for sport, taking fingers for trophies, snapping pictures with a kill like it's a four-point buck. War's the greatest intimacy. We get bashed in the press for not knowing the culture, and maybe that was true at the outset, but very quickly you get to know your enemy or you get killed. You meet them at their most essential. How they wash, what they wear, when they eat, where they shit, and why they fight. Learning these things keeps you alive and makes you a better-prepared soldier. Most of the guys and gals on the front line know their enemy better than they know their spouses. That's what we have to confront when we come home.

I've got a plan.

If you're making plans that involve me, I better damn well be on the planning committee.

We take a road trip. First stop, Jersey.

Atlantic City?

Highlands. Take you to meet my mother.

You're not serious.

Dead serious. I haven't seen her in, oh, five or so years.

Okay.

Then we go down to Key West. Spend a little time.

You know I'm one of those Floridians who's never been.

Well this'll be new then.

Why Key West?

I want to ride from the southernmost point in the US to the northernmost. Want to see the whole shebang and everything in between.

Northernmost point somewhere in Maine?

I want to go corner to corner. All the way to Deadhorse, Alaska. Farthest north you can drive on Alaska's road system. The route that takes you through as little of

Canada as possible's about 6,000 miles. Supposed to be some 150 hours of driving, give or take. Called the Iron Butt Ultimate Coast to Coast Challenge.

And in what kind of vehicle do we make this ass-numbing road trip across America?

Not in, on. A motorcycle. And I want to make detours. Three detours.

We could visit my daddy.

That's what I was thinking.

My daddy, and then Travis, to serve divorce papers.

That's stop three.

And in between?

Fort Knox.

No.

You can't go confronting your husband with your deserter wrap hanging over you.

Hell. The fuck. No.

Can't get to Alaska without going through Canada. Rather not have to make an illegal border crossing coming and going.

Can't we just go to the tip of Washington State?

We could, but that doesn't solve the problem of your husband, which doesn't solve the problem of birth control, which doesn't solve the problem of my marrying you if and when you get pregnant.

And when we gonna start this road trip?

Come spring. Road to Deadhorse is impassable in winter.

I'm not spending 6,000 miles on the back of no fucking bike.

I will.

You'll ride bitch.

I'm man enough.

Be serious.

We'll get a sidecar.

And our gear?

Ok, two side cars.

We gonna have a lot of gear?

One for our gear, one for your dog.

You gonna get me a new dog?

I'm gonna get you your dog.

Fucking could not understand why so many fucking Iraqis just would not stop at the fucking checkpoints. We were lighting up cars of women and kids. Fucking kids. Couldn't imagine what they were thinking. Big signs, bigger guns. They kept right on fucking coming. The fuck? Know what we realized? They couldn't see. Fuckers. No one could afford glasses or eye exams. Didn't stop them from fucking driving but it stopped them from fucking stopping when we wanted them the fuck to stop. So they got shot. It's all so stupid as fuck.

■ ■ ■ ■

During an early January warm spell, Ray comes into camp from a forage with a handful of spindly mushrooms, what he says are Phrygian caps.

Found them in the empty alpaca paddock. Most of the animals are gone from the Standard. A few rabbits and chickens left.

Hope Vessey's all right.

Studies show psychedelics help with anxiety and battle stress.

Feed me, Seymour.

Bellum stands dreamily, fuck-drunk, her posture regimented even when at ease, even when exhausted. She'd been a good soldier, he sees that. She makes him attentive, keeps him from clicking out, prevents the vibes of the yurt walls from becoming the indifferent cosmos, the two of them in karmic orbit around the radiant idol at the far end, the woodstove, indistinct, mute, omniscient.

All this time together, and he hasn't considered the best way to off her. Hasn't even occurred to him. Maybe that's a soldier's love. Being with someone you can't think to kill.

She's something else for sure, reminds

him of no other woman he's known. He pulls her down, and she rolls on her belly.

No need to be gentle.

Yes, ma'am.

My daddy was abusive. Mostly growing up, it was verbal. He's mean, and creative with his meanness. When I was a girl, he'd lash me, hard, with a fan belt. As I got older, he seemed to get meaner. What I remember most is the last time he got rough. Grabbed me between my legs. Said, Grrl, they don't call this a snatch for nothing. You don't start behaving, stop screwing round with them niggers, I'm gonna be the one to give it you and it aint gonna be pretty. He never did, but the threat of it felt real fucking real. And his threat worked. I stopped seeing Lamar. I was sixteen, and the next day I started planning to get out. Went to the ROTC office at school and joined up. Second I graduated, I was off to boot camp.

I've got some sexual abuse in my past.

What, you date rape some poor girl in high school?

My brothers and me had a babysitter, Jimmer. His dad owned an arcade on the boardwalk. Italian kid, fourteen, fifteen. I was all of six or seven, which made my brothers five and three, thereabouts. Started off Jimmer showing us porn mags. It was instructive, you know. Educational. This is a pussy. This is a penis. This is how they fit together. This is a blow job, this, anal sex. Then we got a lesson on how to masturbate. We were told to touch his come. To taste it. If we refused, we got punched. We had to jerk ourselves off. I was having dry orgasms. Boys don't produce semen till they hit puberty. This all happened over a couple years. A slow schooling. I eventually graduated to jerking him off. Him humping my butt while I wore my undies. There was never any penetration, not that I remember. My younger brothers had smaller roles. I got the lead, which was a theme of my childhood. Abusive babysitters, my mom's abusive boyfriends, her headcase of a second husband, they all keyed in on me, the oldest. Then I trickled it down to my little brothers. Ass kickings, mind you, never anything sexual. My molestation didn't make me a molester. Isn't true what they say. Molested grow up to be molesters. Cycle of child abuse is a myth. Makes a good story, easy, but that don't make it true. Fact is, there're far more child molesters out there who were never molested. Mine made me supersensitive to the slightest suggestion of sexual abuse, and maybe to everything else. Don't relate to sex the same way other men do. Made me a bit of an outcast in the service. Sex for me's more emotional, more complicated, than for most men. Never had me a one-night stand.

How many women you fucked?

Six. My wife was the last, before you. You?

Women? Just one.

And men?

You will think me an absolute slut. I never needed to feel love in order to fuck.

You earned the right of a little promiscuity after eons of sexual repression.

That's kind.

So what are we talking? A regiment?

I always confuse brigade and regiment. Regiment's a thousand?

That's a battalion. Regiment and brigade's the same thing, three to five K.

Nice. But no. I'm easy but I'm not a professional near to retirement.

A company?

This little game's making for some unflattering images. But no, not a company.

Company's what — it's been a while — 62 to 190?

Say a platoon that's taken some losses.

Platoon's 16 to 44. I can live with that.

That's where this is going, a number you

can live with?

For the rest of my natural life.

Why don't you tell me about your wife?

My second tour, we were in Baghdad, doing night raids. Couple months earlier, during the invasion, we seized the Haditha Dam on the Euphrates. Night raids were a Sunday walk by comparison. Got some skewed intel. Stormed the house of a nice family in the al-Dura neighborhood. We called it Dora. Scared the bejesus out of a striking young woman coming out of her bedroom. She had a kid brother, three younger sisters, a mother. No father. They were scraping by, and only just. Youngest girl, Larsa, had scurvy. I started bringing them food a few times a week, lots of citrus, would eat dinner with them when I could. Graduated to hounding a couple of neighbors challenging their claim on their house. They were squatting in their own home, feeling the squeeze. They were Iraqi Christians. Chaldo-Assyrians they call themselves. Maryam was eighteen. I was twenty. Knew each other less than a month — she was helping me with my Arabic — when I asked her to marry me. Told her it'd have to be secret. You know. US CENTCOM forbids intimate relations with foreign and local nationals. I'd've lost my security clearance. She probably wanted it kept secret more than me. She told me, Mumkin. Mumkin became my nickname for her. Means maybe. Rajaa'an, I said. I'm begging. She answered, Na'am.

Yes, a formal yes.

Month later, we had a secret wedding. Small ceremony in Amman. Didn't bother to tell my mom or brothers. They still have no idea I was ever married.

This is incredible.

Nah. Had a war bride. Used to be one of the reasons we went to war. Freshen the bloodlines, stir up the gene pool.

It's so . . . romantic.

Yeah, well, four-year tour was getting close to done. This was '04. Things were getting worse. *Sectarian violence* we called it. Don't have to tell you. All-out civil war at that point. Neighborhoods being ethnically cleansed by death squads. Plain genocide, no bones about it. But the Christian neighborhoods in Baghdad — Mansour, Baladiyat, Dora, al-Sana — were mostly left alone. In Mosul, things were already getting bad for Christians. They fled for Baghdad. It wasn't yet like it was in '10, when that kill squad from the Islamic State of Iraq stormed the Cathedral of Our Lady of

Salvation, taking three priests hostage before offing fifty-plus worshipers. If you're a practicing Catholic, guess there's no better place to die. ISI didn't stop there. Families of the mourners hung funeral signs outside their homes. Follow-up squads used the signs as targets for their mortars. But in '04, we weren't ready. No precedent. Went to check on them one night. Like most nights. Were my in-laws by then. There was a couple of old women there, cooking keşkek, Iranian dish, and cleaning up bloodstains. Dumped their stew all over the freshly mopped floors before they told me the whole family'd been hooded and hauled off. Men in Iraqi police uniforms. I'm not squeamish, but what they found of her, of them, even to this day.

Took leave afterward. Followed one cold trail after another. Almost got myself a still on Dead TV. Three weeks went by. Camped out at the Baghdad morgue. They'd just opened the screening room. Four computers and a flat-screen television arranged in front of rows of blue plastic chairs. Saddest damn audience you ever seen. Image after image of Fulan al-Fulani and Fulana al-Fulaniyya. Unidentified Iraqi murder victims, John and Jane Does. They flash by, each image lasting no longer than a heartbeat. Blue-faced men who've been hand-cuffed, gagged and tortured. Headless corpses, corpses without limbs. Bulging eyes. Bullet holes. Burnt faces, frozen mid-scream. Want me to stop?

Yes, but don't.

Wives and husbands, mothers and fathers, they wait for their turn in the screening room. They'd pass out and throw up. Shake and wail. Guy smashed the back window. One of the employees I would talk to said at first his nightmares were of the lifeless bodies, but they'd gotten worse. Worse? I said. How could they get any worse? They'd become the faces of the families watching every day. So I get a call. They tell me they found a bag. I said, What do you mean a bag. They said, A bag. Only parts, but we've identified one of the sisters. Go down there, and it's not even in the main building. In a portable, one of those cooler cars like a dou-blewide. They tell me they're not bringing the bag out till I sit, like a good dog. They set this Hefty bag between my boots. Looks filled with soccer balls. One guy's tearing up.

Oh, god.

Open it, paw through looking for Maryam's face. Didn't see it. See her brother and three kid sisters. Girls were nine, six, and five. Keep moving them aside. The two morgue guys are getting antsy now. I dump the contents on the floor. Heads roll. The morgue guys step back. Among the parts are two pair of breasts. I could tell which were Maryam's.

Oh, Ray.

Mahdi Army drilled holes through them. Way the blood coagulated, they'd done the drilling while they were alive. Week later, bodies of Maryam and her mother — what was left — were found in with a dozen others. Empty peacock cage at the Baghdad Zoo.

If I'm gonna be the one spending all my time in the thing, shouldn't I have some say?

First off, we'll split the driving. I'm gonna be spending as much time in the sidecar as you. Number two, I'm paying. Number three, the sidecar I have in mind's one I've wanted for a long damn time, I've just never had justification to spend the seventy-five hundred.

Where you gonna get that kind of money?

I have money.

We could buy another bike for that.

A used bike that runs on tamari and would only give us problems.

You sound like my daddy. I can't believe you've had a bike in storage all this time. Let's go get ice cream.

You're gonna love it. Sidecar's a Steib S500. Looks like a *Flash Gordon* rocket. You climb in, you'll feel like Major "King" Kong riding the bomb backwards into oblivion.

This Major Kong one of your Ranger COs?

Character in *Dr. Strangelove.* You never seen *Dr. Strangelove?* Every soldier should see *Dr. Strangelove* as part of Basic.

We catch flack for Abu Ghraib. Expected to be above the fray while in the thick of it, while instigating it. Doesn't work like that. Poor Lynndie.

Lynndie's a dumb cunt who got what she deserved.

Rumsfeld deserves what she got.

Rumsfeld deserves what your wife got.

Nobody deserves that shit. Not even the people who did it to her. Taken me all these years to be able to say that. Not saying they don't deserve punishment. That they're not guilty of war crimes. All I'm saying, for me to move on, to stay sane if not whole, I've had to try to understand their motives. Try to sympathize, sick as that sounds.

You're either a better person than I am or

you're a bigger pussy.

This, sweetheart, this is me just trying to justify my cowardice after getting burnt out. But you got to find a way to keep open to the world. And the people in it. Even the people doing terrible things. Maybe them most of all. Because, as you know, anyone can do a terrible thing you put them in a warzone. Any fucking one. Difference between your martyr and your insurgent's a matter of choosing sides. Can only imagine what the final hours of their lives were like. Spent the last however many years trying not to. Finally realized I've got to, imagine I mean, in order to put them to rest.

Ray wakes in a sweat, alone. He dresses shivering outside the yurt. It takes him minutes to remember Bellum's gone to the Standard for the day to check on Vessey.

While she's away, he's responsible for ordering their sidecar. On the hike down, he visits the salon in the village before placing his conspicuous call. He finds that Crystal's Cuts doesn't open till ten.

Tempted to go make his call unshorn, he sees himself fending off a horde of firefighters come piling out of their front door while placing his order for a European sidecar. He decides — then, there; here, now — that he wanted to realize his future with Bellum, not jeopardize it. Determined to be careful, he would kill time along the Neversink Reservoir, making a mental list of anything at camp they should take on their road trip. An hour later, he returned to the salon and stood with his hand gripping the ornate brass knob. He didn't pull. Inside, someone overweight with a shaved head, back to the door, fussed with blue-bathed combs.

Ray's breathing shortened, his muscles strained, and he took a few expansive breaths to stretch his chest and calm himself. Here he was, more angry, more anxious, than he'd been in years, panicked even, before a shave and a haircut.

He could let go of this knob and hike into Liberty alone. Clean out his storage unit, hop on his bike, and ride solo into the sunset. Be done with this whole phase of his life, Bellum included. Their time together beautiful. If anything, it lessened his need for answers. He no longer cared so much who was behind Baum.

The barber looked in the mirror. Face of a woman. A woman barber with a shaved head. Her reflected frown, its harsh judgment, coupled with Ray's confusion, his mistake of her gender — it obliterates the future he imagined. He about-faces. Takes two, three steps down the sidewalk before the salon door dingles open.

"I help you?" Unmistakably a woman's voice.

He raises a hand but doesn't turn, doesn't stop.

Behind him, footfalls scuff on the bluestone slabs. She's coming for him, and he whips around to face the fat lady.

She smiles, says, "Hey, it's okay. Come on in. It's a little early but I'll open. I'm happy to get you trimmed high and tight if that's how you like it." Her sympathy, her absence of embarrassment for him, and for herself — she looks like a bald Mama Cass who survived the ham sandwich — it knocked him backward on his worn boot heels. She held his forearm, her nails bubblegum pink, and pulled him to her salon and inside, locking the door behind her. She was drawing him back into the promise, the hope, not phony, of riding that Blue Ridge wave with Bellum.

She commanded him to sit, and he sat. He closed his eyes, to better appreciate the electric tingle of the woman's plastic-tipped fingers scouring his scalp, could see another Ray Tyro take his cash and head up into the Adirondacks. Buy a rocky parcel, build his own timber-frame cabin. Enroll in a furniture-making class. Spend the rest of his life by himself making deck chairs and —

"I volunteer at a shelter in Liberty once a month." She got his neck situated in the snug curve of the sink wall, and he sat straight up, gasping, reaching a hand to his throat.

"Easy," she told him. She got him resituated. "Not saying you look vagrant now, just saying you're not the first ruffian I've cleaned up, and I've got a sense about these things. Caught one look at you through the window and just knew. After I'm done with you, you're gonna break a heart or two. First one just might be mine." She rinsed out the shampoo and shampooed him a second time. "You're gonna clean up real nice. This" — she twisted tight his hair at the back of his head and wrung out the ponytail — "this is nothing. Now my inclination's short on the sides and tussled on top. But don't let me influence you unduly. You've got a Jude Law under there yearning to come out. And I'm not talking about the Jude Law in *Road to Perdition*. Can hardly believe . . ."

On she went, Crystal, his eyes closed the entire time. Her endless uttering, a salve, didn't keep him from crying behind closed eyes when she clacked on the Oster clippers, ran them over his chin, his cheeks, the sides of his head, the thrum of the razor the same as those used by Army barbers the world over, from the first day of boot camp to the last shampoo, shave, and a trim you get before they dress you in blues and lay you in your box.

He had a hard time fighting his way out of the plastic sack of the barber smock to wipe the tears from his shorn cheeks, so she wiped them for him. When she said, "Have a look," he shook his head. "Scared," he said, the first thing he'd said to her.

"Howbout I describe you to you, then you take a look."

He nodded.

"Didn't find my Jude underneath," she told him. "There's a hint, but not the young Jude." She cupped her hand on the back of his head. "Hair's thinning like his, here." She traced a circle on his crown. "And receding, so I cut it close. Not as close as mine mind you. You got the face to pull it off. Bone structure of a Woody Harrelson. Left the scruff on your cheeks. Till you get some sun, you should keep what I call a midnight shadow. You ready?"

He opened his eyes. The sight of himself, his face unmasked, made him grin painfully and his eyes filled.

"I'm so relieved to see you smile," she said. "Oh no, are those more tears? Oh, honey. You look beautiful. Ready to reenter the world and take it by storm."

He nodded. He wasn't sure if he liked it, didn't want to reenter the world, but he was ready to try in the company of Bellum. "Thank you. What do I owe you?"

"This one's on the house."

"No please, let me pay."

"Honey, you'd have to kill me before I took your money."

The Standard seemed unchanged. Silent in the melting snow. Empty. And Bellum found Vessey in the Library of Esther House, a rotting wing-backed chair pulled close to the hugely inefficient hearth. An alpaca fur draped over his legs and lap. He fussed with something. The smell in the great room was bookish and smoky, and an erratic ticking came from Vessey. His head bowed, she'd think him asleep if not for the blur of his hands. Knitting needles. A basket at his side.

"Vessey, you knit?"

He didn't look up from his work. "How you doing, darling?"

"We're doing okay."

"I'd say so, if you're talking in the plural. Was worried about you." He looked up, looked ten years older than the last time she saw him. "But then I remembered you can take care of yourself."

"Where's everyone else?"

"Gone, everybody but Wiz. Having him around's worse than being alone."

"And Milt?"

"Thought about scattering him here somewhere, but I've got no idea where. And they're gonna raze this place, or worse. All kind of parties tromping through. So I decided I'm gonna keep him. Take him with wherever I go. Say hi." He pointed to what looked like a 105 mm howitzer casing on the mantel over the hearth. "Why don't you come back here? Help me do like he did. Keep Standard Company going. Till we find someplace else."

"Can't," she told him. "Got to get my shit sorted. Do something about my desertion. Divorce my husband. Know what I keep thinking? What if that woman died cause I was afraid of getting arrested? Don't think I'd'a been able to live with myself."

"Well she didn't die, thanks to you."

"You know if she's still at Vassar Brothers?" When he said he didn't, she asked him if he wanted to go for a ride.

"I'm gonna stay, but the van's yours for the taking."

■ ■ ■ ■

Evangelína's neck was wrapped with gauze
so white it was nearly blue. She rasped but
she didn't sound like Milt. Milt's rasp had
been dry, the rattle of stubborn winter
leaves. Evangelína's rasp sounded like
Daddy wet-sanding the clearcoat off a
factory-finish paint job.

They talked for a half-hour, gossip mostly,
girl talk, Evangelína doing most of the talking. She was open and withholding both,
seemed not to care why Smith was there,
nor who she was. They didn't talk about the
mauling, and Evangelína didn't know Smith
helped save her life. Evangelína said she'd
started collecting workman's comp but she
was sure she'd be fired. When Bellum asked
if she had family in the area, Evangelína
said, "Mamí doesn't fly. One of my bosses
flew up. I refused to see him. Doctors are
trying to get me home by New Year's. I'm
being airlifted in a few days." When they
said their awkward goodbye, Evangelína
fished out a business card, SW&B Construction, and Bellum stared at it, thought to ask
questions, but this woman was in no condition to offer answers or advice. Besides,
Smith didn't care. She wanted only one

thing: to be back in the yurt with Ray.

At the payphone outside the fire station, Ray placed his call to Hudson Valley Custom Cycles, and while on hold, the burly firefighter Ray roughed up for the fuckall fun of it walked out the door.

Ray had cover behind the small stall of the payphone, and he reached and touched his Bloodshark in the small of his back, the only blade he brought, but he didn't pull it.

The firefighter came around to get a better look, and Ray obliged him, stepping out from behind the payphone. He raised a hand, waved like a runner-up beauty queen.

Cocking his head, squinting, he nodded, not recognizing Ray without the beard.

The voice over the phone said the Steib could be there in three weeks. "Aint cheap but it's pretty, and it'll look intense on that Dark Horse of yours. I'll be excited to see it."

The wind is strong and whistles through the seams of the yurt, making it breathe like a living thing, Smith inside the belly of it. Waiting in the half-dome feels dreadful — she knows that this, the guilty pleasure of their time together, can't last.

She's not alone long, but when she hears

someone, or something, busying outside the camp, she storms out red-blind with rage. There stands a stranger. She charges punching, clawing, manages to bite a hand, and he — the stranger — wraps her up, drags her screaming into the yurt. Their ground-and-pound fight stops when she feels his face against hers, sees the clean-shaven skin of his cheeks, so sickly pale, chafed, but beautiful. His hair cut short, his hair thin but his head so wonderfully rounded. She pleads, kisses him, Ray, and their fight becomes foreplay, rough, he the angry one now, tearing her frayed clothes, ripping her tattered panties from her waist, the elastic cutting her skin, he plowing into her with a pleasure so intense she can't tell it from pain.

Afterward, he's apologetic, and she doesn't respond, ashamed for feeling like she's just received the best punishment she's ever had.

When the sidecar's ready, they hike into Liberty, to Hide-Away Storage and Ray's unit. He pulls a wee key from his boot lace and pops the tiny padlock. "Bigger the lock," he says, "more they think you have to steal."

Before he rolls open the door, he pulls his kerchief from his pocket, tells her turn round. She does. He ties a blindfold over her eyes. It smells so powerfully of him that she feels something somersault in the hollow between her hips. Then follows a twinge of fear, that he's hiding something — he feels the fear too, though the objects of their fear diverge. She's afraid of what he's withholding; he's afraid of what he's lost. He wants to include her, and he promises himself that after these last kept secrets, he will tell all, give all, and from that moment on, they'll be of a mind.

He pulls open the storage door to the daylight. All looks in order. He checks the stuffing of the camel saddle. The cash is there along with the BlackBerry phone and an old wedding photo; his chest eases. He pulls out a bound stack, a hundred hundred-dollar bills. He figures in the cost of the sidecar, gas, splurges, leathers for Bellum, maybe a second bike, a possible detour down to Houston, and he pulls out two more $10,000 stacks. He puts the cash in his pack along with the thin Canek file, and he pockets Baum's phone. He unzips the plastic suit-bag hanging from a stamped notch in the sheet-metal wall. He pulls out his basic black leathers — pants, riding jacket — and zips the bag on his dress blues. After he draws off the canvas throw covering the motorcycle, he rolls the bike into the sun and finds it ridiculous, this matte-black street scrambler, not the look of it but the expense. He re-covers it. Through the stupefying heat of his embarrassment, he asks, "Ready?"

When she nods, he unties her blindfold. Then, he yanks off the canvas.

Underneath is a motorcycle like a flexed black muscle. A Kings Mountain Indian, before Polaris bought the brand. The bike's dark curves are a femme fatale's but the underlying mechanics, so chrome they glare white, are masculine.

"Wow."

"You don't think it silly?"

"A little." She smiles. It's a motorcycle like a marble Adonis reclining in a tight black dress. She doesn't say that it's maybe the sexiest vehicle she's ever seen. All in all, a dead-serious bike.

"Here's my favorite part." On the front fender, there's the iconic accent: a die-cast chief's head wearing a stylized steel warbonnet. The glass face of the chief is a backlit lamp that glows from within. "Take her for a spin."

She says she'll wait but he insists. Distrustful, a little confused, she pulls on his half-helmet, cranks the ignition, and it tumbles slowly over, struggling, the winter a drain on the battery. Then it catches and rumbles between her legs. She guns the throttle and grins. The bike hops ahead and she's off.

Before he shuts things up, Ray gets the contact info for his former colleague, Joe Ginsu, a PO box in Sierra Vista, Arizona.

In the Hide-Away office, Ray talks to the manager, a geriatric gearhead with whom he has a rapport. Asks if a package is shipped to the office, could it be placed in his unit.

"Sure thing. Do it all the time, especially for the boys over doing the fighting. We get a box, so long I can lift it, I put it in. Least I can do."

Ray wants to thank him and go, a powerful need to be out of these shady dealings he's hiding from Bellum. Even though it's reckless, Ray puts the phone on the countertop. On the phone he puts the mailing address. "Box'll be information. Dangerous in this day and age." Ray peels off five hundred-dollar bills. "If I pay for shipping, and for your trouble —" He puts the hundreds beside the phone. "— might you mail this?"

At the bike shop Ray does the talking, and

the dealer winks at Smith and ribs Ray for riding bitch. The dealer tells them the Steib's still crated, give him three hours, so they eat lunch at the diner two doors down.

In public with their relationship for the first time, she feels like a high-school sophomore in love, horny as humanly possible, making out in every nook, decency be damned. When they go to collect the bike, it's parked out front in the sun. It's slowing traffic. The in-house mechanic meets them with a long, low whistle of admiration. Ray pays cash and they take the Kingston-Rhinecliff Bridge across the Hudson, ride down to Ranting and Raving Leathers in Hopewell Junction. There, Bellum's fitted for a pair of leather pants and a leather jacket, both tawny brown. Together, Ray and Bellum are black and tan.

We just gonna leave all this behind.

That's right.

We're not taking anything?

Everything I have of value's in my storage unit except my NVGs, which I'll deposit before we leave. I'll take my Bloodshark and tomahawk, some clothes, and you.

What'll I take?

If you're gonna travel with me, one thing you won't take's that pistol. I just might be the only soldier in the history of American soldiering against the Second Amendment.

Only thing I still have given to me by Travis. How should we get rid of it?

Should do what the Iroquois do. Iroquois warriors would bury weapons under a white pine to seal a truce. Tree would then become a tree of peace.

Sounds — of Mamí making saffron tea in Chichí's copper kettle; of a hummingbird juddering at the window, trying to sip from the red sash on the other side of the glass; of the straw broom whispering over the Saltillo terra-cotta tiles laid throughout the house, tiles handmade by Tlaxcalteca artisans, a few in the hall outside Evangelína's bedroom impressed with the paw prints of a coyote, and it's with these prints that Mamí takes special care, standing barefoot on baked Mexican earth, sweeping out dirt that drifts into divots made by a criatura mexicano — these sounds, and the images in her mind they inspire, are her salvation. Each tells a story Evangelína's been deaf to. She tells these stories to herself until Mamí enters her bedroom, bearing a glass of horchata, checking the bandages on her neck, the gauzy wrap around her lower abdomen, the small incisions for the surgery to sew together her Achilles tendon. The nurse is in the house somewhere.

Evangelína feels she's doing time in solitary, Mamí the warden. Gradually, Evangelína's getting better, stronger, and she expects her new hearing to flag. But it hasn't. Vividly, sometimes painfully, acute. When Evangelína tells Mamí, Mamí says she's now hearing with the ears of the cat that tried to kill her. To Mamí, her attacker was balam, the jaguar, lord of the jungle, it was Chief Jesús taming the serpent, and it was Papí.

Smith and Ray ride from Liberty to Highlands in the rain. They arrive sopping and cold. Ray pulls into the lot of a B&B, Grand Lady by the Sea, and the room they're given smells like the name. Before Ray strips off his wet leathers, he uses the room phone to call 7-Eleven. He asks for Sharyn and, after a pause, wants to know when she works next. He hangs up. "Tomorrow early," he says. "We'll drop in, say hi. Then be on our way."

"You're not gonna warn her?"

"Element of surprise."

Next morning, they wake and ride. He shows her his old Catholic school, Our Lady of Perpetual Help. They coast down a hill,

398

highest point on the eastern seaboard south of Maine, and into the little town like a crab trap.

7-Eleven smells sweet and slick, syrup and grease. Ray raises his finger to his lips.

An overweight older woman, under a gray bob haircut, holds a small computer, doing inventory for the store.

As Ray draws nearer the woman, Smith inches closer.

He steals from behind and taps the woman's shoulder.

"One second. I'm counting." She types a number. "Then yous can have my undivided attention." Her wrinkles say too much sun at the shore, the red webs over her nose tell of too much booze in the sun — but Smith sees she was beautiful, and maybe stunningly so. Under her smock, her torso's all chest.

Smith has an urge to walk right up and rest her head on that soft sprawl. She resists. As she does, an image of Smith's momma flashes before her open eyes gone fuzzy — all emaciated angles, a woman like a heap of burnt sticks, a fire pit gone cold.

Not turning, the woman says, "What do you want," her voice hard-edged, tired.

Ray leans over her shoulder and sniffs.

His mother swats at him but still doesn't

turn from her work.

"You still smell like a Slurpee," Ray says.

Her neck straightens, her shoulders fall. She doesn't turn.

"What, not happy to see your eldest son?"

"I . . ." Her voice — it's shattered.

"You what, Ma?" The tenderness in Ray's response, and the tears of his mother, infectious, fill Smith's eyes.

His mother shakes her head.

"What, think I was dead?"

Her shoulders shudder, and she nods. Her face is frighteningly white, bloodless, no color in her lips. "I . . . I can't."

"Can't what, Ma? Come on. Look at me. Might not recognize me. I shaved."

She again shakes her head, forcefully. She inhales and says, "Go away."

Ray looks at Smith; she sees the hurt in him, an old wound torn open. He turns back to his mother, his anger evident in the cock of his head, the clench of his jaw. "That's the hello I get? *Go away?*"

"Please," she says, "just go. I can't, Ray, not now. I'm at work."

"Fine, Ma. Be like that." He jams his hands in his pockets, and Smith feels terror like a stitch in the side, nearly doubling her over. He's going to hurt his mother. He takes a step to her, his chest against the back of the old woman. He reaches his arms to her, his hands open, empty, and wraps them around her. He smells her hair, shuts his eyes, and holds her like that, in an awkward embrace, unreciprocated, for a moment.

Held, his mother leans her head against her son's arm. She too closes her eyes, and two tears land on her red smock.

Ray lets go, steps away. He looks at Smith, tips his head toward the door. "This is Bellum, Ma. Brought her by to meet you. But you're not ready. That's okay. We're taking a ride up to Alaska anyway. Maybe after you'll be ready." Ray holds out his hand to Smith, saying, "Love you, Ma."

Smith takes Ray's hand for fear she'll drift away, holds hard, guilt overcoming her, for the violence she imagined in him, for the hate she felt for him in the moment.

She cries and, starting, she can't stop as Ray leads her to the exit.

His mother says, "Ray."

They stop but he doesn't turn.

"I got a check for you."

"Keep it, Ma."

"It's for you not from you."

"Don't want it. You can't use it, send it to Shane for his commissary. I'll call you, Ma." He pulls Smith out the door, and she offers Ray's mother a stupid wave.

With Smith in the sidecar, he's saying, "It's my fault. Didn't occur to me she'd be . . . old. Look like I nearly killed her. Hey, it'll be okay."

"That's not it."

"What then?"

"I thought you might hurt her in there."

"Hurt my ma?" He smiled weakly. "Nothing I could do to hurt her more than I already done."

For most of the rest of the ride, Smith's uncomfortable — sweaty or shivering, rained on or sunburned, her crotch itching or her saddle sore — but even in discomfort she's giddy. The late-winter air is cool but the sun is warm, and they've brought along an alpaca hide, E. Prince, to use as a throw. When she gets cramped or cold riding in the chubby torpedo of the Steib sidecar, Ray takes a turn, folding himself inside to nap.

The looks they're shot, at gas stations in southern Jersey and outside diners in Maryland, she parking him, astound her. Monstrous, burly bikers — like the ones she grew up with, anarchic teddy-men with ten-year-old beards and taut, globe bellies — these mean men give them thumbs-ups, bouncing unhelmetted nods, peace signs angled low to the road. Their diabetic women let go of the great livers of these men to clap and whoop.

When her hand's on the throttle, her mind is the landscape winging by. But in the sidecar, she's merely herself, antsy but not panicked, and she finds herself — despite herself — thinking: Are we in love?

At the empty Rocky Knob observation area, Ray pulls her over to a picnic table. And when she says, "At the lookout? Are you kidding?" he shakes his head and says, "From behind, so we can both look out."

In the gray light before it's over, she says, over her shoulder, she always liked the name Shenandoah. "Shenandoah — Smith — Tyro." When he doesn't answer, or when his answer comes as harder fucking, she thinks she's angered him. Then he's coming, cooing like a raccoon pup, and instead of pulling out to come, for the first time, he pushes farther in. When it's over, the sun nudges up over Rock Castle Gorge. He says, "Shenandoah. Any idea what it means?" In the low-angle, early light, she doesn't answer, doesn't need to. There's plenty of time.

Tucked in the sidecar, she yells over the rush of air, "Ready to turn myself in!"

■ ■ ■ ■

They'll enjoy the Keys first. When they cross Seven Mile Bridge and are on Little Duck, Ray knocks on her helmet leaning against the padding of the sidecar wall. She opens her dreamy eyes to the half-moon shining over otherworldly water, a sea of warm darkness. Heat lightning fills the luminous bellies of thunderheads in the distance, like zeppelins on fire. Here is heaven, she thinks, now I can die.

In Key West, they find a little B&B on Elizabeth Street. Ray and Smith intend to see the sights in the bright brochures, and you'd think having spent the most intimate winter of their lives together, in close furry quarters, that they'd have lost some of their need, but the opposite is true. They attribute this to the tropical heat, the outside air an atmosphere of sopping sex, and in the wet warmth they can stand naked before each other and not freeze. They bask in the sight of one another uncovered by fur or filth. They spend two full days in bed — some love made soft, some hard, some dreamily in between.

Raw, sore, and besotted, but not tired, not sated, they check out and get back on the road, heading north.

Takes Smith all the way to Key Largo before she can holler over the rushing air, "You still want to drop in on my daddy!"

"Depends!" he shouts back.

"On what!"

"Our aims!"

"You mean're we aiming to kill him!"

"Here in the homeland, I don't approve of killing a man I don't know!"

"Maybe just to introduce you! After, you can decide if you want to kill him!"

"Sounds like a plan!"

In Carnestown they turn north, between the Big Cypress and the Fakahatchee Strand preserves. Five miles from her daddy's, she makes Ray turn off and stop so she can pee and breathe. She doesn't want to arrive empty-handed so she buys a twelve-pack of Daddy's beer, Miller High Life. When she comes out, Ray insists she take them the last leg home.

North of Bithlo, they pass a few Orlando exurbs in the making. "Daddy's just up ahead. He don't like nobody on his property. We're risking getting peppered with rock salt by showing up unannounced."

"So you're saying I need to be on my guard."

Just off the road stands a ranch archway, a post-and-lintel entrance built of three telephone poles at the head of a dirt drive, its cattle gate padlocked. Hanging from the lintel by two chains is an old stinger plow blade, rusted, scooped, and sharp. She tells Ray that Daddy was Army Corps of Engineers. Drove a Cat D7 dozer in Nam, outfitted with a Rome plow built in Rome, Georgia. Thing must weigh a ton. Two flagpoles stand atop the archway at either end. One pole flies two flags: the black POW/MIA flag over a sun-bleached Jolly Roger. On the other side, at the top of the other pole, perches a mailbox, its red flag up. On its side, stenciled in red, it reads, *TAXES*.

"Your daddy Tea Party?"

"Daddy's an anarchist. Doesn't believe in parties."

There's just enough clearance for the Indian with its sidecar. Cicadas tick madly, like telegraph operators on methamphetamines. A mangy tabby sleeps in the middle of the sandy drive and refuses to move. They ride around it, more cats lazing in the sun.

The trailer stands on cinderblocks, cinderblock stoop, the frame of an old Chevy pickup on blocks, blocks weighing down a blue plastic tarp over a heap of who-knows-what, blocks holding up the two listing poles of a clothesline — boxers, jeans, tees big and small, one tiny pair of shorts, a few pairs of wide-waist thong panties, and two bras.

"Less your daddy's become a cross-dresser, he's got intimate company."

She parks and revs the motor, the tailpipes trembling. When no one comes to greet them, she cuts it, dismounts, and knocks hard on the flimsy screen door.

A young Hispanic woman answers but doesn't open. She stands squat in a too-small tube top and teal spandex shorts. Sweaty, she's all curves and cleavage. "¿Eres tú la puta que ha estado llamando?"

Smith turns and shoots a look at Ray, who says from the sidecar, "Got a tiny bit of Arabic and Dari, but zero Spanish."

"I don't have much, but I know *bitch* when I hear it." She turns back to the door. "I'm looking for my daddy, Increase Smith. Mi padre." She points to the clothesline. "Those're his underwear. All these years and you'd think he'd get a few new pairs. I'm Antebellum Smith." She points to herself. "Ant."

Ray says, "Ant?" climbing out of the sidecar.

The woman has a few years on Smith, at

most, but her scowl is older than anger. The woman tries to open the door. "Con permiso," she says, and Smith backs off the blocks.

From inside the trailer, through the open door, the woman screams, "Poquito!"

Smith flinches.

"Poquito!"

Smith can't help but laugh. Unless she's misunderstanding, the small sexpot is calling Smith's six-foot-tall daddy Little One.

"Poquito! Sal de ahí. Encuentra tu papá."

From out of a doorless, hoodless, trunkless Buick Skylark, a boy climbs, barefoot, wearing only a bathing suit.

Smith looks at the mamasita, back at the boy. He's maybe four years old. Skin darker than his mother's but he surely spends all his time outdoors, same way Smith did twenty years ago. She tries to see her daddy's resemblance, hints of herself.

The woman holds up her tube top with one hand and points into the distance. "Llévelos a tu papá."

Smith says, "Papa?"

The woman shrugs.

The boy walks to Smith, smiles a forced smile that's more endearing than anything genuine coming from an adult. He blinks and holds out his hand.

Smith squats, reaches to shake. "Hi, what's your name? Nombre?"

"Carlos." He takes her hand and pulls. "This way, please." The boy has no accent.

Ray points to himself, and Smith nods. The three of them walk along a swath of close-cropped crabgrass.

The mosquitoes are fat and loud as hummingbirds but they're not bothering the boy, who releases Smith's hand and runs ahead, disappearing over a grassy ridge. The peak of a pole barn new to her rears over the sharp palmetto fronds. Clacking comes from the barn. They top the ridge and there in the shade of the open roll-up doorway sits Increase, hatted, hunched over an antique Singer treadle sewing-machine cabinet, his dirty bare feet resting motionless on the wide cast-iron pedal. His toenails curl over the ends of his toes like snail shells. The machine, tucked under the cabinet, is the same he used to patch her pants and hem her skirts. On the cabinet sits an old typewriter she's never seen. He drips sweat on the keys, grunts, hammering away with two middle fingers.

Sitting high on Daddy's head is a grimy, floppy straw hat, wide brimmed, the sort worn by middle-aged women weeding gardens. A turkey feather pokes from the loose weave. She can see some of the sunblock slathering he's given himself. He wears a wild, unfamiliar look. The sight is crazy and it hits her — he's lost his intimidating mind.

The boy stands at Increase's side, careful not to interrupt.

Smith and Ray wait. She reaches and takes Ray's hand. Not five feet away, Increase doesn't look up from his maniacal typing.

"Ah, Daddy?"

His middle fingers freeze over the keys. "Yeah?" One hand fumbles to the surface of the sewing machine cabinet, finds a pair of eyeglasses. He pushes them up the bridge of his nose with one of his typing fingers and then pushes back the hat brim. "Ant, that you?"

"Glasses, Daddy?"

"Getting old, darlin."

"Sunblock, Daddy?"

"Getting cancer's part a getting old."

"Typing, Daddy?"

"Guy told me, Increase, you ought've wrote a book, so I did. Wrote my life story. Now I'm writing the sequel."

"That make it the story of your afterlife?"

"Comfort to see you still got that smart-ass mouth. But look at you. Standing before me a woman." He strikes a key. "Done finished the first volume. Published it my own self."

"And him?"

"This here, this's Charlie."

"He my half-brother?"

"Charles aint mine but ought well as be. Right, Charles? Charlie, say hi."

Carlos waves.

"He's my interpreter. His mother don't speak a wet lick of English but she keeps good trailer, cooks a mean barbacoa. Can be a downright banshee in the bunk. Viagra, best thing since the invention of the electric starter."

"Daddy, please."

"Aint never filtered my talk around you, grrl."

"We brought your beer."

"Yall hungry? You staying for dinner?"

"That my stepmom? A Mexican?"

He nods, tips his hat. "Never expected to live this long, see this much. Black President? Hot damn. Only in America. You know we got Neanderthal genes? Took Esperanza and little Victor Charlie here — they're El Salvadorian, by the way — they come here, they just want to fit in. Work mighty damn hard. Espy was juggling three jobs fore she shacked up with your old man. For a country, in the space of 200 years? Go from a civil war fought over slavery to electing a mulatto? To live in the White House with his wife and their two niglet daughters —"

"Now there's the daddy I know."

"Like him or not — and I sure as shrimp don't — world's crazier now than it ever was, Ant. Must say, I love it all the more for the craziness. So, barbacoa?"

"I don't know, Daddy, I just wanted to introduce yall."

"You aint the Missourian."

Ray steps forward. "No, sir. Name's Ray. New Jersian." He offers his hand.

"Yankee, huh?" Increase climbs creakily out from behind his sewing cabinet and takes Ray's hand. "Call me Crease."

Ray squats to Carlos's level and the two wordlessly shake hands, smiling at each other. Ray rises and says to Increase, "You and your daughter got a pair of names. How'd you settle on Antebellum?"

"Ant here's lucky she didn't get saddled with my momma's name, Sookie. Maiden name of Pettipice. No middle name, just like Ant. My middle name's Swerc. Always hated it. Sound a cat makes coughing up a hairball. Promised I wouldn't do that to Ant."

Ray turns to Smith. "Never said your dad calls you Ant."

"All I've ever called her."

"Might have to join in, Ant."

"You gonna tell the story now, Daddy?"

"Don't got to. Yall can read it in my book. Get it off Amazon."

"Daddy, you hear from Travis?"

"Your Missourian talked me into fronting him three thousand dollars worth of mixed meds. I scored em from a croaker in Ruskin. Missourian won't return my calls. Tracked him down on Facebook, made an alias, been hounding him that a way."

"You're on Facebook?"

"I'm old but I aint dead. I was five years younger, didn't have me a hemorrhoid the size of a French cruller, I'd —"

"Daddy, for the love of Pete."

"Peter's a pussy. Always favored me Paul. Late to the party Paul. And a hemorrhoid's no joke now." He points at the rusty folding chair behind the sewing machine. "Been sitting on that inflatable donut for months. Had it to do all over, I'd a straddled me a bike with a little less rumble in the ride."

"We rode up on an Indian."

"Well now, dear daughter, few years back I'd a run you O-F-T, but now? Hell, I'd trade in my knife-and-fork arrangement for an overstuffed Indian seat with some spring. Yours a bagger? Got all kinds of tassels dangling off?"

"No sir," Ray says, "I'm anti-tassel."

"Attaboy. Her other one, he's all tassel. Tassels surely hanging off his testicles. I was a little younger, I'd stove in his head with the heel a my boot. Sure pills'd spill out."

"We're headed up to see him, Daddy. Serve some papers."

"First divorce."

"Like father like daughter."

"Let's hope not. You give your soon-to-be ex a message?"

"Depends."

"You tell him those pills are my gift."

"You have changed."

"Some." He sits, wincing as he gets centered. "But this gift's a curse, cause he's headed for an overdose or worse. Seen it happen a thousand and one times. He'll hit headfirst and someone'll get hurt. Hopefully just him. You're right to get on out. You need some gas money?"

"No."

"Need a car? Can piece something together for you, if you're willing to hang around a few days. Got a tent we can pitch." Another cat, balding, greasy with motor oil, pads from the warm shadows and jumps on Daddy's lap. He gives it a moment to settle in.

"Haven't seen the Green Machine."

"Sold her. Money got Esperanza, Charlie and myself through most of this here Great Recession, which in central Florida's been a downright depression."

Carlos leans against Increase, who raises his arm to make more room.

"Even had enough left over for some decent schooling for Victor here. Got him in a Montessori school. Guy —"

"You're paying for Catholic school?"

"Montessoris aint Catholic, Ant. But don't ask me what they are."

Not wanting their talk to end, she asks if he's working on anything.

"Oh," he tells her, "you know me and my projects. Been trying to nig—" He glances down at Charlie. "To *jury*-rig a steam power plant. Did what they did for their '69 Chevelle — aw but you two don't want to hear an old man yammer on about his projects." He pats Carlos's head. "Right Vic?"

Carlos shrugs and smiles, and Smith can't keep herself from saying, "He doesn't look like he gets the same hard friskings I got."

Increase says to Ray, "I was a ruffian raising a daughter on his own, and she was turning woman before my eyes. Never had an easy time with women. Always treated em rough. I switched Ant's toosh, but I never smacked her around like I did her momma. That woman asked for it. By asking I don't mean she had it coming. She'd get down on hands and knees and beg. Resisted best I could. But I got a low tolerance for resistance. Last thing in my life I wanted was her to wind up like her mother, or, worse, wind up with a man like me, but I —"

"Talk to me, Daddy. I'm standing right fucking here."

"Trying." He turns to her but doesn't meet her eyes. "Wanted to save you from this." He points out at the rusting wrecks, weeds growing in them, one even supporting a mature strangler fig. "It's a bearable existence, Ant, and I can bear it but there's better." He looks at Smith, into her. "Just didn't know how to give it you. Then I got that call from you, right before you shipped out the first time. Just knew. Not that I needed to approve of your Missourian. But when you couldn't even let me see the man? Or let him see me? Well, what I knew to be true was maybe what I expected all along."

"What's that, Daddy."

He says to the cat in his lap, "You found you a fuckup, same as your old man." He turns to Carlos. "Don't let me catch you repeating that now." He faces Smith full-on.

"You wound up with a no-good son of a skunk. Same way I wasn't no good for your momma. Simply could not reach that woman. Even when I was half a foot up in her. Your momma and me, we were BTDC." He waits.

"I know BTDC," Smith says.

He points a typing finger at Ray. "What about you?"

Ray says, "Before top dead center."

Increase smiles. "This one's a keeper."

"What's this got fuckall to do with momma?"

"Your mom and me, we had spark but we'd advanced before top dead center. BTDC. Thought about this an awful lot now. Wrote all about it in my book. I ought've waited till she got clean fore messing with her. Had I been able to delay my gratification, she might still be here. And you, Ant, might've had some motherlove." His lips tighten. "I gave you what love I had. And then some. Wasn't the best brand of love a little girl could get. Can say, looking back, I loved you — love you — more than I ever loved any thing in this life. What that's worth." He stands dry-eyed and, not without trouble, lifts up Carlos, saying, "Ho now, getting heavy." He hands Carlos to Smith. "Told myself that, just maybe, I could do right by you, little bit at least, if I could do a better job caring for another little one."

Carlos hides his face in the crook of Smith's neck, his breath warm and tickling.

"All right, that's it. Apologies for getting windy and sappy. Busted-up biker ought to get a few graces. Now yall git. I do appreciate you stopping by, making introductions."

"Good seeing you're doing good. You don't look good. But you sound good, Daddy, real good."

"Take what I can get. And, Ant."

"Yeah, Daddy?"

"Nothing."

"Go on. Don't start filtering your talk now."

"I am sorry."

"For what?"

"For everything."

She hugs him. "Everything's enough." He smells of sweat and motor oil, and she breathes him deeply before pulling away. "We'll call, Daddy."

"Don't call. Friend me."

"Okay, Daddy."

Without word, Ray reaches out a hand and he and Daddy shake. Ray ruffles Carlos's hair, and with the same hand he takes Smith's.

They walk back to the dusty motorcycle. Before they leave, Smith knocks on the trailer door, gently this time, and when Esperanza comes to it, opening it a crack, Smith says, "Muchas gracias, Esperanza, muchas, muchas." She backs away waving.

Near Elizabethtown, at the start of a Kentucky dusk like a distant barn burning, they ride North Dixie to the cloverleaf that exits toward Bullion Boulevard and Fort Knox. Smith curls in the sidecar, burying her face in her knees.

Ray rests his palm on the back of her neck. "Incoming."

An M24 Chaffee light tank aims at them, parked atop a two-tier brick platform. The road widens to four lanes. Flanking the road are two more platforms, where an M1 Abrams and an M2 Bradley face off, tank versus tank. They both read *Welcome to Fort Knox.*

"It's only going to be a few days, right?"

"Cording to the internet," he tells her, "long as you don't bring up any issues the Army has to investigate, we're talking three, four days. Today's Tuesday, and they in-process into the PCF on Wednesday. Out-processing's Friday morning."

"What are you gonna do while I'm in?"

"Got an errand to run."

"Please tell me you're not gonna go see Travis."

From the Wet Ones tub in a saddlebag he counts out ten bills. "Here."

"A thousand dollars? No, Ray."

"Case something happens."

"What are you gonna do?"

"Got some unfinished business in Houston I need to see to."

"The fuck does that mean?"

"Means I want someone to tell me why I spent a year at the Standard spying on Wright." He turns over her hand, opens it. "Key to the little lock on my storage unit. Remember that camel saddle?"

"This a joke?"

"Saddle's got a ratty leather cushion. Cushion's got a seam on the underside. Something happens to me, you go get that cushion. What's in there's yours, you understand? Not my mother's, not my brothers'. My mother'll get my life insurance."

"Feeling sick."

"Motorcycle's yours too."

"Stop dictating your fucking will to me!"

"I'll be back by Friday."

"And what if you're not? How do I get ahold of you?"

"Ant, I'll be here."

"Don't *Ant* me."

"Look, I'm all in. If I'm not here on Friday, it'll only mean one thing."

"Don't."

"That I'm being detained or I'm dead."

"That's two things, two entirely different fucking things. Detained I'll forgive you for. But if you're dead, you fuck, I'm gonna be so fucking furious at you I'll never —"

"Then I'll be sure to live forever."

Her eyes narrow and he sees her harden. She's a good soldier. Flipped the switch, her fear gone from making her anxious to making her angry. "The Standard is not Iraq."

"I know that."

"You think you're gonna go there and conduct an interrogation till some muckety-muck caves? Says they thought Milt had a stockpile of WMD? Under the armory? The big bell. So they ousted him. Maybe poison him. Make it look like cancer."

"Believe that before I bought the golf horseshit."

"If you got to do this, then do it, but just know this."

He waits, feels himself flinch.

"And maybe it's selfish of me," she says, "but I'd rather have you beside me and absent some of the time, off in your own dark head space, than not have you at all. You understand, you asshole? What I'm saying is I want all of you, however you are. Now kiss me and pull up to the gate before I change my fucking mind. The guards are eyeing us like I'm riding inside a fertilizer bomb."

The guard, a pimply kid in a civvy security uniform, nods. His nameplate reads Hoyt.

"Here to turn myself in," Smith says. "I'm a deserter."

"Need to see ID. Military and driver's if you got both."

She hands them over.

"Hold tight. I'll give the MPs a call. They handle the trip to the PCF." He smiles at her. "Nothing to be concerned or ashamed of. Alright?"

"Preciate it."

"It's in our blood, what I like to tell yall. Country was founded — hell, and filled — by folks running away. Deserting. Few things more American, you ask me. Maybe that's why we treat yall like we do — nice. Worst thing about it's the corporal tunnel you're sure to get filling out all the paperwork. And the food."

Ray says, "Carpal."

"Beg pardon?"

"Don't mind him," Smith says. "He's worried for me's all."

"Well no need to worry, sir. She'll be doing a ton of TV watching. Got a thousand channels in there." In his booth, Hoyt places a call. He returns and says, "Excuse me," before giving Smith a gentle, thorough going over.

The MPs show, a man and a woman wearing ACUs.

The woman says to Hoyt inventorying Smith's things, "Busy evening."

Hoyt says to Smith, "Word's out Wednesday's in-processing. We get a good showing. Fourth one today." He turns to the MP. "She's good to go." He touches Smith's forearm. "Ma'am, it's a long road leads here, and it'll all be over before you know it."

The woman MP says, "This here your husband?"

Ray stands straddling the motorbike. "Fiancé."

"You'd think," the man MP says, "we'd come up with a word wasn't so French."

The woman says, "Normally I'd have to cuff you. But seeing how your *betrothed* is here —" She shoves her partner in the shoulder. "— and you've surrendered, if you want, your man can drive you."

"This man aint my fiancé, ma'am. That

was just another of his clumsy proposals. To which," she turns to Ray, "I say, Fuck no."

Hoyt says, "Ouch."

"If you're here waiting for me when I get out," Smith says, "I'll reconsider."

Ray nods. "It's a date."

She strides over and kisses him hard, feeling a terrible urge to tell him she loves him, an urge she's able to resist.

Overnight on the interstate, and in just under twelve hours, Ray makes the ride from Fort Knox. By the time he's welcomed to the Lone Star State, skirting Texarkana, he's worked and reworked a tentative plan short on specifics, what his onetime commanding officers called a Concept of Operation.

He'll know more when he gets to Houston for reconnoiter. Meantime, all the op needs is a name. From Queen City through to Linden, he rattles off operations he recalls, some he doesn't. Op OK Corral. Op Tapeworm. Op Soda Mountain. Outside Carthage, he says one aloud, "Operation Snakehead," and the rushing air puffs out his cheeks. Resaying it, "Operation Snakehead," makes it real, makes him giddy, recalling that night with Baum on the reservoir. The first honest talk he had with another man in a long damn time.

Exhausted and chilled through his leathers, Ray's shivering, starving, and riding a mean depravation high. Across I-69, in the Deerbrook Mall minutes after it opens, he has a momentous occasion. He clothes-shops, more jittery in retail stores than he'll be on raid.

He visits a bathroom to shave and shut himself in a piss-rusted stall. With his fixed-blade, he cuts out the right pocket-lining of each pair of shorts and pants. To his thigh he straps the Kydex sheath and slides in the knife.

In downtown Houston, he pays to park in a locked-down garage and then humps it the mile and a half to the Cullen Center, a skyscraper complex, connected by second-floor pedestrian footbridges, that includes the headquarters of IRJ, Inc.

He walks to the Wells Fargo branch in Wells Fargo Plaza and activates a prepaid debit card, wanting to deposit $5,000. A bank manager is called over, and he's told that anything over $2,000 requires a photo ID and a forty-eight-hour hold to be placed on the card. He deposits nineteen hundred dollars, and repeats the process at the nearby bank branches in the JPMorgan

Chase Tower and the Bank of America Center.

At the Crowne Plaza Hotel registration desk, he asks for a room, one overlooking Smith Street, gives his card for incidentals — "Thank you, Mr. Wright."

The gravitational pull of the king-sized bed nearly overwhelms him. He slaps his face, makes a cup of black coffee like liquefied cardboard, and stands at the window sipping it.

A rearing bore of a building, IRJ Tower is as American as a box of instant mashed potatoes. In his tiredness, his weakness, Ray has a McVeigh moment: a powerful urge to blow it up — the company, the country — demolish it spectacularly.

Using the computer in the business center of the hotel, he visits the website for the FedEx company store and orders a 40th Anniversary Lanyard, 40th Anniversary Pen, a men's Pima Pique Polo in medium, a FedEx Value Cap, a FedEx Waterproof ID/Media Pouch, and has them shipped to the hotel FedEx Standard Overnight.

At discountofficestuff.com, he orders a roll of Gorilla Tape and a box of Kimberly-Clark Purple Nitrile Exam Gloves. The purple's a little off, more Grape Ape than FedEx's shade of Purple Heart, but it should do.

The last item he has overnighted, from to-talapps.com for fifteen hundred dollars, is the handheld computer used by FedEx employees the world over, a Motorola MC9500-K.

Sitting at the computer, having a hard time pushing up and out of the office chair, he suffers a moment of doubt. All he wants is to talk, gain a little understanding, but he can imagine things going wrong and F. Bismarck Rolling ending up dead.

Be nice to have a third option, the middle ground. Ray visits one last online retailer: supertattoo.com. Thinking of Bellum behind bars a coin's throw from the Bullion Depository back at Fort Knox, he orders the Money Maker tattooing starter kit with the Gold Slinger tattoo machine, a gilded, powder-coated frame shaped like a dollar symbol.

Drowsing at the computer, he pushes away the chair and kneels at the desk. In this position, he crams, reading everything he can on F. Bismarck Rolling — there isn't much — and then turns his attention to FedEx. Training process and services.

At the website for Brookfield Office Properties, he finds IRJ Tower, which Brookfield manages. He goes through the tenant handbook, taking notes left-handed to help keep awake. The section "Deliveries/Loading Dock/Freight Elevator" offers the loading dock's location, where all deliveries are made. Use of the freight elevators after business hours may be arranged by contacting the Management Office.

He visits the Montrose address he has for Evangelína Canek. Spends an hour smoking across the street from the two-story townhouse on Lovett. No one comes or goes.

Resolved, he rings the bell. Behind the wrought security gate, the door opens on a woman kneeling. Dressed in red. Her chest-high face is red-veiled. Ray shakes his head hard.

She's not kneeling. She's tiny, four nine maybe. Her dress reaches ankles wormy with veins. Her feet are bare. Callouses pancake her heels, her nails painted ox-blood.

He does some quick figuring to justify his muddled operational awareness — awake for over thirty hours.

She stands regarding him on the far side of her gate, in no hurry to ask him in or usher him along. She lifts the veil. It's not just her skin, small stature, and gray hair threaded with black that remind him of his murdered mother-in-law, it's that the little old woman is so plainly worldworthy.

When he says hello, she nods and smiles, waiting. She raises a fist to her mouth, as if she's about to cough. She spits something into the loose curl of her fingers and grips it in her closed hand. The thing spat was green and gleaming, like a tree frog, and he sees her anew: he's standing before a mad-woman.

He tells her he came to check on Ms. Canek, see how she's faring.

The woman's eyes narrow. She looks him over, and her regard is basic, bestial.

She opens the fist she spat into. On her papery palm rests a green semiprecious stone, polished, shining with her spit.

Delicately, she sets the stone on a side-board, where rest two tall votive candles, flickering, one adorned with an image of what looks like the blue-veiled Virgin Mary, the other in the same attire and posture as Mary but skeletal, a draped Death, holding in each hand an empty scale, balanced, and a crystal ball. Candy skulls adorn the sideboard, brown ants crawling on them. A dried ear of corn, its kernels red as pome-granate seeds, its husk pulled back. There's a carved stone creature, jade maybe, vaguely feline. At the center of the makeshift memo-rial is a framed portrait of Hugo Chávez wearing a red beret and holding up a green parrot wearing a red beret.

She opens the door and waves him in, saying a word that sounds like Contra.

He hesitates. Feels like he's being shown the future scene of his murder, terrified by the tiny woman in red. Ray can't laugh at the absurdity, because all at once he's in his haphazard history — back at the Jalal home in Dora. It's the Jalals' of the present, their home after the Jalals had gone, butchered, long after the two old women had mopped up the messes — first the blood, then the spilled keşkek they cooked to mask the smell. It's the Jalal home whisked up and deposited in Houston, now occupied by a Bolivarian septuagenarian lunatic.

Shaking his head hard enough to spark a starry ache inside his eyes — he enters. When he passes her, she says something else he doesn't understand: "Fumar te matará."

When he shrugs, she points to Chávez. She makes a peace sign — Ray's desperately confused — and she puts the V of her two fingers to her lips. She points to one of the sugar skulls and again kisses her peace sign.

He fights the urge to run, an urge that in Iraq he would've overcome by hurting the person inspiring it.

"Momentito." The woman bows her head

430

and disappears down a hall.

The MPs cuffed Smith gently, loosely, arms in front, and drove her to a long three-story building painted Swiss Miss brown. There, she was photographed and fingerprinted and she filled out the initial paperwork. They escorted her upstairs to the Personnel Control Facility, where all her possessions were inventoried.

The in-processing paperwork at the PCF was more extensive. She was told, "You can speak to a JAG lawyer now if you need to, if you're worried about self-incrimination."

Smith shook her head.

"Next, I'll read from DD Form 485, your charge sheet. You ready?"

She nodded.

He read an affidavit, and Smith signed her name so many times her hand ached.

Next, her clothes, save her underwear, were taken. She was given a new PT uniform: T-shirt, sweatpants, and a zip-up windbreaker. The boots were gently worn and dusted with foot powder, like bowling shoes.

Handed a hair tie, she was asked to pull back her hair. She was given a huge set of ACUs for work details. When she asked for a smaller size, the woman shook her head.

Shown to her shared room, she picked one of three empty beds.

Her guide of a guard said, "Food's provided by the RCF and it's awful, but that's your worst punishment."

"And we're in the PCF?"

"Right. RCF's Regional Correction Facility, the real prison."

"This isn't real prison?"

"This is like day care. That there's the playroom. As you can see, it's co-ed."

Three men and two women sat watching *Oprah* reruns. The men turned and waved. They were clean-shaven, their cheeks chafed, like they all shared the same cheap razor. A man and woman at a table in a corner played cribbage.

"You get to lounge around all day," her guide told her. "If you want, you can go on a detail. Picking weeds along the track, that kind of thing. But you don't have to. You can go outside. There's a basketball court. The females have an officer go out with them at all times. You can use the payphones. Man in charge is Lieutenant Laplace. Not an Army LT. He's a cop LT. Tomorrow you see the doc for a physical, then you meet the JAG lawyers to gather up your legals requesting a Chapter 10 OTH. If you accept the Chapter 10, and they sign off on it, you're practically out the door."

"If I only knew."

"If you knew, then everybody'd know, and if everybody knew, no one'd be fighting the wars we need fought."

Evangelína sat up in bed, pulling the duvet tightly round her stomach. Naked from the waist down, she hadn't worn panties in ages, eons since she'd pulled on pants, pants she'd be unable to button. Her painkillers, the Roxicodone, made her chiflada, loopy, and estreñida, constipated. They made her fat, or the laziness they inspired — or the liveliness they uninspired — made her fat, but they also made her uncaring of her newfound fatness. When she wore underwear, the elastic waist was a torture to her thoroughfare of a surgical scar, itchy but not aching. Under it, strangely, she was more keenly aware of the absence of her appendix than she was the emptiness where there once was uterus.

Before the man — both young and old, tired and wired awake — could introduce himself, she was apologizing, then adding: "She's in mourning." Evangelína's voice felt raw, sore, but every day it sounded a little more like her, the voice she remembered, but with perforations. "Poor old widow's reliving her grief for my father. Chávez, he's transference." She thought maybe he was an IRJ man just off the links, from legal, here to offer a settlement, but he didn't have the right posture, for golf or for law.

"Maya," Evangelína said, "wear red when mourning." She offered him the seat by her bed, its king size sprawling to the ends of her room. She was coming down. She reached for the pill bottle on the nightstand, found it without looking but didn't open it.

When he said he'd rather stand, she thought he must be a messenger sent by Bizzy.

"Didn't know Chávez died," he said. He ran his hand over his shorn head, a gesture he seemed to be trying out. "Been out of the loop. Cancer?"

"Mamí thinks not." She rattled the pill bottle like a sad maraca, a dried cuia with too few seeds. "Mamí thinks murder."

He nodded. "You know who I am?"

She moved to shake her head but stopped herself, the turn of her neck plucking the guywires supporting the towering pain that ran from her clavicle to her chin.

"Early Bird," he said. "Worked for Ellis Baum to gather information on Wright. Then he, Baum, asked me to track you down after your covert landing in the

Catskills."

When he didn't say more, she said, "Well you've found me back at home in bed. What took you?"

He smiled and tipped his head, and she could see he'd mistaken her comment for a come on, this incompetent general contractor who'd hunted her down months too late.

As if she were answering a question she'd remembered, she said, "Yes," and then felt ashamed. Wearing a T-shirt, no bra. Having not brushed her teeth coated in a starchy scrim. Her tangled, unwashed hair, heavy, hurting her scalp. Aware of her own smell wafting up through the bellows of the bedclothes each time she moved.

She felt her eyes drift closed.

He was saying something, that he should go.

"No, please."

"My . . . fiancée told me about the cougar attack."

"You're engaged," she said, not following him, this man paid to hunt her.

When he shrugged, her eyes filled, and the evening light in the room spangled. She dabbed tears with the bedsheet and apologized. "Please," she said, "sit down. Let me have Mamí get you something. Tea? Tequila?"

He shook his head. "You need your rest. Not even sure why I came. Other than I know that Bellum — she'd be mighty pissed to hear I made the trip and didn't check in with you, see how you're holding up."

Bella: the name was familiar. He meant Bella Smith, the one person to visit Evangelína, and for no apparent reason, at Vassar. "That's nice."

"Is it?"

"You're concerned for the concern of your fiancée." She hoped she made sense.

"How they treating you?"

"They who?"

"Company you work for."

"Don't work for them anymore. Can't talk about it. Case pending."

"Wondering if maybe you couldn't save me a trip to visit your boss."

There was a sound outside the door, and Evangelína, in her loudest voice, painful, said, "Mamí, vete." The hissing shuffle of bare feet scuffing over terra-cotta. "She's shameless." Evangelína, with practiced ease, popped open the childproof bottle and swallowed two pills with a hurtful gulp of water. "You were saying."

"Saying I shouldn't've come."

"To see Bizzy?"

"Who's Bizzy?"

"F. Bismarck Rolling."

"Want him to tell me what it was for."

When she shook her head, cringing at the pain, he added, "Why the Standard?"

Maybe he was an undercover federal agent. "If Bizzy clues you in," she said, "I'd be eager to know, and so would my lawyer. All I ever got was that caca about golf." She pointed to the closed closet. "Inside, on the shelf, in a shoe box, Louboutins."

When he opened the closet, she pulled the bedsheet up over her face, flushed, her neck on fire. Embarrassed, not by the number of shoeboxes — though there were easily a hundred — but that she'd taken photos of each pair of shoes, and then taped the photo to the side of the box so she knew at a glance what lay inside. She drew the sheet to the bridge of her nose, saw him regarding her in a new way, his exhaustion gone.

He was vibrant, and frightening — she lowered the sheet to her lap.

He took a breath, and to get some air back into the room, she said, "There, the big one that looks wrapped in brown paper."

Setting the shoebox beside her, he sat on the bed. He reached and touched a scar on her neck. She leaned back into the pillows propping her up. Offered her throat, exposed her stomach. He looked closely at the closed puncture wounds, set a fingertip in what felt like every last one. He shifted his attention to the scars between her pubic hair and her bellybutton. The wide surgical scar, the thinner mauling scars, the scars of the sutures and staples. She was aware of, but not embarrassed by, her tummy, its two rolls meeting at her splayed bellybutton. This lack of embarrassment emboldened her. "Subtotal hysterectomy," she said aloud for the first time in her life. The words meant little. To give them more meaning, she added, "No more womb," which sounded silly. She smiled. Her smile made her cry.

He stood, and she felt a shockwave of affection for this man, this stranger. He felt brotherly.

She removed the cover of the box. Inside, wrapped in tissue paper, sat the Standard Grande file. She patted it. "Sure a lot of what's in here you're well aware of, seeing how you did the fieldwork, but maybe you can spot something I couldn't." She replaced the lid and pushed it toward him. "I've got another copy. My lawyer does. I'd give you my keycard to the building, but I'm sure they voided it the moment I filed my wrongful-termination suit, which is bankrupting me. You don't happen to want to buy an eight-acre plat in Costa Rica overlooking the Pacific?"

He shrugged.

"Silver lining is if it does, bankrupt me, the ACLU may step in. Do me a favor?" When he nodded, she said, "When you see my boss, please pass along my worst." She closed her eyes, and was asleep almost instantly.

The temporary residents of the PCF were in a torpor, Smith included. A hangover that followed months and sometimes years of dread, dread that turned out to be unfounded, and so all the more demoralizing and debilitating. They were once again in the care of Uncle Sam, and they'd each forgotten how generous — tempting if not attentive — he could be.

At her physical exam, lying on the examination table, Smith opened her eyes. A woman doctor, stoic and middle-aged, stood over her saying, "Inhale and hold," pushing the drum of the stethoscope, not gently, on one side of Smith's stomach, then the other. "Guess you won't be seeking reinstatement to your former command."

Smith straightened. "Didn't know that was an option."

"I just mean you couldn't if you wanted to. At least not for the next six or so months." The woman narrowed her eyes. "You have any current medical conditions we should be aware of?"

"Like panic attacks?"

The doctor made a note on her form. "Anything else?"

"ADD."

Another note. "And?"

"Feel like you're trying to get me to say something."

She set the clipboard in her lap. "You know you're pregnant?"

"Ma'am?"

She nodded.

"Oh fuck no."

"Fuck yes," the doctor said, "which is how you wound up where you are."

"You sure?"

"If we hear a heartbeat, you're at least eight weeks along. You know, if you don't get your period for a couple months, that's usually a pretty good indication."

"Haven't been having regular periods. Diet's been not so good."

"We'll I'm getting you started on prenatal vitamins right away."

"What if I don't want it?"

"The prescription?" The question was plainly, painfully insincere.

Tears filled Smith's eyes and she shook

her head.

"That's your business," the doctor said. "Keep in mind that in the state of Kentucky, after the end of the first trimester, that's week thirteen, an abortion's a class D felony."

Near sunset, Ray walks back to his hotel, shoebox in hand, unsure what just happened, unsure what's happening. Two, three, then a fourth businesswoman smiles as she passes him. What are they drawn to? The killer in him? They must smell it on him, because before he and Canek shared their tender moment, he'd reached for his fixedblade. For a sickening instant, he thought she'd sent him into her closet to shoot him in the back. Almost gutted her, gutted her again, practically in front of her mad mother, in her own bed, in her own home, a home that felt hellish, a hell he'd revisit in a heartbeat. Confusedly, it occurred to him he'd always been there, would always be there, his life on a loop. But if there's any justice, any goodness, he'll do it incrementally better each time, a shade brighter. This time, passing through his hell, he didn't hurt anyone. He might've even helped that woman, and she might've helped him.

On the sidewalk, another passerby smiles at him, and he understands it's not him but the shoebox these Texas women beam at.

He feels a panicked pride, a sad relief: here is the finished product of his long, hard work over the last year, the presentation of it. A document in his possession that isn't his, produced by others. The document, not his deeds, would survive him, outlast his service to his country, endure his selling out to a half-dozen security companies. Maybe someday he, like old, sweating, bare-chested Crease Smith, would have time, and a typewriter, to hunt-and-peck out his story. Because if Ray didn't tell it, someone else would, the way IRJ got to tell the story of the Standard Grande, a story that should've been Wright's to tell.

He has the document Baum compiled but he doesn't have Baum's phone or the information therein. Doesn't have a clear objective, which seems about right. Standing over traffic on the skywalk, he tells himself if he runs into resistance at any phase of his op, Op Snakehead, he'll abort, he'll retreat back to base, Fort Knox.

Meantime, he's here, in motion, in action. What else would he do while Bellum's locked up?

After an exhausting fourteen-hour sleep,

where he dreams through the impossible minutia of his plan, first thing in the morning, Ray visits a computer terminal in the hotel business center and tracks his packages. They're out for delivery. The concierge tells him FedEx usually delivers before noon.

He takes a run, two passes by the IRJ Tower loading dock on Louisiana, coming and going, stopping to tie his shoe on the return, noting the sidearm of the lone attendant.

At his hotel after lunch, a stack of boxes waits for him at the front desk. In his room he opens them. Fixedblade strapped to his thigh, he dresses in the makeshift FedEx uniform. After a few minutes going over his lines, delivering them to the mirror, cheat sheet in hand, he dials the number for F. Bismarck Rolling, and when a woman answers, Ray says, "I'm going to have to cancel my five o'clock today with Mr. Rolling."

"Who may I ask is calling?"

"This is Jim Jones? I'm junior vice president at Honeywell? Engineering, Operations and IT. I was scheduled to come by at five today?"

"I don't have you down here and there are —"

"There any way I could come by a little earlier?"

"I don't think so . . . Mr. James is it?"

"Jim James — Jones." He mouths, Fuck, to the mirror. "Jim or James or Jimmy. Call me anything you like, just don't call me late for my meeting."

"Mr. Rolling's very busy today. He's booked all afternoon."

"Later then?"

"I know he has an appointment after work so I imagine he'll be leaving directly at five. You said Honeywell? Would you've made the appointment with me?"

"You know what, it's alright. It was more just to say hello. I'll try again next time I'm in Houston. Sorry for any confusion."

When he hangs up, he strips to his new underwear and opens the tattooing kit. He reviews the instructions, plugs in the tattoo gun, enameled in gold and shaped like a dollar sign, its four-amp power supply with banana-jack outputs, its foot pedal like that of a sewing machine, which is all it is, ink instead of thread.

He wipes Vaseline over both bare thighs. He inserts a liner needle, fills the tube with water from the tap, and steps on the pedal. The gun buzzes in his hand like an old DC doorbell. He practices on himself. Raising watery welts that weep blood, he painstakingly draws little symbols no bigger than nickels, symbols that would fit on a forehead, anything that comes to him: a bull's eye, a peace symbol, the Islamic crescent, a question mark.

On his other thigh, he tries text: *I ♡ mom.* A number he knows by heart, the count of US armed forces killed in Iraq before he left: *4425.* He can't recall the number of Iraqi dead leaked from the classified Iraq War Logs. Wants to know the number of killed contractors. He'll check the business-center computer, come up with a grand tally, more symbolic than scientific.

He hopes these wet-run, inkless tattoos he's giving himself won't wind up permanent, a wingding scarification collage on both thighs. In case they don't go away, he gives himself one more: *Antebellum Always.*

He showers and when his thighs stop bleeding, he changes. Into the FedEx box that contained the FedEx clothes, he packs the roll of Gorilla Tape, the tattoo gun, its power source and foot pedal, a couple of liner needles and one half-ounce bottle of ink, Black Buddha Ultra Black.

He visits the FedEx Office and Print Center on Louisiana. There, he prepares the box for shipping, sent Direct Signature, to

Marisol Soto-Garza at the IRJ Tower address. The moment after the cash transaction completes, he feigns exasperation, says he forgot to put the birthday card inside. When he's handed back the package, he asks if he has to wait in line again after he repacks it. The surly clerk tells him no. Ray fusses at a side table, then walks out with the box.

He wastes the rest of the day with the Standard Grande portfolio. The only thing enlightening is the scope and extent of the surveillance, and the veracity of Wright's financial and physical ill-health. On paper, with this level of detail, Wright looks legit. Most of the rest of the intel Ray's familiar with, but he goes back through one more time, feeling like he's cramming for written exams. It's a read more stultifying than the *Ranger Handbook,* which to its credit has beautiful, simple illustrations.

From the phone in his room, at 16:50, with a script he drafted three times and rehearsed, he calls the management office of Brookfield Properties. When a woman answers, Ray launches into his monologue: "I know you're about to leave for the day but I've got a FedEx Custom Critical delivery requiring a direct signature from a Marisol Soto-Garza and I'm worried I'm not gonna get there before five, I'm running a couple minutes late, it's all of my third day on this route and my guy showing me the ropes called in. No biggie if I miss her, I can still play dumb, I shouldn't get canned, I'll just have to do it first thing tomorrow before business hours."

"What's your name?"

"Travis."

"Travis what?"

"Travis Wright."

"From FedEx?"

"That's right."

"Not what my caller ID says."

"I'm calling from the Crowne Plaza. Where I just finished a delivery. I am so late."

"Alright Travis. I'm the property manager. I'll call over to the attendant."

"Loading dock on Louisiana?"

"That's right. And Travis?"

"Yes?"

"Relax, I know Marisol, and she's never out of there by five."

"— under current Army policy, you will be given a Chapter 10 general discharge under Other Than Honorable terms. Generally referred to as a Chapter 10 OTH. This discharge will not ruin your life. An OTH gives you TRICARE until you get your discharge papers. When you walk out these doors, you're free to go where you please. Military resources are at your disposal. After your discharge, the federal government will still employ you. It's untrue that you can't get a government job with a Chapter 10. You get no GI Bill, but you're still fully eligible for all other federal financial aid. All the good stuff to get you deep in the red. Now, once you have your discharge papers, you lose TRICARE. But if you get your OTH upgraded, you get your benefits back. Upgrade would help for any number of government claims." Obviously devoted to the sound of his well-drilled voice, the JAG lawyer in PCUs waited.

A man Smith couldn't see said, "For example."

"Say, if you choose to keep your OTH, you can never re-enlist."

A woman asked, "And if I wanted to go back to my unit?"

A man's voice said, "You crazy?"

"It's a good question. An upgrade would help, but it's no guarantee. Without an upgrade, you'd do time in the RCF, depending on your situation. One to two months is the norm, then back here to PCF while you wait for your paperwork to go through."

Someone said, "Without an upgrade, could I join the CIA?"

The lawyer laughed. "You could not."

Thinking of Vessey, and trying to buck herself up, Smith said, "What if I wanted to start a nonprofit company?"

The lawyer laughed again, this time with some meanness. "We've got a big-government entrepreneur in our midst." He winked at Smith. "In all seriousness, if you wanted to start your own 501(c), I'd say an upgrade would help your application. Now," he added, "this is your chance to write a statement asking to have your discharge upgraded. You're not gonna get an Honorable, but if you're honest, if it's deserved, you may be granted an upgrade from Other Than Honorable conditions to a General under honorable conditions. Out of the some hundred discharges I've dealt with who were Chapter 10 seeking an upgrade, I've only seen ten or so denied. Who needs a pen?"

At the loading dock on Louisiana, Ray taps a rubber-gloved finger on the bulletproof Plexiglas, sweating and bowing, giving his name, holding the modest FedEx box like a late-arriving magi offering myrrh.

The seated attendant has at his hip a small

sidearm with yellow grips, a Taurus .38. The security monitors are four low-def color screens, all exterior shots.

Ray says into the speaker, "My brother's got one of those. Though his isn't so yellow. That company issue?"

"Tis indeed." The squat guard holds up a finger like an uncooked bratwurst and pushes a button on the base of the desk phone, dials four numbers. Misdials. Tries again. Gets it on the third try. Must have a hard time finding the trigger on his sidearm. No way he could navigate the wee virtual buttons on a smartphone, his texts sent to women garbled, unreadable, man doomed to failure, unable to procreate, destined to die alone, all because he had the gene for ham hands — Ray can't help feeling happy. He's missed this, missed what happens to him on raid. Ready to kill and be killed, he's most alive.

Over the phone intercom, broadcast through the speaker of the security window, comes a woman's voice; it seems to say, "Carousel."

"FedEx for you. Needs signature."

"Again?"

"All day, every day."

"Okay, send him up."

When the guard buzzes the door and

opens it, Ray says, "Brazilian make? Isn't it designed to be a concealed carry?"

"It is, small and cheap. But bright as sunshine."

"Why would they make you wear a weapon that looks like a toy?"

"Got me. I keep telling them they might as well've issued me a DeWalt drill." He waves Ray in and asks if he knows where he's going. When Ray says he has no idea, the guard gives directions to the freight elevator.

Inside the elevator car is the little fisheye of a camera lens. Ray stares into it for the interminable ride up, imagining what may come: when the elevator doors ding open, you'll exit into a service hall. Marisol waiting for you. Closed doors on either side, an empty service corridor. Hand her the package and the handheld computer. Offer her the stylus, three things at once, fluster her. Then press your knees together. Say, Hate to be a tool, but I'm new to this route and haven't figured when to take bathroom breaks.

She'll direct you down the corridor, using her keycard to the men's room. Inside, wait a moment. Prop the door with the computer. Rush her and, from behind, slip a chokehold, latexed hand over her mouth, drag her kicking backward, into the rest-room and a stall. Sit her on the toilet, your hand clutching her face, saying, Easy, Marisol. Easy.

Ray blinks at the elevator's fisheye camera lens, again focusing on it, rather than through it to a visualized outcome. Thirtieth floor, seven to go, now six. At floor 34, he imagines Marisol wearing the red-soled Louboutins pictured on the side of Canek's shoebox. When the freight elevator door opens at 37, standing there, in a gray wool three-piece suit and old brown desert boots, is F. Bismarck Rolling.

I, Specialist Antebellum Smith, went AWOL to avoid my third deployment. I also needed to get away from my husband and his drug problem. In addition, we were having financial troubles. After returning home from my second tour, this one from Afghanistan, I was diagnosed with PTSD and medicated for anxiety. I believe these led to my neglidgent behavior. While AWOL, I wound up living and voulanteering at a halfway house called Standard Company for military veterans in the Catskill Mountains of New York State. While there, with Standard Company, I aided the owner/operator Milton Wright, a

452

decorated Vietnam War Vet in the upkeep and maintainence of the shelter. We tended a herd of Alpaca, cut and split endless cords of wood to get us through winter, dug up winter crops, and etc. The experience taught me how to be self-suficent as a civilian; and has inspired me to maybe open my own such shelter some day, so that I might help vets who feel they have no where else to turn. I'm seeking an upgrade so that I might one day qualify to start my own not for profit organization. Thank you, and I'm sorry.

Rolling is trim as a retired greyhound. His eyes, too, are old-dog. The lower lids droop, wet and pink. He extends his hand.

Ray offers the FedEx box, saying, "Sir," slipping a loose fist into his unlined pocket.

Rolling doesn't take the box. The two men stand there a moment. Neither moves. When the elevator doors begin to close, Rolling stops them with his well-worn desert boot.

Ray expected something a little more rodeo, more longhorn, maybe understated but a cowboy boot for sure.

"Old man extends you his hand, son, even if you are wearing gloves, you take it."

Rolling is surveilling him, has been for a

year or more. Evangelína, or her mother, tipped Rolling off. Maybe Bellum's working for him. Wright, too, before he died — if he's dead — and every vet at the Standard. Everyone in Ray's path is under the employ of IRJ, Inc., all so they could entrap him. Urge him here, to this moment. His free will nothing but an illusion. His free will nothing. Nothing. Ray braces himself before he realizes he's going nowhere. Needs something to grasp. Letting go the knife concealed in his pocket, he takes Rolling's hand. In the old man's grip, Ray regains some of himself.

Rolling's handshake is firm, not an affront, but he doesn't let go. "When I heard you coming up," he says, "I sent Marisol home. Come in." Rolling pulls Ray off the elevator car, releases his hand, and — untethered, untouched — Ray again feels vertiginous, bottomless.

Rolling doesn't hesitate to turn his back and lead the way down the service corridor. His self-assurance is a product of supreme confidence in his security, an absolute certainty that Ray won't, can't, hurt him.

To steady himself, Ray reaches into his pocket and pulls his knife, the dark blade dividing the air between them.

From a side door, they enter Rolling's office. He waves a rheumatoid hand at a bank of live-action monitors suspended from a corner. "I've seen you before. We record all security operations, for legal purposes, as you well know. I've reviewed the videos of a few of your jobs. One at the Baiji refinery, where you saved the life of your colleague. That stunt helped you get recommended for the Standard assignment." He offers Ray a seat.

Interrupted only by the ExxonMobil Building — flat and gridded as a sheet of graph paper — the view makes Ray feel above it all. Without facing Rolling, Ray adjusts his posture, loosens it the way he once would before contradicting a CO.

Rolling steps behind the standing desk, leans on it. He points to a small mahogany cabinet. "Offer you a drink? Bourbon? Getting close to quitting time."

Ray shakes his head. "This view . . ."

"One of the perks."

"I don't know, sir. Behind glass? All the Southern-fried sprawl? Sad you ask me. Seems so dull compared to the gulf views I've come accustomed to. Dubai, Abu Dhabi, they make Houston seem like such a shitty little backwater. A petrol latrine."

"That's because," Rolling tells him, "those cities didn't exist as such before the sixties.

Dubai didn't have electricity, telephone service, an airport, till the fifties. And historically Dubai and Abu Dhabi have been at war. But oil heals old wounds. When it was found there, two of the most outrageous cities in history were born. To mention Houston in the same sentence, that's like comparing apples and Gomorrahs."

Ray turns from the view. "But which is which, sir?"

Rolling smiles. "Dubai and Abu Dhabi," he tells Ray, "are Miamis with monarchies." Rolling adjusts his bifocals and winks a pink-rimmed eye. "Houston's an oilgarchy." He points a bent finger at the FedEx box. "If I open that, will it explode on me?"

"Inside, among some other gear, is a roll of duct tape."

"Few things with more uses."

"Planned on taping your secretary to the toilet while you and I talked."

"Not called secretaries anymore. You planning on taping me to the john?"

"Thinking about it, sir."

"Then what?"

"Not sure. Didn't come up here with much in the way of preconceived notions. Wanted to see for myself, and hear."

"So you come to talk. I've got a five thirty. What if I cancel, take you to dinner? Early

Bird special."

"Can't be seen with you at your club-house, not if I'm here to bust out one of these windows." He etches his knife point — *scritch* — down the plate glass. "Splash you all over Smith Street."

"If you were here to kill me, I'd be already dead."

"What if I want information first? After I get it — easy way or the hard way don't matter, might even prefer the hard way — then I kill you."

"So what do you want to know?"

"You get married in those ratty old tactical boots?"

"You didn't come here to ask questions about my boots."

"A starting point," Ray tells him.

Rolling looks at his boots. "No need to try misdirecting me, soldier. Too old for games." He raises his foot off the ground, looking like a great blue heron, and hikes up his pant leg. "Been wearing these every workday for a decade. My lucky boots."

"And you didn't wear them on your wedding day?"

"Please. Got married in '54. My wife would've put a stop to the ceremony before it got started. Wore patent leather wingtips, which I rented. But how about we cut to the chase. This about money? We not pay you enough?"

"I've got plenty of money."

"Good for you. What then?"

"Why was I there. And don't give me that bunk about a stop on the PGA Tour."

"Your superiors," Rolling says, "they thought highly of you. Your evaluations were outstanding. You fit the profile. You were collecting disability — says here thirty percent — but you weren't operationally disabled. What?" Rolling taps the open file on his desktop. "Get the data, we like to say. We've had upwards of fourteen thousand employees in Iraq, but only a fraction are security contractors, and only a handful of those were collecting disability when we were looking. Of that crop, you stood out. Did your service with an elite unit. You'd been with the company since we acquired it. No red flags in your file — which is why I'm confident you'll do the right thing here today."

"What else that file say about me?"

"Not everything, never everything, but enough for us to make informed choices. It's all actuary work. Financial impact of risk, uncertainty. Assessments — some expert, some not — of individuals, properties, of systems, of assessments. War, too, is actuary work."

"So you're a bean counter. Sound like McNamara."

"Guy could do worse than be compared to the Whiz Kid. Man responsible for applying systems analysis to the most confusing decision facing an executive."

"Which tax shelter to use?"

"When and how to wage war."

"This you killing time till security bursts in here and subdues me?"

"You believe in evolution?"

"All conversations with you go like this?"

"Not all conversations," he tells Ray, "no. But I feel like I'm making my closing statement before sentencing. Giving it all I got. Aren't many people a guy like me can be candid with. Man holding a knife is one. Only other one's my wife. I understand you could be recording all this, but I've got a hunch not." He looks at Ray over the thin silver frames of his glasses. "Could you reassure me?"

Ray shakes his head.

"Maybe you know this already," Rolling tells him, "but after Rumsfeld resigned, I was approached about succeeding him. Thought Wolfowitz might leave the World Bank for the post, but he was even more divisive than Rummy. Gates was a safe choice. Good man. He and I sat together on the president's Iraq study group. I was kept out of serious consideration by the appearance of a conflict of interest, which is not the same as a conflict of interest but can be more insidious — few people know that better than the Bushes, except maybe Cheney. That, and Edith didn't like the idea. IRJ was also going through a messy divorce at that time. Speaking of, when I don't show up at my five thirty, folks will worry. You get to be my age and tardiness translates to lying dead somewhere."

"Let them worry. I want to hear what you have to say about evolution. Maybe after that you can work your way on over to why your company wanted the Standard, because I'm about to get impatient."

"We don't want the Standard," Rolling tells him, "not anymore. Sad fact of life — hard to want what you have. We're now the proud owners of the Standard. Our bid won the foreclosure auction. Won't tell you what we paid. Will say it was north of the ten million that the Concord sold for at auction. But evolution. In evolution, there's no grand design other than the underlying order. What follows is awesome chaos. Now this is where you might be interested. War's the same way. War is awesome chaos. Realistically, there can't be long-term goals. Goal-oriented thinking doesn't do war justice. Doesn't take into account its humbling complexity. Once upon a time, war was simple arithmetic. Technology — from the first club on up to the atom bomb — complicated the calculations. These days, the systems are so grand war has entered the realm of higher mathematics."

"And what do you know about war. Other than the numbers and what you see on TV."

"I've got skin in the game."

"Investments and business interests isn't skin," Ray tells him, raising his knife.

"Life is a conflict of interests. Competition — for food, for resources, for space, for mates — makes the world go round. Has now for some, oh, three billion years. Surely more, if you believe in Panspermia, which I do." His tone shifts — like a politician about to go off-prompter — from speechifying to confiding: "But when I said I have skin in the game, son, I mean I served, and I mean my oldest grandson, who's survived six deployments in the Middle East, is with the 4th Infantry Division."

"Ivy."

"That's right. Iron Eagle. Alexander's a Black Hawk pilot. Medevac unit. Airborne," Rolling says, "like you. I'm wearing the boots he wore on his first deployment."

Ray lowers his knife but doesn't sheath it, has to gather himself before he can go back on the offensive. "You serve during peacetime?"

Rolling looks up from his boots. "Makes you say that?"

"You've got that peacetime air about you."

"Do tell."

"Peacetime soldiers — and they're all your generation, Boomers — you're insecure. Failure of sympathy."

"Technically," Rolling says, "I'm pre-Boomer. Silent Generation. Sometimes called the Lucky Few. But what you're talking about has little to do with serving during peacetime. What you're talking about is old-ass age, plain and simple. Wise old man's a myth. Bitter, insecure old man — an old man is a dirty, dirty thing — now that's God's honest. Let me tell you an anecdote."

Friday morning, day of discharge, Smith received her paperwork for Excess Leave. Before she finished filling out forms, a bus arrived. No motorcycle waited out front. The civilian desk clerk flipped pages and asked, without looking up, "Airport or bus station?"

"Don't know. I'm supposed to have a ride."

"Well, you can't wait here. Airport or bus station."

"How will my ride find me? Neither of us have phones."

"Same way people found folks since time immemorial. He comes by here, he'll ask around, and he'll be told all out-processed either go to the airport or to the bus depot in town. We'll tell him we took you to one or the other. Which'll it be?"

Across the street from the bus depot, Smith ate lunch at the Gold Bar and Diner. When done, she left a huge tip for her server, Audrey, a woman with hair died the red of a hot candy apple. She took a long walk, came back for dinner and told Audrey some of her story, asked if she'd keep an eye out while she, Smith, got a room over at the Cloud 9.

While the motel manager talked, Smith nodded vacantly, thinking that she was pregnant, pregnant with no way to reach the father. And then it hit her: no longer a deserter, she'd been deserted.

During World War II, Mother and I lived briefly in Coronado, California, while my father was stationed on a carrier in the

Pacific. War ended, Father came home, and we moved back to West Texas. When I went off to Cambridge, Mass., for college —

College in Cambridge. Always means the false humility of the Harvard man.

After Harvard, I joined the Navy. Served from '54 to '57.

You're class of '54. Telling. Korea was, what, '50 to '53? Year war breaks out, you decide to go off to college?

You a reader?

Some.

You fly?

Didn't pilot airplanes, Ray tells him. Jumped out of them.

Well I did both. And your condescension's a bit confused, son. Because there's no such thing as peacetime. Especially during the Cold War. And the people making the decisions in this country all have skin in the game.

Ironic you should talk about skin in the game.

Why, you up here looking for a pound of flesh?

Not much of a taker. Debating whether to cut your throat or give you a tattoo.

Must say, if you're offering me a choice —

We'll start with the tattoo, go from there.

Where will it be?

Take your coat off. Roll up your sleeve. We'll do you standing up, like men. Ray moves the tall desk to a wall near an outlet.

Almost got one on a few occasions. Chickened out each time. Rolling offers his forearm, resting it on the desktop.

Ray turns Rolling's arm over. It'll hurt, but you'll survive.

Will I?

The tattooing.

What're you going to give me?

Gonna surprise even myself.

I'm guessing you have a few.

Wouldn't put you through what I haven't been through. Close your eyes. When Bizzy does, Ray wipes a thin coat of Vaseline on the fishy underbelly of his forearm. Ray steps on the pedal. The machine jumps in his gloved hand. He goes to work.

Hurts more than I thought.

Bleeding more than I thought. You on blood thinners?

One baby aspirin a day, all the medication I take. He hands Ray a hankie.

Hold still. Eyes closed. It'll be over in a few minutes. Meantime, tell me what you're planning on doing with the Standard now it's yours.

You ever hear of the Gaia hypothesis?

By way of an answer, Ray blots blood with

the hankie.

Can't work in hydrocarbons and not consider the Gaia hypothesis. All life on Earth functions as a single organism. Mother Earth defines and maintains her survival. Climate deniers, and I'm not one of them, they're the ones coming from a position of humility, albeit self-serving, saying we can't know. System's too complex. The Earth and its weather is too awesome to behold. Like war that way. We can't figure it out. They, too, have a few facts on their side. That during the reign of the dinosaurs, Earth's surface temperature was nearly twenty degrees warmer than today. Carbon dioxide in the atmosphere was a thousand parts per million. Today, it's under 400. We're talking boreal forests at the North Pole. And there were no coal plants spewing CO_2 into the atmosphere.

When Rolling falls silent, Ray asks, And what's that got to do with the Standard?

Oh, you know, we were planning on building a massive under-mountain bunker so the nation's elite, which of course includes me, can survive Armageddon.

Ray lifts the tattooing needle off Rolling's skin. He studies the old man's face, the lenses of his bifocals flaky and greasy.

We had a few contingencies, too, Rolling

tells him. Wasn't in the Standard file you helped put together, but maybe you're well aware that Sergeant Wright was one of the demo experts hired to carry out the false-flag operation otherwise known as 9/11. You and I both know the fall of the Towers was a controlled demolition. Overseen by Mossad. Sergeant Wright was a Mossad agent if there ever was one. Rolling opens his eyes but doesn't look down at the tattoo-in-progress. He locks his gaze with Ray's, says, There's your smoking gun, and closes his eyes. The old man then says, Of course, I tell you all this only to distract you from our real plans.

Ray steps off the pedal; the tattoo gun quiets.

Because the aliens, Rolling says, who seeded the Earth —

Ray stomps the pedal and presses hard into Rolling's skin.

— this is that Panspermia I mentioned earlier — the aliens have picked the Catskills for the landing site of the mother ship. Rolling's grin is mischievous, wacky not wicked, but Ray wants it gone. He gouges with the vibrating needle. The harder he presses, the better the numbers will look.

IRJ's been contracted to build the alien landing pad — ow. Apparently, airspace over

Area 51's gotten too congested with UFOs.

Alright, I get it.

Do you? Because conspiracy theories are the last refuge of the powerless now. Gap between information and understanding. We know so damn much, grasp so very little. Harder you look for the pattern, worse the world seems. Take the Gulf of Tonkin, which some of us lived through. The *Maddox* was attacked. Torpedoes two days later were probably dolphins. Just because the mistakes of the second day lead us to the Tonkin Resolution doesn't mean the whole thing's a conspiracy. Paranoiacs and crackpots see mistakes as grand plots. Which, in the end, is all well and good. Makes the decision-makers, ones making the mistakes — old white men like me, on their way out — seem a lot smarter than we are. Rolling opens his eyes. Besides, if I told you what we were planning at the Standard, you'd have to kill me.

Ray nods, says, Keep your eyes closed, Bizzy. Almost done. When the old man does as ordered, Ray works in silence for a time. In it, he realizes he's come to like the old coot. He's got spine, stooped as it is. Maybe it's all a ploy, but Ray's having a hard time caring enough to cause any more harm.

Ray steps off the foot switch and studies

his work. Six simple digits — *114944*. He blots bloody ink, begins to understand the bean counter's compulsion. Make the seemingly infinite feel finite. Almost lends a sense of closure. When Ray says, I'm done, he's not talking about the tattoo.

You made me a Jew?

Out of duty, a decent soldier following through, Ray tells Rolling, I've got Baum's phone. So I'll ask one last time. What's your interest in the Standard? If you don't say, you now know I've got a way to find out. Baum's phone offers all sorts of sordid details. And I can tell you the data pulled from it isn't meaningless. That's the reason I'm not recording this. Already got plenty of evidence to incriminate you. Enron'll look like a misdemeanor.

What do you want?

An apology.

That it?

And howbout an admittance of guilt.

What am I guilty of? What am I apologizing for?

Everything.

You want me to say I'm sorry for everything? Admit to being guilty of everything?

Ray nods.

By everything, do you mean Iraq?

For starters.

That's easy, because I am sorry, and I do feel guilty.

But.

But we, too, got the bait and switch. At the beginning, Iraq felt like an alignment. Turning a profit and doing some good in the world. It was only after the ball got rolling did we — and by we I mean the executives here and the board — only then did we realize, slowly, the alignment was false. By then, it was too late. Pulling out, changing course, would've done more harm.

To the bottom line.

Sure, but to the Iraqi people too. Here we are, over a decade later, and we're still trying to figure out how to leave without the whole thing falling into the wrong hands. So I say to you, I am sorry. When I'm being honest with myself, I'd have to say that, on the whole, I feel more shame than pride. That is *the* reason I'm still here. Working to tip the scales before I get fired or die. So my successor doesn't have to clean up after me.

Ray hands back Rolling's handkerchief, stained with the old man's thin blood. It's not enough, but it's something. In the red Rorschach of it, shapeless, Ray sees that there won't be an end to war, but there can be an end to any part he plays in it.

He packs the tattooing equipment into the FedEx box, the dollar-symbol gun, the Motorola computer. Then he removes the needle, unplugs the tattoo gun, and tosses it to Rolling.

He catches it one-handed. That's it?

Thanks for your time, Bizzy. I'll show myself out. He turns to go, then turns back around. One more question?

Rolling waits, studying the tattoo machine. Ever the engineer, figuring out the mechanics.

How's your landman doing after the attack?

You know how she's doing.

Want to hear it from you.

She's suing us is how she's doing.

She going to win?

Known her all her life. Worked with her father. Close to her mother. I had my druthers, we'd settle. But these days, corporations are not dictatorships, benevolent or otherwise. Accounting runs the numbers. Fair amount of money can be saved by stalling till her savings runs out.

Bet you know to the penny how much she has in her accounts.

She could have some cash socked away. He sets the tattoo gun on the desktop, and with his handkerchief he blots his forearm.

471

Walk you to the elevator.

Bizzy pushes the down button. And this number?

You're a bean counter. You'll figure it out. You can't, you can always hire a contractor to crack the code.

Tell me, you're how old?

Twenty-nine.

You've got everything before you.

Doesn't feel that way.

Never does, son.

Riding out of Houston, Ray felt — not satisfaction, not resolution — a simple, unmistakable sense of being finished with his soldiering days. He'd done his duty. He wasn't sure what came next, but he was sure it would come, and fast. He made even better time going north — he was still a day late.

After asking around at Chaffee Gate, at the Welcome Center, getting no information, he rode to the Greyhound station in downtown Louisville, unable to imagine why she'd opt for the airport. He inquired of all the Greyhound ticket tellers — nothing.

He stood outside, watching the Ohio River, the milling Louisville homeless, their winter jackets open in anticipation of a spring just around the corner. Desperation roiling in his gut like hunger, he went into the diner across the street.

Before getting seated, he asked the only server if a young lady'd been in, by herself, about yea tall, long brown hair, brown leather jacket and pants.

She smiled brightly behind her school-marm glasses and bit her tongue ring between her front teeth. With a menu she pointed to a booth.

Bellum sat glaring.

Survived my deployments, Ray thought, decade as a shooter in Iraq, only to be killed by a look in the Gold Bar and Diner. He walked over, head down, and without looking up, said, "Seat taken?"

She didn't answer.

He sat heavily, apologetically. "Look, I'm so very sorry."

"Don't matter."

Way she said it made him certain they were done. "Ant, please, it matters and I'm sorry. I'm good now."

"I don't think I like you calling me Ant." She gave him a look he'd never seen from her, withholding and worrying.

"Has something happened? Anybody hurt you in there?"

"You hurt me."

"And, know what? I can't promise I won't do it again, hurt you I mean."

"You motherf—"

"Hush. Don't curse me. Let me finish. Hurt's part of what this is all about. Willingness to hurt one another, as little as possible, and then getting over the hurt, together. I am sorry for hurting you."

"Another *I'm sorry.*"

"And I'm sorry for being a day late."

Smith said, "You get the answer you were looking for?"

"Did not. But, like you, I did get an apology."

She pushed away her plate of sandwich crusts, a pickle wedge missing a bite. "Okay."

"Okay what?"

"Okay I'll marry you."

He motioned to the server, who strode across the bustling room, and Ray said, "Could we have the check? We've got to find a justice of the peace and fast before she changes her mind."

The server did a little hop in her Doc Martens, saying, "I'll have my manager comp it. No one's ever proposed in here before, except for the time . . . Oh, you don't want to hear about that."

When she was gone from the table, Ray

said, "But first, let's get you a divorce."

They spend a full day in bed at the Cloud 9, stopping between fits of lovemaking to eat from the vending machines, before checking out.

The six-hour ride from Fort Knox to Devils Elbow is, for her, an anxious blur, sunny and blinding; for him, it's a welcome blue emptiness. The only thing she remembers of it is the stop at Office-Max to buy, for $31.99, a Socrates Divorce Kit, most of which she fills out riding in the sidecar, clutching the fluttering pages, all the while kicking at and crumpling other office paper carpeting the floor of the sidecar, a mess Ray says is nothing more than the dandruff of bureaucracy.

In Rolla, Missouri, a couple hours after nightfall, they switch spots, and forty-five minutes later she parks them at her ranch house. Travis's truck isn't in the dark drive. She puts a hand on Ray's helmet and tells him to wait outside.

"You want my knife?"

"He aint here. Foxtrot either. Too quiet."

"First sign of trouble," he says, "I'm blitzing in there like Tillman after Lynch."

She kisses him, hands him her helmet, says, "Don't fucking damsel-in-distress me."

Through the front window, the TV, huge and new, casts shimmering, swimming-pool light from one full wall. Shoshanna's watching alone, in the same spot on the microsuede loveseat Smith once occupied, eating from a yellow bag of chips.

Smith knocks.

Shoshanna answers, saying, "Oh, lord, girl, I don't know," an oniony smell on her breath.

"Shoshanna, I just need to get my important papers is all."

"I don't know. I should call Travis."

"We're just passing through." Smith points to the motorcycle, Ray watching from the sidecar.

"Oh, I still don't know."

"Legally, Shoshanna, this is my house. My name's on the mortgage. Not you, not Travis, can keep me out. Now you're welcome to keep an eye on me. All I want is the box of docs under the bed. Birth certificate. High school diploma. Medal citations. Passport. You two can have everything else. I want to cause no grief for you. I'm glad for you."

"Now you lying on me."

"Am not. I got somebody else."

"That him there?"

"It is."

"You rode up on that thing? Your new man in the buggy?"

"Please, Shoshanna."

"He finds out I just let you in here, he'll . . ."

"He hit you?"

"He alright when he's high, Bell. You know. It's when he's sober's the problem. Right now he's trying a little clean living. Makes him madder than I-don't-know-what. Keep trying to get him stoned."

"Look, don't let me in. Just go in the bedroom, under the bed, get that box of papers and bring it out to me."

"We got a new bed," Shoshanna says. "Slept fine in you'alls but screwing in it was a little messed up. In my head, not on account of the mattress. So we bought one of them space-agey memory-foam ones? You seen these? Now our sex's fine in my head, but on that mattress? Like screwing on a giant marshmallow."

"Shoshanna, you know where that box is? I'm begging you."

"One night," Shoshanna says, "I come home from work. Pulled into the drive. Big plume a black smoke, awful smell, burning plastic, nasty. Thought the house was on fire. Run round back, and Travis there, tending a bonfire in the middle of the yard. I asked where LaLa was at. He said asleep. What you doing, I says. Know what he answers? Says, Overcoming. Overcoming what? I ask. He answered me with cusses, then tossed some things on the fire. Clothes mostly, which hurt me to see. He was saving your box for last."

"No."

"Yes. Asked what was in it. He said all your important papers. Record of your life, he said, and he was gonna smoke it. Well I went right over there and picked that box up, him calling after me, and put it in my car. He fumed but he didn't get violent, not that time. He knew he was crossing a line. He's not a bad guy, Bell. Now I aint saying he good — he aint that neither — but you should see him with LaLa. Her daddy never treated her so sweet. Shoot, treats her better than he treats me."

"Where's the box now?"

"My granny's. You can go get it now, if you like. She don't sleep a wink." When Smith said the morning was fine, Shoshanna wrote down the address and gave her a hug. Then she shut and locked Smith's front door.

Near midnight they pull into the Big Papa's parking lot, and before they're parked Smith says, "There's Foxtrot." She lurches to a stop, not bothering to turn off the ignition.

She runs to her dog, helmet still on, and when Foxtrot sees her, he wags his entire lower half. She gets to her knees and hugs him, and he licks her cheek, her ear, peeing on her leather pants. She unclips his leash, so wrapped and wound up that he can hardly move. "That asshole. Not even a bowl of water out here."

Around the open tailgate of a parked pickup, a crowd of men drink from bagged bottles and cans, same as the morning she left.

Ray comes and sits Indian style at the feet of her dog, offering a hand. "Hello, Foxtrot. Heard lots about you."

Foxy-T's all over Ray, slobbering, pawing, whining, and Smith knows right there, right then, that this man is the best she's ever going to do. "Let's get out of here," she says. "Let's just take Foxtrot and go. We'll send the divorce papers through the mail."

"We came all this way." He pets Foxtrot in a way that makes the dog drool. "Let's finish it."

She sees Ray calm as can be — taking comfort in conflict — and she's livid, furious at him for getting her pregnant, for making her love him, jealous of how her dog is all over him. "We came all this way to get *my* dog. Now let's go."

"We don't start the ball rolling on this thing, it won't get done for years. I got a feeling this Travis isn't the most responsive under the best of conditions. Let's get it moving, let him know you're serious."

"He's probably got a gun."

Ray shrugs. "You want me to go in?"

"You like this shit."

"What?"

"Fucking combat."

"This aint combat. We're just gonna hand him some papers."

She needs to get away from Ray's self-assured face. "If I'm not back in one minute," she says, "come get me."

Travis is where she left him — he hasn't budged — and it hurts her. She's seen so much, faced a full lifetime of trials in ten-odd months, and here he is, in the same spot, thinner, a lot thinner. She remembers he's handsome, intense. She feels bad for him. As he sits, in the moment before she breaks the spell, she can see — given the distance gained by her leaving — how it all went wrong for him, and for them.

She puts a hand on his back. "Buy you a soda?"

His head tips quickly up, like he's just heard a voice, felt a touch, he's been waiting nearly a year for. He doesn't face her squarely, doesn't meet her eyes. She can feel the force of his pride, a trembling anger. "Travy, how you doing?"

He shows her his hard face, sharp and squared. His blue eyes like butane flame. He hasn't been this hot since she left, hasn't been this gaunt since their courtship. His eyes burn with something that scares her.

When she asks him outside, he nods and stands. "After you."

She pushes through the front door, and gasps for breath, reaching for Ray.

Travis says, "Who's this?"

"I'm Ray." He offers his hand.

Travis leaves the hand hanging. "Don't give a fuck who you are. You're at *my* club, in the company of *my* wife, holding the leash of *my* gotdamn dog. You don't back the fuck off — and let go that gotdamn leash — I'll have MPs here in no time to collect this deserter."

"Easy, cowboy."

"Travis, we've just come from Fort Knox, where I turned myself in."

"We? Fucking we?"

"You can gohead call the MPs," she says. "They'll take one look at my ID and hand

481

it back. When they do, I'll tell them you're dealing pills to soldiers."

"Horseshit you turned yourself in."

"Travis," she says, "*I'm* taking Foxtrot — and leaving you with some papers to sign."

From the waist of his jeans, Travis pulls his pepperbox. "Show me right where you want my John fucking Handcock, bitch." He points the gun at Smith's face. "Here?" He aims the gun at Foxtrot, its barrels inches from the dog's snout. "Here?"

Foxtrot puts his nose to the gun muzzle, sniffs. The quad barrels catch his breath and whistle.

"Travis," she says. "Travis."

He ignores her, doesn't raise the gun from the dog.

Ray says, "You ever even fired that four-banger, cowboy?"

Travis shifts the gun off to the side of Foxtrot's face, blindly aiming at the couple of meters of slab sidewalk separating Travis and Ray.

The muzzle flashes, warm, followed by a second flash — a scattered spark — on the cement, and the two-tone sound attending the flashes is a deafening *buc-beow*.

Foxtrot bounds away onto the hard dirt of the lot.

Travis stands nodding at Ray. "That

answer your question, *cow*boy?"

Ray takes a step forward. "Does indeed." Then he sidesteps off the cement slab.

When Travis says, "Take another step, next one's in your eye," Ray sits. Ray crosses his legs, like he did before Foxtrot.

Travis raises the gun to Ray's head. "You banging my wife? You steal her away?"

"Travis," Smith says, "you made your point. You're one mean motherfucker. Now put the gun away."

Ray grabs his knees and pulls them to his chest. He lies back on the hardpack of the dirt lot, staring up at the night. He blows big breaths from his mouth.

"Ray?"

Travis steps to Ray's side, aiming the pistol over him.

"Travis, stop."

Travis leans in, takes a close look at Ray, then turns to Smith, his face a wreck. He points in her direction, with the pepperbox. "This is your fucking fault. Fuck."

A man approaches. "Travis, you douche, what'd your dumb civvy ass do this time?"

Travis lowers the gun, turns, and dashes for his truck. He climbs in, has a hard time starting the Toyota. When it turns begrudgingly over, he peels out, throwing a rooster tail of dry dirt, heading in the direction of home.

The stranger looks familiar. "He hit?"

Foxtrot stands over Ray, licking his face.

"Ray," Smith says, "you okay?"

Ray laughs, nods, not lifting his head off the dirt. He points at her cheek.

The man says to Smith, "You're cut."

"Got nicked," she says. "Saw the slug spark off the cement."

"Must've got hit with a piece of it. That or a splinter of lead."

"Ricochets are the worst." Ray's breath is short, shallow, his voice wet, thick.

"Specially around cherries and civvies," the stranger says.

Ray says, "Who're you?"

"Name's Travis."

"You're Travis?"

"I'm Travis, too. Travis Saterstrom."

Smith says, "Ray, you hurt anywhere?"

"Had he aimed at my chest," Ray says, "I'd probably be missing a toe."

"Ray."

"It's nothing." Ray reaches up. The movement of his arm works like a pump handle. Blood, so dark it looks black, burbles out of a long narrow tear in his shirt.

Travis uses two fingers to rip open the tear — a disk-shaped entry wound.

Ray raises his hand to his chest and moves Travis's hand. His fingers find the hole and he slips in two, middle and ring. "Entry wound's elongate. Slug must've flattened out when it hopped off the concrete. Slipped right between ribs four and five." He closes his eyes. "That's not good." He opens them wide. "Think my fingers're in my heart."

Smith says, "Someone call an ambulance!"

Someone says, "They're on their way."

"Least it's still beating," Ray says. "Little arrhythmic." He closes his eyes. "Never did call my mom."

"Oh, Ray, if you die on me —" With both hands she forces pressure on his fingers inside his chest.

In the sherbet light of the sodium vapor lamp humming over them, she can see the color leaving his face — she starts chest compressions. "Ray?"

He opens his eyes, tightens his lips and forces out a few breaths. "Feeling nervous."

"Nothing to be nervous about. Understand? I'm here and I love you. You just keep looking me in the eyes, look me straight in the fucking eyes. It'll be alright."

"Let me move my hand." When he takes his red fingers out of the entry wound, blood gushes a half-inch off his chest before settling into a visibly rhythmic surge.

She watches, stunned, for the duration of two pulses. Then she covers the wound with her hand and feels each warm rush, and after a moment she thinks she feels each warm rush grow weaker.

He stares into her eyes, through her eyes, then he refocuses. He shakes his head. Something over her shoulder holds his attention, and she feels him fighting it. His eyes jerk back to hers. He gasps, catches his breath. He shakes his head, grins faintly, and his eyes shift over her shoulder.

"Ray." She feels his body slacken beneath her hands, lose all tension in a way that strikes her as wonderful — absolutely at ease, even his grin is gone — before a second later it registers as horrible. In her shock, she has a moment of clarity: even if death's preceded by panic, it's absolute relief at the end, she can be sure of that. She can be sure, too, that Ray's no more. With this, she lets herself spiral down, collapsing at the boots of the onlookers shuffling in the dirt. She butts her forehead against the ground, regains herself. The only thing that keeps her sane is the work of compressing Ray's chest for the short lifetime it takes the paramedics to arrive.

■ ■ ■ ■

SPRING
2013

■ ■ ■ ■

In the Catskills, the season is mud. Not the nostalgic mud of Yasgar's Farm down in Bethel — playful, sexy, dopey. Nor is it the constructive mud of the Middle East, where earth is crafted into dun three-story townhomes. In spring of 2013, the iron-tinged mud of the lower Catskills seems bloody, a rusted mud. It's sucking, deathly. Drown-the-dog mud. Squelching mud that swallows herds whole. Mud letting go of roots, felling age-old trees. A cold, ungodly mud. Muddling mud. Mud that fucks all logistics and tactics. No-man's-land, Never-Endian mud. Mud of the trenches mud. Mad, mad mud. Each stretched moment itself becomes mud, space and time a thick suspension between solid and liquid, a slop. That's how it feels to Smith, anyway, in the murk after Ray's death, she not entirely sure how, or why, she's back in the foothills of these mountains of mud. She tries to be grateful for small, sad things: at least it's not sand.

To escape the mud, she settles at the Rip Van Winkle Motor Inn west of Woodstock near Bearsville, where her bed feels like a foxhole she can't climb out of. Foxtrot tracks mud everywhere. Threatened with additional cleaning fees, she pays the $100 charge with a single bill, starched cash given her by Ray.

Here's what she has in the world: a soggy box of personal documents, some cash, her dog, and Ray's motorcycle, which she's coming to hate. Every time she straddles the seat, visceral memories pass through her like a current, make her want to toss a lit match into the teardrop fuel tank. Then, there's the unwanted attention it attracts.

The bike, obnoxious and racist, parked outside the Rip, stops the sparse traffic on Route 212. Paunchy, furry white men woken from their winter Harley hibernations, men with too much money, too much spare time, the ones most adamant about lowering taxes and spurring freeloaders to work harder, these men pull over to gawk.

At either end of the Rip's twelve-unit, single-story building, a man, on the western side, and a woman, on the east, tinker with junked Oldsmobiles. The man's automotive project seems slightly more sensible. A second-generation, bicentennial-year Toronado. The woman's project is outright insane. It, too, is a Toronado, a '69 Jetway 707. The stretch limousine is four-doored on each goddamn side. Off blocks it's supposed to coast on six tires, but it will never get off blocks. Despite this certainty, Smith has to fight from lending a hand, getting greasy. Over days, she discovers that the woman, Caryn, and the man, Kip, were common-law until they split a year ago. "That's right, honey, we separated by all of ten, tight-ass motor-inn units." Divvying up their possessions, Caryn got first choice of Olds.

An hour after Ray's murder, Shoshanna scooped up sleeping LaLa in her footed pajamas. She grabbed her purse, her daughter's hooded faux-fur coat, and sneaked from the house Travis was about to lose to the Armed Forces Bank of Fort Leonard Wood. With that fool somewhere inside holed up, Shoshanna called 911 from the front lawn. "You best get on over here, cause my boyfriend come home out-of-his-Ozarks, saying he shot some other whiteboy by accident. But I don't know."

The standoff on Tidal Road lasted ten

hours. Camera crews camped across the street. Neighbors tailgated, grilling burgers for the cops and news crews. Then the masked, helmeted SWAT unit forced the front and back doors simultaneously and stormed the house. They found Travis Wallace unconscious, overdosed but breathing, erratically, in the attic, the murder weapon, loaded, by his side, and over a hundred babyblue Roxicodone scattered about him on the plywood.

Smith passes herself off as a widow. She's told no one she's pregnant, but it must be starting to show. Patchouli Caryn and the other women of the Rip notice. The scruffy men simply stare at her aching, expanding breasts. She wonders if they know, better than she does, why her nipples are darkening.

   Among the lost tribe of charity cases paying by the fortnight at the Rip, she and Foxtrot, the newest members, are apparently the most deserving of charity. They find takeout lo mein left at their door, number 9, a fortune cookie for each of them, and an oily paper sack of home-baked dog biscuits shaped like legless cats.

The interim feels to her like months, but

it's been a week since Ray died. The morning she steps on a purple crocus pushing up through mud, she splashes vomit on her desert boots.

The scene she revisits over three insomniac nights — lying propped up and awake with indigestion, heartburn aching her sternum — is not Ray bleeding out in the dirt lot of Big Papa's. It's the image of the boy she ran over in Saydabad.

Poor kid had roundworms. Worms that, with the catastrophic trauma to the warm little world of the boy's body, exited their host moments after it expired. It lay there, the lifeless body — he lay there, the dead boy, half on the road, his cartoonishly flattened lower half. He'd fallen finally silent, and from out of his nose and mouth came no spirit, no soul, no rūḥ threading up to Muḥammad's subservient sun. Out came worms.

With the impending funeral down in Jersey, Smith worries Ray's storage unit might contain something the family will need, something of sentimental value. The stash of cash Ray mentioned, she's decided, is hers. Holed up in her motel room, sobbing over the tiny key on her palm, she feels guilt at her decision, and at the idea of not opening the unit with the Tyros, but she refuses to go against Ray's expressed wants.

She sets the key on the nightstand, next to the unplugged clock and the unfilled prescription for prenatal vitamins. She can't fight her way out of a fixated thought: had she told Ray she was pregnant, he would be alive. He would've held on for the paramedics, or, better, he would've stood down, turned from Travis. She and Ray on the road this very minute, aimed for Alaska. On the front bike fender, the glowing glass face of the Indian leading and lighting the way. Some part of her knows her thinking is the worst kind of black magic, wicked even. There are no miracles. Not in a warzone, not in the homeland.

The morning before the funeral, she and Foxtrot ride down to Hide-Away Storage. On her cheeks, the warm spring sun is an affront. Foxtrot disagrees, biting the breeze, happy, muddy, fattened up on takeout. The dog hops from the sidecar before it's parked, raises a hind leg to ping his piss on the sheet-metal wall. Together they find Ray's unit. When she bends to insert the tiny key into the tiny lock, she sees the hasp has been cut. She pulls off the lock, pockets it and the key, and rolls up the door.

The unit is ransacked. Things of value

haven't been taken. Ray's pair of covert military-issue night-vision goggles. A small wooden box with a couple of sterling bracelets, a gold high-school class ring, OLPH.

In the cardboard box that once kept his motorcycle helmet, she finds a mess of medals. Tangle of ribbons, streamers, brass. She recognizes most of them: Purple Heart, Meritorious Service, Army Achievement, National Defense Service, Global War on Terrorism Expeditionary, Presidential Unit Citation.

One by one, she untangles the knot, placing each medal in a row atop the box. When they're lined up, she can't help herself — she stands at attention.

At the first righting of her posture, she feels stupid, sentimental and hysterical. Yet she lifts her arm in one swift, pendulous motion, without flourish, raising her flattened hand till her fingertip grazes the edge of her eyebrow, focusing on the arranged awards, and smartly snaps down her hand.

Having run a gauntlet of her every last emotion, she stands at ease. The camel saddle, overturned, splays its four short legs in the air like a dead Shetland pony. Expecting the cushion to be cut, gutted, and looted, she flips it. On the underside, she finds the seam laced with an old leather cord soft as chamois. She unties it. Right inside the opening — as if there to hurt her, or to prove he wasn't a fraud — is a photo.

Ray and an Arabic woman, a woman so striking — black hair cleaved down the center of her head; earthy eyes; skin more toasted than tanned — Smith's drawn not to her but into her. The kind of Middle Eastern woman whose beauty is a burden she must bear into late middle-age, if only she makes it that far, a burden not just to her but to everyone in her company, her loved-ones especially. The kind of woman warlords kill for and mullahs fear, afraid of themselves, their own desire. A shameful beauty, a terrible beauty, and Ray, all of twenty, stupidly standing proud beside that beauty in his dress blues.

An understanding, disorienting, hits Smith like a stone striking her head. This young woman and her family weren't butchered because they were Christian in Baghdad, but because of their tie to an American soldier. Ray's the reason this woman is dead.

She wipes her dumb eyes.

Ray's not looking at the camera. He's looking at his stunning new bride in her no-frills wedding dress. Her smile is distanced, distracted. She looks happy as a refugee, lovely as a last breath. Her smile hints that there's a marginal difference between the Middle East and the Midwest.

Under the photo is cash, a lot of cash.

Wanting to close herself in the storage unit and pour her wet face over every object, Smith tucks the photo into the saddle cushion, not wanting Ray's family to find it. She sets the cushion on the seat of the sidecar, where it fits snuggly. Half hoping someone will steal it so she won't have to deal with it, she goes back and yanks Foxtrot's snout out of a small tin. Inside — a severed owl foot, mummified, talons like black glass. She rolls down the door and swears never to return.

At the management office, she asks if it's okay to bring in her dog, and then she sits and reports that Ray Tyro's unit has been broken into.

"You his wife?"

When she starts crying, Foxtrot whines and paws at her knee, muddying her filthy jeans, and the old man comes around the desk and awkwardly pets her dog. He retreats behind his desk, an old bachelor made uncomfortable, compromised, by a crying woman. "Kept meaning to put this in the unit for the guy. But round here it's like the march of history — one fecking thing after another. I get plum distracted." When he asks if she wants to file a claims report, she shakes her head, and he sets on the counter an Amazon box.

At the Rip, she hooks the *Do Not Disturb* sign on the knob, locks and bolts the door, and feeds the dog. Pulls shut the rubber curtains. Cranks up the noisy AC unit in the chilly room. She doesn't open the box. Not her daddy's book — too heavy — unless he wrote a doorstop. Could be more cash. A big brick of opium tar. It could be information. These days, nothing's more valuable — ask demoted US Army Specialist Bradley Manning — nothing more dangerous.

She opens the saddle cushion and dumps its contents on the bed. Neatly wrapped 10k bundles. Finished counting in a moment, she recounts and then counts yet again to be sure, coming up with the same number three times: $190,000. She repacks the cash, thinks to hide the cushion above a panel in the depressing drop-ceiling like the ever-lowering lid of an asbestos coffin. Instead, she hides it in plain sight, leaning it against the laminate headboard, a worn leather throw-pillow on the poorly made bed.

To have a grand total, she counts $722 in

her wallet. There, slipped inside, she finds the business card of Evangelína Canek. The cougar attack flickers before her open eyes as she stares at Foxtrot bolting his dry food, occasionally pausing to crunch a nugget. Her dog, unlike Egon, would've turned tail, pissing the snow as he fled. She's shocked, mystified, by Egon's courage, and by her own idiocy. She wonders how Vessey's doing.

She almost leaves for Ray's service in Jersey without opening the Amazon box, but she decides she wants to know before she goes, in case it's something she needs to convey. Using the motorcycle key, she cuts the tape and finds on top a quart-sized Ziploc bag. Inside, an ancient BlackBerry and a thumb drive. Beneath the sandwich bag is a bound ream of 8 1/2×11 office paper. On the blank cover-page is a yellow Post-it and, scribbled in dull pencil, a no-name note: *We'll always have Nama.*

She spends a minute turning pages before she needs to get ready to ride south.

Frommer and Frommer Funeral Home in Highlands is surrounded by great rundown houses partitioned into efficiency apartments.

Smith parks at the edge of the lot lining the impeccable lawn, and ties Foxtrot to the motorcycle. She'll leave the saddle cushion in the sidecar, where Foxtrot will guard it with his good humor. She pours water in a traveling bowl. Admires the building. A sprawling, glorious Victorian in perfect condition, painted in somber grays with maroon trim. The most beautiful old house in any American town has inevitably become a funeral home.

She ties back her hair and slips on her new heels. Teeters across the asphalt. Enters the foyer, ornate woodwork smelling of almonds, glinting glass chandelier that's nearly a sound, a shattering. In the open parlor, a dozen people mill under the high ceiling.

Beside the closed casket draped with the flag, two dotty old vets stand at ease, trifocals sliding down their varicosed noses. They're in dress blues and gold-piping garrison caps from the local VFW. No rifles, no bugle. The military funeral detail is a VA honor guard, not an honor guard from a nearby base. She's certain that someone looked into Ray's file, saw he spent more years as a private security contractor than as a Ranger, and sent the blow-off squad to give the send-off. On a folding chair, the old vets have a portable stereo with a CD player. They're surely going to need help figuring out how the fuck to switch it on.

Smith stands alone, embarrassed by the newness of her black dress, unbalanced on the heels that have bloomed blisters on her feet in a matter of minutes.

From a corner of the room comes an ambush feeling. Ray's mother, in draped black and deep purple, huffs her way over to Smith.

Smith clenches her fists at her sides.

Before Ray's mother squares her feet, she's reached up and slapped Smith's face.

Beneath the sting, not unexpected, Smith can't help but admire the woman. Here's someone who knows the element of surprise. Smith nods, says, "Ma'am."

"Your husband murdered my boy," she hisses. Ray's mom jabs the short space separating them with an ink-marked finger. "You should not be here."

"All due respect, ma'am." Smith's soft voice booms in the silent room. "I'm fucking staying. You can smack me around all you want."

The woman's eyes fill. She raises her hand to her lips. The ink mark on her finger is a word. Through her unspilling tears, she sizes up Smith, a regarding that makes the gaze of randy soldiers and Rip Van Winkle denizens seem heroically empathetic.

Slouching toward abortion, Smith took care to buy a black rucksack of a dress, but the woman, the potential grandmother, is not working by sight. She sniffs, as though she can smell fecundity, can sense the kindred cells multiplying inside Smith.

To distract her, Smith says, "Right before Ray was . . . before he was murdered, while he was dying, ma'am, he —" Smith steps out of her heels. "He didn't relay any kind of word. But he was thinking of you. Felt bad he didn't call you like he said."

Ray's mother turns her attention to a young man, about Smith's age, who sits out of earshot in the first row, watching. "Ray'd been a bad kid — they all three were — but a smart bad kid. Made it worse and harder both. That boy could justify anything. Joining the service was the best thing for him, cause he would've ended up like his youngest brother, in Rahway, or worse — that's what I always thought anyway. The service saved him. And here he is." She glares at the closed casket, or at the American flag. "I wound up with *or worse* anyway." She looks at Smith. "My boy was safer in a war than he was at home." She dabs her nose with her thumb. "Stay if you got to." She looks toward the ceiling. "And if that there . . ." Her voice breaks as she points to Smith's midriff.

Smith reads the smudged word written on the pad of the woman's pointer finger — *breathe* — and reading the word makes Smith gasp.

Ray's mom reaches out and takes Smith's hand. "Don't say anything, sweetheart. Not till it's real." She tightens her lips. "But I promise, here at the funeral of my oldest boy, I'll do everything I possibly can for yous two." She turns and walks slowly away, sitting heavily in a front-row seat next to the young man. She rests her head on his shoulder and sobs. After a moment, she says something in his ear.

He stands nodding, and walks to Smith, head bowed, his posture poor. He's hurtfully handsome, and Ray is plainly, painfully, in his brother's features.

When he looks up, his eyes are green flux, the kind of eyes that make it hard to look the person in the eyes. Before he reaches her, he's saying, in an overloud voice, "None of us ever thought we'd make it to thirty." Something about him reminds her more of Travis than Ray. "And Ray didn't." His laugh, like his eyes, is disarming and changeable, makes her want to get lost in him, but not for long. "Ray always had to be first. Even in this. Prick." He smiles, his teeth the color of caramel, an eyetooth chipped, teeth that confirm the wreck she was expecting. "I'm Dean."

She steps back into her heels, and they shake hands. "You want his motorcycle?"

"No shit?"

"I got to get rid of it."

"Cause you're pregnant?"

"Cause I'm heartbroke."

"Hear you. How much you want for it?"

"Nothing."

"No shit."

Two wigged women, old and odored as the parlor, press fingers to their grossly painted lips and shush Dean's cussing.

He raises both middle fingers, holding them at their flinching faces. "Anyway." He points to Smith's stomach. "Know what it says, you showing up here pregnant?"

"Says go fuck yourself?"

"That's my kind of mouth." He's assessing the small crowd, shaking his head. Those gathered are all older, over fifty. "Thought more fuckers would show for a fucking war hero. What happens, I guess, when the hero never comes home. Most of these assholes I ran into over the last however many years thought Ray'd already died. Prepared me for today I suppose." He turns to her. "What kind of bike was he riding?" When she tells him, he winks and says, "Anything I need to do to get her?"

She says he has to clean out Ray's storage unit, and when he asks how long he'd been in the States, she says a little over a year.

"Fucking asshole. You probably know him better than me. Heard yous two dropped in on Ma a month or so ago. Could've taken a minute to fucking come call on me. Haven't seen him in . . . ah fuck." He shields his eyes, his fingernails chewed short.

With those eyes covered, Smith feels a degree of relief, like stepping out of the desert sun into hot shade. "One other thing you can do is go with me to a car dealer. Then the bike's yours. Title's in his storage unit."

He says he totaled the last hand-me-down. "Glad for a second shot. Make it up to him, the memory of him." He shuffles his feet. "Come sit with us."

"Don't think so."

"Come on. Don't be a cold bitch. We'll lose our fucking shit together. You can have Shane's seat. We saved him one, same way we do for every family occasion."

"That's kind of you."

"Fucking fucked of us is what it is."

"I didn't mean . . . doesn't matter. I don't think your mother would appreciate me sitting with yall."

He takes Smith's hand, pulls her along, and guides her into the seat beside his mother. "Welcome to the carnival," he says, still standing, and when his mother nods and pats Smith's hand, he adds, "Don't say I didn't fucking warn you."

Smith doesn't attend the off-site cremation after the service, but she arranges to pick up Dean later. He lives with his mom in half of a sad duplex in a sadder part of town, by the marina along the waterfront. She's not sure she's seen a more depressing neighborhood with harbor views, and Dean's outside before Smith sounds the horn.

He stands at the sidecar, gives whining, slobbering Foxtrot a dog-person's rubdown. He reaches into the pocket of his cracked, black leather jacket. He flips her a small ceramic cylinder, which she catches.

"Your share of Ray." He leans in to kiss her. It's brotherly, and then it's not.

She punches him away, saying, "That was wrong in so many fucking ways."

Rubbing his ribs, he says, "Can't blame a guy for trying."

"The fuck I can't."

He shrugs one shoulder. "I have to ride in there?"

"If you want the bike you do."

"Helmet?"

She tells him Ray's is in the sidecar, somewhere under all that paper. "His tomahawk and knife are too. All yours but my dog and that cushion."

At Highlands Used Autos, Smith stands crying with her field pack slung over her back, Foxtrot's leash in one hand, saddle cushion in the other.

Dean, sitting on the running motorbike, asks if she needs help picking a car. When, through her gathering mucus, she tells him she thinks she can manage, he thanks her and rolls the throttle. "I'll be sure to take better care of this one." There's sincerity in his voice, but sadness, too, desperation even — she knows it too well, having married it — and she's sure he'll sell the $30,000 bike and sidecar for a fraction of its worth, go on a two-week rip, and then spend the rest of his life regretting it. But what does she know. Maybe this moment is the one that turns his life around, sets him down some other road toward a job, his own place, a cleaner mouth, whiter teeth.

She pats the glass Indian head on the front

fender. She pats Ray's helmet on his little brother's head. "Take care of yourself, Dean."

He revs the throttle, points to her belly. "And you take better care of that than you did my brother." He races off down the road.

Smith drives back to the Rip in her used four-door Jeep Wrangler, one she bought for just under 10k cash so the dealer wouldn't need to file a Currency Transaction Report.

After a lost couple hours with the Amazon document, she determines the ream of paper is the contents of the phone, plus additional information gained by hacking the phone. The phone belongs to Ellis Baum, a real-estate lawyer working out of Kingston, living in Saugerties. She recognizes SW&B. Understands that it operates under a parent company, IRJ, Inc. She reads occasional mention of a contractor, Early Bird, sometimes simply EB, who she takes to be Ray, and frequent mention of Evangelína Canek, or EC, a frequency that achieves hysteria with the final email exchanges. The last email in the *Sent* tab reads: *Our contractor has offered a safe rendition of Canek that can incriminate Wright. We interested?*

She flips back to the *Inbox* tab: the last received message is a thank-you from the Dalai Lama Foundation for a donation. The second-to-last email is a reply to the rendition query. It's from the email address marisol.soto-garza@irj.com and it is one lowercase word without punctuation: *yes*

Before a first, reactionary thought crosses Smith's mind, she's wetted by a dank sweat, a lurching twist of nausea. She tries desperately to bring back what Ray said about kidnapping Canek, and finds that the harder she grasps, the further she gets from holding Ray's words. Whatever they were, she wants to believe them.

She also wants to believe she's entitled to his money, but she has no idea what to do with it. Not how to spend it but simply where to keep it. Stashed in a cushion on the bed won't do for much longer. She can't just walk into a bank, hand the cushion to a teller, and open a checking account. She thinks of her daddy, wonders what old Increase did with the money he got from selling his Rebel Machine, sees him digging a hole in the dark, or supervising, the scalawag, while Carlos digs. She considers Milt's lawyer, Lependorf.

Switching on the BlackBerry, surprised to find it has a charge and gets reception and service, she dials Evangelína Canek's number.

When the phone rang in the kitchen, Evangelína sat up at her bedroom desk and listened — slow shuffle of Mamí's widening feet, the padding of her soles thickened and flattened.

"Ah-lo?" A pause. "Se habla Español? Okay. Uno moment." Mamí entered, her toenails painted Maya blue. Shrugging, she handed the phone to Evangelína.

"How are you?" a gringa voice said.

"Who's this?"

"Bellum Smith. From the Standard. You gave me your card. Number's disconnected. Had to track down your home phone."

Evangelína waved Mamí away. "When did I give you my card?"

"The hospital in Poughkeepsie."

Evangelína tried to remember. "My time there, New York, is one cold blur."

"And the attack?"

"That too, thankfully. My mother's read me a few of the news stories."

"Any mention of me?"

Evangelína said she didn't think so, and Smith asked how she'd been doing since.

"Bored," Evangelína said, "but better, getting better. Getting fat. I'm up and about.

Haven't done a bit of exercise since . . . well."

After an awkward silence, Smith said, "I have a question for you, couple questions. Didn't know who else to ask. Man I spent the winter with, he told me he went to see you. That's the reason I'm calling you. He trusted you, and you —"

"I'm sorry I'm slow. I'm putting all this . . . You mean Early Bird?"

"Yes, Ray Tyro."

"I hoped maybe I'd hear from him," Evangelína said. "Find out if he learned anything from my old boss. When I didn't, I figure he'd gotten stonewalled. Or . . . Is he okay?"

"He . . ."

"Jail?"

"Killed."

"Ay, Dios. Here in Houston?"

"No, in Missouri, by my husband."

"You're married." Evangelína didn't know what else to say.

A muffled crunching came from Smith's end.

"Your husband," Evangelína tried, "he didn't . . . Did he happen to have ties to my former employer? That you know of?"

"Travis has no ties to nothing."

"But that's exactly the kind of person they'd use as a contractor."

"Contractor?" The gringa's tone grew loud, shrill. "You mean contract a killing?"

Evangelína pulled the receiver a foot away from her ear but could still hear the outburst. She had a hard time following, but she got the last sad part. She pressed the phone back to her ear and said, "Don't hang yourself."

"Okay, I won't. Scout's fucking honor. So let me ask you something else. Say I came by some money. A lot of money. Cash. I want to know if I can keep it."

"More than ten thousand dollars?"

"Yeah."

"You come by it legally?"

"Well," Smith said, "I don't know. Ray left it to me."

"Is there a will?"

"If there is, I'm not in it, that I know of."

"Well, if you go to deposit the money, a bank must file a Currency Transaction Report on anything over ten thousand."

"Used car dealer was just telling me the same thing. It's close to two hundred thousand."

"Wow."

"Yeah."

"Any next-of-kin?"

"Does the fetus I'm carrying in my fucking belly count?"

"You're pregnant?" When Smith didn't respond, Evangelína cleared her voice, with difficulty, and said, "Legally, no. Not now. But children born after the death of a parent — probate law calls them after-born — are entitled to a share in their parent's estate. But because all fetuses don't come to full term, the right to inherit's only realized after birth."

"After-born, huh. Not sure this one's gonna get born, least not in one piece."

Evangelína got the sense that the gringa was trying to upset her.

"The daddy," Smith added, "Early Bird, was Airborne."

Again there was the crunching sound, as if the pregnant woman — contemplating abortion or suicide — was crushing chicharrones in her wet fist. It made Evangelína feel loco. She swallowed hard, hurt, then reminded herself she'd been warned about this: sensory triggers. The reminder calmed her enough that she could hear Smith say, "He's got — had, fuck — a mother and a couple brothers."

"Early Bird does."

"Did. Ray."

"They know about the money?"

"No."

"I imagine it'd be hard to be excited, given

the . . . well."

"Excited about what?"

"Having a baby."

"Come on." A moment passed in stiff silence, and then the gringa said, "You still trying to have one?"

"How did —"

"You mentioned it, at the hospital. You and me had a real female bonding moment, very sisterly, at Vassar Brothers. I was there, you know, for your attack."

They shared another silence broken by Smith launching into the story of the mauling and her role in saving Evangelína's life. It didn't feel like Smith was telling it for Evangelína's benefit. The telling felt mean, but when it ended, Evangelína — hurt, unsettled — was grateful for the telling. A hole had been filled, partially, and Evangelína wanted to ask questions, but she hadn't yet formed them.

Smith was saying: "I'm a bit bummed you don't remember me as your Florence Nightingale. Thought my use of tampons was mighty clever TCCC. That's tactical combat casualty care for you civvies."

"I won't ever need another tampon," Evangelína said. "Can't get pregnant either. Surgeries made sure of that. I've some eggs in deep freeze. Paying to store them, which

I don't think I can afford. Not covered by insurance. You wouldn't want to buy an eight-acre plat overlooking the Pacific in southern Costa Rica? I'd give you a deal. Two hundred thousand?"

"Maybe. What'd you pay?"

"Thirty-five," Evangelína admitted. "That was ten years ago. Bought it imagining an early retirement, that I'd build a house. Eased adoption laws down there. Saw myself taking care of my aging mother by the sea. What better place than a Spanish-speaking country with no army. That was the dream anyway. The reality's poor old Mamí taking care of me. But you don't want to hear mi cuento triste. That's sob story for you gringas. The money, you mind paying taxes on it?"

"Taxes provided my way of life in the Army, way of life I'd take back in a second."

Evangelína advised Smith that as long as she didn't mind paying taxes, the government wouldn't care. Found money, when declared, was taxed as income. Same as gambling earnings or a lottery win. On 200k, 33 percent was the federal rate. Plus state tax. "State of residence, not the state where you found the money. You'll keep about sixty percent."

"Still a lot of money."

"Know what you'll do with it?"

The crunching stopped; a scratching sound started, followed by a whining. "Need to go," Smith said. "Other reason I called's because I've some information you might be interested in. Information Ray came by. Don't know what it means. Don't know if I should take it for what it is or if there's some other explanation. Makes me worry I never knew him. Makes me not want to have his baby. But that's neither here. Where should I send it?"

In Kingston Smith pulls the Jeep into the Planned Parenthood lot. No protesters wave posters of butchered fetuses, and inside she spends the better part of the first day in a group waiting room, watching hour after hour of an infomercial for Xpress Redi-Set-Go, a kind of knockoff George Foreman Grill. She comes to think this kitchen appliance is a Planned Parenthood sponsor. Before she meets with a healthcare tech, she sits through a gruesome counseling session with a social worker, who starts by saying not to worry, abortions are very common. When Smith asks what's common, she's told that one in three American women have an abortion by age forty-five. This makes her feel worse. She's told she has options, and notices the woman doesn't say *choices*. When asked when she last had her period, she says they haven't been regular, but the last one was early November maybe.

If she's right, she'll need an in-clinic procedure, and they don't do them there.

When Smith asks about adoption, she's told there are two kinds: open and closed. Open adoptions happen when the birth mother and adopting family have contact. She asks what if the adopting family's a single woman, a lesbian, living with her mother.

Agency adoptions have more restrictions, but with an independent adoption, where she knows the person, whatever that person's proclivities, everything's handled through a lawyer. You should have your own lawyer to represent you and your interests, no matter how much you trust this woman and her mother. In an independent adoption, you can still receive counseling and guidance through a local adoption agency, if you want.

She's told that during her pregnancy, she has the right to decide on adoption and, even after the baby's born, to change her mind. If you choose adoption, you will have to sign official relinquishment papers after the baby's born. "If you don't sign, you can keep the baby with no repercussions. If you do sign, there's no going back."

Outside with Foxtrot, she makes herself a deal. She'll call Evangelína. If the woman wants the baby, Smith will carry and deliver it for her. If she doesn't, Smith will abort.

When Evangelína answered, Smith said, "You get my care package?"

"I did. Thank you. I owe you tremendously. I might owe you everything."

"Don't forget I also saved your life."

"Yes, I do forget. Thank you for reminding me."

"Want to pay me back?"

"How?"

"Take this baby. Because if you don't want it, I'm gonna get rid of it."

"Where are you?"

"Depressing motel in the Catskills."

"How far along are you?"

"Twenty weeks."

"Ay ay. Hold on. Give me a second. Lot has happened since we talked last. If I say yes, what will you do?"

"Part of me wants to reenlist. Be much easier if you took this baby off my hands. I helped you, now you help me."

"When's the latest you can have the . . . ?"

"Abortion, you can say it. Got four weeks to decide, but I can't wait that long."

Trembling, Evangelína tried to conduct herself the way she would during a business deal, hopeful but noncommittal, wanting to believe. "Tell you what," she said, "you think about it for a week or two. Try to imagine delivering a little boy or girl —"

"Got a feeling it's a girl."

"You getting morning sick?"

"Morning, noon, and night."

"Mamí says bad morning sickness is sure sign of a girl. Imagine delivering a little girl, getting a look at her, and then saying goodbye. If in a week or so, you think you can go through with it, you call me. I'm interested, very. Give me a call either way."

After filling her prescription for prenatal vitamins and opening a checking account, Smith signs a two-year contract with a cell-phone carrier that comes with a slick-glass smartphone. She's reentering society, and it makes her anxious. On her phone, she types in a Google search while sitting in the AT&T store — *travis wallace devils elbow* — and the top hits are newswire sites all running the same story:

The Strip Club Shooter, Travis Wallace, of

Devils Elbow, confessed to accidentally shooting and killing Ray Theodore Tyro, of New Jersey, a former US Army Ranger. Wallace avoided trial on a murder charge by pleading guilty to involuntary manslaughter. Under the plea agreement, Wallace would be required to serve at least five years in prison and could receive up to seven years.

A week to the day, Smith texts Evangelína: *U still want it?*

Evangelína calls, and when Smith asks how she's doing, Evangelína tells her that she's better than she's been in years. "Not allowed to talk about it — signed a nondisclosure agreement — but I can say that after my lawyer saw your package, we filed a whistleblower disclosure. IRJ settled in two days after some hard negotiations. Held out as long as I could. Wanted to see my old boss squirm. It paid off, in more ways than one. Thanks to you, so long as I'm careful, I'll never have to work again."

"And about this baby?"

"You tell me."

"When I left my husband and my post, only thing I regretted was not taking Foxtrot with me. My dog. Afraid this, not taking my baby, could be infinitely worse. If that's true, I won't make it. But I don't know."

Evangelína says, "What if we get things started. I'll pay for all the legal work. We'll proceed with adoption plans, and when you have this baby, boy or girl, if you get a look at it and want to keep it, you do it, and you raise it the best you can."

"Okay."

"In the meantime, what'll you do?"

"Keep being pregnant," Smith tells her. "After that? Don't know. Know it's crazy, but part of me can't stop thinking about going back to my unit. Try to make up for deserting them. Or do something else along those lines. Become a UN Peacekeeper — I don't know. There's a volunteer program in Jordan I've been looking at. Working with disabled children. I'd have to pay to go, which seems shady. But I've got the money and the time. Been in contact with my unit. Waiting to see if my discharge gets upgraded. Got support letters from people who knew me in the service, so I'm hopeful. That doesn't work, I could try the National Guard, maybe go active over time. Other thing I keep thinking about is Fort Irwin."

"In the Mojave?"

"My outfit trained there before I shipped out my first time. Almost all outfits do.

National Training Center."

"I know the area some. One of the IRJ subsidiaries, Clark Nova Energy Group, is building a huge solar installation there."

"Been thinking," Smith tells her, "maybe I could do what Milt did. Vets of these wars would get more out of a halfway house in the desert. At the NTC, they simulate the Mideast to get troops ready. We should use the desert as a jump point back into civilian life. Been thinking I might be able to find a defunct motel close to Fort Irwin, convert it to a home for vets. Want to help me?"

"Help you how?"

"We could go in on it together. Be partners in a nonprofit. You and your mother could help me raise my baby."

"Sounds nice, like a storybook, but I don't think so. I could help you find a property though. Help you make an offer. It's what I do for a living — what I did."

At the Standard, new *No Trespassing* signs have been posted, but there's nothing stopping Smith from pulling up the winding drive.

She parks in front of leaning Standard Tower. Leashed Foxtrot pulls her toward the Alpine village, where smoke rises from the cook fire. A person, not wearing an alpaca hide, tends a giant kettle. She hopes it's Vessey, worries it's a stranger.

As she nears, she recognizes Wisenbeker. Leaner and taller, his hair higher, his beard longer, he's got a cauldron boiling. Smells like laundry.

Wisenbeker says, as if their conversation were interrupted by nothing more than a sneeze, "Been selling scrap. You know the Zaborskis? Stan and Gary? Stan's coming by this week, and Gary next. Hate each other. When Gary split off from Stan, who kept the family business, Gary went and opened Stan'z just to fuck with his brother."

Smith unleashes Foxtrot, who sniffs around the jammed door of the Kosher Konditorei. "Stan did."

"No," Wisenbeker says, "Gary." Then he says, "You must've found a home, got on the path. Gotten fat."

"Pregnant."

"How far along?"

"About four months."

"Doing the arithmetic here." Wisenbeker squints, tapping his thumb on the fingertips of one hand. "It Milt's?"

"Vessey still here?"

"Milt's dandy lawyer come by telling us to vacate, handing out checks. Best eviction notice I ever got. Recouped all my disability.

That, plus what I'm planning on getting for that bell, I'll be set. Pound of scrap brass is going for a buck fifty. That thing's supposed to weigh close to forty tons. You got the math to figure that out?"

"Tell me."

"We're talking 120k. Even if I pay a crew 25k to come in with a crane and a flatbed to hoist up both halves, I'm still making out. Someone should, now that Milt's gone."

She realizes Wisenbeker's stealing and selling scrap that belongs to the company that bought the Standard; she's tempted to help him. "You hear anything about the other boys?"

"Little here and there. You hear Luce died?"

"No."

"Found him in a cattle car. Bet you my balls it was a hit job. Botes reenlisted. Stone's in Coxsackie. Prison a little further upstate. Story goes that after he left here on the day it rained bats, he went to a firehouse in Neversink. From the payphone out front, he called the firehouse. Ordered a sixpack of Coca-Cola. Reverend told him it was some code for a drug buy, and poor Stone was hard-up enough to believe it. Whole fire company stormed out and started beating on him. He pulled a knife and stuck one of them before the cops got there. Took a serious walloping. Hear he aint the same Samuel Stone. Judge threw the whole shelf at him in addition to the book. They're seriously protective of firefighters in this state since 9/11. Got twenty years."

The sentence is nearly four times what Travis got for killing Ray.

"Luckson made a rap CD," he says. "Calls himself Hazard Us. I got one here somewhere if you want to hear it."

"It any good?"

"Nothing to play it on. STD's been seen in the city."

"At a shelter?"

"Times Square. Hands out tracts. Got God or God got him. He's a deacon for the Seventh-day Adventist Church in Harlem. Ephesus it's called. They think Saturday's the seventh day of the week and the Second Coming's coming any day now. They're even vegetarian."

"And Vessey?"

"He still eats meat."

"He still here?"

"Somewhere. What about Reverend? He hasn't been up at his camp."

From the pocket of her leather jacket, she pulls the small ceramic urn.

"Hell's that?"

"His remains. Portion of them."

"Get out."

"Taking them up to his camp to scatter them."

When Wisenbeker asks what happened, she whistles for Foxtrot, who comes bounding over. "Merced?"

"Went back to Hoboken. Apparently the dude did have a wife and kids. Came up here and carried him off. Kind of an intervention."

"And the cougar, any sightings?"

"Big search party gathered here. Before they come through, we had a couple of foresters spray-painting orange Xs on trees, but Merced and me, before his wife abducted him, we went in right behind them with cans of olive drab and painted over their Xs. Slowed them down. Property went into foreclosure before they could start cutting. Then surveyors came in a day after the sale. Day after that it was a bunch of crowd-sourced grassroot environmentalists. Auctioneers are next. After that, maybe demo. Who knows. Why I'm trying to score a buyer for the bell while things are in-between and the new owners are none the wiser. Couldn't stand downwind of those treehuggers and not smell weed. They were furious about all the illegal snares, threatened lawsuits. Told them, Hard to sue a dead man, but not impossible. They turned up scat, some tufts of fur that were probably bobcat. Before he left, Merced spent a month hunting it. Setting traps. Swears he came close. But me? I'm convinced it don't exist — that you, Vessey, Merced, and that little Tex-Mexican — you all fabricated the cougar after some crazy psychosexual foursome gone wrong. That Luce witnessed the whole deviant thing, so you offed him. Am I warm?"

On Slawson Mountain, the yurt still stands. Its walls are slack, its domed roof sags, the flue pipe tipped at an odd angle. The flap that replaced the hide of E. Prince hangs by a catgut cord. The camp looks inactive, the fire pit washed out by the spring rains. Foxtrot finds the little dammed basin, and he drinks for a minute, the hike up hard for him and her, she having to stop to rest, to pee, half hoping the exertion would bring about a miscarriage.

The yurt is empty but for the woodstove. She holds open the flap, breathes the air — their air — till Foxtrot goes in and lies down. He looks up at her, waiting.

Outside, she unscrews the top of the urn. A knotted plastic bag. She unties the knot and folds the mouth of the baggie over the rim of the urn. Ray's ashes are just that, gray dust with little white masses that must be bone or teeth. She wets her finger and dips it in. Ray coats her fingertip. She tastes him — salty, chalky.

The child-to-be inside her — a her for sure, it feels overwhelmingly female, because a daughter would be harder for Smith to bear — maybe she, Shenandoah, would like to have something of her father's some day, even if it's only his remains. Smith reminds herself that she won't get to name the girl, the girl won't have a father, and that she, Smith, won't be the mother. Shenandoah, a stupid name anyway, every bit as stupid as Antebellum. Like mother like daughter. Maybe years down the line, after a reunion, mother and daughter can make a road trip from Key West to Deadhorse. There, the girl, whatever Evangelína names her, can scatter her daddy's ashes at the end of America.

She reties the bag, screws on the cap, shoves the urn in her pocket. She collects three small slabs of bluestone and balances them on top of each other.

Beside the yurt, she approaches the cliff. It's her duty to consider throwing herself over. Not proper mourning if there's no thought of suicide. What she feels at the idea

— overlooking the valley about to break, at any moment, into leafy green — is shame.

Around front, she opens the flap, wanting nothing more than to curl up inside next to her dog and cry herself to sleep.

She wakes to the whines of Foxtrot, alert, listening for sounds outside.

A voice says, "Knock, knock," and it's careworn.

She falls out of the yurt, picks herself up and stumbles into Vessey's open arms. "Easy, sweetheart. Hike up nearly did me in." He hugs her till it hurts. "Alright now. Wiz told me you were pregnant."

Foxtrot pokes out his head and whines.

"How about you introduce me to your four-legged friend here."

After he gives Foxtrot a thorough petting, he rights himself, wincing, one hand in the small of his back.

She says, "Come stay with me, Vess, at the Rip Van Winkle. My back's killing me too. And I bet I'm more incontinent."

"You mean leave all this?"

She nods, and when he says lead the way, the three of them hike gradually downmountain.

"Okay," Evangelína says, "so I've got a few

listings."

Smith shrugs the phone to her ear. "I'm peeing. So you know. I'm always peeing."

"I understand."

"Anything promising?"

Evangelína tells Smith that one stands above the rest. Little defunct motel for sale in Newberry Springs, two towns away from Fort Irwin. About an hour drive. Can't get much closer to the base without living on it. The motel's in terrible shape. On three-and-a-half barren acres, right on what used to be Route 66, which is now National Trails Highway. Property's not listed, but there's a hand-painted for-sale sign on it with a phone number.

"How'd you find it?"

"Took my mother on a little road trip. We needed to get out of Houston. I called the number, left a message, and the man called back in minutes. He was asking 125k."

"That's too much — I've still got debts to square."

"Wait," Evangelína says. She tells Smith that she compiled a comparative market analysis. In '05, in a town two hours east of Newberry Springs, a buyer bought a Roy's Motel and Cafe, which was in very good shape, and in working order. In addition to the motel and café, he bought the entire surrounding town of Amboy and all of its near 1,000 acres. Paid just over 400k. "I told this to the man on the phone. Made mention of the bursting of the housing bubble, the Great Recession, maybe he'd heard of them? And then I offered him five thousand dollars. He said ten, and we settled on seventy-five hundred. It's yours if you want it. Now you can hold out for something a little better. There are a few others I found, but they're further away and not nearly as affordable. You should probably see it first. I don't want you to have any misgivings. The place is not just in bad repair. It needs a ton of work, but the structure's sound. And there's one more thing."

"It's on the site of a former nuclear testing ground."

"Right next door is a little diner where they shot a German movie in the eighties. Name of the place is the same as the movie, the Bagdad Cafe."

"You're joking."

"Can't make this stuff up."

"Anything else nearby?"

"Town of Barstow's twenty minutes west."

"I know Barstow. Almost got a tattoo there. Seventy-five hundred? Shit."

"This guy wants cash. Price goes up ten

percent with a check."

"You let me think about it?"

"Take all the time you need," Evangelína tells her. "Seller admitted the place's been on the market for over a decade. You have other things you're considering?"

"Still waiting to hear if my upgrade will go through."

"If it does?"

"Hell if I know. You sure you still want this baby?"

"I'm sure. You taking your prenatal vitamins?"

"Yes, ma'am."

"My lawyer has all the paperwork ready," Evangelína says. "When he sent it over he reminded me, as often as not with independent adoptions, birth mother backs out. So just know I'll understand if you have a change of heart. I'll be disappointed but I'll still owe you."

"Sick and tired of changes," Smith said, "of heart or otherwise. I should go. The Bagdad Cafe? I'll be."

Smith spends the next two insufferable months waffling, retching, and expanding at the Rip. She hates being pregnant, wants her fucking body back. Using her phone, she self-diagnoses: hyperemesis gravidarum.

Her OB offers an official diagnosis, pregnancy, and tells her she's free to seek a second opinion. Her vomiting has eased some, but she's queasy more than not. Takes two ondansetron a day. Her list of ailments and discomforts gets longer by the hour. She got Vessey a room three doors down, and he works it off preparing meals she throws up, making sure she takes her vitamins, walking the dog, doing the wash at the Next to Godliness Laundromat in Woodstock.

At week thirty-four, she can no longer slide her tummy under Caryn's Olds limousine to tinker with its shot transmission. A week later, she goes to pee, feeling indigestion and stomach upset, constipated, crampy, her lower back seizing. Blood pressure's high, her feet swollen, her breasts weep. When she wipes, the toilet paper is blood-tinged. She stands.

In the bowl, the water is pink, and something, a fleshy mass, reddish and wormy, is sunken at the bottom. Here's the miscarriage she's been dying for. She reaches her hand into the pissy water and fishes out the fleshy bit. There're none of the bones she's seen in the sonograms. She runs her hand over the globe of her belly, still tremendous.

When she calls her obstetrician — Dr.

Dyssegaard in New Paltz; Smith wanted nothing to do with the Woodstock patchouli doulas — she's passed along to the gynecologist at the two-woman practice, Dr. Carlson, who tells Smith she's not holding a miscarriage. "It's your mucus plug. Toward the end of a pregnancy, it turns pink, sometimes red, which is why passing the plug's called the Bloody Show. Dr. Dyssegaard's here. Her hands are full at the moment. She's saying loss of the mucus plug by no means implies labor's imminent. But this is early, and given that you were born preterm, she wants you to go straight to Vassar Brothers. You need to remain as still as possible. Don't drive yourself. Have someone drive you or call an ambulance. She'll meet you there in less than an hour."

The flight from Houston carried Evangelína over the volcanoes of Nicaragua, three of them smoldering outside her window — Cerro Negro, San Cristóbal, Concepción — smoke puffing out of their blasted peaks. After a rough landing in Liberia, Costa Rica, she flew aboard a puddle-jumper to the Nosara airport for the groundbreaking of her hilltop property overlooking Playa Garza and the Pacific. She'd yet to sell the parcel she owned outside Ojochal, on the northern edge of the Osa Peninsula, which hadn't stopped her from purchasing the three acres she stood atop.

Her builder, an expat Californian surfer thickening around the middle, spoke Costa Rican Spanish like the Ticos, who didn't roll their Rs, and was working closely with the Nosara-based Blue Morpho Architecture, the boutique firm that had designed her sustainable home-to-be.

Mamí was unhappy with the plan, but resigned to it. Move-in was three years away. Mamí said she wouldn't live to leave Houston. Evangelína had overseen enough construction projects in Central America to know that three years likely meant five. She also expected the job to go 25 percent over budget.

In the heat, 80s year-round, she refused the shovel offered her, content to watch the backhoe dig its first gouges into the red-sand earth that was hers. A troop of howler monkeys in the nearby trees bellowed competitively at the excavator's engine.

She signed documents, wrote checks, and said her goodbyes to walk downhill, dirt switchback after switchback sending scary shivers up her repaired Achilles tendon. Stepping over a procession of leafcutter ants waving green flags, she approached the house she'd rented from one of her eventual Vista Royal neighbors. She called Mamí, told her how the landscaping had been described, the plans for hillside terracing, the list of fruit trees — mango, papaya, granadillas and guanabana, rambutan, and the chicozapote you asked for, though the Ticos call it níspero — then she sat out by the rental's pool overlooking the panoramic view of the Pacific, some six kilometers away and a thousand meters down. She opened her laptop and, after checking her email, ran the Google search she'd been performing once or twice a week for months: *F Bismarck Rolling.* Her search yielded two new hits.

The first was an IRJ press release titled "IRJ Announces Organizational Changes." In fewer than 500 words — a quarter of which constituted the disclaimer about forward-looking statements — Bizzy received little more than passing mention: *Former COO F. Bismarck Rolling is retiring after 33 years with the company.* No direct quote from the chairman, president, and CEO. No thanks or praise. No mention of the ensuing SEC investigation. Just as they'd done with Evangelína, the company had yanked the rug out from under poor old Bizzy and swept him under it. They'd

even gone so far as to name a woman —
Rosalyn Johns, formerly Vice President,
Corporate Compliance, at Fluor, one of
IRJ's main competitors — as the new COO.

The other hit her search turned up was
"Litigation Release No. 20701 *Securities
and Exchange Commission v. F. Bismarck
Rolling,* SEC Charges Former COO of IRJ,
Inc., with Extortion." The webpage at
sec.gov read:

The Securities and Exchange Commission
announced today that it charged former
IRJ executive F. Bismarck Rolling with
violating the anti-corruptions provisions of
the federal securities laws. The Commission alleges that Rolling and others partic-
ipated in an extortion scheme to coerce a
private-property owner and take control of
the property with the potential to lead to
construction contracts worth more than $3
billion.

The Commission alleges that beginning
as early as 2011, Rolling, with help from
contractors working in New York, determined it necessary to frame the private-
property owner in a kidnapping plot. Contracts would then follow to build a large-
scale infrastructure project. To conceal the
extortion, Rolling used his executive as-

sistant to approve the kidnapping of a fellow IRJ employee, a crime that was ultimately never acted upon.

Without admitting or denying the allegations in the complaint, Rolling consented to the entry of a final judgment that permanently enjoins him from violating the inchoate offense of attempt and conspiracy, with prosecutors charging the aforementioned to be established by proof of a probable or potential impact in accordance with the provisions of 18 U.S.C. § 1951(b)(2), popularly known as the Hobbs Act. Rolling has also agreed to cooperate with the SEC's investigation, and to offer closed testimony before a senate Subcommittee on Energy hearing.

The minute she was back in Houston, Evangelína would have her attorney start the process of making a Freedom of Information Act request for the report ultimately produced by the SEC's investigation.

Smith rides shotgun while little contractions pull across her lower stomach. Foxtrot stands on the backseat behind her, his face out the window. They're stuck in traffic going over the Kingston-Rhinecliff Bridge.

Vessey idles in neutral, shuffling the stack

of six quarters for the toll. "It's ten thirty in the morning, where the hell could everyone be going?" He pats her knee, saying sorry, he should've shot down 9W and gone over the Mid-Hudson.

"It's fine, Vess. I'm not having this baby now anyway. Even if I am, I'll be handing it over. What do I care." She looks hard out the window, but all she registers is the roiling ache in her uterus, the ambiguous sadness in her chest.

At the tollbooth, Vessey shouts at the attendant that he's got a pregnant woman in the Jeep. When the woman, with inch-long, unpainted fingernails that curve like horn, asks, "She giving birth?" Smith answers with an irate, "No."

The attendant says, "If you're giving birth, I could radio a cop to give an escort."

"I'm not giving fucking birth."

Vessey asks the ETA on getting over the bridge, and the woman tells him traffic thins about halfway. Fifteen minutes here to there.

They creep forward.

"Vess, tell me something to take my mind off this baby and what the fuck I'm gonna do with it."

"What do you want me to tell?"

She shuts her eyes. "Anything, I don't care."

"Alright. So Wiz was saying the Great Recession never happened. Or it happened but it wasn't because some global housing bubble. What happened, cording to Wiz, was the US, the UK and the EU've been siphoning off trillions of dollars, pounds, and euros since climate change was confirmed. Says *housing bubble* became code for the ATSS."

"Which is?"

"Advanced Technology Space Station. They've been building it at Dulce Base in New Mexico in conjunction with the Large Hadron Colander in —"

"Collider."

"What'd I say?"

"You said *colander.*" She breathes, winces.

"Well the LHC in Switzerland? Sweden? Wiz was saying it's the public face of a top-secret project. Half underground, half outer space. Just like our good old government. Make a big show of saying they're shutting down the space shuttle program. Next day they launch the X37-B. You know about this? Classified space drone. Funded by the Pentagon's black budget. Can fit it with an atomic weapon that drops radioactive rods, tungsten or some shit, on enemy targets. Rods from God, they're called. Wiz says he's seen it taking off and landing near the Gunks. Thinks there's some secret base in the Catskills. We have no idea, sweetheart. Or we have —"

"Think I'm about to succumb to preeclampsia over here."

"Don't joke. You want that cop escort?"

She opens her door. Before she steps out, she pulls her ratty desert boots over her bare feet, her stomach in the way, and folds over the tops. When Vessey asks where she's going, she says, "To walk aways. Look out at the river. Come pick me up. If I beat you to the other side, I'll wait there." She scratches Foxtrot's jowls, and the dog squints his little-boy eyes. She plants a kiss between them. "Be good for Vess now."

The wind blows, defining the shape of her, describing her ends. It parts the tight leather jacket she can no longer zip. She breathes deeply, reaching for the waist-high cement wall topped by a guardrail.

On the far side is the rolling horizon of the Berkshires, gentle peaks of the Catskills at her back. Between these two beautiful rises runs the Hudson River Valley, the wide silver swath of open waterway. A tug pushes an empty barge upriver, hardly advancing against the current, a current washing toward New York City like a faraway scream.

The more she walks, against her orders, the further the vista vanishes. She imagines what life's like for the little body inside her body; she refused to learn its sex. Is it anxious to get out, or is the anxiety all hers, her body needing to rid itself of the drain on it?

When Smith has left behind the banks of Ulster County, passing over the choppy Hudson, she shuts her eyes, one hand on the cold, curved cylinder of the guardrail, one hand on the warm curve of her belly — what a plunge it would be — her hair whipping up around her head — and then a queer thing happens. She feels the spiral sensation that foretells one of her panic attacks, but she doesn't feel the fear, paralyzing, and the spiral isn't downward and inward. Everything and everyone isn't inside her, a mad construct of her disordered mind. It's as if here, on this bridge, with her eyes brightly closed, she can know their minds, know their lusts and trials, can understand — vaguely, mysteriously — what Travis's life was like over this last year, and Ray's life, too, and Milt's and Evangelína's, the vets of the Standard — the cougar's even — they're all there for her to fathom — momentarily, mistakenly — they're all a part of her being, imperfectly imagined and misunderstood, but it's okay, it's something, she's trying to know them, and it's the trying, not the knowing, that's everything.

A car honks. Inside her, a human floats. What a rude awakening it's bound to get, squeezed from a warm, dense sea into the thin air of planet Earth. But it's too soon for all of that. Smith's only in her thirty-fifth week. She marches harder, faster. She has another month or more to go. As she thinks this, it's as if the hooked thought — she has time — brings to bear its opposite — it's time. She feels a pop, submerged, near the floor of her pelvis, and from out of her pours a warm flood, filling her untied boots.

APPENDIX

Evangelína got a call from the Nosara cart-
ero, who said she'd been sent a large envelope with a USA return address. She and
Mamí left the house early. They'd pick up
the girls after their errand.

They wended precariously down to the
main road, rough-and-tumble 160, the four-
wheel-drive engaged. Mamí, asleep before
the gate to the drive closed behind them,
dozed in the passenger seat, her head
bouncing disconcertingly, like an infant's.
Past the Nosara Yoga Institute, where Evangelína took classes five mornings a week.
She stopped in Garza to let pass a mixed
herd of livestock. Two pigs. Goats. One
water buffalo. A dozen thick-skinned Brah-
man cattle, droopy ears, their dewlaps draping in folds down their chests. The livestock
were herded by a vaquero on horseback, a
lasso looped in his gloved hand. Three, four
calves trotted to keep up. The sight of them

sent a tremor up Evangelína. She'd been told by a Chorotega rancher that one in five becerros in Guanacaste were eaten by jaguars.

Evangelína hadn't thought to consider Costa Rica's wild jaguar population when deciding where to retire. She had — hopefully, wistfully — settled on Nosara because of the education offered by the Del Mar Academy. An independent co-educational day school with a culturally and economically diverse student population, DMA offered an innovative, bilingual English-Spanish immersion program for her daughters, Monserrat and Maura.

The fifteen-kilometer drive to the post office would take forty-five minutes. The roads were abysmal, gravel that, in the dry region during the dry season, churned up great storms of dust that settled over the lush tropical foliage, making the leaves and fronds, the creeping vines and vivid flowers, look blanketed by fallout ash.

Located between the airport and the Red Cross, the post office stood shabbily, a white block building, blue trimmed, with a corrugated red sheet-metal roof that deafened in the downpours of the wet season. Carteros in Costa Rica were detectives. One in five letters were delayed or disappeared. Letters came in addressed to: *Cedar tree, 500 meters up, house with iron railing, painted blue.* Or: *Building, on the left, metal gate, just down from fig tree, old man out front, smoking.*

The return address on the envelope mailed to her was destroyed but recognizable: from her attorney in Houston, a business relationship she'd maintained for the Byzantine bureaucracies facing the expat single-mother of two adopted Tica orphans with dual citizenship.

Evangelína and Mamí arrived early at the Del Mar Academy, and Evangelína parked in the wet dirt lot. A blackstrap smell seeped into the closed cab of the SUV and put her in mind of burnt flan. Homeowners and businesses controlled the Guanacaste dust with monthly dousings of thinned molasses.

While Mamí slept, Evangelína opened the envelope, ignoring her attorney's cover letter. She skimmed to determine what the document was — the result of her years-ago Freedom of Information Act request — and then, skipping the title pages, she read the transcript starting with Bizzy's opening statement.

STATEMENT Of F. BISMARK ROLLING, FORMER COO Of IRJ, INC.

[Certain information has been redacted in accordance with IRJ's FOIA request for confidential treatment.]

Mr. ROLLING. Chairman Franken and Members of the Subcommittee, I am pleased to appear before you this afternoon to discuss the charges brought against me.

In fall of 2012, we sent —

The CHAIRMAN. Mr. Rolling, my Senate colleagues have deferred to me, because of my interest, but if you would jump straight to the events immediately precipitating the arrival of Ms. Canek in New York State, the Committee would be grateful.

Mr. ROLLING. It just so happens, Mr. Chairman, if you'll allow me —

The CHAIRMAN. I'll allow you.

Mr. ROLLING. Ms. Canek was laying groundwork for what promised be the largest ████████████████████████████ Once it was up and running, we wanted Evy to —

The CHAIRMAN. Evy is Ms. Evangelína Canek?

Mr. ROLLING. It is, Mr. Chairman.

The CHAIRMAN. And do you have an

intimate relationship with Ms. Canek, sir?

Mr. ROLLING. If by intimate you mean friendly, Mr. Chairman, I am a family friend.

The CHAIRMAN. Ok, proceed, Mr. Rolling.

Mr. ROLLING. Mr. Chairman, we eventually wanted Ms. Canek to be regional officer in charge. But her mauling complicated things.

The CHAIRMAN. The cougar, was it?

Mr. ROLLING. Cougar, mountain lion, puma, panther, all the same thing apparently.

After we won the foreclosure auction, activist environmentalists started pushing the idea that the cat was an Eastern mountain lion. A roundup yielded DNA they're claiming shows it's distinct from the Western mountain lion. As such, it's eligible for protection under the Endangered Species Act. A bogus claim, a stalling tactic, but Cuomo —

The CHAIRMAN. Governor Cuomo.

Mr. ROLLING. Governor Cuomo, the second, asked the US Fish and Wildlife Service to conduct a review.

The CHAIRMAN. We're aware.

Mr. ROLLING. Then you're aware development is on hold indefinitely. The concern at IRJ, and in Albany, is that the stoppage will keep us from ever breaking ground. The rush to development is because you allowed a popular incentive, ▮▮▮▮▮▮▮▮▮ to lapse. You renewed it in January. You might renew it again in '14, but we can't be sure. So we sit —

The CHAIRMAN. I remind you you're no longer an employee of IRJ.

Mr. ROLLING. They, excuse me, Mr. Chairman, they sit on the Standard plat, which in the end they got for just above market value.

The CHAIRMAN. Please tell us more about Ms. Canek.

Mr. ROLLING. We wanted her to have been there from the start. The thinking was that would've given her the authority to manage what would become a three billion dollar project. But we didn't tell her. Plan A on the table at that time started with ▮▮▮▮▮▮.

The CHAIRMAN. IRJ has ▮▮▮▮▮ ambitions?

Mr. ROLLING. You make it sound like we're Iran.

The CHAIRMAN. That's not an answer.

Mr. ROLLING. No, not as far as I know.

The CHAIRMAN. And plan A?

Mr. ROLLING. If anything it was ▮▮▮▮▮

The CHAIRMAN▮▮▮▮▮▮▮▮▮▮▮▮▮

Mr. ROLLING.▮▮▮▮▮▮▮▮▮▮▮▮▮

▮▮▮▮▮▮▮▮▮▮▮▮tremendous engines toward reviving the two most depressed local economies in the state.

The CHAIRMAN. Why not just build ▮▮▮▮▮▮▮▮▮▮ on state land?

Mr. ROLLING. Republicans in the state legislature are the ones working toward environmental conservation, keeping more of the parks "forever wild," as the state constitution says, but that's a secondary aim for them. They want economic revitalization for two regions of the state that vote conservative.

The CHAIRMAN. But that's not it.

Mr. ROLLING. I'm not sure what you mean.

The CHAIRMAN. I mean the plot to extort

the landowner.

Mr. ROLLING. The answers to these questions are always a bore compared to what the imaginative mind dreams up. In the end, it's business, drab and undramatic, meeting after meeting, followed by the moving of money. Every once in a hundred meetings, you get results that lead to something getting built. That's the payoff. The making of things.

The only people who think there's a second coming of the Borscht Belt heyday, like my wife, are the ones bedazzled by sentimentality and nostalgia. Someone with a little ice in his heart has to come in and say, Tear it down. Start from scratch with something else.

Now instead of a depressing, soul-sucking casino, imagine a ███████ there. ███████ ███████████████████████████████████ ███████████████████████████████████ ███████████████████████████████████ ███████████████████████████ for a geezer like me, to see a shift like that, that would be very rewarding. Might even help balance out what harm I've caused.

If it weren't for those moments, I'd've retired at 55. Built my own airplane.

The CHAIRMAN. Very rueful, Mr. Rolling. Heartwarming, really. But what about the attempted extortion? The plotted kidnapping of Ms. Canek? We have the emails in front of us. We have Ellis Baum's deposition.

Mr. ROLLING. Look, I'm responsible for those emails, and all of their incriminations, because Marisol and Ellis were under our employ, but I didn't authorize them, I did not write them, and I do not believe they did either.

The CHAIRMAN. Who then?

Mr. ROLLING. Chinese government. Some primary schooler in Kamchatka. A former employee. IRJ has been an ongoing target in something called Operation Shady RAT, gets in the neighborhood of 100 attacks a day on its . . .

The CHAIRMAN. Yes?

Mr. ROLLING. You've dragged me into deep water here, Mr. Chairman. You've got me talking tech. Point is, it wouldn't be the first time our email accounts were hacked.

The CHAIRMAN. Ms. Soto-Garza is facing serious charges. You're going to let your lowly secretary take the fall?

Mr. ROLLING. She's not lowly, Mr. Chairman.

The CHAIRMAN. Were you having an affair?

Mr. ROLLING. With my secretary more

than half my age?

The CHAIRMAN. Answer the question, and keep in mind you're under oath.

Mr. ROLLING. I was not having an affair with my secretary.

The CHAIRMAN. That wasn't the question.

Mr. ROLLING. May I have time to consult with my counsel?

The CHAIRMAN. Please.

[. . .]

Mr. ROLLING. Mr. Chairman, we're going to take the Fifth.

The CHAIRMAN. I see. The buck stops with Ms. Soto-Garza.

Mr. ROLLING. I won't be baited, sir. But I would like to thank you, the other Members, and the SEC for the opportunity to testify before you today. And if I may add one more thing, Mr. Chairman.

The CHAIRMAN. If you're expecting to have the final word here, Mr. Rolling, you've come to the wrong place.

Mr. ROLLING. Please, Mr. Chairman, if I may. We, IRJ while I was there, were changing with the times. We were doing our damnedest to tap into reserves here. As you know, the president supports Alaskan drilling, including offshore Arctic development. And IRJ's already there, raring to go.

This isn't drill, baby, drill. This is drill or kill. Irony of the last two presidencies is, the oilman waged war while the law professor drilled for oil. The latter understands that nothing weakens our adversaries like ██████, and does so as peaceably as humanly possible. From al-Qaeda on up to Venezuela, Russia and China.

What I'm saying is that the Standard Grande — and that's "Grande" with an "E" for your stenographer — was part and parcel with national security. Indirectly, and a very small part, on a relatively miniscule parcel. But IRJ doesn't move on an investment like the Standard unless there's a whole host of options. One of which may ultimately be ████████████████████ ███████████. But plan A was beautiful. Plan A was clean. Plan A was trial tested by an earlier initiative, Sunrise at Seventeen Seventy. Plan A was aligned with your progressive, conservationist interests.

Thank you, Mr. Chairman, and my wife, in helping prep me for today, wanted me to tell you she loved you in *The Coneheads*.

The CHAIRMAN. Yes, well, thank you, Mr. Rolling. You may be getting a number of questions from Senators for a response in writing. And might I suggest, given the energy you've shown here today, you should go ahead and build that airplane.

With that the committee's adjourned.

[Whereupon, at 3:42 p.m., the hearing was adjourned.]

Evangelína's huffing, panting anger roused Mamí, and Evangelína was glad for it. The old woman felt somehow to blame for Bizzy's smugness, his chummy, clubby grilling by a C-list celebrity gringo senator.

Bizzy, having an affair? With Marisol? The preposterousness of that line of inquiry made Evangelína doubt the authenticity of the entire document. And Plan A? Bizzy sounded like Mamí talking about the Maya God A, a catchall that could be almost anything. And the redactions! And the misspelling of Bismarck!

When Evangelína threw the transcript fluttering into the backseat, Mamí blinked her dry eyes, tasted her dry mouth.

Evangelína barked in English, "Mamí, get the girls."

When the old woman didn't budge, Evangelína stabbed her finger at the school surrounded by jungle.

Mamí was confronted with the button of her seatbelt. Still strapped in, she fought with the door handle.

Evangelína released Mamí's seatbelt, feeling like she was the mother of three, reached over Mamí's lap and heaved open the SUV door, offering no hand during the long, precarious minute it took little Mamí, getting littler by the day, to climb down and out.

When the passenger door failed to close, Evangelína yanked it shut and read her lawyer's cover letter, blindly at first, then with some comprehension. He noted that the redactions fell under the fourth and fifth exemptions of the Freedom of Information Act. The transcript was a Congressional Committee Print, not an official Committee Report. Prints were viewed as internal publications. This likely prejudiced the Federal Communications Commission in IRJ's favor.

Evangelína knew, too, that the FCC got in far more trouble for releasing information than for withholding it. Her attorney noted the date of the original filing: the request had been placed nearly four years ago. The holdup was caused by the government-wide practice of giving companies a chance to object to the disclosure of requested documents. One of her former coworkers had likely read the transcript, stalled for two or three years before recommending redactions, which the FCC then approved or denied.

Her lawyer closed by telling her she still had options. If she wasn't satisfied with the FCC response, she could appeal. After an appeal, they could then file a civil lawsuit in US District Court to try to force more disclosure.

She jammed the cover letter into its battered envelope. She thought to go back, tear through all the documents she'd amassed: corporate, clandestine, the emails, the endless trails of paper and data. She could try to recall all the conversations. There were certainly clues to be found, signs and inklings that would reveal what IRJ intended for the Standard Grande. What did Bizzy mean that Plan A was trial tested by an earlier initiative, Sunrise at Seventeen Seventy? What did Sunrise have to do with the Standard? She had the sense — general, vague — that all she needed was the wherewithal, and the time, to find the answer. But she also needed to care.

As she sat in the air-conditioning, she couldn't bring herself to want more waiting.

Her two daughters came bopping out of Casa Building, on either side of Mamí, nearly as tall as their grandmother, each holding a bony hand. Mamí kept up, shuffling her sandaled feet over muddy molasses. At six and eight, the girls had both overcome their developmental delays, mostly minor. Monserrat, whom they called Bunny, with her surgically repaired cleft lip, which Mamí said meant she'd been conceived during a lunar eclipse; and Maura, older but shorter, her free hand scratching her stubborn patch of eczema, likely exacerbated by her since-treated congenital syphilis. They were adorable, giddy girls she'd saved from a dirtfloor orfanato, and they helped Evangelína to fit in among the peaceful people of Costa Rica.

Evangelína's resentments and suspicions vanished, for a time, as she watched an old woman skip hand-in-hand with her granddaughters. She vaguely remembered when the idea of a child seemed to offer not just an answer but *the* answer. Then, she'd taken custody of these girls like two open-ended questions. Here they were — asthmatic, unbelievably messy, mostly healthy — two beautiful, bottomless wells of inquiry. Question after question, asked in three languages, one of which Evangelína barely grasped, until Evangelína began to question why she'd wanted children in the first place. Eventually, inevitably, they tired. They fell asleep on the shady patio couch, with its heartswelling view of the Pacific, nestled into their Chichí, all three of them snoring, and Evangelína had her answer.

Bicycle Lake Army Airfield recedes in the Humvee's rattling sideview mirror. Three klicks up ahead, a small Middle Eastern city shimmers beyond the heat haze. Flooded and distorted by the desert, the city is an island in a silver lagoon. On the far side of the city, the wavy road narrows to nothingness beneath brown mountains.

Ant drives her three-man team. As they draw nearer, the dome of the mosque, stratosphere blue, looks more Russian Orthodox than Islamic. A pair of minarets flank the dome. The sun — white, insistent — feels like a daylong interrogation halfway done.

In the up-armored, crows-mounted M1114, the chunky tires sing against the sandblasted asphalt. They ride high. Sixteen inches of ground clearance — and four-wheel, double-wishbone suspension — lets them sink into kettle-holes and bounce out the other side without busting an axle or throwing the differential.

Every jolt feels to Ant like the beforeshock of a blast. She has to remind herself she's not in the Middle East. She can only imagine how her passengers feel, these three boys. Their combat's closer in tow. Especially tough for the two in the tight backseat. The boxed-in windows offer what might as well be the view from a microwave.

She turns up the AC and loses a hundred horsepower. She wants to calm her crew. First, she needs to calm herself. Be cool, be careful. Total the Humvee, this little program will end at the beginning.

As they draw nearer, her thoughts muddle; her heart quickens. She has a hard time recalling the names of these soldiers — soldiers she's led for months — but she knows her sense of displacement will pass.

At the approach to the simulated city, Jersey walls line up unevenly along both sandy shoulders, more scattered than situated. A green sign with white Arabic lettering over English reads: *Yekiti Bajar.*

"That's it," she says, "pretty sure." She tells them that the command here, at the National Training Center, changes the city names from conflict to conflict. "Supposed to have a couple Russian towns left over from the Cold War. Hear they're fully operational yet again. When I trained here in '07 it was Iraqi. Think this was Medina Jabal."

Riding shotgun, Dopp says, "For me it was Ertebat Shar, sim Afghanistan."

"How come I didn't train here?" Goodman asks from the backseat.

Steed pounds the heel of his fist lovingly into Goodman's shoulder. "Cause you're a blue buddy, served in the Chair Force, piloting a D4D."

"Didn't know you flew," Dopp says over his shoulder. "What's a D4D?"

Steed laughs.

"Technically, *I* didn't fly," Goodman says. "D4D's a desk, four drawers."

Ant recruited her three boys in San Julian Park, downtown LA, two hours away, found them scuffling among the other Hollywood homeless, bivouacking in the streets.

A concrete-block footbridge, slathered in gray stucco, angles up and arcs sharply over both lanes of the two-lane road.

Steed says, "Ambush in wait, right there."

A flagpole stands at the center of the footbridge. On the pole, at half-staff, a Syrian flag luffs in the sizzle breeze.

"Well, boys," Ant says. "We're a tad early. Don't see anyone, so we'll sit loose and wait for the welcome araba."

"This fake town," Dopp says, "this Yekiti Bajar was supposed to be Medina Jabal in your time?" At her right, Lance Corporal

"Big" Ike Dopp is her favorite, nervous, compact, and canny. His acne blurs the line of his strong chin, bubbles his honed cheekbones.

She looks hard at him questioning her. In his clear eyes, it's there: not long ago, when called upon, he was capable of doing severe harm. The violence in him, like with all of them, was circumstantial not constitutional. Once Dopp gets a little more distance on puberty, Ant's sure he'll be decent, and handsome. She's trying to fix him up with the pretty petite bartender at Lil's Saloon in the Calico Ghost Town turned state park. But riding shotgun, picking his pimples while challenging her command, he could pass for a zitty eighteen, a cherry inductee daydreaming about the legal prostitutes of Kuwait. "I don't think so, ma'am," he says. "Think this must be Medina Wasl. Or what was."

"Big Ike," Steed says, "how the hell you know?"

Dopp shrugs, pinches a red welt on his neck he's been fussing with for days.

Ant swats his hand, and when he apologizes, she throws the Humvee into gear, drives under the fortified city gate of the footbridge.

Well trained, they part their mouths and

breathe in quick gulps till they're released out the other side. Smack-dab into a narrow, nameless street tight as a tourniquet. The two-story buildings look designed to disorient. Walls an inch or more off plumb. Windowsills unleveled. An ensnaring cat's cradle of electrical wiring hangs overhead. The rooftops are arrayed with gray satellite dishes aimed every which way.

She knows her boys are stiff with dread — the shit talk's gone silent. They pass an open-air butcher shop, no butcher. A skinned goat, bloodied, hangs from the ceiling beam. On a stainless-steel table rest three slabs of meat. The sight is gruesome, but no flies buzz. No sweet-metallic smell wafts through the door Steed's opened to get a better look.

Goodman says, "Like everyone bolted in the middle of whatever the hell they —"

Steed slams his door. "At's how they do when they know an IED's about to blow."

Her heart's up now, and she rounds the traffic circle at the center of the village. Five roads branch off at odd angles. There, surrounded by Jersey walls and in between a pair of dead palm trees, is the three-story international hotel, the Lyndon Marcus Jr., which was in Medina Wasl not Medina Jabal, far as she can remember. "Month after next," she says, "if we don't botch this mission coming and going, we'll spend the night there."

"Goody and Dopp get one room," Steed says, "you and me share the honeymoon suite?" A lapsed black Mormon turned lackadaisical Five Percenter, Private First Class Ruffin "Steady" Steed talks on occasion about his deceased father, who didn't believe military service was a substitute for missionary service, and so disowned him.

They drive past the mosque visible on the approach. A slice of crescent moon, golden, perches over it, sharp as a Soviet sickle.

At the center of the traffic circle stands a clumsy cement statue, cast not sculpted. The head of the towering woman is covered in a hijab, and one hand clutches her abaya, raising the hem to outrageously show her ankle. She holds up her other hand, palm out — she's either waving or she's commanding, Wadrega!

More and more, Ant believes they're in the wrong damn medina.

There's a bicycle repair shop. Pile of dusty tires and rims, pile of rusty frames. An archway shows a sign to the souq, the open-air market. They pass a closed gift shop.

"Amazing," Goodman says. "I want a souvenir."

The gift shop does it. "You were right, Big Ike. This must be Medina Wasl not Jabal. Or what was Wasl." She exits the traffic circle first chance she gets.

Steed says, "What if we're in the wrong damn medina and they're conducting live-fire exercises in this here one?"

"If we're in the wrong medina," Goodman says, "we'll be late for our rendezvous."

"We'll double-time it to Jabal," she says. "Seven klicks separating the two medinas."

"How many medinas they got?"

"Whole slew," Ant says. "Secretary of General Staff, LC Perry, toured me through Medina Wasl and Jabal, or whatever they're now called, one right after the other. Month passes, I guess they blurred together on me." She pulls into a driveway and, without a rear windshield to see through, makes a blind K-turn. They take another spin around the traffic circle.

"Making Goody dizzy," Steed says. "He's gonna sick-up."

"This is our first run at this, boys. Maiden voyage. Yall are my guinea pigs, so we've got some problems to work out."

"Ah, Houston?"

"There's no danger, Steady. Relax. The Box here's all a secure part of Fort Irwin."

"Second I relax's when the world ends."

Dopp asks, "World or the war?"

They find the route out of the faux-Arabian ghost town. Head east-southeast toward the Chocolate Mountains on a rougher patch of road. The heat opens like a furnace door.

"Big Ike," Goodman says, "how'd you know that wasn't the right medina?"

He tells them that he did three weeks of MILES training out here way-back-when. "Jabal means mountain. Mountains're up ahead there." He flushes, his pimples turning purple, and says, "Did well on the DLAB."

"Which is what?" Behind Big Ike, Goodman cracks his knuckles. When done with those, he'll start popping other larger parts of himself. None of her boys can sit still, keep quiet, not even while asleep, when they tremble and whimper like pups with distemper.

"Defense Language Aptitude Battery. Enlisted to become a Marine cryptologist. Was sent to Monterey, Cali-forn-i-a, where I flunked out of the DLI, lasted —"

"Don't acronym us to death." Goodman pulls a knee to his chest with a liquid snap.

"Defense Language Institute. Did okay in conversation, but there was something about the text, which goes right to left like your Hebrew, Goody, that I couldn't wrap my head around. Flunked out. Got the swift desert boot. Fore I knew it, I was in Fox Company, 2nd Battalion, in southern Helmand, reinforcing Brit and Estonian forces at Now Zad."

"Big bullshit, Big Ike." Steed flings open his door — hot air floods in — the door bangs shut. "You mean to tell us you fought the Battle of Now Zad? How we just hearing this?"

"Know how it is, Steady. Marines do most the fighting but you Army boys do most of the talking and the dying."

"You my brother from another mother, Dopp, but that don't mean I wont drop you, eat the eyes straight out your skull, part your eyelids like labia, and have me my merry fucking way with your head."

"Alright, Steady," Ant says, "that's about enough of that."

"Sorry, ma'am. I get overexcited. Talk about it, Dopp."

"Bout getting skull raped?"

"About Apocalypse Now Zad."

Dopp laughs like a boy too often bullied. "Shot a lot." He stares out at the desert.

Over these months — hell, years — Ant's been waiting for and working toward this moment. Get vets to let down their guards in the desert. She says, "Go on, Ike."

"Got shot at a whole lot more. Sampled some poppy pods. Pashtuns eat em like crab apples. Reason their teeth are falling all out their beards. Opium's everywhere in Helmand. They grow poppies way we grow corn. Combat I was part of went house to house. Field to field. For six straight months. Had a few firefights in acres of blooming poppies."

"Man, I can see it," says Goodman. "Kabloom."

"I can't."

"Well, wish I couldn't, Steady. Most unreal thing I've been party to. Also, most real. White and pink poppy flowers everywhere. Wore em in our helmet bands for added camouflage. Muzzle fire like orange poppies. Bullets and bees zipping past. Got bee stung on my damn neck and thought I was a goner." Dopp fingers the welt he's been worrying. "Getting high at night. Fighting all the livelong day. Wake up, shit in a sandy hole, too beat to cover it over, scarf some eats, go on patrol, find a fight that fills the hours, head back to base camp with heat-bent barrels. Eat, get some shut-eye, repeat. Didn't see the end of it. Lima Company relieved us. Brits and Estonians were reassigned at the same time. Those bros needed out and bad. Brits are one thing, but the Estonians? Man alive. Dudes're something else entirely. Nother order. Polar Bears they call themselves. Estonians at Now Zad were on a vodka drip. No joke. They had an IV bag on a pole filled with Viru Valge. They'd plug in for a minute, no one bothering to change the dirty needle. They all had phlebitis. Bad strain of meningitis went through their ranks. Were trying to get sent rearward. Brits didn't think the IV and their shot immune systems was the cause. Said the Estonians were all buggering each other, passing the bug around that way. Those dudes'd turn on this DJ Coone jumpstyle song, *I got something for your mind,* was the refrain, and in unison, like someone flipped a collective Estonian switch, they'd all start hopping around like Arian fascists in some Nazi fucking musical."

Steed sings, *"The hills are alive . . ."*

"I know that Coone song," Goodman says. "Catchy."

"Well, got its hook in me. For damn sure. Dance they did was part dubstep, part goose step. Stechmarsch. *Got something for your mind,* alright. Be hearing it on repeat till the day I die. Probably be my dying words. Shit would send me spiraling. Still sends me spiraling. You want to fuck with me? Give me a full-on anxiety attack? Play that song. I'm straight back in Now Zad, mesmerized. Taliban trying to murder my ass with ABIEDS."

"I know VBIED," Ant says. "What's ABIED?"

"Animal-borne IED," Goodman says.

Steed says, "Donkey bomb."

"There, it was goat bombs. All the bombing, improvised or otherwise, turned Now Zad into a wasteland. We were wasted as the place. Bombed-out town'd blown our minds. Snugged at the foot of the Hindu Kush. Got water from an aqueduct built by the Brits in the sixties. Was an honest-to-god oasis apparently. Electricity in the homes, a bazaar, a health clinic, a school. Place even had a gas station. Taliban started using it to rest up between fights. In '08, Brits bombed the region to clear out insurgents and moved in on foot."

"Queen giveth," Steed says, "and the Queen taketh away."

"We followed. That was it. My war. Rest's just bookends." Dopp nods at the desert. "Still there. Living terribly ever after. Here in body, but part of me, sometimes most of me, is stuck the fuck in the Now Zad."

After a hurtful silence, Ant says, "A life is

just a body keeping pace with time, boys. All it is. Our hearts and minds, on the other hand, aint bound by time. Free to roam. Recall the past, fantasize about the future."

"I've got a fantasy for you, ma'am."

"Can you let the lady talk a minute, Steady, without sexually harassing her?"

"He's all right, Goody. I understand Steady Steed has a hard time showing affection in a way that aint preteen."

"Alright, ma'am. Apologies, you were saying."

"Part of me's still stuck in a parking lot, Steady. Place I lost someone I loved."

Steed says, "Your babydaddy?"

"When I'm in one after dark, have a hard time getting out. In heart and in mind. Sure I always will. I'm what you might call heart stuck." She feels a downward tug, losing some of herself. To combat the loss she says, "What was I saying?"

Goodman and Dopp say at the same time, "Heartstuck," and Steed says, "Jinx."

In the crook of two mountains, Jabal comes into view, its sunbaked cluster of buildings smaller than Wasl.

Ant slams the brakes.

Her passengers brace themselves, and the Humvee skids sliding to a halt in the sand. The snaking column of dust they were kicking up swallows them and, through the belly of it, the sunlight filters red.

Ant makes eye contact, in turn, with each of them, torqueing herself to see Steed first. Looking at him, it occurs to her that this was how Milt felt — self-assured and insecure both — driving her up to the Standard. She saves Dopp for last, glares into him, and in his skittish eyes she sees the disconnect — he averts his eyes. She puts two fingers on his knee. "Kind of like your vehicle died on you in Now Zad and you ditched it there."

Steed says, "This another one of your paramilitary parables?"

She points up ahead to Jabal. "You been traveling on foot. You're tired. You keep thinking about that vehicle you abandoned, wishing you hadn't just ditched it."

Dopp asks, "Vehicle's my heart or my mind?"

Ant pats his knee. "Our job's to get it up and running. Got to get a little dirty. Check the plugs. Change the starter maybe. Sometimes rewire. Sometimes hotwire. Jumpstart. We've got to revisit the place, or pretend to, and do so in a safe, secure way. Might surprise you, but what we should be doing right now is playing that song."

Goodman says, "I got something for your mind."

Ant revs the V8 turbo-diesel engine. "We Americans like to talk about chasing dreams. But first —" She revs again. "— you've got to chase your fears. To do that, you got to identify them." Another rev. "Woman I see in Barstow, therapist who's not a script writer in the pocket of Big Pharma, she specializes in EMDR, eye movement desensitization and reprocessing. She can help. When you're ready. Cause if you don't figure out your fears, dreams'll never be within reach." Ant slams the gas, throws the Humvee into drive. The gearbox grinds and the overburdened vehicle lurches forward, shooting two modest rooster-tails of sand. "All we're trying to do is get your mind out of that time so you can live in ours." She pats Dopp's knee. "Together, here with us. Do that, terribly ever after will lose some terror. Won't ever be happily. Promise you that."

Steed slams his door — it bounces back open.

Dopp touches the bump on his neck. He presses it but doesn't squeeze it.

Steed leans up and says near Ant's ear, "Weren't you an 88-mike?"

"Was indeed, Steady Steed."

"Then hows come you don't know where in tarnation we're supposed to be?"

"My driving's better than my navigation."

"I'd say." Steed leans back, closes his door and reopens it.

Ant says, "You don't like the females in charge of things, Steady, you best stop the world and hop on off. That or emigrate to the Islamic State caliphate. Cause we women'll be running the show here in the States for some time to come. Get used to it. Now take it easy on that door — that's an order."

"Yes, ma'am, but do tell the door to take it easy on me. Thing won't stay shut. Spent the better part of fifteen months living out of one of these fucked-up up-armored kegs. You white motherfuckers, yeah you, playing that grindcore shit nonstop. Band names like Hog Decapitation, Dead Baby Tree, Veil of Maya. Laugh, Goody. You think I'm making these names the fuck up. I aint. Sickass whiteboys. Took me six months and winning an arm-wrestling tournament left-handed before I got them to concede to some old-school, hardcore Body Count." He kicks open the door and shouts out at the desert, "Shit! Like doing my goddamn service in a busted-up diving bell! My daddy was right! Should've went off to Haiti to raise churches. Had I wanted to be a sub-motherfucking-mariner, I'd've signed up for the pussyass Navy. Next time, MTO Smith, I want an M998, wide open to all the elements, the Cadillac convertible of Humvees. Can I make that one damn request, pretty fucking please?"

"I thought you boys would want AC."

"What I want's to be able to breathe."

"Alright, Steady, easy, you got it. Next time. Keep in mind this is a joyride. Cruise with the door wide open if you got to. Only shrapnel might come flying in's the shell of an armadillo. This all's an exercise. And I feel it too. Just like you. Right here's the scene of most of my worst nightmares."

Goodman says, "Have this recurring one. I give Muslim women Brazilian waxes."

"Nice," Steed says. "Wait, where's the nightmare? You gay, Goody?"

"Not far as I know."

"I'm not criticizing."

"Bothers me how they're all lined up," Goodman says. "Waiting for me, depending on me. Gives me the heebies. Got a sky-high stack of wooden waxing sticks. Pot of hot wax. And I go to work. One by one. Yanking their pubic hair out. As-salāmu 'alaykum, I say. Wa'alaykumu s-salām, they say. Next."

"Goody," Steed says, "you do live up to your damn name. Bet even your war crimes're wholesome."

"As if all war aint a crying damn crime."

"What about you, Coach?"

"My war crime?" She drives in silence through the desert. There's her answer. But she says to Steed, "The one time I did my own Brazilian wax."

"Don't be flip now. Why we're here, aint it? Supposed to be swapping sob stories?"

"Maybe at lunch, Steady, if you behave."

Steed says, "You sure you don't want me up on the .50 cal?"

"No one's manning the machine gun, Steady. If you didn't notice, mount's empty."

Steed grabs the joystick on the control group behind Ant's seat. To Goodman he says, "Want to play a little *Call of Duty?*"

"Looks like a scaled-down version of what I flew." A blue-collar Chicago Jew, tall, with gypsy ancestry and what Steed calls a young-Gaddafi mop of hair, Airman Asa "Goody" Goodman passed for Chilean, Greek, Palestinian, French, Algerian, on and swarthily on.

Dopp says, "Thought you didn't fly, Goody."

"I was 18-Xray. UAV driver. Ninth Attack

Squadron."

"You," says Dopp, "a drone jockey?"

"Don't believe him," Steed says. "Yids are all full of stories." He pushes his door wide open and the desert air washes in.

Dopp says, "One job I wouldn't want."

With a sudden jerk of his head, touching his ear to his shoulder, Goodman pops his neck. "What's the Reaper pilot say to his sensor operator?"

"Tell us," Dopp says.

"Says, What'd we hit?" Goodman waits.

"Well?" Steed says.

"Sensor operator answers, Either a funeral. Or a wedding . . ." Goodman looks out the window. "Or a funeral for a wedding."

Steed says, "Damn."

Ant brakes at the entrance to the city. There's movement. "Okay, keep in mind, this is a peace mission we're on. This is to recast your wartime experience with one that requires no vigilance and no violence. Understand?"

"Affirmative."

"What's our objective? Steed?"

"Our objective's to eat lunch, ma'am."

"That's it?"

"That's it."

"That's right."

Dopp says, "We're not here to rescue the *Kobayashi Maru*?"

"Ike," Steed says, "no one has no idea what you're babbling about in North Korean."

"I do," Goodman says, "and I don't believe in the no-win scenario."

Steed sits up and points out the windshield. "Hajji COB-V, one o'clock!"

"We're a COB-V, Steady." Ant honks the horn. "We're civilians, on a battlefield — albeit simulated — in a vehicle."

A rusted-out, dinged-up jingle truck rolls by. Metal tassels hang from the undercarriage of the Hino, its windows tinted impenetrably black. The truck slows as it passes. On one wall inside the open dry-freight box, the handle of a push broom aims out.

"Here they're flying the Afghan flag."

"And here we go again."

The moment they're inside Jabal, the Humvee is descended upon. Steed holds closed his door. In the middle of the street, vendors have road-blocked the way with tables displaying wares. There's no getting around them. Ant leans on the horn. A crowd, some seven or eight men and women, push platters of fruit and dried fish toward the Humvee.

"Must be the place."

"They're putting on some serious show for us."

A vendor in a qaraqul hat, of the kind worn by Karzai, wraps on Steed's window till he opens the door. "Khaakandaaz. Khaakandaaz." The vendor makes a peace sign, then shows two shovels, one without a handle. "Khaakandaaz. Twonty Afghani."

"Twenty, motherfucker, twenty?"

The man nods.

"D, motherfucker, D."

The man shrugs. "Twonty. Twon-ty."

Steed holds up ten fingers. "Howbout ten?"

The man makes a noise like a goat, "Baah," spits in the dirt, and turns his back.

"Nice attitude," Steed says. "Hajji spits but hajji don't surf."

A boy, no more than eighteen, sprints down the street. All heads turn and watch. As he swipes a toaster oven off a table, Ant waits for him to explode. The cord trails behind him in the dust like a tail. A woman in a shami dress screams, "Wudrega! Ghal!" Her chador falls from her graying hair.

The thief dashes down a passageway too narrow for vehicles, pursued by two blue-uni Afghan police.

Kebabs sizzle over an oil-drum grill. On a tinny portable radio, anasheed chanting sounds like it's sung from inside a drainage pipe. A woman sells pirated DVDs.

Then the afternoon azan, the call to prayer, blares from the cloverleaf of horn loudspeakers perched on a minaret of the mosque, this one gold-domed.

Two old men don't budge from their backgammon game, talking through smoke they pull from a shisha pipe, placing bets with big brass coins.

In the circle of the town center, a woman in a perahan tunban and Jackie-O sunglasses sells naan stacked in towers and tied with string. Through Steed's open door, Steed serving as middleman, Goodman buys a stack for five dollars. He doesn't haggle. He says, "So we don't come to lunch empty-handed." He sniffs the stack and nods.

"Black sesame?" Steed says.

"Nigella seeds, I think." Goodman points his chin at the woman backing away holding her lone stack of naan. "You look closely, you see the tells. She's wearing a Seiko."

"You see their shoes?" Steed says. "Every villager's wearing American-made boots."

A woman in a burqa over a shami dress and white pants, white chador, comes out of the town center accompanied by a man in an embroidered linen perahan tunban, a red camel-wool pakol, like a burlap beret, worn back on his head. They wave.

"Now those two waving there," Ant tells them, "they're who we're meeting for lunch. We're gonna park, get out, and with not a single weapon between us, without even securing a perimeter, we're gonna sit down — look, they set up a Bedouin tent — and eat us some hummus and tabbouleh and we're gonna break Goody's naan with them. Maybe drink a little hibiscus tea. How you boys doing?"

"How you know they're the ones?"

"In the town center, we're to meet a couple, man in a red hat."

"Could be a setup."

"All they did was set up lunch, Steady. Okay, I'm pulling around and parking."

"We do this how often?"

"My agreement with the LC's that we schedule a Sunday a month to bring vets of the Bagdad Grand on base to one of the villages. Have a nice time, then we go. Calling it Operation Homeward Surge."

They park and fall out. The woman looks like an Afghan refugee, kohl eyeliner; the man could be too, that or an Arab-American language specialist, this a part of his training.

"Naame ma Zamda ast," the woman says.

"My name is Zamda. This is Lakhkar." Her English is exceptional, her accent not glottal Pashto or Dari but lilting British.

"Kindly pleased to meet you," Ant says. "Apologies for being late. Got a little lost along the way."

"It's alright, though it doesn't leave us much time. But please, make introductions."

"I'm Ant. This here's Ike, Ruffin, and —"

"That's Young Gaddafi," Steed says, a potshot followed by his white flag of a smile.

"Yes, I see it," she says to Goodman.

Goodman smiles shyly, bows his head and hands Zamda the bound naan. "For you . . . Zamda is it?"

"Zamda, yes."

"It's beautiful," he says. "What does it mean?"

She laughs awkwardly and to Lakhkar says something in Dari. She turns back to Goodman. "Not my given name you understand. Staged name." Zamda lifts the naan by its tie. "Very kind." She gestures under the tent. There, a dastarkhan is laid out on the ground, a large tablecloth spread over a Persian rug and, on the cloth, a feast.

They duck under the tent. Zamda holds up a copper basin. "Aftabah wa lagan." She nods. "We wash hands." She goes around, first to Ant, pouring warm water. There's a hand towel for each of them.

"Remember," Ant says, "never step on, or even over, the dastarkhan."

"Oh, it is okay. We are not fundamentalists here. Sit, sit." Zamda moves like a woman with formal attan training, her hand opening like a bird stretching its wing. "Relishes and torchi, pickled peach, lemon, eggplant. Basmati rice, qabili palao, fried raisins, carrots, and pistachios. Kufta, meatballs. Tea is in two copper teapots. Help yourselves." She pulls Lakhkar's sleeve. "Will you please excuse us? We must make a call. Continue enjoying."

When they're out of sight, Steed says, "Managed not to get beheaded in Baghdad, here I'm gonna get my head cut off at a picnic in the motherfucking Mojave."

Ant tosses a leek dumpling at Steed. "Fill your mouth, wouldja?"

Goodman says, "You tell us your war crime, Specialist Smith?"

"My war crime." She bites a dolma, lemony and moist. She pulls a grapeleaf vein, stringy as floss, from her mouth. "Plowed over a boy in Saydabad with my HET."

"Yeah?"

"Wasn't no accident. Swerved to hit him,

not avoid him. Bout cut him clear in half."

Steed asks, "He a threat?"

"He was a boy, Steady, twelve years old at most."

Steed tells her it don't mean nothing. "Had a kid fire an RPG at me. Recoil hadn't knocked him on his ass? Sailed the rocket over my head? I'd'a been done. Blowback slammed him into a wall. Knocked the wall over and knocked him out. Sidearm was this ancient, rusted-out revolver. Two dud rounds in it. Looked leftover from World War I. I zip-tied him, wrists and ankles. Kicked living hell out of him before handing him over. Sure he was back on the street in days. Maybe he's who you hit with your HET."

"Tried that kind of thinking. Only made me paranoid." She tastes the kufta, greasy and delicious. "Trick's to try to forgive yourself for killing a kid without making the kid a villain." She pours tea into a small brass cup. She smells it, ginger. "Anyone else, hot tea?"

They all shake heads.

Steed and Goodman, sitting across from her, look up from their plates perched in their laps to a spot over Ant's head. Goodman gives his head another shake, subtler, seeming to say Please stop instead of No thanks.

Ant ignores him. "Kid I killed wasn't evil. Wasn't no savage. Neither was the kid who tried to kill you, Steady. They were kids. Kids trying to survive a war. You got to find a way to hold on to the qualities that keep us open, to the world and the people in it." She sips. "That there, boys, is not only the lifelong mission of the military veteran — it's the duty of every single human being. You think our two hosts have it any easier than us? Uprooted from their homelands? Refugees relocated from who-knows-what warzone?" She sips again. "It's good, ginger and chamomile, I think. You should try it." She finishes her tea. "Does get easier. Never easy. For a time, couldn't get behind a wheel. Now I'm taxiing you boys all around, even if I am getting us lost. But better to get lost along the way than not go. For that, for your willingness to get lost with me, gentlemen, I'm thankful." She raises her empty cup. "But that's just one woman's opinion." She feels a hand on each of her shoulders — they're tender and they startle her.

Zamda and Lakhkar stand behind. Her voice husky and off-key, Zamda sings:

Oh Earth, the tax you exact costs far too
   much,
you devour our youth and leave the beds
   deserted.

"It is prettier in Pashto," she says, "and I'm
better dancer than singer. We have a Pashtun
tradition. The landay, means *short poison-
ous snake.*" She smile-shrugs. "There is
another I think of every day. I won't sing,
I'll just say: *The exiled woman never stops
dying, turn her face, then, toward her mother-
land so she may breathe her last.*" Zamda
looks to the sun angling under the tent. "It
is hard here for us." She turns to Ant. "But
we are women, you and I. Better to be
women here than anywhere else in the
world. Yes?"

"Yes," Ant says. "And I'm not sure I
could've said that a few years ago."

"No? Well, when I get too homesick, I
listen to Radio Azadi. May I tell one more?"

"Please."

"It's said to be by Malalai, a Pashtun poet
and woman warrior, a folk hero, who fought
alongside Ayub Khan. It goes: *When sisters
sit together, they praise their brothers. When
brothers sit together, they sell their sisters.*
That's how it is still, there, for women." She
shrugs. "Please forgive me. I'm strangely

589

nostalgic for Herat."

Goodman wipes his mouth with his sleeve. "How did you come here, Zamda?"

She tells them that in the weeks after the fall of the Taliban — in 2001, months after you lost your towers — she sought asylum, with help from a professor. "Tony Blair was very hospitable, and I was given a fellowship to attend University of London. From there, I went to grad school at Cal State, San Bernardino, where I now teach. As adjunct. This" — she sweeps her hand out — "I do on the side. As thanks. And it pays better than teaching." She shrugs. "Now, I'm sorry, but we must bring lunch to an end. There's another exercise. May we give you anything to take?" She steps the toe of her American hiking boot on the dastarkhan, reaches, her bangles chiming, and lifts the tied stack of naan. When she steps back, the dusty half-bootprint is glaring, and Ant pats it till it's mostly gone.

Zamda hands the naan to Goodman. "Take this at least. Thank you dearly for thinking of us. And we hope to see you again, next month, when we'll have more time. Lakhkar and I will be sure to be here." She turns to Ant. "We're very excited about what you're doing. Making peace."

Lakhkar nods and bows a little.

"We'll look forward to it," Ant says, "and we'll be early."

They pile into the Humvee and pick their slow way through emptied-out Jabal. Not a role-player in sight.

"Oh man." Dopp chuckles.

Goodman asks, "What's funny?"

"Sign on the spice shop. In Arabic and English. English translation said: *In place of Omar for all kinds the spices.*"

Steed says, "All your spice are belong to us," and it's the last thing anyone says, till, talked out and tired, in Fort Irwin proper, after a ream of paper-signing, Ant swaps the borrowed Humvee for her Jeep Wrangler. They put the soft top down for Steed.

First thing he does is ask Goodman, "I borrow your flatbread?" Using the naan as a pillow, Steed rests his head on the rollbar, closing his eyes to the low sun, the rushing air, for the seventy-five-klick drive back to Newberry Springs and the Bagdad Grand.

They exit the main gate of the National Training Center, pass Painted Rocks, where units training at Fort Irwin each decorate a boulder with unit insignia and date. Ray painted one of those rocks, and on her first visit to base, she found it. It's visible from the road. There. Her eyes find the faded sun and star split by a red lightning bolt on a green and blue shield, and then it's out of sight.

The desert road calms, reassures. It also excites. At the far end waits a warm welcome. No one talks. They're each deep in their own heads, and she knows the vets in her company brood in dark corners. Her hope is that they might get to a spot lit like hers, out in the open, where she's found a few devotions — her place, her vets, her dog, her boy — that get her through her days, and sometimes even eagerly.

They spend forty dusty minutes on Fort Irwin Road, she slowing once for a rattler S-ing across the asphalt, before taking Old Yermo Cutoff. She considers making a pit stop at the Calico Ghost Town to buy a round of sarsaparillas, letting Dopp flirt with the bartender, but they're all napping.

She takes Daggett-Yermo and, then, they're on the last leg, National Trails Highway, formerly Route 66. Old Mother Road once supported hundreds of small towns along its narrow bends. But no more, and here Ant is, a single mother living and working on some 650 feet of frontage along that storied road made defunct by progress.

Living and working just off of this ramshackle road lends her comfort. Any moment she could lift her boy and her dog into her Jeep and speed off. Visit Florida or Jersey, venture far south to Costa Rica or way north to the end of Alaska. Not that she would. She's set down roots. They're shallow and in loose sand, but for the time being and for the foreseeable future, she's bound to her small patch of scorched earth.

In her first few months at the Bagdad Grand, when it was just her, Vessey, Foxtrot, and infant Wright, they painted red the lone, low building of the former Henning Motel, same shade as the Bagdad Cafe next door.

A short time on the National Trails and there it is, the vertical

M
O
T
E
L

sign left over from another era, its neon gone. Under the *L* it reads horizontally:

HENNING
FREE TV

Under the sign — her sign — the company chickens peck and scratch in the dust. At the scattered center of them, Wright and Foxtrot dig a hole. Her filthy boy and her filthy dog. Two beautifully browned creatures making busywork not three meters from the empty road. This makes her anxious, angry. The tragedy she envisions most — too perfectly fated — is of little Wright run over. The more deserted the road, the easier it is to imagine.

His sitter, Vessey, watches from the swinging chair chained to the front porch of the red barracks. He rolls a cigarette, a lit cigarette in his lips, a can of Drum tobacco in his crotch. His eyes narrow on his charges. She knows his worn soldiering bones and tired muscles would quicken and strengthen under duress, that he can be counted on, that he'd kill himself, to keep her boy safe.

The older boys in the cab of the Jeep are unsound asleep. Her vets found a little ease in her vehicle with her driving. Reluctant to break the spell, she slows before the turn and takes stock: her brood, her dog, and her boy fuss on land she owns outright, land found for her by a woman whose life Ant saved, land supporting a nonprofit business she started with money Ray earned as a merc, a business, of her own making, trying to darn a hole or two in the frayed national fabric. She wonders how much worse off she'd be — how long she'd've been dead, who else she might've killed — if not for the Standard.

When she pulls into the drive, the boys in the cab rouse.

Foxtrot and then Wright look up from their digging. The Jeep's open top allows in their calls — hard to tell dog from boy — yelps and giddy whines that enter into and course through her like a warm inoculation. She isn't sure how she managed it — it's all unreal — but she feels lucky and indebted, forever obliged to forces far greater than she.

Her boy and her dog scramble out of the hole. Wright drops something and stops to fetch it. Foxtrot heels and waits wagging his tail. You'd never know the boy'd been born nearly two months premature — 4 lbs., 10 oz. — spent his first twelve days on the neonatal intensive care unit. There, she came to know him, tiny Wright Tyro Smith, came to love him, decided to keep him, he a little fighter from the start, hungry for life, hungry for her. Had he been on time — fat, all secure — she might've surrendered him.

Wright holds up what he dropped. A plastic tan Army man, gift from Goodman, who took care to give only Army men not bearing arms: the scout with the binoculars adhered to his eyes, the mine detector, the radio operator. Displaying the retrieved toy soldier, Wright runs toward Goodman.

Ant cuts the engine, opens her door, hops down, and shouts, "Wright! You best get your little tokhes on over here now." She takes a knee in the dust.

Wright beams, hoots, and happily changes course. Foxtrot skids to a stop, cocks his head, then follows. He reaches Wright and nudges him, leans against him while they run, behaving more like a herder than a retriever. The long, reddened shadows of the boy and the dog wash together on the red earth in the lowering sun red at their backs. Over their eager, bobbling heads, the old road narrows into the distance, and everything's behind them, everything before them.

ACKNOWLEDGMENTS

While I won't acknowledge the socioeconomic schizophrenia of corporate personhood, I've come to believe in the notion of the novelist as person incorporated. A publicly traded company. Call me I, Inc. When a character in Exodus asks God's name, God, ever the smart aleck, answers, "I Am That I Am." Had He bothered to write the Old Testament, God might've replied, "I Are We." That gets at the metaphysics of the novelist, I think. I are we, and we am I. And we've been raucous. Even when I wanted, I could not shut us up. We woke me countless times in the night. We fought each other, fucked each other, talked to each other and to me. We lived and drove, loved and died, all inside of me. That's how this novel came to be. Now that I'm rid of it, I still hear us, but we grow distant. We disturb me less, and I miss us. In the time it took us to write this — nearly every day for over five years — we learned that if I'm not actively bossing us around, and being bossed, my imagination turns on itself. Then I am me and me alone. I'm much better — more engaged, less crazy — for the company, and so here's to us, my characters, for keeping me from going out of our mind. We must next, as part of this initial public offering, recognize Jennifer Carlson, agent extraordinaire and cheese connoisseur. Jen helped me narrow this novel down from 800-plus pages and, over interminable years, she's ushered me gamely through rejection, failure, and, finally, into the hands of my remarkable, artful editor. Elisabeth Dyssegaard labored ardently for my novel and me. She's a writer's ideal — part Maxwell Perkins, part Pippi Longstocking — and she helped me to realize this, my most drawn-out desire, with fewer flaws and greater force. Gratitude to the devoted, determined, and book-adoring folks at St. Martin's Press and Macmillan, chiefly Alan Bradshaw, Bill Warhop, Talia Sherer, Laura Apperson, Laura Clark, Courtney Reed, and Dori Weintraub; and to the likeminded, indie-spirited owners of Bookbug in Kalamazoo, MI, Joanna Parzakonis and Derek Molitor, doting shepherds who tend a wonderfully wide-ranging, ever-wandering flock. An ovation to Josh Ritter for his glory of a song, "Girl in the War," and for permission to use a few lines as half of my epigraph; and to Meena Mohammadzai, for her smoke-flower translation of Nadia Anjuman's poem. Appreciation to my former sister-in-law, Specialist Nicorvo, for the inspiration despite — or maybe due to — the difficulties. Snappy salutes to Maj. Todd Perry and Brandon Davis Jennings, the finest pair of veteran drill instructors a novelist could ask for. Stiff debts — stiffer drinks — are owed to my spendthrift writing teachers: Ray Wonder, Scott Ward, Peter Meinke, Frederick Reiken, John Skoyles, Margot Livesey, Pamela Painter, Dennis Lehane, and especially my mentor — and adopted papa — Sterling Watson. If not for Sterl, instead of writing this sentence, I'd be selling sinkhole insurance in south Florida, or building picnic tables in prison. Cheers to Don Lee for making me the Ripper all those years ago, and to Martha Rhodes for welcoming me into her Four Way home. Susan Weaver helped keep me (reasonably) sane. Thank you to Ellen Levine for her generous gift from the Ellen Levine Fund for Writers, and to Jeffrey Lependorf for his nomination. Also, thanks to the National Society of Arts and Letters for a Career Chapter

Award. A shout goes out to the founding members of the Phenomenal Nobodies: Michael Dopp, Clintel Steed, and Matthew Aaron Goodman. Love to my immediate family: brothers Shawn and Dane; aunt Gail Guscott; mother-in-law, Myra Nissen; and my mom, Sharon. Mom spent the better part of thirty years behind the counters of umpteen 7-Elevens, working harder for less than anyone I've ever known. Because of her example — the willingness to give most of her waking life in desperate support of the half-wild creations she brought into being — I was able to keep writing for so long with so little to show. (This, the first novel I've published, is the fourth novel I've finished.) I owe everything else to Thisbe Nissen — best friend, first and last reader, wife — who sustained me in all ways during this outrageous, years-long flight of fancy. We go far for small things. And to our son, Sonne Niscorvosen (I hope I spelled that right), who put his little hand in mine and pulled me toward the grace that comes from trying to see the world through the eyes of others. This list could go endlessly on — my apologies to those not acknowledged by name — and that hints at the embarrassing extent of my grand fortune. Finally, I want to recognize US service members, including those who abandon their posts. Whether or not we approve of war — or vote for representatives who do — we, by virtue of being citizens of the US republic, are responsible for our wars nonetheless. One way we can acknowledge the service of veterans is by actively trying to imagine what they live through. If we do, we may better appreciate what they die for, and why.

AUTHOR'S NOTE

I'd be remiss if I didn't confess to my dependence upon the following sources: Larry Chambers's *Death in the A Shau Valley: L Company* LRRPs *in Vietnam, 1969–1970*; Elizabeth D. Samet's *Soldier's Heart: Reading Literature Through Peace and War at West Point*; Frank Johnson's *Diary of an Airborne Ranger: A* LRRP*'s Year in the Combat Zone*; Keith Nolan's *Ripcord: Screaming Eagles Under Siege, Vietnam 1970*; Azar Nafisi's *Reading Lolita in Tehran: A Memoir in Books*; Tania Grossinger's *Growing Up at Grossinger's; The Long Path Guide*, edited by Herb Chong; Paul Fussell's *The Great War and Modern Memory*; Maxine Hong Kingston's *Veterans of War, Veterans of Peace*; Denis Johnson's *Tree of Smoke*; Robert Young Pelton's *Licensed to Kill: Hired Guns in the War on Terror*; Dexter Filkins's *The Forever War; Songs of Love and War:*

Afghan Women's Poetry, edited by Sayd Bahodine Majrouh, translated by Marjolijn de Jager; Tim O'Brien's *If I Die in a Combat Zone: Box Me Up and Ship Me Home;* John Edgar Wideman's *Brothers and Keepers: A Memoir;* Friar Diego de Landa's *Yucatan Before and After the Conquest,* translated by William Gates; *The Book of Chilam Balam of Chumayel,* translated by Ralph L. Roys; Kevin Powers's *The Yellow Birds;* Jeremy Scahill's *Blackwater: The Rise of the World's Most Powerful Mercenary Army;* Kim Hopper's *Reckoning with Homelessness;* Ben Fountain's *Billy Lynn's Long Halftime Walk;* Donald Anderson's *When War Becomes Personal: Soldiers' Accounts from the Civil War to Iraq;* David A. Snow and Leon Anderson's *Down on Their Luck: A Study of Homeless Street People; Operation Homecoming: Iraq, Afghanistan, and the Home Front, in the Words of U.S. Troops and Their Families,* edited by Andrew Carroll; Steve Fainaru's *Big Boy Rules: America's Mercenaries Fighting in Iraq;* P.W. Singer's *Corporate Warriors: The Rise of the Privatized Military Industry;* James Ashcroft's *Making a Killing: The Explosive Story of a Hired Gun in Iraq;* John Geddes's *Highway to Hell: Dispatches from a Mercenary in Iraq;* Brandon Davis

Jennings's *Waiting for the Enemy;* Dan Briody's *The Halliburton Agenda: The Politics of Oil and Money;* Myrna Katz Frommer and Harvey Frommer's *It Happened in the Catskills: An Oral History in the Words of Busboys, Bellhops, Guests, Proprietors, Comedians, Agents, and Others Who Lived It;* the films *Full Battle Rattle,* directed by Tony Gerber and Jesse Moss; *Restrepo,* directed by Sebastian Junger and Tim Hetherington; the songs "Hell Broke Luce" by Tom Waits; "Sam Stone" by John Prine; "Written on the Forehead" by PJ Harvey; "A Love Supreme" by John Coltrane; "Trouble in Mind" by Nina Simone; "Handsome Johnny" by Richie Havens; "Sovay" by Andrew Bird; the websites sofrep.com, warisboring.com, famsi.org, wikimapia.org, nytimes.com; and on and on.

ABOUT THE AUTHOR

Jay Baron Nicorvo lives on an old farm outside Battle Creek, MI, with his wife, Thisbe Nissen, their son, and a couple dozen chickens. His writing has appeared in *Salon, Poets & Writers,* and *The Believer* and has been featured on NPR and PBS News-Hour. He's published a poetry collection, *Deadbeat,* and served as an editor at *Ploughshares* and at *PEN America.*

The employees of Thorndike Press hope you have enjoyed this Large Print book. All our Thorndike, Wheeler, and Kennebec Large Print titles are designed for easy reading, and all our books are made to last. Other Thorndike Press Large Print books are available at your library, through selected bookstores, or directly from us.

For information about titles, please call:
(800) 223-1244

or visit our website at:
gale.com/thorndike

To share your comments, please write:
Publisher
Thorndike Press
10 Water St., Suite 310
Waterville, ME 04901